Emily Kerr has been scribbling since she learnt how to write. S is based in Yorkshire.

She can generally be found with her nose in a book, or hunched up over her laptop typing away, though she has been known to venture outside every so often to take part in various running-based activities.

www.emilykerrwrites.com

 twitter.com/EmilyKerrWrites
 facebook.com/emilykerrwrites

Also by Emily Kerr

Duvet Day

MEET ME UNDER THE NORTHERN LIGHTS

EMILY KERR

One More Chapter
a division of HarperCollins*Publishers* Ltd
1 London Bridge Street
London SE1 9GF
www.harpercollins.co.uk
HarperCollins*Publishers*
1st Floor, Watermarque Building, Ringsend Road
Dublin 4, Ireland

This paperback edition 2022
1
First published in Great Britain in ebook format
by HarperCollins*Publishers* 2021
Copyright © Emily Kerr 2021
Emily Kerr asserts the moral right to be identified
as the author of this work

A catalogue record of this book is available from the British Library

ISBN: 978-0-00-843360-4

Printed and bound in the UK using 100% Renewable Electricity
by CPI Group (UK) Ltd

To the Kerrs and the Raws, with love

Chapter One

'No pass, no entry.'

'But I'm due on air in less than ten minutes,' I pleaded into the intercom, hopping anxiously from one foot to the other as I tried rummaging through my handbag yet again to find my missing ID. I racked my brains to see if I could work out when I'd last seen it, but my memory of last night was a little patchy. Mornings will do that to a person, although it could also have had something to do with the open bar at Barry the security guy's retirement bash. Given my early alarm call, I should probably have given it a miss. But as I remind my mum when she drops one of her frequent hints about me needing to be sensible and settle down, if Lucy's life is boring, so is Lucy's radio show. Besides, it would have been rude not to have given Bazzer a decent send-off.

'That's what they all say.' Barry's replacement on the other side of the door sounded supremely indifferent to my plight. I could just about make out his shadowy form through the glass. He was lolling behind the reception desk, hands behind his head. If I wasn't very much mistaken, my frantic ringing of the buzzer had woken him from a nap. I don't really blame the guy. I would much rather have been asleep too.

'How many people do you get trying to break in at stupid o'clock in the morning? People aren't that desperate to get hold of the coffee cups we give out as prizes.'

I regretted the words instantly. If I was going to get into the studio on time to wake up the good folk of the UK with the effortless stream of cheery banter that they'd come to expect from their favourite breakfast radio presenter, then I needed to get this bloke onside, and fast. Unfortunately, it's a little hard to charm someone into submission when they're nice and cosy inside, and you're stuck out in the dark, freezing your butt off. I settled instead for the unsubtle method of rapping my knuckles against the door frame until the persistent banging irritated him sufficiently enough to drag himself up from his seat, turn the lights on, and come across to inspect me at close quarters.

I practically genuflected when he finally opened the door.

'I'm so sorry for disturbing you, and I promise I won't forget my pass again, but it's an emergency, and if I don't get into the studio in the next five minutes, the breakfast show won't get on air.'

'But the breakfast show is presented by Lucy Fairweather.' My adversary folded his arms and frowned disapprovingly.

'That's me,' I said trying to maintain a friendly demeanour while inwardly screaming in frustration.

He looked at me, then pointedly glanced across at the triple-sized poster of my face which decorated the wall behind reception. He studied the image for a moment, then turned his attention back to my sorry features and shook his head in disbelief, leaving me feeling as attractive as the before picture in a magazine makeover. Yes, my appearance is a tad different from the poster girl version of myself, but show me a breakfast presenter without dark circles and bags under their eyes big enough to use instead of a suitcase for holidays. Getting up at 3:30am every weekday takes its toll on a person. Besides, I spent four hours getting contoured half to death for that picture and they were extremely generous with the airbrushing afterwards. To be honest, I look nothing like that image, even on the rare occasion when I've had the energy to make an effort on a morning.

'It is me,' I pleaded. 'I'm Lucy Fairweather, wishing you fair weather for today.' I cringed as I put on my radio voice to do my trademark sign off, in the desperate hope that it would spark some kind of recognition from the guy. His expression remained impassive. I was about to whip out my driving licence to see if he'd accept that form of ID, when my producer Mike, aka the grumpiest man in broadcasting, stomped into reception and greeted me with his usual glower.

'Where the bloody hell have you been? I was about to call the network and tell them they'd have to put out the emergency show. You're meant to be in the studio saying that kind of nonsense, not prancing around reception showing off to the help.'

'And a good morning to you too, Mike. Really sorry I'm cutting it so fine. I misplaced my pass again, as I was explaining to our very diligent new security guard.' My attempt to ingratiate myself with Barry's replacement was met with stony silence, but he did at least move away from the doorway, so I could squeeze past his mountainous form and into the building.

The on-air light outside the studio flashed, giving us a warning that we had only three minutes until I was due to broadcast. Mike's expression grew more thunderous and I braced myself for the traditional round two of him making a snide comment about women and timekeeping, but thankfully I was saved from my daily dose of sexism by the arrival of our newsreader.

'Morning, Lucy, it looks set to be another gorgeous autumn day. I've got some really heart-warming stories lined up for the bulletins today, you're going to love them.' Skye breezed towards us, smiling with the calm assurance of someone who'd already been up doing yoga for hours. If she wasn't such a lovely person, it would be easy to resent her for being so ridiculously perfect.

'Typical,' muttered Mike under his breath, momentarily disarmed by Skye's general aura of Zen. He rolled his eyes and clomped into the studio, still grumbling about the unreliability of the female sex. Skye winked at me and surreptitiously passed across a page of notes as we followed him in.

'A few things I thought might interest you, Luce,' she

whispered. I looked down at the paper and saw she'd compiled a list of some extra talking points and quirky stories to help me fill the show, something which Mike was meant to do as a fundamental part of his job, but had never bothered with. The woman deserved a promotion. Four hours is a long time to single-handedly fill with chat and make it sound effortless, especially when one is slightly fuzzy of head. I don't know what I'd do without her.

I logged onto the computer and briefly scanned the day's music playlist before sending Skye a quick instant message so Mike wasn't privy to our exchange.

'You're a star. I owe you a massive drink.'

'As long as it's one of those gorgeous smoothies of yours, you're on,' she pinged back with a spattering of thumbs up and smiley face emojis. 'I'm off alcohol for the moment.'

The cheesy jingle announcing the start of the Lucy Fairweather Breakfast Show prevented me from enquiring further.

As Skye launched enthusiastically into the headlines, Mike threw a packet of throat sweets at the side of my head, and held up a bit of paper on which was scrawled, 'Take these or you're going to sound as hungover as you look.'

The live microphones stopped me from answering him back, so I had to content myself with sending a dark glare in his direction. Hungover? How dare he? Of course I wasn't hungover. Admittedly I felt a bit grotty, but there had been a bug doing the rounds of the office, and I was pretty sure I was coming down with it. And I drank no more than anyone else at Barry's leaving do. Why shouldn't I let my hair down with everyone else? The breakfast show may be the slot that everyone would kill to get, but no one talks about the cost it can have on your social life. If I was fixated on getting my eight hours before work, I'd be going to bed at 7pm or earlier.

Skye finished her bulletin with a cute story about a dog that had saved its owner from drowning, then handed over to me. I hastily swallowed my medicine as instructed and turned on my microphone.

'Oi oi, here's a shout out to the early morning heroes.' I started off with my customary greeting, although maybe it didn't have its usual pizzazz as my voice was admittedly rather more gravelly than normal. I was definitely succumbing to the lurgy. 'It's five past six in the morning, and if you're awake and fully conscious, then you are winning at life. You're doing better than me, guys, that's for sure. Let's kick off with a big tune to start your Tuesday morning.' I looked up and caught Skye shaking her head and pointing at the digital display on the wall. 'Oops, your Wednesday morning. Just keeping you on your toes, folks, you know what I'm like.' I forced a raucous peel of laughter which left my brain vibrating in my skull.

I moved the fader up and hit play. As the strains of 'I don't like Mondays' blasted out of the studio speakers, my head started throbbing even more.

I don't know how I got through the show. Mike seemed to have decided to punish me for my late arrival by making me play all the noisiest tracks, plus he kept putting through all the difficult callers on the phones, abandoning me to handle them live on air which my brain really wasn't up to. As the clock ticked towards ten, my stomach was grumbling so loudly I was afraid listeners would start texting in to ask if there was an earthquake in the studio. Skye, bless her, had offered me half of her scrambled vegan egg substitute, but it turned my stomach just looking at it. Mike had smugly eaten his cornflakes at eight o'clock, bang on time as per his usual schedule, and then locked the cereal box away, pointedly not offering me a share of the bounty. Classic demonstration of his attitude towards being a team player.

Finally, it was thirty seconds to ten o'clock and I dipped the music on my last track (a particularly long one that I'd chosen to give myself less time for talking) and signed off from the programme.

'We've got the news coming up shortly, but that's all from me today. If you're not at work yet, hurry up, you're running late. Jonno's up next with his Wednesday Whiners, sorry, Winners, lots of chances to get your hands on some cash, but this is Lucy Fairweather, wishing you fair weather for today.'

I fired off the final jingle, leaned back in my chair and briefly closed my eyes, relishing the brief respite from the brightness of the room.

'Am I going to have to wheel you out of here on that thing? Because you currently look like you're not capable of standing up and walking in a straight line,' said Mike, slamming his headphones down on the desk with such force I thought he was going to snap them in half. Skye flinched. For a journalist, she's surprisingly squeamish when it comes to any kind of conflict. I shot Mike a warning look.

'Calm down, Mikey,' I said. 'No need to get your knickers in a twist.'

I sent a reassuring smile in Skye's direction, and deliberately removed my headphones with great care. After a good old stretch, I pretended to stagger towards the exit to make her laugh and dissipate the tension in the room.

The heavy studio door swung open and Jonno shambled in, his nose still deep in a newspaper.

'Hey, Jonno, the place is all yours. I'm off in search of breakfast. Watch the producer headphones, they're looking a little fragile now.'

He glanced up from the headlines, many of which seemed to feature the antics of his reality-TV star girlfriend, Serenity.

'All good at home, Jonno?' I asked. In my book, tabloid coverage was never a good thing.

'Tip-top, matey,' he said. 'Thanks for warming up the airwaves for me. That was quite the show, as always. Cheers for the plug, though I'd rather you didn't refer to my listeners as whiners.'

He grinned at my contrite expression and moved the microphone into position. Before he pushed the fader up to broadcast, he turned back towards me.

'It was a great night last night. Cheers for letting me crash at yours. Don't worry, I posted the key through the letterbox. Oh, and a friendly warning, you might have to smooth a few ruffled feathers at The Crown before you go back. I know it's a dive, but even they draw a line at tap-dancing on the bar.'

Tap-dancing? I hadn't, had I? A vague memory of doing a few shuffle-ball-changes filtered through the fogginess of my memory. Oops. I'd wondered why my feet felt sore this morning. I certainly had no recollection of inviting Jonno back to mine. I hadn't seen him when I'd set off, so I guess he'd spent the night on my sofa. Maybe I had underestimated just how into the party spirit I'd got last night.

Jonno laughed at my horrified expression and hustled me out of the studio so he could get on with his show.

Now that the adrenalin of broadcasting live to the faithful listenership of Star FM had subsided, a wave of tiredness hit me. I needed fuel, and I needed it fast before I crashed. Mike, however, had other ideas.

'We need to talk, Lucy,' he said cutting me off before I could reach the kitchen and examine the contents of the fridge.

'Does it have to be now? I am so ravenous I could eat my own arm. It's not a good feeling.'

'That's the problem with excessive drinking, it gives you the munchies,' said Mike.

I didn't like his gleeful tone. Was he enjoying watching me suffer?

'Oh bog off, Mike. You're one to talk about the munchies, sitting there shovelling all that cereal into your mouth. Half a box was it today? And I've not been drinking excessively. I'm getting a cold, that's why I'm so hungry. You know what they say, "Feed a cold and starve a fever".' I didn't give him a chance to reply. 'Wow, guess who's coming down the stairs,' I said, pointing to the empty space behind him. He's so gullible, he actually fell for it and turned to look, giving me a few seconds to duck out of his way and reach the front door.

'We'll chat when I'm back,' I shouted over my shoulder as I zipped out of the radio station.

The fresh air and autumn sunshine instantly perked me up. I much prefer weather that is like my surname. Starting work so early means being constantly confronted with the dark. I hate this time of the year anyway, and the lack of daylight makes things so much worse. The thick gloom makes me feel sluggish and down, everything becoming so much more of an effort to do. It's not surprising I sometimes run behind schedule because of it.

I pushed all guilty thoughts about lateness to the back of my head and set off in search of sustenance. On a day like today, there was only one solution for my current state of bleurgh. I made a beeline for my favourite place. Across the road from the radio station was one of the city's best-kept secrets. There are not many independent greengrocers still surviving in the battle against the supermarket giants, but Mr Martin's place was somehow hanging on in there, even though in all the times I'd visited, I'd never seen another customer darken its doors. It was their loss. The shop was a cavern of wonders, filled with the most mouth-watering delights your imagination could summon; the juiciest of fruits, the tangiest of herbs, and a sheer rainbow of scrummy vegetables.

'Good morning, Miss Fairweather. And how are you

today?' Despite the fact that I urge him to call me Lucy on practically every trip, Mr Martin still insists on addressing me formally.

'I'm suffering somewhat, Mr Martin, but I feel sure that you have exactly what I need to perk myself up.' He smiled with pleasure and passed across a collection of paper bags. I wandered around the shop, picking out a scoop of tiny dark chia seeds, a handful of blueberries which were practically glowing with freshness, a couple of beautifully ripe bananas and a tub of thick Greek yoghurt.

As I handed over my credit card to pay, he added a chilled bag of spinach into my basket.

'Helps with detoxing the system,' he explained.

'As long as it gives me the vitamins I need to fight this cold,' I replied cheerily. Seriously, did I need to make a 'Poorly but definitely sober' sign to hold above my head?

He cleared his throat and packed the ingredients up for me.

I texted Skye to let her know I was on the way back and she kindly let me into the radio station's side entrance so I didn't have to go through the faff of trying to convince Barry's replacement to let me in without a pass all over again.

'What are we having this morning?' she asked eagerly, as I unpacked the ingredients onto the worktop in the communal kitchen. I probably should have given it a bit of a wipe down first, given the amount of gunk on the surfaces, but maybe the cure to my ailment was lurking among the bacteria there, the world's new penicillin if you will.

'Ah-ah,' I tutted, waving her away from the counter. 'I

owe you a drink and this is what I'm providing. You put your feet up. If you're very lucky, I might even let you in on my secret recipe. Trust me, it's guaranteed to perk up a person even when they're feeling their absolute grottiest. I like to call it "Lucy's Hangover Vanquisher". Not that I'm hungover, of course,' I added hastily. 'Or you for that matter.'

Skye pulled up a stool and watched carefully as I chopped a banana and tossed it into the blender along with the fresh blueberries, a tablespoon of chia seeds and a couple of handfuls of the spinach which Mr Martin had so generously gifted me. I added a mug of coconut water, then hesitated. 'What will make this really zing is some Greek yoghurt. Wonderful for balancing out the digestive system and restoring order, or so the healthy eating gurus say.'

'Go for it,' said Skye. 'I'm not being strictly vegan these days.' She paused. 'For some reason, the baby seems to crave dairy products.'

I nearly didn't hear her over the sound of the blender. I turned around and saw the contented smile on her face.

'No way, seriously?' I asked.

She placed her hand self-consciously on her stomach. 'I was sure you'd worked it out ages ago,' she said quietly. 'I've been dropping little hints. I didn't want everyone to know, but I wanted to tell you. I thought you'd got it, but I guess I was being too obscure. But I can't get away with keeping it a secret much longer. I'm definitely showing now.'

I kicked myself for not paying proper attention over the past few weeks. Skye was such a good friend, as well as being an amazing colleague. She deserved more kindness from me than I gave her.

'I don't know what to say. That's amazing news. You and Henri must be absolutely thrilled.' I wrapped her in a huge bear hug, then pushed her back to her seat, not quite sure how to treat her now she was an expectant mum. Suddenly the gulf between our very different lives seemed wider than ever.

'Let's toast your life as Mummy Skye,' I said, injecting a note of jollity into my voice. 'That baby has hit the jackpot getting you as its mum.' I poured us both a tumbler of smoothie and we chinked our glasses.

'That's such a sweet thing to say, Luce. It all feels rather overwhelming at the moment. Exciting, but still a lot to think about.'

'You are the most sorted person I know, Skye. You and Henri are going to be the best parents ever. Look at you, you're already giving off a magical glow. And your tummy is still flatter than mine, lucky cow. I'm madly jealous of your perfect life.' I kept my tone light-hearted and fun, trying to ignore the unsettling feeling of inadequacy which was once again niggling at the back of my mind. Every new year, I vow I'm going to be more like Skye in my approach to life, but come January the second, I always slip back to my usual ways. Maybe next year I'll manage it.

Skye laughed and took a tiny sip of smoothie, then a great big gulp. 'That is delicious. I can practically feel the healthiness oozing into every cell of my body. You have a serious talent, Lucy.'

I took a few restorative mouthfuls myself and waited for it to work its magic on my general feeling of malaise.

'Yes, when it comes to the liquid diet, there's not a lot our Lucy doesn't know,' said Mike, stomping into the kitchen and interrupting our moment of quiet companionship. 'Shame she doesn't bring such dedication and drive to the rest of her life.'

I buried my head in my glass and downed some more of the liquid before I said something I later regretted.

'When you've quite finished dealing with your hangover, we need to have that meeting. And you might want to speak to your rep beforehand, as I'm calling in HR to intervene. Your near lateness this morning was the final straw, Lucy. Your work is simply not up to scratch and I don't know if we can trust you on the airwaves.'

Suddenly the smoothie didn't taste quite so good anymore.

Chapter Two

The meeting with Mike and HR was about as fun as a pool party where the pool has been concreted over, it's raining, and nobody remembered to order drinks. Mike spent the entire duration of it glowering at me across the desk, probably inventing a million ways he could push me down the stairs at the radio station and make it look like an accident. Before long, he'd got so into his diatribe, he was actually jabbing his finger onto the desk. It looked pretty painful to be honest, but that wasn't stopping him.

'The thing is, Lucy,' he said in his best patronising voice, 'You've been out of your depth from the moment you started on the breakfast show. Listeners want someone with more gravitas, someone less flighty, less high-pitched first thing in the morning.' I rolled my eyes, knowing that when Mike said that, he actually meant someone with more XY chromosomes and less of that pesky oestrogen. 'That's why they're not tuning in any more. And don't get me started on your erratic behaviour of late. People are beginning to wonder why you say the wrong date and stumble over your words. They don't want to be woken up by someone who is still slurring from the night before.'

I felt a stab of fear. I'd always known Mike had a problem with a woman being in the big job, but these were serious accusations he was making, and I couldn't afford for them to stick. Word about things like that gets around. After all, in an industry where people talk for a living, gossip is the main currency.

'I was not slurring my words. How many times do I have to tell you that I have a cold?' I snapped back, vowing for the hundredth time to cut back on the fun times so I didn't get myself into scrapes like this. 'Yes, I made a couple of mistakes this morning, but that can happen to anyone. I love this place. Most people book themselves off sick all the time, but do I? Oh no, I drag myself in however ill I am. It's because I care. And to say listener numbers are down is an out and out lie.' I was warming to my theme now, determined to prove that regardless of what I got up to outside of the radio station, I still did a damn good job when I was here. 'I'm inundated with texts and phone calls throughout the show. People love what I do. They love that I keep it real. They want entertainment, and that's what I give them.'

I would normally die rather than cry at the office, but I'd got myself so het up that tears were pricking at the back of my eyes. Charlie from HR pushed a box of tissues across the table and patted my wrist awkwardly, before quickly snatching his hand away, no doubt terrified that any form of physical contact could bring a sexual harassment claim to his door.

I sniffed a few times, and blew my nose pathetically while Charlie made comforting 'There, there' noises.

'Perhaps I should head home and see if an afternoon in bed will make me feel better,' I suggested, figuring it was best to make a strategic retreat and gather my thoughts before I made even more of a fool of myself.

'Yeah, that's right, hide under the duvet to nurse the rest of your hangover,' said Mike.

'I think that's enough for now, Michael,' said Charlie. 'That sounds like an excellent plan, Lucy. Are you well enough to drive yourself home, or do you want someone to give you a lift back?'

I took another tissue. 'I'll be OK. Thank you for your understanding.'

I walked out of the room forcing myself to hold my head up high. Before I closed the door, I swear I heard Charlie laying into Mike for giving me such a hard time. Served him right, the sneaky so-and-so. How dare he go creeping to Management to stir up trouble? OK, so maybe I had been letting my hair down a bit too much of late, but working in media, it's practically compulsory to join in with all the parties and awards ceremonies. It's important for promoting the show. It wasn't fair that I should be punished for doing everything I could to get people to tune into Star FM.

Skye was hovering around the corner, an anxious expression on her face.

'Shouldn't you be reading the bulletin?' I asked, glancing up at the clock.

'I've got a minute to go.' She hopped from one foot to the other as if warming up for a running race. 'Plenty of time. I wanted to check that you're OK. I was so worried when I heard Mike threatening you with HR.'

I forced a smile. 'Don't worry about me, Skye. Mike's just being his usual charming self. It'll all blow over.' Or at least I hoped it would. I massaged my forehead. The headache was getting worse, despite my earlier restorative smoothie. Today was turning out to be extremely trying. 'Sorry I'm not going to be around for the weekly planning session.' Actually, I wasn't that sorry. The weekly planning meetings normally turned into a passive-aggressive standoff between Mike and everyone else, and they tested my patience at the best of times. 'I'm heading home for a quiet afternoon.'

Skye checked her watch. 'Fifteen seconds to go. I suppose I'd better get down there now otherwise I'll be out of breath when the jingle goes. Hope you feel better soon, Luce. Make sure you get plenty of rest.'

She scurried away before I could urge her to do the same. It was only when I got outside that I remembered that my car was still parked outside The Crown. Thankfully, the pub wasn't far away, and there were a couple of shops along the route where I might be able to get a present for Skye. It wouldn't make me feel any less guilty about not picking up her hints that she had something important she wanted to share with me, but better to celebrate her good news late than never.

As I stared at the bright displays in the windows and tried to focus on deciding whether to get a treat for Skye or something cute for the baby, my mind instead wandered off to the things Mike had said about the listening figures. Despite the bravado in my response, I was worried about what he'd implied. The world of radio is a ruthless place, where change is a constant and there is always a threat from the shiny new up-and-coming presenters. I'd been lucky being awarded long-term contracts and gradually working my way up the presenting ranks until I'd finally got the dream position as breakfast host on a show which was syndicated to stations all over the country. But where was there to go from here? There were plenty of people who'd do anything for my job and I couldn't afford to rest on my laurels. Some people would say the next career move to make was the gilded land of television, but radio was my passion. That and smoothie making, but I was hardly likely to make a living out of that. If my show started haemorrhaging listeners, then my days at this radio station were numbered, and once that happened, there wasn't an obvious place for me to go.

I forced that uncomfortable thought to the back of my mind and tried to channel Skye by mindfully enjoying my surroundings. I managed about fifteen seconds of attempting to appreciate the claggy, polluted air of the street, before an empty crisp packet flew in my face and snapped me out of it. As I still hadn't managed to decide whether to get a gift for Skye or the baby, I settled my dilemma by picking out items for both. The shop assistant declared himself to be a huge fan of my show, and asked for a selfie when I was paying, which was rather embarrassing but flattering nevertheless. Given that I was meant to be heading home sick, I should have said no, but the request made me feel a bit better about my listening figures, so I gave my best grin and made him swear not to post it on social media until at least tomorrow.

I was massively relieved to arrive at the pub and see my car, all four wheels still attached and windows un-smashed. Time to go home. Of course, things were never going to be that simple, because then I couldn't find my keys in my handbag. I concentrated hard until a vague memory floated back into my mind of Chris, the landlord of The Crown, putting them safely behind the bar for me. I smothered a smile as I wondered if that had been before or after the tap-dancing. There was nothing for it, I'd have to go in and hope I could charm Chris into returning them.

I swung open the heavy door and marched in confidently. The Crown, in keeping with its less-than-illustrious surroundings, was a complete dive. It was what you might generously call a 'traditional' old man's pub complete with sticky floors and catering consisting of a few pork pies wrapped in clingfilm behind the bar. But the drinks were cheap, it was close to work and the atmosphere was welcoming, well, to a select group of people anyway. Consequently, it was rare to walk in there and not see someone from Star FM propping up the bar. Sure enough, the first person I saw was Jonno, enjoying a pint and one of the aforementioned pork pies in celebration of another successful show.

'You ought to be careful eating that thing.' I nodded

towards his lunch. 'God knows how long those pies have been out of the fridge for. Surely Peace will have a go at you for all the additives it contains.'

Jonno took another mouthful. '*Serenity* believes in free choices. Besides, she's off filming another series of "Britain's Best Biscuit" or some other tosh, so while the cat's away and all...'

Chris emerged from the back room, a dusty-looking pint glass in each hand.

'Lucy Fairweather, I wondered when I'd be seeing you. And how dare you cast aspersions on this establishment? I'll have you know those pork pies were purchased from the cash and carry by my good self not a week ago now.' His eyes twinkled good-naturedly behind his thick-rimmed spectacles. He placed the beer glasses down and folded his arms expectantly, an expression of mock anger on his face. 'Have you got something to say to me, Lucy? Maybe an apology for the scratches on my tables which weren't there this time yesterday?'

He gestured at a few lines on the surfaces, but to be honest the furniture looked no more battered than it usually did.

I tried to look remorseful. 'Sorry, Chris. I've got a cold. That drink I had must have gone to my head quicker than usual.'

Chris pursed his lips. 'That drink, and then all the others. Tap-dancing, I ask you. Much more of that and I'll have to apply for a special entertainment licence from the council. Never mind, we won't say anything more about it. Though if you fancy making recompense, you could give me a shout out on your show. Anything to get the punters in.'

Jonno pulled a face. 'And get normal folk in here interrupting our peace of an evening? Don't you dare, Lucy. I'll buy you both a drink if you forget about that idea right now.'

I looked at my watch. It was well after midday. I really should be heading home and getting that rest I'd told Mike and Charlie I so desperately needed.

'Go on,' urged Jonno. 'One for the road. Where's your sense of fun? Let's toast Skye's baby. Did you see her round-robin email? It's worthy of a celebration. That child is probably going to come out of the womb meditating. It'll never cry because it'll be too busy doing baby yoga and mindfully drinking breast milk.'

I lightly punched his shoulder. 'Don't be so rude. Skye's an angel, and you know it. She's way above the rest of us.' I hesitated, Sensible Lucy battling it out with Fun Lucy. As always, it wasn't really a fair fight. I pulled up a barstool and settled myself down. 'Go on then, let's wet the baby's head. Or is that what you do after it's born? I don't know. Either way, it would be a shame not to celebrate such a special moment in our favourite newsreader's life.'

'The usual?' asked Chris, reaching over for a large glass.

'Why not?' I said. 'Though perhaps you should make it a small one. It's still only lunchtime after all.'

The small glass ended up being not quite so modest as I'd intended, but I stuck to my word and only had the one, though I had a horrible feeling that Jonno topped it up when I nipped to the loo. It was good to have some relaxation time, and I felt the stress of a difficult morning start seeping away.

As the strains of the *Doctors* theme tune finished playing on the ancient TV in the corner, Jonno checked his watch.

'Better be heading back to work. And am I right in thinking you're skiving off this afternoon?'

I blew a raspberry at him. He laughed, and helped me on with my coat before we headed out to the car park.

'Can you give me a lift down the road, Luce?' he asked. 'I'm going to be late for the weekly planning meeting otherwise.'

I shook my head. 'Afraid not. If Lucy's had a drink, then Lucy doesn't drive, that's my motto.'

It's a rule I always stick to, even if I've just had the one. There are some things you don't mess around with.

A flicker of irritation crossed Jonno's face, but then he leaned in and gave me the standard media-luvvy farewell of a kiss on both cheeks.

'Laters, Luce. Feel better.'

I'd actually been feeling better ever since arriving at The Crown, I guess thanks to the walk in the fresh air to get there. However, the chances of being caught out if I spent any more of my unexpected time off shopping or doing something fun were high so, being a good girl, I caught the bus home to go to bed, only deviating from my journey to get some more cash out.

Unfortunately, the duvet day didn't proceed as planned because my mum was hovering by my doorstep, a classic look of disappointment filling her face when she saw me arrive.

'Hello, Lucy. I've been worried about you the past few days. You look terrible, by the way.'

Only my mum could cram concern and condemnation into the space of six seconds. She turned to the dog, who had dared to raise his bottom so that it was now hovering a couple of inches above the ground.

'I told you to sit!' she barked.

Freddie slammed his backside back down onto the pavement and we exchanged a look of doggy–daughter solidarity.

'Hello to you too,' I said.

I fumbled putting my key into the lock and could feel her disapproving stare boring between my shoulder blades. As soon as the door was open, she strode in, Freddie trotting neatly at her side.

'Yes, please do come in,' I muttered under my breath. 'And, Freddie, feel welcome to leave as much hair as possible when I've just cleaned the place.'

My mum swung round. I always forget that she's got ears like a bat, attuned from many years of listening out for trouble in her job as a playground supervisor at a particularly rough primary school.

'It doesn't look like you've cleaned recently, Lucinda. I'm surprised all this dust isn't setting off your asthma. And don't get me started on the state of your kitchen counters. You should keep on top of your recycling. All those glass bottles cluttering up the place make you look like an alcoholic.'

'Gee, thanks, Mum, way to make a person feel like

they've got a problem. They're from a party I hosted at the weekend, because I have a social life.'

'A bit too much of the wrong kind of social life, if you ask me,' she replied.

I laughed. 'I was wondering how long it would be before you launched into a lecture. This must be a record-breaker, Mum. You've been in the house for less than two minutes and you're already having a go at me about my life choices.'

Freddie whimpered at the tension in the air. For a few moments, a mother–daughter staring match was in full force. Eventually Mum caved and pulled a face. 'I'm sorry, darling, that was perhaps a bit harsh. You know it's only because I care about you that I say these things. I only want what's best for you.'

However, I was on a roll now and in no mood for accepting her apologies.

'I think I'm grown up enough now to know for myself what's best. I'm Lucy Fairweather, I'm a successful radio DJ and I like to have fun. I'm not hurting anyone, so why don't you let me get on with living my life without coming around to judge me all the time? What are you even doing here?'

As soon as the question was out of my mouth, I wished it away, because I already knew the answer. There's a painful reason Mum comes around more often at this time of the year, and it's because of that same reason we're both more likely to end up in just this kind of slanging match. But acknowledging it to myself, and being able to talk about an incident I still find agonisingly raw are two very different things. I teetered on the edge of trying to say something, but while I was grasping for the right words, Mum clicked her tongue at Freddie. He leaped to her side, throwing me a disappointed look that his visit was being prematurely curtailed. She fixed me with a stern stare which would have had me whimpering in moments in my teenage years.

'You think you're not upsetting anyone, but I can think of quite a few who are hurt by your actions, not least one of whom is yourself. Come along, Frederick, we're not wanted here.' Freddie's ears went back as Mum yanked him away from some cereal crumbs which he'd managed to find on the floor. 'Call me when you're in a better mood, Lucinda. I deal with enough sulky, immature children at work. I'm not going to waste my spare time doing it as well.'

Chapter Three

I decided to fix myself a hot toddy for medicinal purposes and took myself off to bed to recover. So far, the day had been rubbish from start to finish. The only good point had been Skye's surprise announcement, but I was in the kind of mood where even that made me feel down. She was the one friend I knew I could rely on, but her priorities were bound to alter over the next few months. I'd seen it happen with other friends. They'd swear that motherhood wouldn't change them and that they'd still have plenty of time to hang out with me, but, before I knew it, I'd be ditched in favour of Tumble Tots and cake meetings with the other yummy mummies. Maybe Skye would be different and she'd let me play the role of Cool Aunt Lucy, but the way my life was going, I'd probably end up more like a lonely Great Aunt Lucy, left behind in the old bears' home in Peru while young Paddington went off to explore the world and have adventures without me.

I put my glass down unfinished on my bedside table.

The whisky in my hot toddy was making me maudlin. Next time I made one, I'd cut down on the booze content, I vowed. I shuffled further down under the duvet and turned the television on, flicking through the channels until I found one showing ancient repeats of some soap opera to distract me from the dark places my mind kept disappearing into. And then I finally drifted off to sleep to a soundtrack of arguing addicts and cheating fiancés.

———————

I woke up with sunlight streaming onto my face from the gap in the curtains. Stretching my limbs like a cat, I rolled over and checked my phone. I must have forgotten to put it on charge last night because there was no sign of life. Normally my own batteries felt pretty flat too, but today I was invigorated by the healing powers of sleep. I spent half my life feeling groggy from my semi-nocturnal existence. It was amazing what difference it made seeing the light. Sunshine had the power to make my spirits soar and ease the tension headache which seemed to constantly pull on my forehead. I took a deep, relaxing breath and relished the sensation of contentment.

And then my heart stopped as the obvious question occurred to me with a cold sense of horror. Why was it so light outside? At this time of the year, I shouldn't normally be experiencing this kind of brightness until I came out of the studio. I leaped out of bed, my pulse suddenly going triple-time. I hit the menu button on the remote control and the time on the TV screen confirmed my worst fears. I was late. Very, very late. In fact, so late, I'd be lucky to make it to the radio station for the last five minutes of the show.

I hopped around the bedroom, trying to pull on my jeans while turning the radio on to see how they'd managed to cope with the situation. I'd properly dumped them in the poo. Was that Skye presenting my slot for me? Why hadn't she rung my landline to wake me up and get me in there? I nearly fell down the stairs as I tried to simultaneously do up my trainers and pull on my old uni hoody, the first item of clothing I'd managed to grab. As I slammed the front door behind me, I cursed myself for abandoning the car in the pub car park once again. To add to my transport difficulties, I couldn't summon a taxi because my phone was dead as a dodo. There was no other option. I'd have to make it to the bus stop. I set off at a run, but no sooner had I got going, then I tripped over my still-undone laces. I went headfirst to the ground, painfully jarring my wrists as I automatically put out my hands to break my fall.

But a tumble wasn't going to stop me. I heaved myself up and continued at a staggering jog pace, picking pieces of gravel out of the grazes on my hands as I went. One bus sped past me when I was still a couple of hundred yards from the bus stop. I put on a spurt, but the sadistic driver waited at the stop until I was ten feet away before setting off on his route again.

If my palms weren't so sore, I would have shaken my fist at his retreating vehicle. Somehow the fact that the bus had a banner on its side advertising my show, complete with a glossy picture of me, made my predicament feel even worse. I collapsed in a heap on the bus shelter bench and fought to regain my breath. My hands were stinging, my lungs were aching and I still had the problem of how on earth I was going to get to work to contend with. Mike was going to slaughter me. And the tears routine wasn't going to work for a second time with Charlie from HR. I was in deep, deep bother.

I sat there feeling pathetically sorry for myself. It felt like however hard I tried, and however good my intentions were, something always seemed to go wrong. I allowed myself five minutes of self-indulgent wallowing, ignoring the niggling voice at the back of my mind telling me that I'd brought this particular disaster on myself. Then I forced my brain into gear. There were practicalities to sort. I needed to come up with an excuse for not showing up, something better than just having slept in.

I don't deal well with having too much time to think. The longer I sat at the bus stop worrying away, the more guilty and uncomfortable I felt about the whole situation. Maybe my mum was right and I am my own worst enemy. I quashed that thought immediately. Part of the reason my programme is so successful is because I'm not afraid of showing that I am that girl next door, you know, the slightly bonkers one, but basically an average human being who makes mistakes like everyone else, and knows how to have a good laugh. Only my mistakes seemed to have got into the habit of being rather bigger than everyone else's.

My train of thought was interrupted by an angry beep. I looked up and saw another bus had pulled up.

'Are you getting on today, love, or not?' asked the driver. 'Only I do have a strict schedule I've got to follow.'

'Sorry, I was miles away.' I hurried forward, accidentally colliding with someone who was disembarking. The dregs of their tea spilled onto my jeans, joining a smear of blood from my injured hands. At this rate, I'd turn up looking like a victim of assault. For the briefest of seconds, I actually contemplated whether that would work as an excuse, before I firmly stamped on the ridiculousness of the idea. I might tell a few little white lies every so often, but that would definitely classify as a dirty great big one.

I scrunched myself up on a grimy seat and spent the journey racking my brain for inspiration. I was so engrossed in my thoughts that I nearly missed the stop for the radio station, and rang the bell when we'd driven past it. Thankfully, the bus driver took pity on my bedraggled state and screeched to a halt, letting me descend in the industrial estate around the corner from the office.

I set off at another vigorous trot, but slowed down again when I heard the thunderous bell of the local church clanging for ten o'clock. My show was over. There was no point in rushing now. My feet grew heavy and every instinct in my body told me to turn around and leave because I was in big trouble. But I wasn't one to shirk my responsibilities. It was up to me to face the music and try to mend some bridges. I reluctantly trudged up the road and turned the bend. Then I stopped in my tracks. Why was there a crowd outside the building? There were so many people milling around, I couldn't even see the front door. At first, I thought they must be doing a fire practice, but as I scanned the faces of the jostling mass, I realised I didn't recognise a single one from the radio station.

However, I soon started spotting the familiar forms of photographers who occasionally descended to get snaps and gossip when we had a big-name celebrity appearing on the show. Perhaps Jonno had a famous guest on today. I looked down at my grubby jeans, far-from-white trainers and tatty hoody. Well, they'd either be too busy looking out for their celeb to notice me, or as fellow media-types they'd hopefully cut me some slack for my less-than-perfect appearance. I lowered my head and strode on, deciding the direct route was the best way through the crowd.

It was a massive mistake. As I moved forward, one of them shouted my name, and then the rest surged towards me. Suddenly phones were being thrust in my face and cameras were flashing enough to blur my vision. I was disorientated and overwhelmed by the sudden invasion of my personal space, but the harder I pushed to try to get past them, the harder they pressed back at me. It was suffocating and noisy and horribly intimidating. People were shouting questions at me, but I couldn't make out what they were saying in all the hubbub. The noise was an assault and the expressions on the faces surrounding me were gleefully predatory. I spotted the smallest of gaps, and scurried through, but still they chased me down. And then at last I was at the front door of the radio station, banging the frame in my desperation to be let in. If someone didn't rescue me soon, I was scared I was going to throw up, or faint, or worse.

When someone tapped me on the shoulder, I lost it. I turned around to the mass of strangers and bellowed at them. I'm not sure what I said, or if it was even words that came out of my mouth or just a noise, but I was completely overwhelmed by the crowd and I wanted them to leave me alone. But they surged closer towards me, laughing at my distress, relishing my obvious discomfort, or so it felt. I shrank against the door, my body feeling like it was turning into a cowering, quivering mess.

Then, suddenly, someone was pulling me inside, the door was firmly shut behind me and the hubbub of the outside world quietened into a dull roar.

'Blimey, they need to calm down a bit,' I said shakily, attempting to inject a note of levity into my voice as I tried to collect myself. Now that it was all over, I felt embarrassed at my overreaction. 'Who's the paparazzi pack's victim of choice today?'

'You are,' said Skye, a fearful expression on her face.

Chapter Four

At first, I thought she was joking.

'Very funny, Skye. What would that bunch of beasts want with me?'

She looked anxiously behind me at the group who were still trying to take shots through the glass doors of the main reception.

'Perhaps we should find somewhere a bit more private to speak,' she suggested, dragging me down the corridor and into Studio Two which had been closed, supposedly for refurbishment, for as long as I could remember. She shut the heavy door behind us and urged me to sit down, looking at me like she was an oncologist about to deliver some bad news.

I was too unsettled to follow her direction. 'I'd rather stand, thanks, if it's all the same. What on earth is going on? Surely all that fuss out there can't be because I missed my show this morning? Great job on presenting it, by the way. I didn't get to listen to much, but from what I did hear, you're a total natural.' Despite my own anxiety, I wanted to let Skye know I wasn't angry with her for stepping into my shoes.

Skye frowned. 'Trust me, missing your show this morning is the least of your worries right now.' She took my hand. 'Please sit down, Lucy. I don't know how I'm going to tell you this, and you're making it so much harder with all that pacing around.'

I'd never seen Skye look so concerned. 'Is everything OK with you, lovely? Nothing's happened to the baby, has it?' She shook her head. 'That's good. Well, whatever's happened, I'm sure I can handle it. Tell me straight. I've still got to smooth Mike's ruffled feathers over this morning, and I suspect I'll have to eat humble pie for Charlie as well. Another standard Thursday morning in the wonderful world of Lucy.' I was trying to sound blasé, but the gurgling noises from my nervously churning stomach probably told their own story.

The words came out of Skye's mouth in a torrent. 'Luce, this is going to take much more than smoothing feathers and eating pie. Look, it's probably better if I show you, rather than tell you.'

She took her phone out of her pocket with shaking hands and scrolled through until she found what she wanted. She held it clutched to her chest.

'I don't know if I can bring myself to do this to you,' she said, her pale face making her look like a ghostly waif in the half-light of the abandoned studio.

'Skye, please don't be melodramatic. I'm sure it can't be as bad as all that. Just show me the darn thing.' I was still desperately hoping it would turn out to be something and nothing. Skye and I do after all have a very different perspective on the world. I was relying on the fact that her definition of a disaster normally qualifies as a minor quibble on my scale of things.

I held out my hand, until at last, she reluctantly passed the phone over.

'Don't say I didn't warn you,' she whispered, folding her arms close and chewing her bottom lip as she waited for me to see whatever it was on the screen.

I looked down and blinked in surprise as I saw a video of me tap-dancing on the bar at The Crown and warbling along to a song about being a gold-digger. OK, it wasn't taken from the most flattering of angles, and my moves and tuning left a lot to be desired, but it was hardly the worst video I'd seen of myself online. After all, as a radio presenter, I regularly end up participating in wacky stunts for the entertainment of my listeners, and they are always filmed and posted on social media. Google my name, and you'll find a host of stuff featuring me looking like a prat. I felt a surge of relief.

'Carry on watching,' urged Skye, pre-empting my response.

All of a sudden, the video changed tone. First of all, there was a clip of me sipping a drink, but whoever had put the thing together had edited it with a boomerang effect so it looked like I was constantly knocking back shot after shot. Then there was some footage of me staggering forward and being caught by Jonno, shortly followed by a clip showing the pair of us getting in a taxi together. Jonno leaned across me to open the door, and I stumbled forwards. He was stopping me falling, but from the angle it was filmed, it looked like I was throwing myself at him, in a prelude to getting up close and very personal. Then the video cut to a shot which must have been filmed only yesterday, because there was me standing close to Jonno as we said goodbye to each other at The Crown. But at the point when we were about to air kiss our farewells, the video faded to black, turning another innocent moment into something far more suggestive. Someone must have been lurking in the shadows to get the shot, because I couldn't remember having seen anyone around when we left the pub.

The video was intrusive and nasty. Watching it made me feel uncomfortable, especially at the idea that someone had been creeping around after me to try and get material which looked compromising.

'Wow, someone's made a lot of effort pulling that together. What are they hoping to achieve with it?' I said, attempting to put a brave face on the situation. My mind was buzzing with questions. 'What's Jonno got to say? I can't imagine he's too happy at this either, especially given that he's meant to be all loved up with Serenity.'

Skye leaned over my shoulder and tapped the phone screen to bring up Twitter. 'I've not been able to speak to him properly yet because he was prepping for his show, but he's tweeted that it was all a big mistake and he's publicly asked for his girlfriend's forgiveness. #TeamSerenity is now trending online along with stuff like #LooseLucy. And that's one of the nicer hashtags to describe you. People are posting some really offensive stuff about you. I'm so sorry, Lucy. It's a complete mess.'

I scrolled through the feed and scanned the stream of vile hatred directed at me. The sheer nastiness of some of the comments made me want to curl up in a ball and hide.

'I don't understand,' I said, my eyes starting to blur as words like 'bitch', 'slut' and 'gold-digger' flashed repeatedly up at me. 'Why would Jonno tweet asking for forgiveness? Neither of us have done anything wrong. There is nothing for us to apologise for.'

I leaped up and resumed my angry pacing, Skye's phone nearly paying the price of my outrage when I slammed it down on the desk. Why did all these complete strangers feel like they had the right to be so rude and comment on something which they didn't know the first thing about? They were obviously enjoying ganging up on me, egging each other on and forgetting that the target of their vitriol was a real person.

'There's another thing,' said Skye, hesitantly. 'We got loads of texts and tweets sent in during your show this morning. I'm afraid the listeners seem to have taken your absence as an admission of guilt. As soon as it became obvious I was doing the show instead of you, the hotline phone started ringing off the hook. The main office numbers have been jammed as well with journalists wanting a comment about the situation.'

'There is no situation.' I threw my hands up and gestured to the ceiling in sheer exasperation. 'I slept in and missed the show, my bad, but it doesn't have anything to do with this horrible video. It's clearly someone with far too much time on their hands who's got it in for me. How can one dodgy video stir up so much outrage? It's not even well edited.' I took a deep breath. 'But I'm not the only victim of this. How's Serenity taking it? I don't want to cause issues for her and Jonno.'

Skye looked shifty. 'I don't really know. You're probably best asking Jonno rather than me,' she said eventually, scratching at the worn carpet with her foot as she avoided my gaze.

'I know you, Skye, and you're rubbish at lying. What is it that you're not telling me?' I tried to lighten the tone. 'Come on, it can't be as bad as that unflattering shot of me on the bar. I mean, did you see how many chins that filming angle gave me?'

Skye couldn't even raise a smile. 'I don't really know, but Jonno was muttering something about it being great publicity for her new TV series. She's posted on Instagram about forgiveness and understanding, but, if I'm being honest, it's got an edge to it, and I'm sure it's going to wind up her followers to hate you even more.' Skye always sees the best in people, so if she was suggesting that, the post must be really bad. No wonder there'd been such a reception party to greet me on my arrival. The tabloids always love social media spats, especially if a reality star with an online following of several million is involved. Serenity had arrived on the scene after being a contestant on one of those dating programmes. She'd captured the public's hearts by calling out the bad guy of the show for cheating on her, and had continued to dominate the headlines ever since with her antics both on and off screen.

'Never mind,' I said shakily, still hoping against hope that the storm would be short-lived. 'Today's newspapers soon go into tomorrow's recycling bins. They'll move onto something more interesting quickly enough and forget all about me.'

'I'm sure it'll all be fine,' said Skye, sounding not very sure at all.

We sat in silence while I digested the thought of my new-found notoriety. I'd seen people destroyed by the online world, whole careers flushed down the toilet in minutes because of a badly judged tweet or a poorly worded Instagram story. It was terrifying to contemplate. At least in the abandoned studio I felt safely cushioned from the hostility of the outside world. Would it be possible to lurk in here until the controversy had blown over?

Unfortunately, my sanctuary didn't remain a haven for long. Mike strode into the room, exuding an arrogant he-man air, determined to sort out the naughty little girl.

'So, this is where you've been hiding,' he said. 'A mighty fine mess you've got the radio station into. You've brought us into total disrepute, not to mention what you've done to that poor Serenity with your selfish behaviour. What are you going to do about it?'

I swear if he had a moustache, he'd have been twirling it like a pantomime villain. There was a distinctly gleeful tone to his voice, and I strongly suspected he was rather enjoying my discomfort.

However, this was not the time to stand up to him and his patronising attitude.

'Mike, I'm really, truly sorry about this morning. My

alarm didn't go off. It's no excuse, I know, but it's the only one I can offer. I will set half a dozen alarms in future, and I guarantee it won't happen again. I've learned my lesson.'

His lips briefly twitched into a disturbing smile. 'We are far beyond excuses now. HR want to see you immediately. And as we've worked together for some time now,' he definitely made it sound like a prison sentence, 'I feel honour-bound to give you advance warning that Charlie's going to suspend you for gross misconduct.'

I nearly choked. 'Gross misconduct? Because I was late on one day, and because some weirdo has made me go viral with a horrid fake video? I'm the victim here. The company should be supporting me, not sacking me.'

Curse me and my big fat mouth. Mike looked even more pleased with himself. 'Nobody's talking about sackings yet, but I wouldn't be surprised if it's on the cards. Of course, there are processes to follow, and statements to be taken from colleagues, but you know how these things work.'

He left me with no doubt that he'd be testifying against me. 'Follow me,' he continued. 'Charlie is waiting for you in the boardroom with the managing director.'

Could my day get any worse? I'd never met the managing director and the only people I knew who had seen her hadn't stuck around long enough to tell the tale. I might as well empty out my locker and sign up at the job centre right now.

Mike held the door open and gestured at me to follow him, like a prison officer escorting the accused to the dock. Skye hissed some words of good luck which I acknowledged with a miserable expression on my face. As we walked through the radio station, everyone went quiet when they saw me, but as soon as I got past, the whispering restarted. I tried to ignore it, but it made me feel even more isolated and alone.

The conversation in the boardroom didn't last long. There was no denying that I'd missed my show this morning with no good reason, and that, combined with yesterday's almost tardiness, meant they didn't have to find an excuse to suspend me from duty. But I knew there was more to it than that. It would be a relief for them to get me off the airwaves for a bit. From what I'd seen so far on social media and the reaction to me at the front door, it was clear what narrative had been built around the viral video. I was to be the villain of the piece, and Jonno and Serenity the poor, innocent victims. The internet loves to gang up on someone, and it didn't make the radio station look good if the presenter of their flagship show was otherwise known as #LooseLucy, drunken stealer of boyfriends and slutty gold-digger. It would be much better for Star FM if they kept me out of sight and out of mind.

What made the whole meeting worse was Mike sending smug, satisfied little glances in my direction whenever the managing director said something particularly damning. He clearly enjoyed every minute of my discomfort and when Charlie asked if Mike was able to speak in support of my work in his capacity as my producer, he remained pointedly quiet. That was what tipped me over the edge. He was the laziest, most patronising producer I'd ever met, content to sit back and let me do all the hard slog of putting together the show. It takes a huge amount of work to entertain a mass audience for four hours every morning, and keep things fresh and fun while people are getting stressed out on the school run or commuting to the office. I couldn't remember the last time he'd actually contributed to the effort. Well, when I returned from my exile, I was definitely going to demand a new producer. It was clear our working relationship was well and truly over.

Of course, that all depended on me having a future at Star FM.

'I suggest you leave by the side entrance,' said Charlie, not even giving me a chance to speak in my own defence. 'We'd rather keep the station's name out of this as much as possible, and I suppose it would be inappropriate to make you run the gauntlet of the press pack at the front again. Mike, please could you escort Lucy to the exit? We're all mature grown-ups. I'm sure I can trust you to leave without making a fuss?' He looked over his glasses at me, and I had a flashback to being a naughty eleven year old being told off by the headteacher.

I nodded obediently. What did he think I was going to do? Nick all the stationery from the cupboard and tap-dance my way out of the building?

Mike tucked his phone away and agreed to walk with me. Charlie and the managing director started putting paperwork back into folders, signalling the end of the meeting, but there were more questions I needed answers to.

'How long are you putting me on leave? Are you going to pay me while I'm off? Because I will be contacting my lawyer if you're not.' I was completely winging it, but I had to at least try something to show that I wasn't going without a fight. I wouldn't know where to start in appointing an employment lawyer, but I saw a flash of fear on the managing director's face. 'I'd like to remind you that when Jonno was late for his show, there was no further action taken, so I can only assume that this is a discrimination thing. I'd also like to point out that I'm the victim of an online hate campaign, and you, as my employers, should be helping me through this difficult time, rather than joining the bullies. I expect there to be a full and thorough investigation into what's happened, and I shall look forward to hearing the results from you at the earliest opportunity.'

I knew it was pointless even saying it, but it made me feel better. At least I might be able to leave this room with my head held high, knowing that I didn't roll over and let them kick me when I was down.

Charlie cleared his throat. 'Jonno was late on that occasion because of personal reasons. We are an equal opportunities employer, and the video has certainly had no influence on how we have decided to handle things today. I think we're done here.'

That was me put in my place. The managing director nodded. Clearly my fate was sealed.

'Can we go down the back way rather than going through the main office?' I hated myself for asking the question and showing even the tiniest bit of weakness in front of Mike, but the thought of being paraded again in front of my colleagues was utterly mortifying. I realised my mistake as soon as I'd asked the question, because he acted like he'd gone deaf and deliberately steered me towards the office.

Nobody wanted to meet my gaze as I was frogmarched through. And then 'Gold-digger' came on the radio and I wanted to curl up in a ball of humiliation. Had they deliberately timed it to this moment to drive the knife home? I pressed my lips together to stop them trembling, and stared directly in front of me, hoping to give the impression I was rising above the whole situation. It was only when Skye rushed forward and pushed a box containing my blender and various bits of desk detritus into my arms that I nearly broke down.

'Maybe you'll have some more time for experimenting with flavours now,' she said, forcing a smile onto her face, trying to look on the bright side as she always did. 'Then, when you're back, you'll have lots of lovely new smoothies for us all to try out.' She gestured around her, clearly trying to get the support of the office, but nobody else was willing to stick their neck out for me.

'Thanks, Skye. I'll keep you posted how I get on,' I said. She opened her arms, moving in to give me a goodbye hug, but I neatly side-stepped her embrace. Kindness would definitely be my undoing and I was determined not to cry in front of this lot.

'See you later. Or not as the case may be,' said Mike cheerily, as he pressed open the side door and practically pushed me outside. He slammed the door behind me, and I could hear him checking the lock as if he was concerned I might try to force my way back into the building. For a moment I stood outside the door, numb with shock at my change in circumstances, and wondering if I'd been shut out permanently.

But I couldn't stay lurking on the fire escape for ever. I crept across the car park, desperately hoping to make a clean getaway without attracting any more attention to myself. I hoped in vain. I was in the most exposed position possible with nothing to hide behind when the pap pack rounded the building and spotted me standing there with the blender in my arms. I realised instantly that this would be a brilliant photo for them to get, me looking like I'd been kicked out with all my possessions in a cardboard box. I threw caution to the wind and set off at a run. I didn't care if this gave them an even crazier-looking snap for the sidebar of shame. I'd had enough. I wanted to get home and bury myself away from all this. Trusting that the photographers would be too lazy to pursue me far, I put on a spurt and didn't look back.

Chapter Five

I dashed to the car park of The Crown to retrieve my car. Much as I was desperate to retreat within the doors of the pub and drown my sorrows, the images from the video of me dancing on the bar and apparently flinging myself at Jonno kept flashing before my eyes. The Crown no longer felt like the safe haven it usually was. I glanced nervously around, wondering where the video-maker had hidden to get his or her shots, not once, but two days in a row. Their persistence felt particularly sinister.

There was a low wall at one end, but I couldn't imagine someone being able to conceal themselves properly behind that. I considered the angle at which the footage had been taken. The only other place was a straggly row of bushes, which looked like they were the main toilet area for the neighbourhood's dog population. Whoever it was must have been pretty driven to hide there long enough to get the compromising shots. Somehow that made the whole thing even more threatening.

I hurried inside and collected my keys from Chris, ignoring his efforts to engage me in conversation. I didn't feel strong enough for speech. Once I'd checked the coast was clear, I hurried back outside and locked myself in my car. It was an effort to turn on the ignition and start driving, when all I wanted to do was grip the steering wheel and wail into the dashboard, but I knew I wasn't safe yet. The pack could still be in pursuit, and I needed to get a safe distance away.

The journey home took all the energy I possessed. I drove at exactly the speed-limit the whole way, double and triple-checking at the junctions, forcing myself to concentrate hard on every move I made. For the first time since I'd got a car of my own, I kept the radio turned off. Hearing my colleagues laughing and joking on the airwaves would have been too much to bear, as I knew they'd be using the same silly tone to banter about my fall from grace as soon as the mics were off.

When I arrived home, I drove past the front door first to check there were no stray paps hanging around outside. I wouldn't put it past them to have found my address and camped out on my doorstep too. Fortunately, there was no sign of the hacks. I guess they'd got all the photos of me looking bonkers that they needed at the radio station. I still scurried from the car to the house with my hoody pulled up over my head, looking like a defendant arriving at court. It was only once I was safely inside that the barriers finally broke. I crumpled to the floor in the hallway and cried like I hadn't done in years.

. . .

The next few days passed in a blur in which I turned into the clichéd stereotype of the unemployed person, dressing in my slouchiest trackie bottoms and relying on regular fast food deliveries for sustenance. I kept trying to tell myself that my suspension was only temporary, but when I turned on the radio to torture myself with the breakfast show every morning, it seemed clear they were doing just fine without me. Mike and Skye were holding the fort, doing a presenting double-act. Skye had a beautifully light touch, and even Mike's total inability to sound relaxed and natural wasn't holding her back. She had stepped into my shoes with ease, and I was professional enough to recognise the freshness she injected into the format. I tried to make myself be pleased for her, telling myself that it didn't matter that she was doing so well, but I was finding it harder and harder to find the energy to be nice in my replies to her regular text messages checking up on me. Eventually, I stopped replying at all.

In fact, it was better to keep my phone turned off. Even though I knew I shouldn't, I frequently found my fingers hypnotically drawn towards the social media apps, and once I'd fallen down that particular worm hole, I'd be trapped for hours, scrolling through the reams of hatred which were still being directed at me. I'd hoped the trolls would have moved onto another victim by now, but some anonymous villain kept fanning the flames, and so it kept on coming. I could cope with the stupid gifs and the vindictive memes people had created with various choice images of me looking like a prat, but of course they didn't stick with that kind of tame stuff for long. Soon, my haters' preferred pastime was tweeting about the inventive ways they'd like to make me suffer. Rape threats were their go-to method of violence. I tried to tell myself that it was only talk, but I couldn't help thinking of all the news stories I'd heard about people who'd been threatened online and then been found at a later date horribly attacked or even murdered.

It disturbed me so much that I rang the local police station. I felt vulnerable picking up the phone, like I was admitting weakness in not being able to shrug off the abuse. It was even worse when the bored-sounding desk sergeant finally answered the call. He made me feel like a silly child for wasting his time with my petty problems. On top of that, he made it abundantly clear that he'd seen the viral video online and thought that I was getting exactly what I deserved. To be fair, he did go through the motions of responding to my concern, but the gist of it was that there was nothing he could, or would, do about the situation. He told me people said all sorts of things on social media, and it didn't normally come to anything. It would all go away eventually, but, if I was really worried, there were a few online support groups he could point me in the direction of. He apparently failed to see the irony in prescribing support in the very place where I was being tormented. I hung up when he was only halfway through reciting the support group's address.

Left to my own devices, I started to get jumpy and paranoid, and took to triple-locking my front door and constantly peering out of the windows to check for intruders in the garden. However much I told myself not to take the cruel vitriol to heart, the words were always dancing there on the back of my eyelids whenever I tried to get some rest from it all. The only thing that deadened the obsessively paranoid thoughts was a stiff drink or two before I went to bed. If my mum could see the extra bottles lining up on the kitchen worksurface now, she'd be really mad, but I still wasn't speaking to her, and she was too stubborn to make the first move after our spat. I comforted myself with the thought that, as the last remaining person on the planet without a smart phone, social media accounts, or any interest in the celeb gossip pages of the newspapers, she'd be blissfully ignorant of the mess I was currently in.

I stared bleakly at the pile of empty takeaway boxes which were stacked up by the bin. I'd inadvertently created my own leaning tower of pizza in the kitchen. Normally, I'd tuck away a line like that to drop casually into my radio show, but who knew when I'd next have an audience who actually wanted to listen to me.

The sound of something coming through my letterbox set my heart racing. I still wasn't used to not being on breakfast show time and needing to take a nap in the middle of the day. With all the neighbours at work, my street was deadly quiet, and the creak of the letterbox flap sounded like an ancient door being opened by a creepy butler in a horror movie. I gave myself a stern lecture. Just because it wasn't the usual time the postman came around, didn't mean there was something sinister about the delivery. I needed to calm down and stop being so suspicious of everything.

'It's official, I'm turning into Loopy Lucy,' I addressed

the empty room. Filling the silence was proving to be a hard habit to lose.

I went into the hall, actually quite pleased to have something to do, however mundane the task. But I should have listened to my first instinct. There was a single envelope lying on my doormat. There was nothing out of the ordinary about the simple white object, but something about it set me on edge. As I moved closer, I could make out my name scrawled in green ink on the surface. It was a standing joke at the radio station that the nutters always used green ink, but I told myself it didn't mean anything. Still, I held back from touching it. The handwriting was jagged, and whoever had written on the envelope had done so with enough force to poke a scattering of holes through its surface.

'Oh grow up, Lucy, you're being pathetic,' I told myself sternly. A diet of daytime television was clearly sending me to the edge. I scooped the letter off the mat and ripped the envelope open. A collection of yellowing newspaper cuttings fell out. There was an article from the local paper about the rise in knife crime in the area, complete with an illustration of some vicious-looking blades which had recently been confiscated from perpetrators. Another article was about a woman being assaulted on her way home from work. The final article was the one which freaked me out the most. It was a cutting about the murder of the television presenter Jill Dando, but my publicity photo had been stuck over her face.

I only just made it to the bathroom in time. I clutched the sink and heaved my guts up. My forehead was clammy and I felt as achy and wounded as if I'd been physically attacked. It was one thing seeing those horrible threats on Twitter when I could turn the screen off and walk away if I chose, but it was quite another to see it posted through my own front door, invading what should have been my safe haven. Someone had worked out where I lived and gone to the trouble of hand-delivering the disturbing articles to my house. That person had been outside my front door, mere inches away from me only minutes ago. Had they stuck around to enjoy the impact the cuttings had had on me? My heart was racing.

Would the police take me seriously now? But the memory of the condescending attitude I'd encountered before held me back from picking up the phone straight away. If I rang again so soon, the snotty sergeant would probably think I was a delusional has-been, desperate for attention at any cost. I couldn't face the thought of it.

Perhaps I should tell the radio station about what was happening. I knew that on the rare occasion when presenters got weird letters delivered to work, the bosses had ways and means of getting the authorities to pay attention and sort the problem out. But I was very much *persona non grata* there. Why would they feel any obligation to help me out when I was currently suspended? Besides, the managing director had nominated Mike and Charlie as my points of contact should I have any issues during my suspension, and I couldn't imagine either of them putting themselves out to come to my aid. I had never felt so alone.

I'm not sure how long I stayed hiding in my bathroom, curled up on the cold tiles, my head pressed against the bathtub. It was a deeply uncomfortable position, but the ache in my shoulders and the pins and needles in my legs were a welcome distraction from the dark terror. I wasn't sure how much more of this psychological pressure I could take.

When the doorbell rang, I jumped so suddenly, I banged my forehead against the sink. I crawled over to the bathroom door and checked the lock was fully turned, my pulse pounding. Had the person who'd clipped up the newspaper cuttings returned to make good on their implied threats? I glanced around the bathroom. The toilet brush was about the only object which I could use to defend myself with, and that was hardly going to make a difference against someone wielding a knife. I decided to stay hidden and prayed that the person at the door would go away.

But they seemed determined to attract my attention. Whoever was there was leaning on the doorbell so it pealed constantly. They only stopped ringing it to rattle the letterbox vigorously. Clearly they were there for the long haul. Should I make a run for the bedroom and phone for help? It was the only sensible option, and I needed to start making more sensible decisions in my life, because look where being impulsive and scatter-brained had got me right now.

I told myself to grow up, unlocked the bathroom door, and crept onto the landing. I was halfway towards my bedroom when the letterbox creaked open again.

'I can see your feet moving around up there, you know,' called Skye. 'Please let us in, Lucy.'

The sense of relief was overwhelming. I had never been

so glad to hear a friendly voice. I rushed down the stairs and hustled Skye and Henri indoors, quickly glancing up and down the street to see if I could spot any suspicious characters lurking around. Bolting the door behind us, I ushered them through to the kitchen so we weren't in a room which looked out onto the road, but then I thought someone might be watching from the overgrown garden at the back, so I shepherded them back into the hallway again. Unfortunately, that meant the gaping letterbox and doormat were right in the centre of my vision, which made me go all clammy and panicky again.

'Are you alright, Lucy?' asked Henri from a long way away. I quickly tore my gaze away from the doormat which seemed to have been growing bigger and bigger in my imagination. The hallway was awfully dark. Why were Henri and Skye moving in such a peculiar way? They were undulating in and out of focus in a most disconcerting fashion.

'I think she's going to pass out,' said Skye, her voice distorted and practically unrecognisable.

I felt myself being pushed to sit down on the bottom step, then Henri was holding a paper bag in front of my mouth, urging me to breathe into it. This seemed like the most confusing action so far, but I'd reached the point where I was convinced I was having a heart attack and about to die, so it was just simpler to do as I was told. I took a couple of breaths, and choked as I nearly sucked a receipt into my mouth.

'Sorry,' apologised Skye, fishing the offending bit of paper out of the bag and then passing it back to me.

She rubbed my back while Henri talked me through my breaths until I was breathing normally. Then the utter ridiculousness of the situation hit home, and I started laughing, which I think frightened them even more than the funny turn.

'Good practice for you, this, Henri,' I spluttered.

'What do you mean?' he asked, his subtly lyrical Finnish accent making the question sound all the more comical to my warped mind.

'Good practice for when Skye gives birth and you're holding her hand and telling her to breathe her way through the pain.'

'Ah, yes, you are right. Very good. Thank you for providing me with this perfect opportunity,' he said formally. I've never been quite sure of what to make of Henri. He always comes across as very serious, which normally makes me want to act in a silly way to counteract it, but that's just my contrary nature. But serious or not, he's a kind man, and I'm glad Skye has him at her side.

'Feeling better now?' asked Skye.

I felt like I'd done ten rounds in a boxing ring, but at least I was breathing normally again.

'Getting there,' I said.

'Perhaps a cup of tea would help,' said Henri. 'I know what you English are like with your belief in the healing properties of tea.'

'Proper tea is theft,' I said, dropping another one of my silly radio jokes.

Skye rolled her eyes. 'She's definitely feeling better if she's doing puns. Henri, why don't you put the kettle on?

Lucy can you show him where everything is? If you don't mind, I'm going to nip and use your loo. My bladder seems to be shrinking as my belly grows. Thank you, little one.' She patted her stomach affectionately.

Henri and I followed our instructions. He insisted I sit down at the breakfast bar, so I directed him around the kitchen and he bustled about boiling the kettle and putting teabags in mugs, all while tactfully ignoring the collection of junk which gave away how badly I'd been taking care of myself over the last few days.

I was about to take a sip of the comforting steamy liquid when Skye burst into the room, clutching the newspaper cuttings in her hands. I could have kicked myself. She must have found them on the bathroom floor.

'Is this what you've been having to deal with?' she said, gesturing at the picture of my face stuck on the murdered TV presenter's body.

'Oh it's nothing, pass them over,' I said, in a lame attempt to steer her away from the topic. It didn't seem fair to inflict my troubles on her when she should be enjoying her life as a newly promoted presenter and expectant mum.

She passed the clippings over to Henri. I tried to intercept them en route, but the pair of them used their superior heights to foil me.

Henri examined the bits of paper with his usual seriousness. 'This is very worrying, Lucy. And was this envelope hand-delivered?'

I nodded before I could stop myself. However much I knew I should spare them from my woes, there was a sense of relief in being able to share the situation with my friends.

'Then it is safe to assume that this individual knows your address. Have you involved the police yet?'

I quickly explained what they'd said when I'd approached them about the internet hate messages.

'I'm not sure I've got the energy to go through all the hassle of reporting it. They clearly don't take me seriously. It's only some crank anyway.'

'You are probably right. We'll leave you to it,' said Henri.

'Please don't leave me alone,' I said plaintively, then immediately gave myself a stern telling off. I was a grown woman, and I could handle this by myself.

Henri smiled. 'I was testing. We have no intention of leaving you to deal with this alone. We will report the matter to the police and they will investigate it. Perhaps they will pay more attention if we are here when you do it.'

Skye nodded. 'Of course, we know you're perfectly capable of coping with this. I mean, look at everything you've been through in the past.'

I shot her a warning glare. I was not feeling strong enough to dredge up that kind of stuff.

She took the hint. 'Well, all I'm trying to say is that everyone needs a friend at their side sometimes. You'd do the same for me. Now why don't you drink that tea before it gets cold, and Henri will call the police. You've got a friend in CID, haven't you, hon? She might be able to help us out.'

Henri disappeared off into the living room to make the call while I went around the house closing all the curtains. It was already starting to get gloomy outside, and I couldn't bear the sight of all that darkness closing in on me, concealing who knows what in the shadows. Was this how the rest of my life was going to be, hiding behind closed doors, constantly scared of predators lurking in the outside world?

'Tessa will pop over as soon as she can,' said Henri, returning from the living room.

'Can I interest anyone in a drink while we wait for her?' I said, itching to numb my nerves. I wasn't sure how much more tension I could stand. 'Sorry, Skye. Didn't mean to rub it in.'

'Perhaps we'd be better keeping off the booze until Tessa's had her chat with you,' said Henri in a disapproving tone.

'Tessa sounds like a sheepdog's name,' I said, lashing out defensively, then immediately regretted the stupid comment. 'Let's hope she can round up whoever it is who's behind all this,' I added, hoping to make up for my thoughtlessness.

'Why don't you go and have a bath while we wait?' suggested Skye. 'It might make you feel brighter. I can put a wash on for you too, if you like.'

I took that as a hint that my lazy layabout wardrobe was starting to fester. I allowed myself to be pushed in the direction of the bathroom, but I drew a line at Skye and Henri washing my delicates for me. I hadn't quite hit that kind of a low.

Skye, with her usual wisdom, was right. I wallowed in the bath for a while, sinking back and allowing the water to cover my face until only my nostrils were above the surface. The water deadened everything to a comforting roar in my ears and the gentle lapping of the bubbles against my skin eased at least some of the tension from my neck and shoulders. It was only when the water started turning cold that I reluctantly sat up and washed the suds out of my hair. As the rather grimy bathwater glugged its way down the pipes, I imagined my troubles washing away with it. If only things were that simple.

Chapter Six

My sheepdog comment had been rather prescient, because Tessa turned out to have a barking kind of voice, which fitted well with her no-nonsense attitude. I got the impression that like her colleague, the condescending desk sergeant, Tessa didn't exactly approve of me. I was getting a lot of that attitude of late. However, to be fair to her, she went through the motions of taking my concerns seriously; scribbling stuff down in her notebook and even looking shocked at the stream of hatred on my social media feeds.

'There are some strange folk out there,' she said. 'It's like people have forgotten that there are actual human beings on the receiving end of this.'

She scrolled through, occasionally pulling faces at some of the more explicit stuff. At one point she even winced. I wondered if she'd come across the video someone had created where my head was pasted onto a porn star's body. In normal circumstances, I'd be amused at being gifted a figure with such inflated boobs and ridiculously pert bottom, but that woman was certainly not enjoying life, given that she was tied up with a succession of men lining up to brutalise her. It had been posted with a laughing face emoji, but I for one was not finding it funny.

'I think we've seen enough of that,' Tessa said, putting the phone to one side. I wished I could be so dismissive of the images. 'Henri mentioned that you'd also received some newspaper cuttings?'

I pushed them across the kitchen table towards her. I suppose I should have stopped touching them, in case there were vital fingerprints on there, but she didn't seem too bothered by preserving the evidence as she picked them up straightaway.

'I didn't realise people still read the local papers offline, let alone keep cuttings,' she said. I attempted a half-hearted smile. Surely once she saw the sinister nature of the articles she'd propose some action. Maybe the police would provide protection? I guess I could put up with a bodyguard around the place, as long as he was from the Richard Madden school of close protection. It was the first positive thought I'd had in days.

Tessa interrupted my brief daydreams involving a hunky bodyguard shielding me from danger with his taut, muscular body. 'This is obviously a very worrying time for you.' She tucked the articles into her notebook and fixed me with a serious expression. I could tell she was trying to choose her words carefully. I sensed Skye hovering nervously behind me, ready to pile in with a comforting hug when needed.

'Little bit of an understatement,' I said. 'Frankly I had no idea I was so famous until I became infamous.'

Tessa nodded. 'It is very easy for trivial stuff to blow up out of all proportion on social media nowadays. People are easily outraged, and once they start egging each other on, it's hard to put a stop to it. I'm sorry to have to tell you this, Lucy, but while this stuff online is absolutely vile, there really isn't a lot I can do about it. We can sometimes get people on the grounds of inciting hatred and violence, but, in truth, it's very hard to track down the individuals responsible and with resources the way they are nowadays, more often than not, those behind the threats get away with it.'

There was a sigh of outrage from Skye, but I merely shrugged my shoulders, trying to pretend I didn't care. Tessa wasn't telling me anything I hadn't already expected to hear.

'The newspaper cuttings are more concerning,' Tessa continued. 'I'll certainly take them to the station and see if there's any more evidence we can glean from them. We'll arrange for you to come in so we can take your fingerprints for elimination purposes.' I felt a tiny burst of optimism. She soon crushed it. 'I'll be brutally honest with you, unless the perpetrator has licked the envelope and left DNA evidence there – which any child who's watched a crime drama knows not to do – there's really not much more we can do. I know this sounds horribly blunt, but I don't want to raise your hopes and I suspect you'd prefer me being honest, rather than feeding you with platitudes.'

'Well, that's a bit pants,' I said, understatement of the

century. I'd resigned myself for some time as a hermit hiding out in my house until the social media furore died down, but now my own home didn't even feel like a safe haven, I was at a complete loss as to what to do.

Tessa stood up briskly and turned to Henri. 'Perhaps Plan B is the better option,' she said. Henri and Skye nodded. I realised that the three of them had been cooking up something while I was wallowing in the bath. I felt my stomach turn over. The events of the last few days had made me feel threatened and isolated, but now that my friends were conspiring with a stranger about what was going on in my life, I suddenly felt even more out of control. I folded my arms defensively and scowled in Tessa's direction. It was easier to direct all my anger and confusion at the stranger in the room.

Tessa was obviously made of strong stuff, because she didn't even flinch. 'I'll leave you to discuss the next step,' she said. 'Make sure you lock the door behind me.'

Reassuring.

Henri and Skye took it upon themselves to escort her out. I could hear the three of them whispering together in the hallway before she left. It was like being transported back to my teenage years when things went so terribly wrong and the adults in my life decided to exclude me from everything that was happening in the misguided belief they were sheltering me from the worst.

'Sod it, I think a G&T is in order.' At least while I was rattling around the kitchen trying to find a clean glass, I couldn't hear the mutterings about the mysterious 'Plan B' which were going on without me.

I poured myself a generous measure and idly swirled the liquid around my mouth while I thought about what to do next. Unfortunately, my mind was as empty as the glass soon became. Why was it that when I was on the radio, I knew exactly what to say and how to act, but when it came to my life outside the station, I was completely lacking in ideas?

Eventually I heard the front door close, and Skye and Henri returned with matching serious expressions.

'You guys look like you're about to stage an intervention.' I tried to inject some levity into the atmosphere.

For once it was Henri who cracked a smile while Skye reminded stony-faced.

'Lucy, I'm really worried about you.'

I held my hand up to stop her. 'Skye sweetie, please don't worry about me. I promise you, this is just a minor bump in the road, and I'm dealing with it. What matters to me most is that you are OK, and that this silliness isn't stressing you out when you've got much more exciting things to be thinking about.'

She didn't look convinced. I tried harder. 'Look, I've been having a think, and I reckon all I need to do is disappear for a bit until all this dies down. I'll find somewhere quiet where people have got better things to do than spend all day on social media, and then hopefully whilst I'm away, the police will lift a DNA profile or some fingerprints off that envelope and we'll work out who put the stupid video together in the first place, and Bob's your uncle, I'll return triumphant.'

It sounded so simple when I said it, but I struggled to believe my own words.

'I agree, you can't stay here. It's clearly not safe. You must come and stay with us,' said Skye. 'Henri and I have talked about it, and we'd love to have you.'

I glanced over at Henri. If I'd been a second slower, I'd have missed the brief look of unease which flitted across his face, before he fixed his features into a polite expression of agreement.

I responded quickly, not giving myself the chance to wimp out. 'Categorically, no. Don't get me wrong, I'm honoured and touched to be invited to stay at *Casa* Skye and Henri, but there is absolutely no way I'm putting you two in the middle of this. I feel bad enough about you coming around here now and pulling favours with the police on my behalf. The newspaper cuttings are probably a stupid prank gone too far, but I am not taking even the slightest risk that there's something more to it than that and putting you two in harm's way. I would never forgive myself.'

'But if you don't stay with us, where will you go?' Skye started crying and wrapped her arms around me. 'Sorry, I'm being pathetic,' she said. 'I'd like to blame hormones, but you know what I'm like.'

'You're a big old softy,' I said, patting her back, trying to ignore the unintentional sting in her suggestion that I didn't have any other friends. I looked over her shoulder and caught Henri's gaze. He gave me a small nod of thanks.

'Have you any ideas of an alternative safe haven?' he asked.

'I'm sure I'll come up with something,' I said breezily,

privately wondering if there was a place left in the world where people weren't glued to their smartphones. 'It'll be fine,' I repeated, more to reassure myself than them.

'Perhaps I may offer a solution?' said Henri. 'Have you ever thought about visiting Finland?'

Skye wiped her tears away and noticeably perked up. 'Why didn't I think of that in the first place? Wasn't Tommi talking about needing extra help at the Outward Bound centre?' She clapped her hands together in delight. 'Tommi is Henri's brother and he's just opened this amazing adventure place in the forest less than ten miles from the Arctic Circle. I'll find you some pictures on my phone. I promise, it's the most special place you could possibly imagine.' She started swiping through her photos, talking at high speed in her enthusiasm. 'We could kill two birds with one stone. You can help him out, and you'll get away from all this rubbish for as long as you need to.' She hesitated for the briefest of seconds. 'I'm sure he'll be up for having you to stay.' She moved on quickly. 'Honestly, it's the most magical place. There are acres and acres of trees, absolutely nobody for miles around, and so much space and fresh air. They chop their own wood to provide fuel for the centre and they get around with kick-sleds. Sometimes they camp out in wilderness huts or make themselves snow shelters. It's so energising. And, of course, at this time of the year it's all gorgeous and snowy and dark most of the time, so you can hunker down and really reconnect with yourself.'

Dark, cold and in the middle of nowhere. It sounded like someone had gathered everything I hated most and put it all together in a place to create my idea of absolute Hell.

There was no way I would voluntarily subject myself to freezing my butt off at the Arctic Circle. There *had* to be a better option closer to civilisation. But then I thought about the newspaper cuttings and all of the online hatred being aimed in my direction. I was already existing in one version of Hell. Perhaps a trip to Finland might not be so bad after all.

Chapter Seven

After that, everything started to happen really fast and my sense of being out of control spiralled still further. Skye managed to smuggle me into the police station without being spotted for the elimination fingerprints, a process which made me feel even more like a criminal. And before I had the chance to have any second thoughts, Henri booked me onto a flight to Kuusamo, which he rather gleefully told me was one of the snowiest places in Finland. I'd be met there by his brother Tommi, who would escort me to his wilderness retreat in Oulanka National Park, fifty kilometres further north, a mere stone's throw from the Arctic Circle itself, which I had a horrible feeling would turn out to be even snowier than Kuusamo.

In normal circumstances, I'd spend every spare minute before a trip Googling the best places to visit and the coolest venues for nights out, but as the internet and I were not on friendly terms currently, I had to rely on information supplied to me by Skye and Henri, neither of whom turned out to have much of use to say. Skye went into paroxysms of delight about her experiences of doing yoga in the sauna then rolling in the snow afterwards, which frankly sounded like a recipe for a heart attack. Henri was more circumspect, not really telling me anything beyond that there was nowhere quite like Oulanka for making you feel the true power of nature. Worrying.

I decided to keep quiet about my departure, even to my mum, until I was safely out of the country. I couldn't help feeling there was something rather shameful about admitting defeat and running away. And the brutal truth was, there weren't many people who'd genuinely care about what I was up to. I didn't live in the kind of place where kindly neighbours would water my non-existent plants whilst I was gone, and it wasn't like anyone from work gave a damn anymore about my whereabouts. Other than a formal letter detailing the conditions of my leave – for the unspecified duration of the Investigation – work had pointedly put me in isolation and I'd heard diddly squat from any of them except Skye. I'd tried to reach out a few times to Jonno about the video, but it quickly became clear he didn't want to know. According to the tabloids, he and Serenity were busy putting on a 'united front' at various glitzy dos, glammed up to the nines, paparazzi gleefully capturing their every move. Each article would also include an image of me, generally one taken from an unflattering angle with an equally unflattering caption underneath it, which didn't exactly help my mood.

And so, within twenty-four hours of the decision being made that I had to go, I was at the airport, suffocating in my biggest, thickest winter coat, and hoping desperately that the stack of ugly thermal long johns Skye had thrust into my hand luggage at the last moment was her idea of a joke. Despite the fact that it was a gloomy day, I was wearing sunglasses indoors, something which I normally ripped the hell out of actors for. But now I understood where they were coming from. It was the first time I'd stepped out of my front door by myself in days, and I felt incredibly exposed among all the crowds at the airport. Behind the shield of the sunglasses, I could watch the world without being seen, or at least, so I hoped. As I looked around at the happy, chattering groups of families, friends and colleagues, I felt even more of a pariah and utterly alone.

I slunk in the shadows, until the boards flashed up information about which check-in desk I needed to go to. Henri and Skye belonged to the sensible, grown-up style of traveller, and so had dropped me off two hours before the gate was due to close, approximately an hour and a half earlier than I would usually arrive at an airport myself. Normally, I viewed it as a personal challenge to get through Security, grab a quick drink in the bar and get onto the plane in less than half an hour. And, I admit, it always amused me to hear, 'This is a final call for passenger Fairweather, the flight is about to depart' blasting out on the Tannoy. There are certain advantages of having a distinctive name, and once the air crew realised I was *that* Lucy Fairweather from Star FM, I sometimes got to enjoy some complimentary hospitality, which was a much more civilised way of spending a flight.

Today, I guess it was preferable to be here with time to

spare. The fewer people who knew I was on this flight, the better. However, there were a few hurdles I had to get over before I could flee the country, the first of which was getting past the guy on the check-in desk.

'Sunglasses off,' was his opening gambit.

Normally, I'd have come back with a sassy, 'And a good morning to you too,' but the last few days seemed to have kicked the gumption out of me.

'I have sore eyes.' I attempted a pathetic excuse. I'm not quite sure why I was making a fuss about this. He was going to see who I was from my passport details anyway, but suddenly it felt really important that I hide myself from everyone around me for as long as possible.

'Medical note?' He held out his hand, a bored expression on his face.

'Sorry, no.' I shuffled awkwardly on the spot, aware that the queue behind me was growing by the second.

'Then glasses off. I have to verify your identity before I can give you a boarding card.'

I shook my head slightly so my hair fell forward to shield the sides of my face. I handed my passport over, and reluctantly removed the sunglasses, my pulse rate quickening. Was it my imagination or were the people at the neighbouring desk staring at me? There was a prickle in my spine as everyone around me seemed to go quiet.

'Did you pack your own bag?'

I gave the tiniest of nods, barely daring to make any movement in the hope that if I kept really still, I'd develop a cloak of invisibility.

'Any of these dangerous items in your luggage?' He

indicated a list of cartoon pictures of bombs, knives and other deadly looking weapons.

The shake of my head was more like a nervous twitch.

The man behind the desk grunted. He tapped away at his computer, then slapped the label onto my luggage with much more force than necessary. He wrenched open my passport and stared at my face. I felt myself go pink under his scrutiny.

'Lucinda Fairweather,' he said. 'The one off the radio.' It was a statement rather than a question.

I cleared my throat nervously.

He pursed his lips. Once again, his keyboard came in for a bashing. Then, at last, he printed off my boarding card and held it out towards me. I shoved my sunglasses back on my face, feeling my confidence rise as my shield went back into place.

'Thank you very much,' I said, trying to inject a cheery note into my voice.

But when I tried to take the boarding pass, he kept hold of it and fixed me with a steely glare.

'I'm Team Serenity, just so you know.'

A red-hot wave of humiliation swept over me. He was looking at me like I'd threatened to kill his first born. The Lucy of a week ago would have come back at him with a smartarse retort and laughed the implied hostility off, but after days of dealing with abuse, all the fight had been pummelled out of me.

I squeaked, 'Sorry.' Though, thinking about it later, I realised I really had nothing to apologise for. I prised the boarding card from his hand, and scurried away to join the queue for Security before I lost my courage altogether.

By the time I'd endured another half hour of queuing, I'd completely convinced myself that everyone in the airport was whispering about me. I was hoping some of it was in my overactive imagination, but there was no mistaking the girl who'd taken a selfie in which she was sending an obscene gesture in my direction. I could imagine the kudos she'd be getting from her friends for publicly humiliating me.

Once I was finally airside, I made a beeline to the bar for something to restore my spirits. Something sparkling with a cheery miniature umbrella in the top of it would put a smile back on my face. But the bar was rammed with lairy types heading off on a stag do and I had a horrible feeling that once they spotted me, I'd become the focus of their drunken chanting, so I swerved away. I helped myself to a couple of the freebie shot samples they were handing out in Duty Free, then I hid in a toilet cubicle until my flight was called.

When I finally boarded the plane, it quickly became apparent how the guy at the check-in desk had chosen to wreak his punishment on me. I was crammed into a seat right by the toilets, which, judging by the smell, were in a sorry state of cleanliness. I was grateful that Skye had insisted I wore a polo-neck jumper, because I buried my mouth and nose in it and breathed through the fabric in an effort to filter out the reek. I was so wound up, I actually flinched when people sat in the seats next to me. Thankfully however, they ignored me, apart from when one of them was kind enough to lend me a napkin when the stewardess accidentally-on-purpose spilled a plate of sausage and scrambled egg onto my lap. Clearly the air crew were Team Serenity too.

However, as the flight went on, I started to feel a tiny bit of the tension easing from my shoulders. Every mile I travelled, I was getting further away from the source of my stress. A couple of weeks in a new place, and everything would be OK.

I leaned forward, brushed another bit of egg from my lap and rummaged around my rucksack to find something to read. As I opened my paperback, an envelope fell out and onto the floor by my feet.

Instantly my heart started pounding double-quick and my palms went damp with fear. The noise of my fellow passengers faded into a background roar and all I could hear was the sound of my own panicky breath as I contemplated the object in front of me. What was in the envelope, and how had it got into my hand luggage? I hadn't put it there, and whoever had done, must have had access to my house in order to do it, a thought too terrible to contemplate.

I summoned up every morsel of courage I possessed, and, with trembling fingers, reached out to pick up the terrifyingly innocuous-looking envelope. At the last minute, I remembered Tessa taking the newspaper cuttings off to the lab for testing, and pulled my jumper over my fingers to act as makeshift gloves to protect any evidence as much as possible. Somehow, I managed to pick up the envelope, but now I was left with a new challenge of how to examine the contents. Every instinct in my body screamed at me not to open it, and to chuck it into the rubbish bag the next time a member of the air crew walked through the cabin. But sod it, I was Lucy Fairweather and I was determined to prove to myself that I was made of stronger stuff than that. Surely it was better to know what I was dealing with rather than conjuring up even worse phantoms in my imagination? In the end, I gave up the delicate approach and forcefully ripped it open.

'Is everything OK, love?' One of my seat companions was looking at me with a very funny expression on their face. To be fair to her, I guess I was acting in a most peculiar way. Because when I tore open the envelope, a card fell out, and there, written in the most elaborate calligraphy, was a message saying, 'Travel hopefully.' Underneath it was Skye's distinctive rounded handwriting wishing me a good trip. At first, I couldn't stop laughing, overwhelmingly relieved that my worst fears hadn't been realised.

But the relief soon turned to sadness. My dad always used to say 'Travel hopefully', and I was touched that Skye had bothered to remember that nugget and send the wisdom back to me. While it wasn't a mantra that had worked for him in the end, I vowed that I would try to take it to heart on this trip.

Right on cue, the captain came over the speakers to announce that we were half an hour from landing at Kuusamo airport. I chose to blank out her final statement that it was minus eighteen degrees centigrade. Surely that must be a mistake on the thermometer? It was time to get my game face on. I made my way to the toilet and tried a quick repair job on my makeup. I wanted to make sure I gave a good first impression to the complete stranger who'd agreed to host me for the next however long.

Peering at myself in the artificial light, I was shocked at how terrible I looked. The bruise-like dark circles under my eyes gave me a ghostly appearance, not an attractive ethereal ghost in a romcom, but a full-on scary ghoul who was about to steal some souls in a horror movie. There was a haunted look in my eyes, and even when I tried smiling at my reflection in the mirror, there was an emptiness in my expression. I decided to throw every unguent and cream in my makeup bag at the job. Hopefully some bright lipstick and a couple of layers of foundation would distract from the lank dullness of my hair and the constellation of stress spots which were making an appearance on my jawline.

War paint in place, I returned to my seat and tried to muster my confidence. It's funny how I could happily witter away to several hundred thousand listeners across the airwaves, but the prospect of meeting just one person, Henri's brother, was sending me into a spin.

A bing-bong over the speaker system signalled that we were coming into land. I leaned forward and peered past the generous bulk of my seatmate. The land below me seemed to be painted in monochrome. Mile after mile of spikey trees stood silhouetted against interminable white snow. Skye had told me that Finland was a country of forest and lakes, but it looked pretty much like solid forest from where I was sitting. The signs of habitation were few and far between, an occasional wooden building poking out from between the endless branches. It was like flying into an ancient land. For the thousandth time, I wondered if I'd made the right decision to come here.

As the land grew closer, my anxiety levels increased as my mind jumped to scenarios where ice sent the plane skidding off the runway and into the spooky forest, or where the plane nosedived into a bank of snow and we had to dig our way out. I pulled my seat belt tighter and reacquainted myself with the brace position from the laminated card in the seat pocket. We were now so close to the ground, I was convinced the plane's wings were going to brush the snow off the tree tops. I shuffled further back in my seat and squeezed my eyes shut, willing that when I opened them, I would wake up and discover that the last few days had been some kind of horrible nightmare.

The engine noise changed and a shudder ran through the plane's fabric. I felt a bead of sweat drip down the side of my nose. And then we were slamming down onto the ground, while my stomach still hovered about sixty feet up in the air, reluctant to catch up with the rest of me. But the dreaded slipping sensation never happened, and instead the plane slowed to a gentle taxi towards the modest terminal building. All around me, people were starting to dig extra layers out of their hand luggage, laughing and smiling as they wrapped thick scarves around their throats and bundled woolly hats over their hair. I glanced down at my winter coat and noticed for the first time how flimsy it seemed in comparison to my neighbours' clothing.

I hung back, allowing as many people as possible to exit the plane before me. I told myself I was being polite, but I can't deny that cowardice was hovering around somewhere there. While I was still in the aeroplane, I was in the safe bubble of limbo land.

But eventually the air crew started marching down the aisle with bin bags and I had no excuse not to stand up and leave. I hauled my rucksack onto my back, reached down to do my coat up and promptly yanked the teeth of the zip apart and the zip-pull off altogether. Great start. What was I meant to do in one of the most hostile environments on earth if I didn't even have a functioning coat?

But it was only thirty yards from the plane to the terminal building, and I asked myself how cold I could really get in that small distance, especially when I was still experiencing a nervous hot flush from the landing. I soon found out. The first step off the plane was fine. I glanced around and there might even have been the tiniest little spark of something resembling excitement as I took in my alien surroundings up close. The second step, however, my surroundings fought back. The dry cold scraped its way through my windpipe and flooded my lungs, while the skin of my nose itched from exposure to the elements. I swear I could feel ice crystals forming in my blood. I wanted to hold onto the handrail, wary of slipping down the steps, but I was scared my fingers might freeze to the metal, so I put my hands in my pockets and inched down nervously, the arctic air making my movements sluggish and clumsy. If I thought it was bitter at the top of the steps, the chill on the ground was something else. It insinuated its way through the soles of my walking boots and danced around my toes so quickly, I actually glanced down to double-check that I hadn't inadvertently got off the flight in my bare feet. I wanted to run to the terminal, but I was terrified of falling flat on my face because I didn't trust my legs to obey my commands. In the end I shuffled along like an arthritic pensioner, wanting to cry at the cold, but not daring to in case the tears froze on my face.

I went through Passport Control and collected my suitcase in a daze, my skin still frozen despite the warmth of the terminal building. The whole environment was an assault on my senses. I was definitely not designed for these conditions.

I checked the piece of paper where Skye had scribbled Tommi's details and nervously scanned the faces of the people waiting by the arrivals gate. Everyone looked sensibly dressed and at home in their surroundings, while I felt so out of place I might as well have had a neon sign flashing 'Sunshine-loving city girl' above my head. I wondered if it might be a better idea to turn around, head over to the booking desk and see if I could get a seat on the return flight home. But the thought of what was waiting for me there was even worse than the prospect of enduring life in the frozen wastelands. I firmly told myself to be brave.

There was one man standing slightly apart from the crowd, watching the people reuniting with their loved ones. There was something about the perceptive gaze of his clear blue eyes which convinced me that he must be Henri's relation. He was as tall as his brother, and had a similar air of self-confidence, but there the similarities ended. While Henri was wiry, bald, and had the pasty complexion of an office worker, this guy clearly spent a lot of time outdoors. He was broad of shoulder, perhaps from all the wood-chopping that apparently went on in Finland, his cheeks were bordering on ruddy, and strands of rusty-blond hair were peeking out from beneath his woollen hat. He looked like he didn't suffer fools gladly.

Time to get my game face on. I summoned up my brightest radio presenter persona and marched across before I changed my mind.

'Hello, I'm Lucy Fairweather. Are you Tommi, by any chance?'

He stared at me for longer than felt polite. I started to panic slightly, wondering if I'd picked the wrong guy and given my identity away to a complete stranger. If word got around that I'd fled to Finland, then I'd have to find a new hideaway.

'Sorry, I don't speak Finnish. I'm Lucy,' I patted my chest, and then gestured towards him, 'Are you Tommi?' I probably came across as the worst kind of Brit abroad, raising my voice and speaking slowly to make up for my own shameful lack of linguistic ability, but I was growing increasingly nervous that I'd made a horrible mistake.

'Yes,' he said. 'I am.' He dipped his head slightly. I wasn't sure whether it was meant as a gesture of greeting, or whether it was simply a practical move to answer me as he was so much taller than I. 'Follow me.' He picked up my suitcase as if it weighed no more than a packet of crisps and started striding out of the terminal building, while I scurried along in his wake, trying to balance my rucksack and the other bits of detritus I'd accumulated on the flight. Just before we got to the exit, he swung round and stared down at me. 'That coat won't be sufficient in this climate.'

His speech was brusque and efficient, his English only slightly accented, just like his brother's. He gestured at the makeup I'd devoted so much energy to perfecting. 'And you'll have to wipe that off your face. It'll only freeze in these conditions.'

My mouth fell open. What the hell was I doing in a place where even the most everyday of things like putting on makeup was apparently hazardous? Maybe being pilloried online and hunted in my home would be preferable after all.

'This way,' Tommi said. He swept past a giant snowman which was standing guard at the entrance to the airport. I looked around for a sturdy four-by-four but Tommi seemed to be striding towards a small car of the type I'd normally expect to see trundling around town on a Saturday morning. It looked in no way equipped to handle the conditions out here.

He pulled open the boot and seemed surprised at my hesitation.

'You are joking?' I said. 'Shouldn't we be travelling in something sturdier?'

'This is perfectly adequate. Unlike other countries, here the world does not stop when there is a little bit of snow on the ground.'

I pointedly glanced at the towering pile of white stuff which had been cleared from the car park. A little bit it certainly wasn't.

I heaved my luggage into the boot, slipping like Bambi on the ground. I hesitated before I got into the vehicle, part of me still wanting to rush back to the terminal building and escape. But the thought of Skye's disappointment after she'd stuck her neck out to support me steeled my nerve and I dived into the car and did my seat belt up tightly before I changed my mind.

Tommi accelerated out of the airport car park like there was a herd of wild bears chasing after us. I gripped the sides of my seat and told myself not to scream if we went into a skid, which was surely inevitable. I assumed the road had been cleared because there were great big piles of snow either side of it, but the Tarmac was still covered in a lethal-looking layer of discoloured ice. It was the kind of conditions where back in the UK we'd be doing endless travel reports and advising people not to drive unless absolutely necessary. But Tommi seemed absolutely indifferent to the potential hazards, rounding corners and accelerating down hills with the calm air of someone cruising along a boulevard in an open-top sports car in the middle of a heatwave.

'Thank you for your assistance, but I can assure you it is unnecessary,' said Tommi as I slammed my foot on an invisible brake for the fifth time in as many minutes, bracing myself for an impact which never came.

I forced my gaze away from the windscreen and tried to distract myself from my growing fear by staring at the landscape out of the window. It couldn't have been more different from home. Serried ranks of trees lined the route, fading into the distance as far as I could see. There was an occasional house, but they were spread so far apart it was hard to work out where the centre of any kind of settlement might be. At one point we passed a children's playground with ski jumps instead of swings and a couple of gleeful toddlers bundled up to their eyebrows in clothing throwing themselves around the snowy obstacles. And then even the houses stopped appearing and we were out in the wilderness.

'It looks pretty isolated out here. Do you ever get scared of being snowed in?' I asked, trying to make polite conversation as the silence stretched out. Tommi didn't strike me as a man for small talk, but I'd been a radio presenter for too long not to feel uncomfortable about empty air going unfilled.

We took a bend at breakneck speed and I only just managed to stop myself squealing out loud.

'In this part of the country, there is the equivalent of a land mass of one square kilometre per person. We Finns like our personal space.'

'In space, no one can hear you scream.' I had meant it as a joke, but Tommi didn't respond. I really hoped it didn't turn out to be some kind of horrible premonition.

Chapter Eight

After what felt like hours of driving, with the roads getting progressively narrower all the way and the forest closing in still further, Tommi skidded to a halt.

'Welcome to Wild Zone,' he said, a note of pride in his voice. The very name of the place made me wish I could hide under my duvet back at home.

I looked around, struggling to distinguish this patch of snowy, wooded land, from the previous snowy, wooded land we'd been driving through.

'Lovely,' I said, because it seemed to be expected, even though I thought it was anything but. My insides were churning away once again. Maybe I had misunderstood what Skye and Henri had said and that when they had referred to it being an outdoors centre, perhaps they had literally meant outdoors, because there seemed to be no sign of habitation whatsoever.

Tommi pointed to a mound of snow in a small clearing.

There was a slight shadow at its base which may or may not be some kind of entrance.

'That is a quinzee. It is the Finnish version of an igloo.'

An igloo? I swallowed. Was that what he was expecting me to live in? An actual heap of snow? I think my life expectancy just reduced by about five decades.

'Those quinzees have been there a while. We will show you how to build one for yourself. It is very easy; a matter of piling the snow up and then hollowing it out from the centre. As long as the base for sleeping is higher than the entrance, it is perfectly safe to sleep in. It only takes a couple of hours.'

I swore under my breath.

'Pardon?' asked Tommi.

'Nothing,' I replied, wondering if I could nick the car while he wasn't looking and make an escape. But I wasn't sure my driving skills were up to keeping the vehicle on the road with all this horrible ice around. If the ground wasn't so cold, I would have got down onto my knees and prayed for a miracle. This was even more nightmare-ish than the worst-case scenarios I'd imagined.

Tommi started laughing. 'I think you have misunderstood me. The expression on your face! Did you think you were going to have to stay in one? This is merely the boundary of Wild Zone. We have actual huts for people to stay in, though guests and staff are always welcome to spend the night in a quinzee, should they wish to have an authentic experience.'

What a bastard. I didn't trust myself to speak.

Tommi chuckled away to himself as he drove the last

couple of kilometres to the accommodation blocks, while I sat in dignified silence, imagining all the different ways I could get my own back on him for making me think I was going to have to rough it in an ice-cave.

After rounding a final bend and whizzing down the steepest hill yet, we finally arrived at our destination. Having been convinced that I was going to be spending the night freezing my butt off (and probably dying) in the snow, the accommodation at Wild Zone looked like a palace in comparison. It had proper walls and roofs to start with. There was a long, low wooden building at the centre of the clearing and then dotted in a constellation around it were a succession of small huts with sweet wooden verandas in front of them, the doorway to each sheltered from the worst of the elements by an overhanging roof. They looked like the house Red Riding Hood's grandmother lived in. Hopefully I wouldn't find a wolf lurking within.

'Follow me,' instructed Tommi. He hauled my rucksack onto his back and I cringed as my various bottles and lotions clattered in the bag's interior. He strode to the hut furthest away from the main building. Someone had shovelled a route to the door, thank goodness, as the cleared snow came up to my knee on either side of the path.

'You're in here. We'll sort you out with some snow shoes and better winter kit once you've unpacked.'

'Please don't put yourself to any trouble,' I said, determined to demonstrate that I was going to be a good guest.

He fixed me with a stern gaze. 'These conditions are not to be underestimated. In this environment, the difference between a good coat and that,' he gestured at my parka, 'is the difference between life and death. You will cause us a great deal of trouble if you don't follow my suggestions about clothing. I don't have time for that, and I certainly don't want to be doing the resulting health and safety paperwork if you freeze, so I really would rather you did as I say.'

'You know best,' I said, hoping I sounded braver than I was currently feeling.

'I do,' he said, without a trace of irony.

I lugged my suitcase up the steps and followed Tommi into my new home. It smelled of freshly cut wood. Despite the fact that it looked no studier than a garden shed, the interior was as warm and comforting as an embrace. A bit of the tension eased from my shoulders as I gazed around my tiny new home.

'I suggest you remove your shoes here by the doorway so you do not tramp melting snow around the place. You are responsible for keeping this building clean and monitoring the amount of snow on the roof. If too much builds up, it can cause the roof to collapse from the pressure. Snowshoes are to be kept on the porch, but I will explain more about that later. The floor is heated, so if you need to dry wet clothing, you can place it on the ground. The bathroom is through that door there. It gets dark at around two thirty in the afternoon, so best to keep a torch with you at all times. Meals are served in the main building and that is also where we keep the winter clothing. Come across once you've unpacked and we'll kit you out.'

It was a very practical speech, full of useful information,

but I hoped he lightened his manner once the paying guests arrived. I couldn't see his gruff nature going down too well with the Trip Advisor crowd.

He turned around and strode away, leaving me in my compact hideaway. I heaved a sigh of relief, glad to have five minutes to myself to decompress. It didn't take long to stow my inadequate clothing away in the cupboard and acquaint myself properly with the space. The bed was small and decked out with sheets and blankets. Aside from a simple wooden chair and a bedside table which both looked like they'd been hewn from the neighbouring woodland, there was no other furniture. This was definitely back to basics living. Perhaps simple surroundings would lead to a simple life. I could but hope.

I felt pretty grotty after all the travelling so I dived into the shower and quickly scrubbed off before changing into a fresh set of clothes. Mindful of Tommi's comments, I washed every trace of makeup from my face. It was so exposing being barefaced when I knew that the stress of recent circumstances was etched into every line on my skin, but the thought of foundation freezing into my pores was no more comforting, so I gritted my teeth and got on with the job.

There were only two tasks remaining before I braved the main building. I'd promised Skye I'd let her know when I'd arrived safely. And then there was the small matter of making the phone call to my mum to inform her of my new circumstances.

I turned my phone on for the first time in a few days and braced myself for the onslaught of horrible messages. But the only text that came through was one from my phone provider welcoming me to Finland. The red notification circles were also wonderfully absent from other apps. I sat up straighter as I let out a breath I didn't realise I'd been holding. Perhaps my flight to Finland had been an unnecessary overreaction. Perhaps the trolls had moved onto their next victim and I was old news. Maybe I could head straight home after all.

Although I'd sworn I wouldn't, I found myself drawn to my social media and email apps. And then crushing disappointment replaced my misguided optimism because I quickly realised why I had no notifications on my phone. Someone had signed me out of all of my accounts. So that was what Skye had been doing when she'd shiftily asked to borrow my phone at the police station. I guess she was trying to protect me from myself. I resisted the urge to sign back in, and instead pinged off a message to her saying thanks for everything she'd done for me. And then I took a deep breath and dialled my mum.

The conversation went about as well as could be expected. It turned out that the kids at school had filled her in on my social media shame and then she'd read about it in one of the tabloids which him-next-door had put out with the recycling. Thanks to their biased take on things, she was not best pleased with me. However much I tried to explain that the video was fake and that I hadn't done any of the things I'd been accused of – 'A homewrecker, Lucy, I'm ashamed of you' – she wouldn't be convinced.

'I've been saying for a long time that your job is a bad influence on you, darling. It was only a matter of time before you got confused between the raucous radio persona and real life. Jenny's daughter has retrained as a teacher. Perhaps you should look into doing something like that. I could get you some work experience at my school, although you might have to wait a little while for the children to stop talking about you being viral or whatever it is they say.'

I clenched my fist and made a great effort not to bite back. 'I'm not sure I've got the temperament for teaching, Mum.'

'You're probably right. Although I'm sure if you applied yourself, you could quieten down and be an English teacher. Or maybe even Media Studies, if you had to.'

She launched into another lecture about me needing to knuckle down and be more like my sensible cousin Fiona who'd dutifully got a boring job as an accountant straight out of university, and had managed to marry and produce two charming children, and was incidentally raking it in, all before she'd reached my age. By the end of it, I was so exhausted I pretended the signal was bad and hung up, feeling the weight of motherly disappointment as much as if she'd physically battered me around the head. I know she meant well and that her desire for me to settle down came from a place of loving concern, and perhaps even fear, but it didn't stop me feeling suffocated by it. I then did the really wimpy thing of texting her to say I'd been calling from Finland, but without giving her the exact address, and then I turned the phone off and hid it in the depths of the cupboard where it couldn't do me any more harm.

Frankly, I felt like hiding in the dark cupboard myself. But Tommi's lecture about the danger of my surroundings had got to me, and I was wary of staying too long in my little haven before I got myself properly kitted out. I was stuck in this situation and I needed to make the best of it. I told myself to woman-up, laced on my walking boots, wrapped my rubbish coat around me as best I could, and tramped across to the main building in search of clothing and some food. I don't know if it was the coldness of my surroundings, or the after-effects of being on the receiving end of my mum's particular brand of loving care, but I was ravenously hungry for the first time in days.

I didn't see another soul on my way across. The silhouettes of the trees were blurred by a covering of snow, and it was hard to work out where the ground ended and the trees began. Even though it was only early afternoon, the sun was already low on the horizon, sending a strange orange glow over the landscape. The snow seemed to deaden the sound of my surroundings, so the only noise came from the soft crunch of my boots on the compacted ice. It felt so unnaturally quiet, that I jumped when the door of the main building opened with a groaning creak.

'Ah, you must be Lucy. How lovely to meet you. I am Johanna, and I am the chef. Come in, come in. Welcome to the headquarters of Wild Zone.'

She beckoned me in and handed me a pair of slippers to change into.

'We are so glad you have come to help us as we prepare for the big opening. In here we have the dining room, kitchen, bar,' my ears pricked up hopefully at that, 'the main reception, although it seems very grand to call it that when it is only a desk, and then below there is the storeroom, and on the very bottom floor there is the sauna. In Finland it is practically compulsory to have a sauna.'

She pronounced it 'sow-na' rather than the British 'sor-na'.

I nodded, wondering which area of the business I'd be helping out in. I prayed it was something involving being in this nice, cosy building. The less time I spent in the hostile outdoors, the better.

'Tommi asked that I help you get some winter clothing together and brief you about a few things that we do differently out here,' continued Johanna.

'He's already given me the lecture on makeup,' I said, pulling a face.

She smiled. 'Yes, unless you have oil-based makeup, it is best to avoid it. I also try to wash my face in the evening before I go to bed and put any moisturiser on then, rather than in the morning. You'll find that the best defence against the cold is the natural oils that your own skin produces.'

Well didn't that sound lovely. At least I was reassured that it wasn't something that Tommi had been having a joke about at my expense.

'I dug out some kit which I think will fit you. The key thing here is layers. They help to trap the warmth between them.'

She led me down to the storeroom and I gasped at the rows and rows of brand-new clothing which was hanging up.

'Yes, it is a lot, isn't it?' said Johanna. A worried expression came over her face. 'Tommi decided that providing the winter clothing would be our unique selling point. He thinks many people would be put off from coming here because they do not have the right equipment.'

'It seems like a sensible plan,' I agreed.

'But an expensive one,' she said, pursing her lips together. 'Never mind. Let us take advantage of this and make sure you have the correct clothing. What size boot do you take? They are over there, along with the gaiters and waterproof shell outer layers. I'll get the other layers you'll need.'

It turned out the other layers consisted entirely of baggy fleece with elasticated cuffs and waistbands. They wouldn't have been out of place as a prison uniform.

'Why don't you try them?' she suggested. 'You have a base layer on, right?'

If she meant the ugly long johns from Skye, then yes, I had bowed to the inevitable and pulled them on beneath my jeans before I came across. They were bad enough, but the thought of wearing a double layer of fleecy tracksuit bottoms with matching fleecy navy tops made me cringe. The trolls would have a field day if they saw me now. Never mind #LooseLucy, they'd be calling me #LardyLucy as the shapeless clothing gave me an unflatteringly rounded appearance. I told myself not to think about them. They had no place in my life right now.

'I'm worried I'm going to cause a fire with the amount of static I'm producing,' I said, as I struggled to pull another top on. I was now bundled up as much as the Michelin man, and looked about as attractive.

Johanna laughed. 'I'm afraid frizzy hair is the price we

pay for living in such a beautiful part of the world. Do not worry, by the time you have a balaclava and hat on, nobody will notice.'

A balaclava? Oh excellent. Got to love a bit of bank robber chic.

'If I were you, I would also avoid wearing jeans. If they get wet and then freeze, it is a most unpleasant experience. Around here, our clothing tends to be more practical and outdoorsy than stylish, but when everyone is dressing like that, it doesn't really matter.'

I nodded, resigned to my fate. The world of red carpets and glam nights out couldn't be further away.

I pulled on the final layer and twirled around for Johanna to inspect me. I say twirled round, but really it was more of a bowlegged lumbering lurch, given that my limbs were sticking out at much greater angles than usual, thanks to the multiple layers covering them.

She nodded in approval. 'Tommi was planning to teach you how to snowshoe before it gets dark, but as that is in half an hour's time, and you've had a long day of travelling, I'm guessing you would prefer some soup and a drink?'

'That would be amazing,' I said, definitely feeling in need of something to revive me. 'Something tall and cold would be perfect just now. A drink I mean, not Tommi.' I laughed.

Someone coughed behind me. 'You will be OK with just the base layer in here if you wish. With the fire and the underfloor heating, it can almost get too hot,' said the man himself.

I certainly felt flushed now, as I wondered if he'd heard my previous words.

'Eat your soup and then I will explain what jobs I need you to do. The first group of guests will be arriving the day after tomorrow, and there are a lot of preparations to finish before then. You need to learn the basics of getting around here before we set you to work, otherwise you will be a dangerous hindrance.'

Well that was me told.

Chapter Nine

I t must have a been a combination of the good food and finally being away from the threats of home, but, by some miracle, I had the best night's sleep I'd had in ages. In fact, I only had time for a couple of sips from my emergency stash of gin miniatures purloined from the plane to celebrate my safe arrival before I was out like a light. Despite the lack of duvet, my bed was super cosy. Tucked up beneath the blankets, the utter stillness of my surroundings felt surprisingly comforting rather than eerie.

When my alarm dragged me from deep sleep, I peered groggily out of the window and concluded that the clock must be wrong because it was still pitch-dark outside. Which is why I rolled over and went back into a dreamless daze which I was only woken from by the sound of banging on my door.

'Lucy, it is Johanna. Are you OK? Tommi was expecting you for your snowshoe lesson half an hour ago. You won't last long around here if you can't get from A to B.'

I checked the clock again and decided it hadn't been lying to me after all. All of this darkness was going to take a lot of getting used to. It was my first full day in Finland and I'd had an accidental lie-in until 11am. Oh bother. This was not a great start. I did not need Tommi to change his mind about allowing me to stay. I pulled on my sexy fleeces (if in doubt, add another layer), laced up the heavy boots which were probably Finnish army issue and stumbled out into the snow, forgetting my hat and gloves in my panic.

Of course, as soon as I arrived at the outbuilding where the snowshoes and skies were kept, Tommi took one look at me and sent me back for the proper kit. The look on his face told me I was already running out of warnings. I vowed to put my best effort into my lesson.

However, snowshoeing turned out to be way more complicated than Tommi and Johanna made it look. It was bizarre to refer to the instruments of torture as shoes in the first place, given that they were basically plastic trays with some lethal-looking metal spikes in the base and a few straps on the top so you could attach them to your boots. My Finnish guides helped me heave them on and then stood back as I took a couple of experimental steps and promptly fell flat on my face in one of the many snowdrifts which encircled Wild Zone.

'You have to lift your feet up higher and then place them more carefully,' explained Tommi, striding out as if it was the simplest thing in the world. 'The walking poles will help you keep your balance and you should only sink down a small way in deep, soft snow because the shoes give you a greater surface area to walk on. When you get to a sloping area, you can dig your toes in to get the spikes to grip into the ice so you won't fall over.'

Johanna demonstrated by gracefully ascending the towering pile of snow to the right of the outbuilding.

'Come and join me,' she said.

What I really wanted to do was go and hide back indoors. But as snowshoeing was apparently a fundamental life skill in these parts, I gritted my teeth and tried to mimic her easy movements. Alas, I ended up looking like a clown trying to get around a circus ring in overly large shoes. I kept tripping up, and because the snowshoes transformed my feet into size 20 monstrosities, I couldn't recover my footing quickly enough and repeatedly acquainted myself with the ground. If nothing else, I was gaining a new-found appreciation for my clothing. Shapeless and ugly it might be, but at least my fingers and toes were still snuggly.

I persisted with my climbing efforts, and eventually heaved myself up to join Johanna, sweat beading on my forehead. I hastily wiped it off with my glove in case it froze in place. I never thought there would be a point in my life when I'd have to worry about frozen sweat.

'Well done. You'll be running around in no time, don't you agree, Tommi?' said Johanna.

He grunted, 'You'll do,' which I took to be the highest form of praise I was going to get. I did a celebration dance, ridiculously proud of my rudimentary achievements, and immediately slid all the way down to the ground on my backside.

Tommi concluded that my glee was a sign I hadn't been taking his lessons seriously.

'The techniques we are teaching you now could be the difference between life and death. In these conditions, there is no option to make mistakes.'

I heaved myself upright and nodded sheepishly.

'You are, of course, free to come and go as you wish, this is not a prison after all, but the rule is that if you go out, you leave a note in the diary in the main building saying what time you're leaving, which direction you are going in and when you expect to be back. This is a rule we will also be enforcing with the guests to ensure there are no mishaps. Given your current level of experience, it might even be best if you try to avoid going out by yourself at all, at least until you become more accustomed to your surroundings. Do you understand?'

'Yes, Tommi,' I said, clicking my heels together and giving a silly salute, trying to inject some humour into the situation.

He shook his head in disappointment. 'I am very busy. Tomorrow I have a group of guests arriving at a business I have spent years working towards establishing. I do not have time for childish behaviour. Please do us the courtesy of taking this seriously.'

He turned around and strode off towards the main building, leaving me feeling very ashamed of myself for messing around.

Johanna checked her watch. 'We were hoping to teach you some of the basics of cross-country skiing as well – it is the easiest way to do longer distances around here – but I need to go and check the supplies are all in order.'

I could tell she wasn't impressed with me either. While I

would never have voluntarily chosen to come here, I appreciated the fact that they had opened their doors to give me sanctuary when I was at my lowest ebb. I could have kicked myself for not being more respectful of their efforts to help me settle in. I could practically hear my mum's voice in my head reminding me that not everything in life is a radio stunt to be played for laughs.

'Can I come and help?' I asked, hoping to make up on some lost ground.

'I think it is better if I get on by myself,' Johanna said.

I felt even more crushed by her response. Why was I always sabotaging myself by acting stupid? I needed to show them that I could be of use and that there was more to me than an empty-headed extra mouth to feed, before they changed their minds about having me here in the first place. But what could I do in this alien environment? I could talk for England and mix some decent tunes, but apart from that, life as a radio presenter hadn't exactly prepared me for anything actually useful in the real world. Once they discovered I was crap at cleaning and the world's biggest klutz, they were going to throw me out in the snow faster than you could say 'Arctic Circle'.

Perhaps the answer was to get to a place where this environment felt less alien. Maybe if I practised hard and got really good at snowshoeing, I could demonstrate my commitment to being a vaguely useful member of staff at Wild Zone? It was a long-shot, but worth a try. I picked up the walking sticks with a new-found sense of resolve and started gingerly making my way around the perimeter of the buildings, deciding to tramp my way round the small settlement until I got used to the weird, waddling motion of snowshoeing.

I tentatively started off on the deeper snow first, reasoning that at least it was softer to fall into. After a few laps without any major stumbling, I decided to brave the icier paths. Concentrating hard, I chipped toe-holes into the sheet ice with the spikes on the shoes, creeping forward inch by inch, using the poles to help keep my balance. My progress was slow, but steady, and I felt a warm glow of achievement.

As I rounded the basement of the main building, I spotted a steep slope not too far away which looked like it would be the perfect ground on which to complete my training. Surely if I could make it up that hill, I could make it anywhere. I set off determinedly, striding out between the conifers, and ducking and diving to avoid some of the lower branches. It felt almost liberating to be out here on my own, like I was a pioneer in a strange land with only my own snowshoe tracks marking the path. I kept on glancing up to check my destination was still in sight, but it was only when I'd been walking for a good twenty minutes or so that I realised that however much I strode ahead, the hill seemed to be just as far away. I picked up my pace, feeling proud that I was now master enough of this skill to be able to vary my speed. But another ten minutes later and I was still a way off. I turned around to measure how far I'd come and realised with horror that I could no longer see the light from Wild Zone's buildings.

I took a deep breath and reminded myself not to panic. Getting back to base would be a simple matter of merely retracing my footsteps, which were clearly there for all to see. I say simple, but it was already starting to get dark, despite the fact it was only just after lunchtime. I told myself it didn't matter. There was so much snow around, what little light there was would be reflected for a while yet. Of course, my usual luck dictated it would never be that easy. I felt a drop of something cold landing on the tiny bit of skin which was exposed between my balaclava and hat. I reached up to work out what it was, then felt another one and then another. Before long, great white feathers of snow were floating down from the sky and speedily covering up the tracks I'd been so proud of making. In any other circumstance, I'd probably have been captivated by the beauty of the moment, but here every single flake of snow represented a threat. I needed to get moving, and fast before I got stuck in the middle of nowhere. But my recently acquired confidence deserted me when I needed it most and I turned clumsy all over again, staggering around and messing up what few tracks remained in my haste to get back.

The important thing was to keep going in a straight line, but it was hard to tell one snowy tree trunk from another and the whiteness everywhere was massively disorientating. I knew I was in real trouble. Tommi's words came back to me about the importance of leaving a note in the book in reception to say where I'd walked to. Why hadn't I paid proper attention and remembered to do that when I'd set off towards the hill? I lurched from tree to tree, trying to spot something, anything which would distinguish one bit of dark snowy landscape from another.

For all I knew, I could be walking around in a massive circle, doomed to spiralling out here in the snow until eventually the cold got to me. I wanted to cry, but frozen eye ducts were the last thing I needed right now.

If only I had my mobile on me, I could at least call for help, although who knew if there was even any signal out here in the back end of beyond. But there was no point in berating myself over 'If onlys'.

'Calm the hell down, Lucy,' I told myself. It was good to hear something other than the deafening silence, even if it was the sound of my own voice. I decided to narrate my way along the route, the pretence of doing a feature on my radio show helping my anxiety to quieten just a little.

'Thanks for joining me on this week's "Spot the difference". Our contestant, Lucy Fairweather, needs to tell one pretty much identical tree from another and there's a lot at stake on this. Oh yes, it's not a cash giveaway this week, there's something a lot more fundamental going on. If Lucy doesn't spot the difference, she's stuck out in these endless woods for the duration, and that's it for her! It'll be time for our next contestant. So, Lucy, which way is it? Left or right?'

I hummed a cheesy theme tune and looked back and forth. Actually, there was something rather familiar about the branches of the tree on the left. In fact, one looked distinctly like the branch which had done its best to jab me in the eye on the way through. Maybe I was heading in the right direction after all.

There was no time for hesitating. I needed to keep moving. I ploughed on through the interminable snow, which in some places sank beneath me until I was nearly up to my waist. Every so often I had to stop and kick loose the blocks of ice which kept forming around the spikes on my shoes. I was getting seriously tired now, and each step forward felt like a huge effort. Every muscle in my body was screaming at me to sit down for five minutes and take a breather, but I was concerned that if I did that, I might not ever get back up again.

Sunset had been and gone. My surroundings were now completely monochrome – black sky, black trees, grey snow. My thoughts had wandered to dangerous places. Would Star FM do a special tribute to me if I died, or would my infamy follow me to the grave? How much more disappointed would Mum be with me if I went and froze to death because of my own stupid stubbornness? And would Skye and Henri ever forgive me for ruining his brother's beloved business venture before it had even opened?

I'd been walking for what felt like forever, face down, eyes straining for tracks, when I suddenly bumped into something solid. I would have mistaken it for yet another tree if it hadn't been for the distinctive rustle of waterproof clothing. I looked up and found myself frozen in the steely gaze of Tommi Laukkanen.

'Where the hell have you been?'

I have never been so glad to be on the receiving end of a bollocking in all my life.

Chapter Ten

Fortunately, Tommi decided to cut short the lecture, and hustled me back to the main building which turned out to be much closer than I had realised. I would have been proud at my navigation skills had I not been so horribly frozen. Quite how cold I was, I didn't fully realise until I was in the warm when the blood started returning to my extremities in a very painful fashion.

'Take your clothes off,' barked Tommi as soon as we arrived back in the warmth of the drying room.

'Haven't had an offer like that in ages,' I couldn't help responding, although my chattering teeth rather diminished the effect. At least my sense of humour was still intact.

Tommi ignored my quip, but I thought I might have seen his cheeks flush a little. I tried to undo my layers as instructed, but it soon became apparent that I'd lost all dexterity in my hands. My fingers fumbled and failed to accomplish their task. Tutting away, Tommi efficiently undid the zips and pulled off my outer layers until I was left standing in the ugly long johns. I could feel the waves of disapproval emanating from his every pore. Although I was still fully clothed, I felt incredibly exposed there under his stern gaze and defensively crossed my arms in front of my chest as if I was trying to cover up nudity. I examined the floor closely, scratching at the grain of the wood with my big toe.

Then I felt Tommi gently lift my chin between his finger and thumb. He tucked my hair behind my ears and appeared to be concentrating fiercely on my lips. Now I was the one blushing as his intense blue eyes focused on every detail of my face, as if memorising it. His steady fingers traced up across my cheeks and then settled once again by my mouth. He moved closer and I could feel the warmth of his breath on my skin. My heart started beating more quickly. I found myself leaning towards him, hypnotised by the intensity of his scrutiny, suddenly very aware of the speckling of blond stubble which traced along his tough jawline, and the power in his strong arms.

'Good, no sign of frostbite where your face was exposed,' said Tommi, stepping back with clinical efficiency. 'Let me check your fingers and toes too.'

I cleared my throat to disguise my embarrassment. There was me imagining we'd been having some kind of special moment, when all he'd been doing was checking my nose wasn't about to fall off. I'd obviously been reading too many romance novels. Why would I even want to have a special moment with a grumpy so-and-so who obviously thoroughly disapproved of me?

He gave my fingers and toes a professional onceover, and then nodded in satisfaction.

'All fine. You have been lucky, this time.'

'For future reference, what should I be looking out for?' I said.

'I am hoping there will not be a next time, but as you are clearly determined to do whatever you please, the key thing to look out for is the skin turning white. It means there is no more blood flow to that area. You need to act before it gets to that point, as once the flesh is damaged by frostbite, there is very little that can be done to save it.'

Every word he said was a reminder of how foolish I had been. I needed to sort my ideas out.

'Thank you. I'm really sorry for going off like that. I wanted to improve my snowshoeing so I could pull my weight, but I ended up being more of a burden, yet again. I'm truly sorry.'

He shrugged his shoulders in exasperation. 'I will be honest. I am not sure if I can continue taking a chance on you if you are going to persist in putting yourself at risk like you just did. I agreed to take you in for Henri and Skye, but there is only so far brotherly loyalty will make me go. I don't want the guests following your dangerous example. Perhaps it might be best if you kept to your cabin while they are here. And I will consider whether it is practical and indeed safe to continue to do as my brother asks of me.'

He left me standing there, pathetic in my long johns, feeling like a naughty child abandoned to fend for themselves. If Tommi withdrew his offer of asylum, where else could I go?

After expending all that energy, both physical and emotional, I wanted nothing more than to go to bed and sleep for a thousand years. It was as dark as if it was the middle of the night, but a glance at my watch told me it was still only four in the afternoon. It felt wrong to go off to my room, when I knew there would be a lot of work to do with the guests arriving tomorrow. Maybe if I made myself useful, Tommi would have a change of heart? I determined to try to help behind the scenes, all while doing my best to avoid being caught by the man in charge. If I wanted to stay here, safely hidden from the trolls, then I needed to make the situation work, however much out of my comfort zone it was.

I hurried to the storeroom to grab a fresh set of fleeces to replace my snowy, sweaty ones. I was in the middle of heaving on a particularly gargantuan pair of jogging bottoms when all the lights went out.

'Hello?' I called between the racks of clothing. 'Is there anyone there?' There was a long silence, during which I peered into the darkness, wishing my night vision was better. There was something spooky about being among the rails of clothes in the dark. The shadows made them look like rows of people lining up ready to attack me at any moment. Clearly this environment was tipping me over the edge into a nervous wreck.

'Hi,' a voice right next to me replied.

I yelped with surprise and tried to take a step back, forgetting that my feet were all tangled up in fleecy underwear. I thudded painfully against the bench, adding another bruise to the collection I'd already gained on my backside from my snowshoeing exploits. I swore under my breath.

The lights came back on and a fur-covered figure loomed towards me, confirming all my earlier fears about strange creatures lurking in the darkness of the storeroom. The being shuffled closer towards me, then a hand emerged from the fur and swept back what I now realised was a giant hood. The tattooed and pierced face of a young guy emerged, only his cheeky grin making him appear less threatening than the dramatic body art would suggest.

'You must be the famous Lucy Fairweather,' he said. 'I recognise you from the internet.'

I cringed as he shook my hand vigorously. Was I never going to escape that?

He must have seen the despair in my expression because he quickly continued. 'Oh not that internet, although yes, I have seen your tap-dancing and the dodgy video. I meant the online stream of your radio show.' He tapped the big disc which stretched out his earlobe. 'I am a big radio nerd and I've been improving my English by listening to your British stations. Star FM's breakfast show is my favourite. Or it was while you were on it. I'm Rudi, by the way. Really excited to finally meet you.'

I felt myself hold my head a little higher. It was nice to meet a genuine fan, someone who was actually pleased to see me for a change, even if they did look like an animal rights activist's worst nightmare.

I smiled back, amused at the way the spider tattoo by his

right eyebrow seemed to dance expressively as he talked. 'Nice to meet you, Rudi. I apologise for my current state of undress. I became a bit too closely acquainted with the snow.'

He shrugged. 'You look very dressed to me. In Finland we get naked all the time. You'll get used to it.'

Another worrying revelation. As if to confirm his statement, he started removing his layers of fur and hanging them on the rails.

'So, Rudi, what do you do around here?' I said, hoping to interrupt his impromptu striptease. I dreaded to think what other tattoos would be revealed as he removed the layers. Despite my boisterous radio persona, I was still too much of an uptight Brit to do co-ed changing with a complete stranger, especially one with what I assumed was the Finnish version of 'love' and 'hate' tattooed on his knuckles.

'I am Rudi,' he said, waving his arms expansively, as if no further explanation was needed. The spider undulated in agreement.

'And…?' I pressed.

'Oh, I am the barman, the handyman, the everyman. You want something, I'll sort it for you.'

'Sounds like you're an important person to know around here.'

He puffed up his chest. 'That's me,' he said proudly. I flinched as another piece of fur was thrown in my direction and averted my gaze as a brown bear started to appear, climbing its way up his ribcage.

I spun around to give him some privacy. He chuckled. 'Do not worry. My girlfriend is not the jealous type.'

'Good for her,' I said. 'But I'd still rather you didn't bare all when I'm around.'

He laughed again, enjoying my inadvertent reference to his body art.

'So, Miss Lucy, is there anything I can do for you that will make your stay with us more comfortable? A little something that will cheer you up while you wait for Tommi to remember how to smile? He does not bear grudges by the way. He is just very serious about his dream. You will grow accustomed to his ways before long.'

'If I get the chance to stay, that is. I need to get myself back in his good books. There's not really much I can offer,' I said.

Rudi let out a distinctly dirty laugh. 'There is one thing I can think of,' he said suggestively.

'Far too many layers to remove to do any of that kind of thing,' I retorted, enjoying the banter.

Rudi snorted. 'You'd be surprised. You'll find us Finns can be most imaginative. By the way, you can turn back around now, I'm decent.'

I still didn't quite trust him. He laughed and appeared in my vision, fully clothed in a startling neon pink and purple onesie.

'Wow, very um, fashion forward,' I said.

'It makes me stand out in the snow. I am bright like the berries on the trees.'

I clapped my hands together. 'Rudi, you're a genius, why didn't I think of that before?'

'I know I am, but thank you for noticing. Am I right in thinking that an idea has come to you?'

I nodded and started pacing up and down as I wondered how I could implement my plan. 'I think I've come up with a way of getting back into Tommi's good books. But I'm going to need a few things. Any chance the Arctic Circle's Mr Fix-It could sort me out?'

He thumped his chest. 'There is no doubt. I can do it. What is it you are wanting?' he asked. 'I can get most legal stuff on a same day turnaround.' He lowered his voice and checked around conspiratorially. 'If you're wanting something a bit shady, then that can take a couple of days.'

'Oh, this is all above board,' I assured him. When he saw what I'd got planned, even Tommi would be able to muster a smile. And I know he'd said he wanted me to stick to my cabin when the guests arrived, but surely he wouldn't object to me zipping across to do something in the kitchen for a short while before then? This idea was guaranteed to make up for my earlier foolishness, and once the guests had tried it, they'd definitely fall in love with Wild Zone. But to make it work, I needed ingredients and I needed them fast.

———

Rudi proved to be good for his word, as, a couple of hours later, I heard a tapping on the door of my cabin and opened it to find a pile of produce on the veranda. I'd spent the intervening couple of hours since enlisting Rudi's assistance for my scheme flicking through the pages of a Finnish recipe book, trying to work out from the pictures what went into the traditional meals of the area. Needless to say, I remained as baffled as I was at the beginning of my research. My idea was to create a really special smoothie for Tommi; something that the guests could also enjoy as a welcome drink, which captured the flavours of Finland and which also said that I was sorry and could be a useful member of the team. Basically, a miracle drink. Still, nothing ventured, nothing gained.

I peered out through the gloom and tried to see if I could spot how many pairs of snowshoes were on the veranda in front of the main building. I thought I could make out a couple, which I hoped belonged to Johanna and Rudi. I didn't think Tommi would take too kindly to seeing me hanging around in the reception area when he'd expressly banished me to my quarters. I'd just have to take the risk and hope I could dive into a convenient cupboard if he happened to be in the vicinity.

I heaved on my cumbersome outdoor kit, manging to do it in a record ten minutes. If I kept going like this, I'd soon have it down to a fine art, though I wasn't sure I wanted to be stuck here long enough to develop that skill. I scurried across to the main building, head down, looking like a prison escapee, and clutching my paper bags of goodies to my chest. Johanna met me at the front door and hustled me into the kitchen.

'Tommi told me what happened earlier. Are you OK?' She squeezed my arm sympathetically.

'It gave me a bit of a fright, but I survived, all extremities intact. I'm definitely in the bad books though.'

Johanna smiled. 'Do not worry. Tommi will not hold it

against you forever. If he came across as cross with you, it would only be because he was worried. He feels responsible for everyone at Wild Zone and he takes his responsibilities seriously.'

'Maybe a bit too seriously,' I muttered. 'He's not around now, is he?'

Johanna shook her head. 'He has gone out to check on the dogs up at the kennels, so you should have enough time to try your experiment.'

'Brilliant. Then all I need is a blender, a sharp knife and a few chopping boards. And perhaps you could talk me through what these orange berries are. I asked Rudi to find me something typically Finnish, but I've no idea what they are.'

Johanna nodded. 'These are cloudberries. They are local to this area and they taste delicious, juicy and sharp and full of goodness. We Finns love eating whatever we can find in nature. Of course, at this time of year, the cold stops a lot of things growing, but we are good at storage and we try to avoid importing produce wherever we can.'

'They sound perfect for my smoothie making. I thought if I made enough, we could hand the drinks out to the guests to make them feel really welcome.'

Johanna hesitated. 'I'm sure they would be delighted,' she said.

'It sounds like there's a 'but' in there,' I said.

'There is no but. It is different from what we had planned, but I am sure it will go down very well. Perhaps you can teach me the recipe.'

I pulled on an apron and rolled up my sleeves. It felt good to be doing something familiar for a change.

'I don't tend to work from a recipe. I try to experiment with flavours and keep on tasting until it zings. Somehow, they're always a hit. They've never failed me yet.'

If only I could make enough smoothies to quell all the abuse from my internet haters.

I chopped and blended, adding fruit until I thought there was enough and then added more to be on the safe side. By the time I'd finished, there were three jugs full to the brim of the most wonderful-looking smoothie, so stuffed with cloudberries they looked like scoops of sunrise.

Johanna poured out a taster for each of us in two shot glasses. We clinked them together and took a sip.

'Wow, that's incredible,' she said, downing the rest of her drink. 'That tastes out of this world. And it's all pure and natural, which is even better. I feel like it's given me enough energy to cook all night.'

'That's the smoothie magic. I might call this one "Clear skies and cloudberries smoothie". Mostly because I'm hoping it will clear the air. Do you think the guests will like it?'

'I'm sure they will love it.'

'And do you think Tommi will mind if I help serve it? I don't want to give you guys extra work, and I'd really like to prove to him there is something I can do around here.'

'Leave it with me,' she promised. 'I'll try and talk him round.'

Chapter Eleven

Despite all the exertions of the day, when I finally got to bed, I found myself lying wide awake, nightmares about being stranded out in the endless snow threatening to surface whenever my eyes did try to drift close. If it wasn't the claustrophobic images of frosty trees closing in on me, it was a succession of my nearest and dearest lining up to berate me for my stupid behaviour.

When echoes of my dad's voice telling me off for being stupid enough to go viral started bouncing around my brain, I got out of bed and took out the cheeky bottle of spirits which I had also requested from Rudi, knowing there was no chance of me being able to hang out in the Wild Zone bar for the duration of the guests' stay. I know there's something rather pathetic about drinking alone, but this was an emergency. I took a couple of swigs, hoping that they would do the trick of knocking me out until the morning. Anything for a decent night's sleep. But although they made my brain fuzzy, they did nothing to quieten the anxiety swirling around my mind. I carried on sipping until eventually the churning of my stomach settled into more of a gentle lull.

I unfolded the piece of paper where Rudi had itemised what I owed him and nearly choked. The berries and smoothie ingredients were about what I'd expect, but the alcohol was ridiculously expensive. Was it made of liquid gold, for goodness' sake? I was going to have to go steady for the duration of my stay otherwise I was going to have to take a mortgage out to afford those prices. Perhaps it would be better if Tommi chucked me out after all.

It was the final straw after a challenging twenty-four hours. Feeling very sorry for myself, I decided that the best course of action was to go on the defensive. The root of all my problems was that viral video. If I could only get to the bottom of who had put the horrid thing together, then I could confront my persecutor, publish the evidence to clear my name, and then everything would be OK. It's amazing the clarity a couple of doses of gin could bring to the old brain. I don't know why I hadn't tried before. As sleep was still miles off, I decided there was no time like the present. I would be brave and undertake another Google search of myself, and from there work out why things had gone so wrong for me. Nothing could stand in the way of Detective Fairweather.

Unfortunately, it turned out that a lack of Wi-Fi signal could. I still wasn't feeling quite brave enough for turning my phone back on, so I decided the only course of action was to haul a fleece or two over my pyjamas and brave the freezing sprint across to the main building. Johanna had told me they always kept it unlocked in case any hikers needed to take shelter during the night. Quite why anyone would want to be hiking in these conditions was beyond me, but it certainly worked to my advantage tonight.

Once there, I did a quick check around to make sure I was the only one in the building, then I opened up my trusty laptop again and settled myself on the sofa in front of the cosy embers of the fire. I'd been expecting the internet to be slower than dial-up, as Wild Zone was in the middle of nowhere, but amazingly I got straight online and was soon confronted once again by the horrors of my public shaming. I could have done with bringing the gin across to steel myself against the images. A few new ones had been added to the collection of memes, all even more horrible than the last lot. Would this thing never die down?

But I told myself I was made of stronger stuff, and started digging around, hoping that I would somehow come across the original video and that it would miraculously reveal its secrets. They always made it look so easy on programmes like *CSI*. But I was no computer expert, and apparently I wasn't much of a detective either, because confronted with page after page of identical versions of the video with millions of views combined, I didn't even know where to start. I wandered to the kitchen, took one of the smoothie jugs out of the fridge and poured myself a glass to help me think. But despite the invigorating properties of the 'Clear skies and cloudberries' smoothie, the sleep which had evaded me earlier started to do battle with my eyelids. I curled up back on the sofa and took another sip. I'd just rest my eyes for twenty seconds to restore my energy, and then I'd get to work properly…

I was caught fast asleep and snoring about eight hours later by the worst possible person.

'What on earth are you doing?' said Tommi staring down at me from his great height.

I sat bolt upright and swore when I realised that a) I'd accidentally spilled smoothie on the sofa and b) I'd also left one of the jugs out on the fireplace and it was already starting to smell a bit whiffy. My heart sank.

'The guests are outside. They are about to walk in and this is the sight that will greet them?' said Tommi, gesturing at me in despair.

I became very aware of the fact that I was wearing unicorn pyjamas, my hair was standing on end, and that I'd fallen asleep on the laptop so probably had a massive great big keyboard crease across my face. I could see his point that it wasn't exactly the professional impression he wanted to create for his first ever paying guests.

'I am so, so sorry, Tommi,' I started garbling. 'This is a terrible mistake.' Yet another one. I'd be lucky if he didn't chuck me out in the snow right now. It was what I deserved.

'There is no time for your grovelling.' He sighed as he examined the orange stain on the formerly pristine sofa. I felt even more dreadful. He sighed again. He'd obviously reached the 'I'm not angry, I'm disappointed stage', which somehow felt so much worse. He took some cleaning implements out of a concealed cupboard and threw them across to me. 'You clear up this mess, while I try to delay the guests.'

'There's more smoothie in the fridge if you want to offer them that.' I tried one last-ditch attempt to make things right. I really should learn when to keep my mouth shut.

Tommi wrinkled his nose as he picked up the jug of slightly fermenting smoothie. 'If you think I'm going to start my business by poisoning my guests, then you are very wrong. Johanna and I will serve them *glögi*, as we always planned. They are in Finland, therefore they will have something traditionally Finnish, not whatever strange concoction you decided to create which got you into this state.'

I opened my mouth to explain that I'd fallen asleep on the sofa because I was tired, and that I hadn't passed out pissed, but realised there was probably no point. He'd already made up his mind about me. As always, I had meant well, but managed to screw everything up.

I heard Tommi taking the guests down to look at the sauna and set to work trying to clean up, knowing that he wouldn't be able to stall them for long as they'd want to relax in the lounge after their journeys. The stuff he'd given me didn't seem to touch the stain, but fortunately, Rudi had something in his secret stock which was powerful enough to do the trick. I poked at the fire so it burned more brightly, hoping that it would have the dual effect of drying out the fabric and distracting the guests from the suspicious-looking damp patch.

I still hoped Johanna would take pity on me and serve the smoothie anyway, but Tommi had obviously got to her first and she refused. I was certainly not going to be able to finish it all, so, after giving Rudi some to take home to his long-suffering girlfriend, with great regret, I poured the rest away. I was burning bridges left, right and centre. It was time to get my act together.

The next day, I was resigned to my fate and stayed in my lodgings as instructed. I'd managed to find a portable radio, although listening to it felt rather like pouring salt onto the wound. Tuning my way up and down the dial, I realised there was only one station which had anything close to resembling a clear signal. I couldn't understand a word of what was being said, but I lay back on my bed and tried to get an impression from the presenter's intonation. Unfortunately, this presenter seemed to favour speaking in a clanging monotone, which nearly sent me drifting off to sleep. He didn't sound like he wanted to be there, and his indifference must have been even more glaring to his Finnish listeners. Every forty-five minutes or so, he'd deign to play a track of music, but the long pauses and the heavy sighs before he did so suggested it was the last thing he wanted to do. It was an incredibly frustrating experience, and eventually I switched it off, the radio DJ in me unable to deal with this lazy approach to my profession.

It wasn't long before I began to appreciate why they call it 'cabin fever', though I kept telling myself that it was better to be hidden away here than out facing the abuse and threats in the real world. I'd just finished counting the number of wooden slats in the walls for the third time – forty-six, if you want to know – when there was a knock at the door. Tommi was standing on the step with a pair of sharp-looking poles in his hand. I took an automatic step back. I know I'd irritated him, but surely threatening me with weapons was a tad extreme. Had he come to literally chase me off the premises?

He looked surprised at the horrified expression on my face. 'Oh, these?' he said, eventually cottoning on. 'I am teaching a cross-country skiing lesson for the guests, and I thought it might be a good opportunity for you to join in. You'll have to learn the skill sooner or later, so it might as well be in the group.'

I was surprised at the invitation. Yesterday he'd been adamant he'd had enough of my presence, but here he was holding out the poles in a gesture of goodwill. Maybe it was a test. Nevertheless, I felt torn. This was a very generous offer from Tommi and I certainly didn't want to shove it back in his face. But on the other hand, hiding out in this isolated little bubble felt safe. The thought of encountering strangers who had probably seen the viral video was enough to send a shiver down my spine.

But Tommi gave me no time to come up with an excuse. He plonked the poles down on my veranda and stomped off, issuing a stern instruction that I was to be by the storage building in five minutes' time 'or else'. If this was the olive branch he was presenting me with, then I would just have to seize it and hope for the best.

Having learned from my snowshoeing experience, I figured skiing called for all the layers I possessed. I even strapped on the oh-so-attractive waterproof gaiters, just to be sure there wasn't an inch of clothing where the damp cold and ice could creep through to my skin. This time, donning the balaclava made me feel like I was putting on a protective mask which I could hide behind. With any luck, if I kept quiet and didn't draw attention to myself, the visitors wouldn't associate this Lucy with the Lucy Fairweather of viral video infamy and I could keep my head down and learn a new survival skill.

There were around fifteen guests, a range of ages, but mostly women, who already seemed to have bonded as a group. I crept to the periphery of the gathering, hiding near the shadows of the storage building in the hope that they didn't notice my presence.

Unfortunately, Tommi seemed to have decided that I was going to be used as the class guinea pig. As soon as he spotted me, he called me to the front of the group to help him demonstrate the first technique he wanted to teach. It was either incredibly trusting of him, or he was taking the opportunity to have a bit of fun at my expense. I quickly decided it was the latter.

He launched into a lecture. 'Here in Finland we often get around by kick-sled. It is taller than a normal sledge as you can see, and you stand up on the rails, hold onto the handle and then kick out at the back in order to move along. Lucy, would you like to have a go and show them how to do this?'

I nodded in what I hoped appeared to be a confident

manner, and tried to mimic the easy kick and slide motion he'd just demonstrated. Unfortunately, my feet went one way and the kick-sled went another, and I ended up spread-eagled between the two looking most undignified.

Tommi swallowed a chuckle. 'That was an interesting attempt. Ladies and gentlemen, it is perhaps best if you think about what Lucy did, and then try not to do it that way.'

Ah, so this was how it was going to work. Fine, if he wanted someone to be the class clown, so that everyone else didn't feel bad when they got it wrong, then I was happy to play that role. After all, wasn't that exactly what I normally did on my radio show? Why did I keep on torturing myself with thoughts about my job? I needed to concentrate on the task in hand. I did a couple more prat-falls, still accidental, but by my third attempt I could sense I was starting to get the hang of the correct kick-slide motion.

Soon everyone was kicking their way along and laughter filled the air. Tommi had a way of explaining things very clearly, but I could sense that his straightforward manner and his habit of intense scrutiny made a few of the class a bit too aware of when they weren't doing well. Some of the ladies had a habit of falling over whenever they felt his gaze on them, though whether it was because like me, he made them nervous, or because they were enjoying attention-seeking, I wasn't quite sure.

Once most people had mastered the basic technique, Tommi opened the doors of the storage barn and started handing out the skis. He took his time over checking that everyone had the right size, and some of the class started muttering under their breath about getting cold. I could sense rebellion in the atmosphere unless he quickly turned things around. There's one thing you learn in radio land, and that's when someone is floundering on the air, you step in and throw them a line. After all, it's what I'd hope someone would do for me if I was in that position.

'How do kick-sleds relate to skiing, Tommi?' I asked, raising my voice so it cut through the discontented chatter of the group.

He looked annoyed at first that I was asking the question in front of the guests, but I could see it dawn on him that he hadn't really explained how the two disciplines were related. I thought he nodded his head towards me in a subtle gesture of thanks, although I could have been mistaken.

'Cross-country skiing is quite different to traditional downhill skiing. The skis are narrower and longer, which is helpful when you are sliding over thick piles of snow in challenging conditions, and when you move, you use the kick-slide motion that you have been practising on your kick-sleds. Once you have mastered the kick-slide technique, you should be able to travel for miles, and do all kinds of terrain with equal ease as going downhill.'

The group muttered approvingly and Tommi seemed to warm with their response. 'Of course, in Finland, we are raised using kick-sleds. Children learn how to walk with them, and then they use them to travel back and forth to school in the winter months. And at the other end of the scale, they become Zimmer frames for our elderly people. In fact, I once saw a lady speeding along on a kick-sled when spring had arrived. Whenever she got to the Tarmac where the snow had melted away, the sparks flew from the rails of the sledge. It was quite a sight to behold.'

The group relaxed still further after that anecdote, and I felt the satisfaction of a job well done. Maybe it would help Tommi think more kindly towards me.

He decided that the rest of the lesson should be held out on the frozen lake, a vast expanse of glistening ice which was distinguished from the snow that surrounded it by the fact that it was the only place not covered in trees. As we gathered in the rough ground by the edges where bits of reed stuck up here and there through the snow drifts, Tommi fixed us all with a stern expression.

'This lake is very deep and, at this time of year, it is very, very cold. It is frozen at least two feet deep for the majority of its area. However, do not go within one hundred yards of that bridge over there.' He pointed to a precarious wooden structure in the distance which looked like it was suspended in mid-air seemingly by magic. 'That is where the river runs out of the lake, and although a lot of it looks snowy and frozen, there is still moving water in that area and so the ice is not thick enough to hold the weight of a human. Do you all understand?'

We nodded solemnly. The thought of plunging into dark, freezing water and being swept under the ice filled me with horror.

'Good. Lucy, where are you?'

I was once again summoned in front of the visitors to be the first one to try my kick-slide moves with the skis on my feet. But whereas I had felt completely out of my depth doing the snowshoeing, this felt more within my comfort zone. There was something almost meditative about sliding my way around the lake, exploring its virgin surface and hearing the gentle swoosh of the skis over the snow. I wasn't sure I'd feel quite so confident once I braved any hills, but here on the smooth, flat snow of the lake I was actually starting to enjoy myself.

'Nordic skiing is acknowledged to be one of the toughest workouts there is,' said Tommi, as a few of the older members of the group started complaining about aching limbs. 'It uses almost every single muscle in your body, so it is very good for developing your stamina and physique.'

'I can see it's certainly had a positive effect on you,' cackled one of the louder ladies. Tommi looked embarrassed.

'Aw, love, sorry, I'm only saying what everyone here is thinking. Lucy is lucky to have a man like you around the place.'

'I'm not his girlfriend...'

'She's not my girlfriend...' we chorused simultaneously.

Chapter Twelve

When we finally arrived back at Wild Zone, my limbs were aching and my skin was tight and dry from the cold, but I felt invigorated. It was good to be physically exhausted for a change rather than just mentally drained. As I helped everyone stow their skiing kit and brushed away the clods of ice which had been tracked into the store room, I felt satisfaction at a job well done. But it didn't matter what I thought. What really mattered was whether I'd done enough to change Tommi's mind and convince him to allow me to stay. Trouble was, he'd been avoiding being alone in my presence ever since the guest had made the comment believing we were in a relationship. It was quite sweet really that a grown man like him could be thrown off guard by such a thing. I preferred to think of it like that, rather than the alternative – that he was embarrassed at the idea of him feeling anything apart from complete contempt for someone like me.

Eventually, I managed to corner him among the rows of drying gaiters and waterproof trousers.

'Are you hiding from me?' I asked. It wasn't the right way to approach the conversation, because he immediately looked confused and then defensive.

'What are you talking about, Lucy?' he asked. 'If you've come to ask if you can stay, I haven't made my mind up yet.'

'Oh.' That was not what I had been hoping to hear.

'However,' he continued, 'I am grateful for the effort you put into the skiing lesson today. I'll admit it was helpful to have an extra pair of hands to assist me. You may consider yourself on probation.'

I resisted the urge to punch the air in relief. Probation was better than nothing, and I'd make every effort to complete it successfully. The thought of having to find another sanctuary had been too awful to contemplate.

Tommi fixed me with one of his stern looks. 'You do not have to avoid the guests, and I do not demand that you hide in your cabin. But perhaps you might offer to help Johanna in the kitchen. She assures me you won't get in her way and suggests that you might even have some culinary talent. I do not care what you do, as long as it is useful and you do not cause trouble.'

'Understood. Thank you for giving me another chance. I hope I won't have to impose on your hospitality for too much longer. It's only until I can get to the bottom of this stupid mess and convince my producer to put in a good word for me, though Hell might freeze over before that happens.'

Was it my imagination, or did his gaze soften a fraction?

'The internet will find another scapegoat soon. People's memories may be long, but their attention span is short.'

I think there might have been an attempt at comfort somewhere buried in there. I pulled a face. 'Even if the internet folk forget, I don't think my bosses will in a hurry. I'm afraid my radio career might be dead and buried.'

'You never know. These things have a way of working out for the best,' he said philosophically. Somewhere underneath the gruff exterior, there lurked a kind man, I thought.

As suggested, I reported for kitchen duty, and Johanna welcomed me with open arms. Although everyone kept saying the Finns liked their solitude, I think Johanna enjoyed having someone to keep her company because she chatted away merrily. Under her tutelage, I learned how to make reindeer stew, only experiencing the smallest sense of disquiet at the idea that I was putting Dasher and Dancer into the pot. The reindeer came from a nearby farm and had been brought up on an organic lifestyle, so I comforted myself with the thought that they'd had the best lives they possibly could. Into the stew went lentils, beans and potatoes, until there were so many ingredients, it was a challenge to be able to stir the pot. It was all terribly hearty, the kind of food I'd never have the time or energy to cook back at home, but here it was exactly what I craved after a long day out in the cold.

I wanted to stay in the kitchen doing the washing up while Johanna served the guests, but she insisted I help her so I could see the result of our efforts.

'What is there to be afraid of?' she asked, as I tried another feeble line about not getting under her feet.

It sounded so pathetic to confess that I was scared that people might recognise me from the viral video.

Johanna saw right through my excuses, and passed me a stack of plates to carry through. 'If they realise that you are Lucy Fairweather, so what? What has happened is a huge deal in your life, I know that, but for most people it is a tiny drop of nothingness. I doubt they will have the courage to say to your face what they write online. They are here on holiday and they want to relax. Besides, Rudi tells me they have been good customers at the bar. They will hardly be aware of your presence. Tipsy guests might cause problems for us later on if they go wandering off when they're meant to be walking to their cabins, but for now, we shall take advantage of that, shall we not?'

Despite her reassurances, I was still on high alert when I walked into the dining room. Although I'd genuinely considered donning the balaclava again, I'd gone with the more subtle disguise of wearing a catering hairnet and making sure my body was concealed by my apron. But Johanna had been correct. Most of the guests barely acknowledged me, and, if they did, it was only to thank me for serving their dinner. My sense of relief was indescribable.

While they were tucking into their grub, Johanna and I settled down in the kitchen to eat our own meal and I discovered a liking for the reindeer stew. And although I'd thought I'd never want to look at another cloudberry again after the smoothie debacle, the cloudberry crumble soon converted me.

'Where's Tommi this evening?' I asked, surprised that he wasn't around. The impression I'd got so far was that he was almost surgically attached to the place.

'Probably seeing Gurta,' she said, shrugging her shoulders as if this was a commonplace occurrence. 'She is very lovely. I expect you'll meet her at some point soon.'

'If I'm around long enough,' I said gloomily. My surprising pang of something which might have been disappointment at this revelation about Tommi's personal life was simply delusional. Of course Tommi was seeing someone. And of course she was perfect. I sort of hoped I didn't have to meet the 'very lovely' Gurta. I wasn't sure I could take feeling even more inadequate in comparison to a woman who was probably a saintly model of Scandi good looks and intelligence.

Chapter Thirteen

The next day the guests were scheduled to try out husky sledding. I stood in reception to wave them off, trying to tell myself that cleaning bathrooms in the warmth would be miles better than freezing outside, even if there were cute huskies around. Whatever I did, I needed to keep myself extra busy for the next few days. Mum had sent me a message this morning about it nearly being Dad's anniversary, not that I needed a reminder of a date which felt no less upsetting each year that passed. I needed to keep myself fully occupied so my mind didn't have time to wander to painful places.

'Good morning,' said Rudi cheerily, interrupting my thoughts as he strode up in his fur outfit, looking hairy enough to be one of the dogs himself. He started a tuneless rendition of 'Lucy in the sky with diamonds' by the Beatles and tried to twirl me round.

I attempted to hush him as several of the guests turned to look in our direction. I really didn't want them to get any kind of association in their heads between music and me, as it was only a small step from that to them thinking about infamous radio DJs called Lucy. He hummed a few more bars until I gave his furry shoulder a shove.

He laughed. 'Tommi says could you come and join us for the sledding? We have a very special job for you to do.'

My heart soared with hopeful excitement. This was a completely unexpected bonus, one of those once-in-a-lifetime experiences that people always talk about.

Tommi himself strode up, carrying a bag filled with industrial-thickness gloves. 'Yes, we need someone to scoop the poop for the dogs. Do not worry. We are a small group today, and there will only be around twenty of them. They normally make a lot of mess at the beginning when they get excited, and you may have to jump off the sledge en route as they don't stop running to relieve themselves and sometimes the poo can fly through the air, but I am sure you will be able to run and catch up with us again.'

And, lo, my starry expectations were crushed. Where could I sign up for the toilet scrubbing? That sounded way preferable to clearing up after twenty over-excited dogs. I forced a smile to my lips. If Tommi was testing my resolve, I wanted to try to show willing.

'No problem,' I said through gritted teeth. 'Where do I find the poop scoop bags? And can I borrow some of those gloves?'

He solemnly handed over a couple of pairs of gloves and several extra-thick bin bags. Just how much excrement was he expecting me to deal with today?

He let me hang for a while and then the men exchanged glances and burst out laughing.

'We are having you on,' confessed Tommi. 'The huskies run through a special area of woodland, where everyone knows there will be traces of the dogs around. The mess soon freezes and is cleared by the guys who run the sledding company, so it does not cause anyone any problems.'

'The poo does fly up in the air when you're going really fast, so watch out,' said Rudi with a delighted expression on his face.

'I recommend you leave that detail out of the guidebook,' I said, trying not to be completely grossed out by the image. I wasn't surprised at Rudi playing the joke on me, but it was interesting to see this teasing side of Tommi emerging again. I hoped it was an indication of his softening attitude towards me, but maybe he was just in a good mood after spending the evening with the lovely Gurta.

'We do not need you for clearing up, but it would be useful to have someone to help the guests on with their extra clothing and wait with them at the minibus until it is their turn to take to the sledges. They will be travelling around in two groups as there are not enough huskies at the moment to take everyone at the same time. Some of them have recently had litters of puppies, so they are enjoying what you might call their maternity leave and not working today.'

I crossed my fingers that I would get to meet the husky puppies at some point. There had to be some compensations for living in this climate. And Skye would love to hear about them. She had been on a mission to persuade Henri to get a husky for years, although, with the baby on the way, I suspected the puppy plans might have to go on the back burner. Even Skye, with her serene approach to life, might struggle to keep up the Zen when trying to wrangle a baby and a puppy at the same time.

Determined not to make Tommi regret inviting me along for the day, I threw myself into trying to be useful. I whizzed around the cabins, knocking on doors and reminding people that we were due to leave any minute. Assembling the guests for the trip was like herding cats. No sooner had everyone gathered by the battered minibus, then someone would need the loo, and someone else would remember they'd forgotten their camera. I also ended up doing a few emergency runs to the storeroom to get extra hats when Tommi warned that it was minus seventeen degrees centigrade today, but would feel more like minus twenty-seven when we experienced the wind-chill factor.

'When you're on the sled, you're just standing there, making only small movements with your weight to help the dogs go around corners. Apart from that, you are expending no energy. It is therefore very easy to get dangerously cold. Lucy, remind us of the symptoms of frostbite again?'

'Watch out for the skin turning white,' I answered quickly, proud to demonstrate that I had been paying attention to some of his lectures, but already concerned that today's temperature might mean I had to put my knowledge to practical use.

'Very good. Everyone, keep an eye on each other. Right, ladies and gentlemen, follow me if you please.'

The minibus only just had enough places for everyone and their extensive kit. I ended up crammed in the front seat between Tommi, who was driving, and Rudi, who was providing an endless commentary on his driving ability to wind him up. We were so squashed together that Tommi kept on accidentally hitting my leg whenever he needed to change gears. The apologising and my reassurances that it wasn't a problem were starting to get a tad awkward and repetitive, so I began tuning into the sound of the engine and then leaning towards Rudi whenever I anticipated Tommi would need to change gear. It had the unfortunate effect of inciting Rudi to even more boisterous behaviour, and by the time we arrived at the husky run, I could tell Tommi had had enough of him. That was probably how Rudi ended up being instructed to do the job I'd been expecting to perform – hanging around the minibus with half the guests and keeping them entertained while they waited for their sledding turn. His misfortune resulted in a promotion for me, as I was enlisted to help Tommi with the husky group.

We could hear the dogs about half a mile before we saw them. The sound of their howls was both plaintive and haunting, especially when the noise echoed endlessly around the hills. The huskies were tied to the trunks of the sturdiest-looking trees, five to a rope, and they were straining at their leashes to get going. They were fluffy and bubbling with enthusiasm, but also had the tough look of working dogs who know they've got a proper job to do.

They scrabbled in the snow, growling at each other and getting into play-fights until a dog who was obviously the leader of the pack bared his teeth at them and they settled back down.

Their handlers were a proper pair of Viking lookalikes, all bearded faces and long hair, and they seemed no less fearsome than their animals. Their strength made Tommi and Rudi look like a pair of weedy teenagers in comparison. They seemed to communicate in barks themselves, one word from them making the dogs lie down on the ground with barely a whimper. It was like stepping back in time, seeing a mode of transport that had gone unchanged for centuries. Our state-of-the art thermal gear seemed out of place in this traditional setting, but I was extremely glad we had it.

A couple of the dogs snarled and then lashed out at each other, rolling towards me as the dispute grew more serious. I leapt away in alarm. I wasn't normally scared of dogs, but these seemed closer to wolves than the domesticated animals I was used to having around.

Tommi mimicked the barking command of the Vikings, and the dogs let out a couple more growls and then separated.

'They have to know who is boss,' he said. 'You know that dogs are pack animals. Well, this is nowhere more true than in the husky herd. Each animal knows exactly what their place is in the pecking order. They have their four-legged leader who keeps them in line, but they must also realise that the human is above even that leader. If you stand your ground, and are firm but fair, they will respect your authority.'

It sounded like his own philosophy for running his business. There was no question where I was in the pecking order of that particular pack – the runt of the litter, and still at risk of being cast out as too much of a burden on resources.

The guests went into paroxysms of delight when they were introduced to the dogs and Tommi had quite a struggle to stop them from taking selfies with their arms wrapped around their furry bodies. It was very quickly clear that these huskies were not into hugging when they were at work. I kept a wary eye on the guests' fingers. It would never do for them to lose them either through over-enthusiastic dog interaction, or from frostbite caused by leaving their gloves off too long while they were doing their photo shoot.

The Vikings clapped their hands together. 'Time to get going.' The dogs instantly went ballistic, scrabbling at the ground and baying in their eagerness to run. Each guest was assigned to their own sled, pulled by a pack of four or five dogs. The huskies were arranged evenly spaced along two ropes for each sled, I guessed so that the weight of the vehicle was distributed among them. In the middle of each group was a chunkier beast, who looked like it was the powerhouse of the pack. While the ropes were checked, the animals kept looking back at the humans, as if willing them to hurry up with the boring talking so they could get going.

The taller of the Vikings briefly explained how to drive

the sleds. 'It is very simple. You stand on the runners, and you hold on with all your strength. The dogs will be hyperactive to start with, so you might wish to put your foot on the brake to try to slow them down.' He mimed jumping back on the brake, which was a narrow slat of metal which ran horizontally between the runners immediately behind where the driver stood. It looked rather flimsy to my untrained eyes. 'When you are going downhill, it is very important to step on the brake so the sled does not start going faster than the dogs and run them over. On the other hand, make sure you are not on the brakes when you go uphill as the dogs may start to struggle. If you are able, lean gently like a motorcyclist when you approach the corners. But do not lean too much as you do not want to tip the sled over. If that happens, the dogs will carry on running until I tell them to stop. Is that clear?'

And that was the extent of the instruction. Tommi gestured me over.

'One of the guys will lead the way, and another will run parallel to the guest convoy with his team. We will be at the back in a double sled to scoop up people who are getting left behind.'

I nodded, feeling a clutch of nerves at the responsibility. At least in a double sled, I wouldn't be driving, I tried to reassure myself. It soon became clear that Tommi had other ideas.

'As it is your first time in Finland, it seems only right that I should let you have the fun of being the driver.'

'You'll be better than he is at driving the minibus,' piped up Rudi who'd wandered over with the remaining guests to see us off. 'Make sure you go super-fast. It is the only way.'

He high-fived me and I tried to return it with the confidence I was seriously lacking. I was beginning to realise that I was about to put my life in these dogs' paws. I really hoped they couldn't sense my nerves.

One by one, the guests set off at breakneck speed, whooping and laughing as the huskies bounded through the snow and hauled them uphill like they were no weight at all. And then it was our turn. I could feel the dogs straining to get going as I gripped onto the sled as if my entire life depended on it. As soon as the tall Viking undid the restraining rope, the huskies set off at a charge, whizzing out of the field at full tilt and taking us deeper into the winter wonderland.

It was like speeding through the magical world of Narnia. The snowy ground was glittering as if it had been sprinkled with silver dust, while delicate particles of frost danced and twirled in the air. The low sunlight bathed the landscape in a gentle yellow glow, softening the dark silhouettes of the trees which stood sentinel at either side of the path. But the icy bite of the wind provided a sharp reminder of the potentially deadly nature of my surroundings, even while the sparkling snowflakes collected on my eyelashes, making everything appear to be edged in delicate diamonds. I wanted to slow down and take in every inch of my surroundings, but it felt like we were doing a hundred miles an hour whizzing through the trees and I wasn't sure there was any stopping these enthusiastic hounds. I desperately wanted to put my foot on the brake to hold us back, but I was scared that any movement I made would send me flying or make the dogs turn off in a different direction.

'Lean to the left, we are coming up to a sharp corner,' said Tommi from his cosy nest among the blankets on the sledge. I know he thought he'd been doing me a favour by letting me have the driving experience, but I couldn't help feeling that his situation looked a whole lot warmer and less precarious than mine. I tried to do as directed, my frozen feet clumsy in their attempts to follow Tommi's instructions, and, as I'd feared, the movement sent me completely off-balance. In one beautifully smooth motion, the huskies swooped the sled around the corner, fur streaming back, wet snouts sniffing out the route ahead. I meanwhile continued going straight on, flying through the air and landing on all fours in a huge pile of snow. I quickly closed my mouth and eyes, praying that the snow was at least clean and hadn't done service as a husky toilet.

Going from the adrenalin high of speeding along to the abrupt jolting shock of the crash, caused my spirits to take a similar dive. The noise of the huskies had already faded into the distance and I was alone in the wilderness. I dragged myself upright, legs wobbling, and attempted to take a deep breath to calm myself down, but the cold burnt its way into my lungs and made me cough. I reached up to pull my hat more firmly over my ears, and the ice in my hair crackled against my gloves. If I stayed here any longer, I was going to turn into a snowwoman.

I started following the tracks, hoping that Tommi would stop the sled and send a search party back to look for me. If this had been a dramatic attempt to get rid of me, I wasn't impressed. Judging by the trail of yellow through the snow, Tommi and Rudi hadn't been making up the part about the dogs relieving themselves en route. I ploughed my way on following the pawprints, until eventually I rounded another corner and saw the husky train at a halt in the distance, a distinctive figure striding towards me in the foreground.

'No bones broken?' Tommi deigned to ask before he pointed out that we were now running late because of my misadventure.

There was only one answer to that. I bent down, rolled a snowball up and then chucked it at him, aiming for the centre of his chest. It struck him right on target. He looked surprised.

'I didn't plan to fall off. In fact, I think you'll find I did a beautiful demonstration of how to go in a straight line,' I said, sending another snowball winging his way. This time he was expecting it and somehow caught it mid-air and threw it right back at me.

'It's a shame the huskies were going around a corner while you were demonstrating that manoeuvre,' he retorted. The snowball glanced off my arm and bounced harmlessly onto the ground.

'Perhaps you'd like to prove your husky sledding skills are better than your snowball throwing?' I said.

I thought I saw a sparkle of something like amusement in his eyes, but he nodded so quickly that I suspected I'd imagined it.

'I'll check the guests are OK, and then we'll get going,' he said. 'Challenge accepted.'

He worked his way down the line, obligingly taking some more photos and then stopped off to have a quick word with the younger Viking.

Once everyone was back in position on their sleds, the tall Viking let loose a whooping cry from the back of his throat. The huskies bayed in return and set off at full tilt again.

'Hurry up and make sure you've got the blanket over you,' was all Tommi would say, then he leapt on the back of the sled and clicked his tongue. If I'd thought we'd been going fast before, then I was very much mistaken, because now we were practically skimming above the surface of the snow. Tommi seemed to have taken on the responsibilities for being on the flank of the group, because we overtook two of their number and then the huskies dived into the darker forest, weaving in and out of the trees. I gasped as a couple of overhanging branches came so close I thought they were going to knock Tommi from his position. Every time I thought it wasn't possible to go any faster, the huskies put on another burst of speed, flying along like they were having the time of their lives. It was invigorating and thrilling and utterly terrifying, all at the same time.

Eventually we arrived back at our starting point. Tommi drove the team around the field in a lap of honour and then we came to a halt. I felt almost as breathless as the dogs looked. The Vikings hurried forward to tie the dogs up so they didn't set off running again, then poured them bowls of water which they lapped up eagerly.

'Now that's how it's done,' Tommi said triumphantly, leaning down and helping me stand up from the sled. My legs felt distinctly wobbly so I kept hold of his hand. He gazed down at me with a warm smile. It transformed his face. I reached up and wiped the frost from where it had crystallised on his eyebrows and stubble. It should have looked ridiculous, but it made him appear distinguished instead.

'You're turning into a snowman,' I said. 'No sign of frostbite though, you'll be pleased to hear. A little thawing out and you'll be OK, I think.'

He returned my scrutiny with a steady gaze.

'You're turning icy too,' he replied. 'Your breath has frozen in wisps in your hair.'

'Maybe I'm getting used to my surroundings.'

He looked at me as if considering the veracity of my statement, then a bark from one of the huskies interrupted his thoughts and he turned away.

'Time to get on with the next trip. Rudi, perhaps you can help with this one? Lucy, wait in the minibus with the guests.'

I felt a wave of disappointment at being cast back into the wilderness again.

Chapter Fourteen

That evening I decided to be brave and hang out in the main building. It was either that, or drive myself mad in my cabin listening to the world's dullest DJ on the local radio station while trying to block awareness of the clock ticking down to the date I always dreaded. Logically, I knew that an anniversary should make no difference whatsoever to the depth of my emotions, but there's not a lot of logic when it comes to dealing with grief. This year, with the added stress of my status of social media pariah, I was finding it almost unbearable. I needed something else to focus on.

I loitered in the shadows of the lounge with a book, letting the guests enjoy the prime positions by the fire. The sweet scent of wood smoke hung in the air and the pitch black outside the windows made the warm lights of the lounge seem even more cosy and comfortable. Once again, there was no sign of Tommi. He was probably spending the evening with the perfect Gurta again, regaling her with tales of the silly English woman who kept falling in the snow and who'd been causing him problems ever since her arrival. Not that I cared what he did in his free time, of course.

By now the guests had really bonded as a group; the challenges they'd shared during the day sparking conversation and laughter among even the shyest of individuals. Most of them had arrived as solo travellers looking for a bit of adventure in the wilderness as an escape from another dreary autumn at home. I hoped for the sake of my new Finnish friends that the trip was living up to the guests' high expectations.

From my safe observation position in the corner, I could see the small cliques which had formed. Although I wasn't intending to eavesdrop, I couldn't help overhearing their conversations, and I kept on optimistically tucking away little gems of anecdotes which would make for funny retelling on the radio. Maybe one day they'd come in handy.

My ears tuned into one bubbly trio in particular. From what I could make out, the women were all high-achievers, holding top roles in the city, law and medicine. They obviously lived their life at home to full tilt, determinedly pursuing their goals and never stopping to take a moment's rest. But the arctic air must have got to them, because here they were set on letting their hair down and rediscovering their rebellious youth. I smothered a smile as they started reminiscing about their favourite university drinks. If they were harking back to those days, then Rudi's bar really was going to make a big profit this week.

'I'm impressed they could make me a Glass Tower cocktail,' said the one who wore trendy media glasses. She was the one who made me the most nervous, purely I think because her eyewear was so similar to the spectacles worn by our head of HR. 'I thought that was just an Oxford drink, but Rudi managed to mix it up. He's a right laugh. And those tattoos. I wonder what he's got on the areas of his body we can't see. Wouldn't mind taking a closer look to find out, if you know what I mean.'

The other girls laughed and clinked their drinks together gleefully. I bet Rudi would be thrilled to hear them speaking like that. I started to feel sorry for his girlfriend again.

The woman with the pixie haircut piped up. 'Actually, I think that Tommi is more my cup of tea. Got to love the strong and silent type. There's usually a lot going on below the surface. Still waters run deep and all that kind of thing.'

Glasses woman pulled a face. 'Yes, but maybe he's a bit too silent. You know, a bit too solemn for his own good. That husky sledding today was meant to be the highlight of the trip, but he was so serious the whole time, I felt like I was back at school and getting told off whenever I laughed.'

The third of their trio, a woman in a startling red jumper, nodded in agreement. 'Yes, I'm afraid his attitude is going to lower my scores on the old Trip Advisor review. I can't be doing with uptight people. They suck the fun out of a place. And I'm here to have fun.'

I noisily turned my page, hoping to keep up the pretence that I wasn't earwigging. My mind was racing. If that was what all these women were thinking, then Tommi was in for a nasty surprise when he got his feedback forms in. Over the last few days I'd seen how much of himself he'd poured into the business. Every detail was down to him. Yes, he was a bit uptight and serious at times, but I'd also seen glimpses of another side of him, one which was a lot more easy-going and fun. He had a wicked sense of humour. Maybe he should let that side of himself show more to the guests. It would certainly help him to boost the review scores from this all-important first booking.

I gazed around the room with a critical eye at the groups of people quietly playing board games and sipping their drinks. I mean, it was all well and good having a cosy evening in, but as those women had been saying, people wanted to let their hair down on holiday and have some fun. It couldn't all be Cluedo in front of the fire and bed at 9pm. If nothing else, a business strategy like that was missing out on one massive piece of revenue – the takings from the bar. Yes, this group were enjoying a few tipples, but I'm sure if they had reason to, they'd be happy to spend much more. And, as I knew, the cost of alcohol in this country was sky-high. It was another area for Tommi to make a tidy bit of profit for himself, without having to get on all the fleecy gear and head out into the hostile cold.

What he needed to arrange was an evening event, maybe a party with entertainment or some kind of theme. That would create a livelier atmosphere and get things going. Rudi would soon be raking it in on the bar. If there was one thing I knew I was good at, it was throwing a decent party, and it would be just the distraction I needed right now.

But would Tommi listen to my suggestion? I sensed he

was starting to have a bit more time for me, but was that enough for him to take me seriously? I was still on probation as far as he was concerned and there was no reason for him to take tourism advice from a radio DJ. There was also the matter of the nagging voice at the back of my head which kept asking whether partying was really Tommi's style. I stamped down on the doubts. The bigger picture was what mattered, and surely when Tommi saw what a highlight of the guests' holiday a party could be, he'd agree that it was a great idea. But maybe I would be better off showing him my plan, rather than just telling him. If I presented him with a done deal, and it didn't make any extra work for him, what could possibly go wrong? I searched in one of the drawers until I found a notebook and pencil and started scribbling down some ideas.

'You look deep in thought,' said Rudi. 'Are you planning to stay up much longer, or am I OK to shut the bar?'

I looked up, startled to find that it was already approaching midnight. I'd been so deep in party planning that I hadn't noticed the rest of the room emptying.

Rudi took a sip from the dregs of a glass and grinned when he caught me watching him.

'It's one way of clearing up after people,' he said, shrugging his shoulders. 'And I was curious to try the Glass Tower that those ladies were so keen for me to mix. It is very strong. Perhaps too strong for me. Do you want to finish it off?'

'No, you're OK,' I said. I needed to keep a clear head for finalising my plans. 'Did you make a note of what goes into the drink?' If the ladies liked it so much, then it would be a good one to serve for the guests at the event.

'It is more a question of what doesn't go in,' he said. 'There are five different spirits involved. It would put hairs on your chest as I think you Brits like to say.'

'It sounds lethal,' I said, gleefully. I'd definitely add that one to the list.

The next morning, I was back in my rightful place, on kitchen duty with Johanna. As I peeled potatoes and prepared the other vegetables for Johanna's hearty soup, I carried on day-dreaming about my plans, which were getting more elaborate by the minute. I figured if the guests wanted to recapture their youth, then the best idea was to go all out with a fancy-dress event, something where they could be really silly and nobody cared what they looked like. And although Wild Zone wasn't quite at the Arctic Circle, it made sense to have an arctic theme. People could borrow Rudi's furs and dress up as bears, or maybe they could wrap their white bedsheets around them and disguise themselves as snowmen and women. With imagination, there were endless possibilities. Maybe we could play games like pass-the-parcel and charades; good old-fashioned fun which was bound to get people laughing. And I'd get Rudi to mix up some arctic cocktails as well, just to make sure the party really got going.

'I think that potato is probably ready to go in the pot now, what little there is that's left of it,' said Johanna pointedly.

I looked down and realised I'd peeled it so vigorously it had shrunk in size so it looked like a new potato.

'Sorry,' I said. 'I was miles away. Lots of things on my mind. Nice things for a change.'

I decided to try out my idea on Johanna. She seemed to have a good insight into Tommi's mindset.

'I've been thinking about putting on a small entertainment for the guests tomorrow night. A few games, maybe a bit of fancy dress. I'll do any extra work that needs doing and you guys can enjoy the fun. What do you think?'

As I described them, I realised I was underplaying my plans a tad, but I figured it was the best way to test the temperature.

Johanna beamed. 'That sounds like a lovely idea. I am sure the guests would enjoy coming up with costumes. I can dig out some spare fabric and other bits and pieces to help them put something together. Have you decided on a theme?'

'The arctic, of course,' I said. 'I thought I might go as a tree. There seem to be plenty of those around here. I just need to work out a way of sticking some branches onto me. What do you think you will dress up as?'

She laughed. 'I am no good at fancy dress. I think I may stick to being an arctic chef and keep my apron on. I will make sure that tomorrow evening's meal is extra special.'

'Thanks, Johanna, I appreciate your support. I'm going to speak to Rudi as well to get his help behind the bar, but would you mind not telling Tommi if you can help it. I'm not trying to keep it as a massive secret, but I thought it might be a fun surprise for him.'

'That should work. He has his day off tomorrow, and Rudi will be leading the activities, so he won't find out until the evening.'

'Perhaps I should put together a costume for him,' I pondered. 'I wouldn't want him to feel like he's missing out.'

Johanna rolled another couple of potatoes in my direction. 'I'm not sure if he is really a fancy dress sort of guy, but I guess it doesn't do any harm to have something ready for him, just in case.'

'What do you think he should be? A cross-country skier? One of Father Christmas' elves? Or maybe the abominable snowman might be more appropriate? Is that Finnish?'

We both burst out laughing.

'The abominable snowman is from the Himalayas,' said Tommi, striding into the kitchen. 'What are you two giggling about?'

'Nothing,' said Johanna, winking at me and then miming zipping her lips.

'Hmm,' said Tommi. 'It looks like you're having far too much fun in the kitchen, Lucy. I need your help outside. Make sure you have your waterproofs on. We'll be out there for a few hours.'

I glanced at the temperature on the thermometer just outside the window. It was hovering at the minus twelve degrees centigrade mark. Positively balmy.

'I'll go and get my long johns on,' I said.

Chapter Fifteen

Today's activity for the guests turned out to be survival skills and as it seemed another pair of hands was required, I was finally going to get the opportunity to see how a quinzee was constructed, though it wasn't really an experience I'd ever felt I'd been lacking. I had no intention of swapping my cosy hut for a night in a snowy mound, however authentic an experience it would be. Rudi and Tommi led everyone down to the lakeside, while I followed up at the rear, bundled up in my usual fleeces, carrying a collection of snow shovels and a rucksack full of flasks of hot chocolate.

Once everyone had gathered around a fallen tree, stamping their feet and rubbing their hands to keep the circulation flowing, Tommi removed a knife from his pocket and carefully carved a few pieces of bark from its trunk.

'Today you are going to learn the most primitive of skills; how to make fire,' he said. He placed the shavings of wood in a neat pile on the snow, leaned forward and did something with his hand so a spark flew out, landing squarely in the middle of the bark. A tiny wisp of smoke starting curling upwards.

'What are the three things fire needs?' he asked, picking on the lady with the media glasses. I willed him to choose another person rather than the one who had been already chuntering about him making things too serious.

'This is like being back in chemistry classes at school. I hated science,' she said. But Tommi continued looking at her with his usual steady gaze. She sighed. 'Fine, if you insist, I'll take a guess. Fuel?'

Tommi nodded. 'Very good. Fuel. We have that with the dry bark. It is very important it is dry, otherwise it is impossible to get the spark to catch. Anything else? I'll give you a clue. It is known as the fire triangle.'

'Ooh, I know, heat, fuel and oxygen,' said the lady whose pixie cut was today concealed by a large hat with a bear's face on it, complete with woolly ears sticking up at the top. Her friends rolled their eyes, muttering about her being a swot.

'Good. So, let's give it more of those things.' He leaned forward and cupped his hands around the smouldering bark and blew gently at the base of the embers. Gradually they glowed brighter until a flame started licking along the rest of the bark. He started feeding it with twigs, slowly adding larger pieces of wood until there was a merry blaze dancing away.

'And there we have it. Fire,' he said.

I have to admit; it was pretty impressive. Maybe it was harking back to cavewoman instincts, but there was something rather sexy about a man who was so capable with his hands. Plus, from a practical point of view, I was glad there was a source of heat in these bitter surroundings.

'But how did you get the spark in the first place? Or can you magically produce them with your fingers?' The woman in the media glasses looked Tommi up and down in a manner which left no one in any doubt about the intention behind her words.

Her companions giggled.

Tommi cleared his throat and sensibly took her question at face value. 'I have a flint. It is standard Finnish army issue. When we do National Service, we all learn how to make a spark with a flint, although most children in these parts will learn it as soon as they can walk. You can also make the spark through friction, by rubbing the point of a stick into the bark, keeping it moving until the flame is produced that way.'

He demonstrated it as he was speaking. Unfortunately, it was a rather suggestive motion, or maybe it seemed that way because of the previous conversation. The giggly trio were besides themselves by now, and even I was feeling hot under the collar. Tommi remained straight-faced as if he had no idea what the fuss was about, but I thought I caught a glimmer of a wink thrown in my direction.

Rudi was keen to get some of the attention from Tommi. 'Ladies, you should see my spark-producing skills. I'm much quicker at making fire than he is.'

They laughed even harder.

'Sometimes quicker doesn't mean better,' said one of them.

Poor Rudi looked rather crestfallen.

'Enough of the lessons, it's time to work and try these skills for yourself.' Tommi divided the group into two, taking pity on Rudi and ensuring that the giggling trio weren't with him.

'You guys will come and learn how to build a quinzee with me, while these people will stay here with Rudi and practise making a stretcher out of the kit you have on you. You never know when you might need to use emergency skills out in the wilderness.'

There were a few groans from the stretcher party group. It did seem like the kind of activity that you'd do on a Scout camp rather than on your hard-earned holiday.

As I had the shovels, I figured I was on quinzee duty, although I would much rather have stayed by the warmth of the fire. There is only so much snow and ice a girl can cope with in one day.

It soon became clear that the main requirements for building a quinzee were brute force and sheer bloody-minded persistence. The guests all worked together to shovel a massive pile of snow, taking it in turns to climb on the top and stamp around in order to compact it down. At first it was fun, with people dancing and pulling funny poses on top of the pile, but then the effects of the hard work started to get to them and I could hear the grumbling beginning.

'I warn you, there's rebellion in the ranks,' I whispered as I heaved another load of snow to the pile. I could empathise with how they were feeling.

'They are enjoying themselves,' said Tommi defensively.

'They are in the outdoors, enjoying nature in one of its most challenging forms. This is an experience they will treasure for the rest of their lives.'

'They're not going to treasure it if all they can remember about it is doing hours of hard labour with no reward. But you're the boss.'

'Yes, I am,' said Tommi. 'Last time I checked, you were an out-of-work radio DJ, not a tourism expert.'

Well that told me. I stomped off, hurt that he'd be so dismissive when I was only trying to help. But something I said must have trickled through, because he searched through his rucksack and produced portable speakers for his phone and set some music playing. His taste was rather eclectic and I wasn't sure it was doing the trick for the guests. If anything, it was adding to their malaise. I watched as their working pace slowed down even more, their faces as glum as if they'd just endured a three-hour conference call.

'Oh give it here,' I said, taking pity on Tommi, despite his grumpiness with me. I pulled my gloves off and scrolled through his phone to create a quick playlist. It took twice as long as it should have done because I kept on having to put my gloves back on to warm my fingers up. That was the disadvantage of touchscreens in these conditions. But, eventually, I'd pulled together a playlist of tunes which I thought would do the trick.

I heaved myself to the top of the snow pile and put on my best radio voice. 'Oi oi, here's a shout out to the snow-shovelling heroes. My name is Lucy F—' I swallowed my surname and moved on quickly. There was no need to spell it out for them. 'And if you're crazy about your quinzees or stoked at the sight of snow, then I've got the tunes for you. Let's get the party started.'

As the strains of 'Ice, ice baby' started playing, I could see the smiles returning to the guests' faces. I retreated to the ground and carried on mixing the tunes as the guests started shovelling the snow in time to the beats, and dancing on top of the snow pile with renewed vigour.

I riffed with my best snow and ice puns, trawling my memory for every single tune I could think of which could possibly be related to the arctic conditions. With no fancy studio effects available at my fingertips, I was forced to rely on my own instincts and quick wit, reading the reactions from the guests and honing my response. It took me back to my early days in radio and I felt a pang of nostalgia for everything that I had left behind.

As the last notes of 'Cold as ice' faded away, Tommi finally declared he was satisfied with the size of the snow pile.

'And now the difficult work begins,' he said ominously. 'It is time to create the entrance and the chamber for sleeping in. I need a volunteer to start digging a tunnel and hollowing out the pile. Lucy?'

I'd been trying to lurk at the back, hoping he wouldn't catch my gaze. Although mixing tunes wasn't exactly hard physical work, it was still tough keeping up the jolly facade, and I was starting to feel tired and more than a little blue. It had been fun pretending to be a radio DJ again, and welcoming back the lively Lucy Fairweather persona, but pretending wasn't half as satisfying as doing it for real on the airwaves. I'd started to hate the bloody pile of snow, seeing it as the physical embodiment of my personal failure. Rather than digging more of the stuff, I wanted to turn my back on it completely and go and hide indoors in the warm. But Tommi was having none of it. He put the shovel in my hands and put me to work, while he lit another fire and handed out the flasks of hot chocolate to the guests, which made me feel even more sorry for myself.

If the initial shovelling phase had seemed like a challenge, this was even more bone-shatteringly exhausting, especially for a person like me who wasn't used to doing physical stuff for a living. For a start, I had to lie flat on my stomach, with my arms at a very odd angle, while I used what looked like a small coal shovel to dig away at the pile of snow and create an entrance. The jumping on top had done its work because it was compacted rock hard. I guessed this would make for a better quinzee, but it meant I was stuck with a huge challenge trying to dig through it. I chipped away at solid ice until my shoulders were aching, my neck had frozen at an odd angle, and I could barely lift my arms. I felt like a prisoner sentenced to doing hard labour.

Eventually Tommi took pity on me, and asked one of the guests to take over for a bit. But despite the hot chocolate and the fire, I felt like I was frozen to the core and would never experience warmth again. As yet another of my ice-themed tunes came on the playlist, I wanted to pick up the phone and throw it as far away as I could as a punishment for mocking me.

Halfway through the afternoon, the guests switched

over, and the other group came to construct their quinzee. My heart sank. Given that the first group still hadn't finished work on theirs, there was no way this one was going to get done before darkness fell. I mustered up my greatest performance yet and managed to repeat the whole music-mixing routine as if I'd just thought of it. But it was a strain to appear enthusiastic and when my whole body started shivering, there was nothing I could do to disguise that.

Tommi checked his watch.

'You have all worked hard today. Thank you to Lucy for entertaining the workers.' He led a smattering of hollow applause. The guests were clearly feeling the cold, too. 'You have some free time tomorrow if you've not signed up for Rudi's ice-climbing class, so if you feel up to it, you can finish hollowing the quinzees out and creating your sleeping shelf, but make sure you leave a note in the book in reception if you decide to do that. You are also welcome to try sleeping in your quinzees, once I have taken a proper look to make sure they are safe for you to do that.'

Some of the group looked eager to try it out. I genuinely thought I'd rather meet my social media trolls in person than spend the night camping out here in the cold.

'I believe Johanna has some more hot chocolate and cakes ready for you in the lounge,' Tommi continued. 'You have earned them with all your hard work today.'

The guests made a beeline for the main building; a chattering, happy group. It's amazing how the suggestion of food could instantly lift their mood. I helped Tommi and

Rudi collect all the shovels and make sure the equipment was stowed away, and then I was left to my own devices.

Hot chocolate and cake sounded tempting, but I was so tired, I was beyond being sociable, so I returned to my cabin. There was a note pinned to the door. It was too gloomy outside to read it so I retreated indoors. Johanna had taken a message on the phone from Henri. Tessa had been in touch with him to say they'd had no luck getting any DNA or fingerprints from the envelope of newspaper cuttings. Although there were no other active lines of enquiry for now, they would keep everything on file in case anything else came up. My earlier shivering returned with a vengeance. I hadn't realised how much hope I'd been pinning on the police tracking down the culprit, until it was snatched away from me. Was I destined to be stuck in exile for ever?

I felt like I would never be warm again. I peeled off my now-damp outer layers, wrapped myself in a blanket and sat on the floor to get the full benefits of the underfloor heating. My muscles ached. My head felt like a steel band was being slowly tightened around it. My fingers were stiff and painful, and when I held them next to my face, they felt like blocks of ice, so maybe that wasn't a purely psychological reaction. Only the fact that they were also bright red reassured me that they weren't about to drop off through frostbite.

I tucked them under my armpits and rocked back and forth a bit, feeling thoroughly sorry for myself. It was pitch black once again even though it was only three in the afternoon, and it felt like the night was closing in already;

another day gone where I was still stuck here, with no hope of regaining the life I'd left behind me. My mood dipped further to match the darkness outside. It was like my life had fallen into a great big dark hole and I couldn't see how I was ever going to climb out of it.

Maybe it was time to try something new and get myself out of this patch of feeling miserable. I remembered the sauna in the main building. I wasn't normally a sauna kind of person, but, then again, I wasn't the kind of person who normally did any of the activities I was taking part in here. Surely the super-heat of the sauna would help me to feel human again. I scooped up a towel, my swimming costume and torch, hauled on my coat before I changed my mind and headed across to the main building through the gloaming. Through the illuminated windows I could see the guests enjoying their treats, laughing as they exchanged notes on how the day had gone. Standing outside in the dark by myself, I felt like even more of an outcast.

I tramped around the side of the main building, slipping and sliding my way down the snowy slope, regretting my decision not to take the easy route inside. It was like I wanted to reinforce the challenges of my surroundings as I indulged in my one-person misery fest.

But thankfully the warmth of the basement changing room brought some welcome circulation back to my body, and I started to feel some of my tension dissipate. It was beautifully quiet. I hoped the guests continued to stay upstairs enjoying Johanna's culinary delights as I still wasn't feeling particularly sociable. I quickly changed out of my fleecy garments and into my swimming costume, the most undressed I'd been since I'd arrived in Finland, apart from when I was in the shower of course.

I opened the door of the sauna and breathed in the hot, pine-scented air. It was very dark, the only illumination being the slight glow of embers in the centre of the room. I made my way to a seat by touch alone and sat back with my eyes closed, letting the heat ooze into my pores. The tightness in my shoulders started to ease and the warmth wrapped around me like an embrace. I sighed and took a deep breath, feeling the heat slipping through my lungs; chasing away the last traces of ice. It was only then that I opened my eyes and became aware of another presence in the shadowy sauna.

'Hello, Lucy,' said a very bare-chested Tommi. He was sitting casually on the bench directly opposite me, the most relaxed I'd ever seen him. The shadows from the embers traced the lines of his muscles, sculpted through hard outdoor work. His broad shoulders tapered down in a classic upside-down triangle to his narrow waist. He could certainly give the gym bunnies a run for their money. Suddenly I remembered Rudi's assertion that Finns like to get naked, and I forced my gaze upwards.

'Tommi. Hello. What a surprise,' I said, my imagination working overtime. Was he sitting there completely starkers, opposite me? I kept my eyes fixed on his nose. A trickle of sweat traced its way down my forehead and into my left eye. I blinked rapidly. 'Lovely day for it.' Trying to appear completely cool with the whole naked sauna scenario, I said the first thing that came to mind, which was inevitably complete and utter nonsense. Lovely day for what, exactly?

Tommi chuckled quietly. 'At the end of a hard day's work, it is good to retreat in here and let the heat take the tension out of the muscles. I find it very relaxing.'

While I, on the other hand, was feeling rather tense.

'Sometimes it is good to do sauna yoga as well, to help the joints get moving. It is especially helpful if you have been involved in quinzee construction. You worked hard today, Lucy. I appreciate it.'

The sauna felt even hotter.

'Sauna yoga, you say? How on earth does that work?' I said, fighting to keep my voice sounding normal as the image of Tommi demonstrating downward dog in his current state of undress came to mind.

'It is not your usual yoga, more a few gentle stretches from a seated position. I might ask Johanna if she can run a class for the guests. Do you think they will like it?'

I was gratified that he thought it worthwhile asking my opinion.

'Why not? Hot yoga is very trendy back at home. I'm sure they'd jump at the chance.'

He nodded. 'I shall add it to my list of possibilities for future groups. Speaking of back home, have you heard from Skye and Henri at all?'

I examined my fingernails, then hastily stopped when I realised it looked like I was eyeballing Tommi's thighs.

'I'm doing what you might call a digital detox. Phone and internet are strictly rationed. It sounds good, but it's me being a coward really. There's only so much abuse I can hack at one time.'

'I am sure Skye would welcome an update on how you

are getting on. I am visiting the local town tomorrow. I am happy to post a letter for you, if you wish.'

Yet another example of how living here was like stepping back in time. I couldn't remember the last time I'd sent a letter. Even traditional holiday postcards had been replaced with Instagram updates and Facebook statuses. Maybe it would be nice to put pen to paper for a change. And I could imagine Skye would absolutely love to receive a letter in the post; it was exactly the kind of quaint, folksy thing she would be into.

'Thank you. I might just do that.'

'Do you mind?' Tommi indicated the pail in the corner and when I nodded my assent, he put a ladleful of water on the hot coals, setting them hissing and steaming. The smell of pine grew stronger. He carried on speaking through the slight mist which now hung in the air. 'Skye texted me. It is not good news, I am afraid. The video is still creating traction online, and the radio station bosses have been speaking to a guy called Mike about changing his contract from producing to presenting. She seems to think this is something you should be aware of. I am sorry if that makes me the bearer of bad tidings.'

The slimy git. Mike, not Tommi, that is. So he'd been making determined moves to take my show off me permanently, had he? I shouldn't have been surprised, but I would have hoped to have inspired greater loyalty from someone I'd worked with for several years. Well, he could talk to the bosses all he liked. Hopefully they had greater sense than to put him in front of the microphone full time. If anyone was going to replace me, and I was still clutching at straws that it wouldn't happen, I'd want it to be Skye, who at least had genuine talent going for her.

I sniffed, the steamy air making my nose tickle. Tommi must have thought I was crying, because he leaned across, revealing that he was after all wearing dark boxer shorts, and gently patted my hand, before chastely moving back into his seat. The gesture from such a restrained man seemed even more kind. I think that's why I found myself confiding in him.

'If only I knew who was behind it all. Someone must have put the video together, and it can only have been a person who's reasonably close to me, otherwise they wouldn't have been able to get all the shots that are on there.' A suspicion which had been niggling at the back of my mind crystallised. 'I bet Mike had a hand in it. He's been on my back ever since I first set foot in Star FM.'

'That is a very serious accusation to make against this man. Is it something you can support with evidence?' asked Tommi sensibly.

'And therein lies the problem. I don't know where to start when it comes to proving it. I'm going with my gut instinct. And that's been wrong in the past, so the whole thing is probably a big waste of time.'

Tommi stretched first one muscular arm and then the other. 'It is worth looking into. With your permission, I shall ask Rudi if any of his shadier contacts know a good IT person. He may be able to help your situation.'

'That would be amazing. If I could expose the culprit and prove the video's a fake, then maybe I'd get my job back. I'd certainly be out of your hair anyway.'

He leaned further back against the pine bench and fixed me with that clear, all-seeing gaze of his. 'I was starting to get used to you hanging around the place.'

I don't know who was more surprised by his words, him or me.

Chapter Sixteen

My letter to Skye was only partially a work of fiction. I told her about the husky sledding and the glittery snow, and glossed over my increasing sense of loss and isolation. She was probably intuitive enough to read between the lines to see what I wasn't saying, but I didn't want to worry her unnecessarily. The letter, which Tommi took with him to post on the way to his day off with the perfect Gurta, was actually the second copy. I'd had a seriously wobbly moment writing the first one and hadn't been able to stop tears falling down and blurring the ink on the page. I'd started over on a fresh sheet, armed with a strong G&T to distract me from my wallowing.

I woke the next morning and experienced a brief moment of blissful forgetfulness before the memory of what day it was bore down on me, crushing me with the weight of grief. The years since losing Dad had long gone into the double-figures mark, but while the shock had numbed over time, the pain felt no less raw. There is no comparing the loss of a career and the loss of a parent, but my current circumstances heightened my sense of bereavement and loneliness, and, lying alone in my hut, so far from home, I wondered how I would find the strength to get through this day.

Before I lost courage, I forced myself to turn on my phone and leave a message for Mum. Part of me hoped she'd break the habit of the last few years and actually pick up, but, as always, she was choosing to get through this day in her own way; cutting off the rest of the world and spending the anniversary in solitude. And so I also turned to the safety of the familiar, and threw myself into party planning with a vengeance, attempting to force all other thoughts out of my mind while I plotted a night to remember.

I raided the office for stationery and created posters to advertise the event, which I stuck up around the main building once Tommi was safely out of the way. Then I helped Johanna put together a hamper of spare clothing, bits of fabric and other props so the guests could root through and create their fancy-dress outfits. My suspicions that the party would go down a treat were soon confirmed, because everywhere I went around Wild Zone, I could hear people discussing it and comparing notes on the status of their costume.

Rudi had been onto his suppliers, and the bar was groaning with every kind of drink imaginable.

'I think we should keep the cocktails on theme. We can have the usual Snowballs and stuff, but let's rename the others so they've got arctic references as well,' I suggested.

'How about a Wild Zone Whisky and a Frosted Mojito? We could even throw a few weather-related drinks in there like a Winter Sunshine Spritzer and nickname the bar the Isobar. Get it?'

Rudi clapped his hands together. 'It should be "Lucy's Isobar". After all, your surname is Fairweather and you're the one who came up with all this.'

I wasn't sure that was such a good idea, but he seemed so enthusiastic about it that I didn't have the heart to say no. Besides, there was always the possibility that I could blag free drinks if the bar had my name above it. He set to work on the sign, creating an intricate design not unlike the inkwork etched on his skin. I wondered, not for the first time, if he'd been responsible for creating some of his own tattoos. Once that was done, he sat in a corner with a cocktail recipe book, studying it as intently as if he had an exam coming up. It was sweet to see him so engrossed in the task.

Back at home if I'd been planning a party, I would have spent days preparing it; shopping for decorations and props and visiting the local trade warehouse to bulk-buy booze and other refreshments. But being several snowy miles from the nearest town, and with no way of getting there other than the dreaded snowshoeing, I decided to use a bit of innovation and imagination, and set to work transforming the lounge into a winter wonderland. I draped white sheets over the furniture, using cushions underneath to make them look like snow drifts, and then artfully arranged some snow shoes to look like they'd just been taken off after a long day adventuring. Remembering an activity I used to do when I was a child, I folded pieces of paper and cut them into intricate snowflakes, stringing them up on thread so they looked like they were floating through the air. They twisted and turned gently above my head, and for a few moments I soaked up the magic of the scene, proud of what I'd managed to achieve out of almost nothing. I set out tables for the food (Johanna had promised to pull out all the stops with a buffet banquet fit for snow royalty) and scattered glitter over them to recreate the sparkling snow we'd witnessed on the husky ride. I even brought a kick-sled inside and a selection of winter kit so people could use it like a photobooth and pose for pictures to share with all their friends. I made a mental note to avoid that corner of the room when the party was in full swing so I didn't inadvertently end up in someone's social media feed.

I borrowed Rudi's phone, surprised at the amount of cheesy pop music I discovered on there, and created an Arctic Party playlist. The collection of tunes varied from traditional disco hits to a few more avant garde numbers, but they were all guaranteed to get people dancing. It felt good to be busy and doing something normal for a change, and the closer it got to the time for the gathering, the more excited I grew. If I was going to be stuck out here, I might as well make a proper go of it. Now the only thing to do was to prepare my party games and we were ready to go. I sat down with one of Rudi's freshly mixed Frozen Mojitos, and got to work. It almost felt like I was back in civilisation.

Bang on seven o'clock, I declared the party started and flung open the doors. The guests poured in, whooping merrily. They had really got into the spirit of the occasion judging by how seriously they were taking the fancy-dress theme. I guess Rudi's offer of a free bottle of vodka to the winner had proved quite the incentive. Soon the main building was populated by skiers, some rather terrifying-looking bears, and even a couple of Father Christmases. I was the only tree, which gave me quite a burst of satisfaction, but given that I kept on shedding leaves and it was extremely awkward to get about with twigs sticking up everywhere, it wouldn't be too long before my branches went onto the fire.

By half eight, the music was thumping, the drinks were flowing, and I'd already led several increasingly raucous rounds of charades. Johanna's grub had been demolished in about five minutes, and such had been the demand for her traditional Finnish sweetmeats, she'd retreated down to the kitchen to make another batch. I looked around the room which was pulsing with energy and fun, and felt satisfaction at a job well done. Tommi would be thrilled at the success. There was nothing quite like a Lucy Fairweather party.

The woman with the media glasses came dancing over to me.

'We've not been formally introduced. I'm Heidi.' She clinked her glass with mine, some of the liquid sloshing over the sides. 'And yes, my parents loved the Heidi books, thanks, Mum and, no, I'm rubbish at yodelling and I never wear my hair in those stupid pigtail things.'

She downed her drink and looked around for another. I reminded myself to check that Rudi was on top of everyone's tab. There was no point in throwing a party if it ended up costing Wild Zone a huge amount of money rather than turning a profit as intended.

'I wasn't going to ask you about that,' I replied. 'We can't help what our parents decide to call us. Mine went for Lucinda, so I got a lot of Cinderella gags at school. I much prefer to be called Lucy.'

She nodded, and her expression turned hostile with frightening speed. 'Oh, I know exactly who you are,' she said, grimly. She lowered her voice and jabbed her finger painfully into my shoulder. 'You aren't fooling anyone, however much you try to hide yourself with all that fleecy gear and the arctic ranger act. We all recognised you as soon as we got here. You may throw a decent bash, but I'm still Team Serenity and I think what you did to that poor girl was wicked. You're not going to change our minds.'

I tried to tell myself she was drunk and that her opinion of me really didn't matter, but her words cut me. Had the group spent the whole time they'd been here talking about me behind my back? Was I not safe even in the middle of nowhere? I was so sick and tired of people believing they had the right to have an opinion about me when they didn't even know the first thing about the real me. I took another gulp of my drink and tried to smile politely at her while calling her a few choice words in my head. I needed to escape from this situation. However much she'd got to me, she was a guest, and I still had to pretend to be nice to her.

A new tune came on and Heidi whooped with delight, her change in mood startling. 'Oh my goodness, this takes me back.' She grabbed my arms and roughly tried to get me to join in with her dancing. Somehow, I managed to extricate myself and took another gulp of mojito to fortify myself against her onslaught.

'We should play truth or dare,' she said gleefully. 'Shots if you tell the truth or do a dare, double shots if you refuse. Lucy, you'll play, won't you?'

'I don't want to get in your way,' I said, trying to turn her down politely. I had a horrible feeling I knew what questions I'd get asked for the 'truth' round.

But Heidi started chanting 'Truth or dare' and clapping her hands, and soon all the other guests were joining in with the intimidating chorus. I glanced across at Rudi, hoping he could save me, but he had a grin on his face and was joining in the clapping too. He gave me a thumbs up and mimed counting all the money that the bar would take during the game. I gritted my teeth. At least the takings would look good to Tommi and prove he should lighten up and do this kind of event more often.

Heidi lined up the shot glasses, grabbed a bottle and then poured the spirit along the line, a significant amount of it slopping out onto the table. I flinched at it all going to waste.

'Everyone grab one to get things started,' she said. 'Come on, Loose Lucy, no hiding in the corner.'

The sharp tang of tequila numbed the pain of her bullying attitude. I hoped it gave me enough Dutch courage for the game because I knew I was in for a hard time. Heidi pretended to close her eyes and twirled around with her finger pointed out. As I'd anticipated, she came to a halt by me so I was the first person to be targeted by the question: 'Truth or dare.'

I looked around at the glazed expressions of the guests, trying to work out which was my safer option. From everything we'd been through in the last few days, I knew there were some daredevils among them, but I still figured taking the dare might be the better route than going for truth. Besides, if they asked the question I anticipated, they would never believe my answer was true.

Actually, I got off relatively lightly, as my dare involved putting on as many winter layers as I could and then sitting in front of the fire for five minutes. I ended up sweaty and red-faced, but, after my time in the sauna yesterday, it felt like a breeze.

But that was the last of the reasonable dares. Before long, there were challenges for people to run naked out into the snow. With the benefit of hindsight, this was a seriously dangerous thing for them to do, but you'll have to bear in mind that I and the rest of the guests were a few sheets close to the wind by this point, and good sense had long since gone out of the window. It's funny enough seeing respectable accountants and IT managers getting their kit off and streaking through the snow, but add a few shots into the mix, and even I was crying with laughter.

However, it wasn't exactly the civilised scene I'd envisaged Tommi arriving back to. There was so much noise, I didn't hear the sound of his car pulling up, so I was taken by surprise when he came into the room, the smell of cold swirling around him. I watched his expression eagerly, anticipating the delight on his face that the guests were having such a brilliant time. But his nose wrinkled and his mouth grew tight. There was a slight pulse by his jaw as if he was having to fight really hard not to say something. I looked around the room and tried to see things from his perspective. I suppose it must have been a shock to return to this, especially when the first sight to greet him when he strode into the lounge was one of Heidi's mates twirling a pair of knickers around her head. She was actually fully clothed by this point, but she'd clearly forgotten to put a few items back on when she'd returned from the rolling naked in the snow challenge.

He paused on the threshold, his eyes searching the room until they fixed on me. He strode across towards me.

'What in hell is going on here?' His voice was calm and controlled, but it sent a shiver down my spine. I caught sight of Rudi ducking behind the bar, clearly sensing which way this was going to go.

'Surprise!' I said. I'll admit the jazz hands motion I did to accompany this was a very bad idea, but I wanted to win him round, and overwhelming enthusiasm seemed like the best way of doing it. 'Welcome to the Arctic Party, Wild Zone's answer to Ibiza. Drinks, games and brilliant Trip Advisor reviews guaranteed.' I waved my arms around, pointing out the happy faces of the guests, hoping he would now understand the genius of my plan.

'I can't image the reviews will be brilliant when it involves making this much mess,' he said, gesturing at the decorations which were now slightly skewwhiff. The room was littered with half-empty glasses, dirty plates and ripped up bits of paper from a rather filthy game of Pictionary. 'The place looks like a tip. Why is all the spare bedding festooned around the place? And tell me that's not sticky tape on my freshly painted walls?'

'I was going for the magical winter wonderland look,' I said mutinously, although seeing it with fresh eyes now; the whole thing did look rather amateurish and tatty. It wasn't stopping the guests having fun though.

The knicker-wielding woman came dancing over, still swirling the underwear around her head. 'Has anyone seen Heidi? She said she was going to take a nap in the quinzee, but she must have had enough sleep by now. It's nearly time for pass-the-parcel and she'll kill me if she misses out. I heard a rumour the prize is amazing.' She catapulted the knickers and they landed on the hearth and started sizzling.

Tommi looked very serious. 'When did she go?' he barked. 'Tell me now.'

The woman pouted. 'Only about half an hour ago,' she said. 'It was right after Kevin did his streak to the ski shed and back.'

She burped loudly, and giggled as she belatedly covered her mouth. Tommi didn't even flinch.

'And was she as drunk as you are?' he said. The woman pouted defensively.

'Tommi, there's no need to be rude to the guests,' I interjected. People were starting to turn around to take a look at the scene which was brewing.

'I'm asking because if she is inebriated, then half an hour in a quinzee is half an hour too long. When people have been drinking, they lose their proper perception. They can think they are warm when in fact they are dangerously cold. It can quickly prove fatal.'

Tommi's words had a sobering effect on me. I blinked rapidly, trying to get a hold of myself, and wishing my brain wasn't quite so fuzzy. How could I have let things get so out of hand?

After that, Tommi acted speedily. He and Rudi pulled on their thickest outdoor coats, collected torches, a first-aid kit and, most worryingly of all, a stretcher. While Johanna escorted the now very subdued guests to bed, the guys headed outside in search of the missing Heidi. I begged them to let me help, but was ordered to stay put.

'One drunk woman out in the snow is quite enough to be dealing with,' said Tommi, his words cutting me to the bone. 'Will you never learn that these conditions are not to be messed around in? You'd better hope the quinzee didn't collapse and suffocate her. I hadn't checked them over and signed them off yet. And let's not even start thinking about the dangers of her wandering around the lake when she's not in control of her senses. The quinzee site isn't that far from the river outlet, and if she's gone through the ice, we'd be lucky to find her body before spring.'

I managed to hold it together long enough to watch the glow of their torches disappearing into the trees, and then I ran to the toilet and threw up. Bile burned my mouth and nose, mixing with the snotty tears which wouldn't stop falling. It was only a party, I told myself. It had been planned with the best intentions and everybody had had such a good time. How was I to know some people couldn't handle their drink and it made them do stupid things? Heidi was a grown woman. It wasn't my fault she decided to go off wandering into the dark like an idiot. But a niggling voice at the back of my head kept on saying that maybe I was the really stupid one. I'd planned the party, I'd created the carefree environment without bothering to consider the risks of getting wasted in the wilderness. And I'd done it because I'd selfishly needed to distract myself from my demons, all the while pretending to myself and others that I'd done it to help Tommi's business out. Once again, my irresponsible nature had caused trouble, and this time it could have potentially fatal consequences. What if Heidi was completely lost in the snow? Could I live with myself knowing that I was responsible for her demise?

I sat on the cold, tiled cloakroom floor, hunched up over the toilet bowl, imagining the darkness of the ice on the lake, the terrifying prospect of sinking into that freezing cold water, and feeling it overwhelming you. Would she know she was dying as that blackness overtook her? How would it feel to hear that terrible sound of ice creaking and then cracking and knowing there was nothing you could do to get away? I swallowed another wave of nausea and punched my fist against the cubicle door, hoping the physical pain would distract me from my emotional turmoil. My head was pounding and my heart racing with fear. I'm not a religious person, but I sent a prayer up to somewhere, anywhere, that Heidi would be OK. I would rather undergo internet trolls a million times crueller than for something awful to have happened to her.

After what felt like a lifetime, I heard a noise on the veranda and the sound of someone stamping snow off their boots. I rushed out of the cloakroom. The lights in reception had been switched off by their timer so only the faintest glow from the snow outside illuminated the room.

'Tommi? Is that you? Is she OK?' I called out desperately.

But it was Johanna unwinding her scarf and undoing her coat.

'The guests are all in their cabins now. I had to leave a few of them with buckets at their bedsides, and there will be some sore heads in the morning, but I think I have managed to persuade them to stay tucked up rather than joining the search for Heidi. We can't have the whole lot of them wandering around out there.'

I could barely look at her in the eye. I was so ashamed of myself.

'Is there something I can do?' I said. 'I feel so useless waiting in here.'

Johanna checked her watch. 'The guys have been some time now. I think maybe I will go and find them to see what is happening. It would be helpful if you could stay here, in case she returns to base.'

She was spinning me a line to distract me and keep me occupied, but I grabbed onto the opportunity.

'Of course I will. I'll boil some kettles too. They're bound to need a hot drink when they get back.'

I could see her hesitating as she wondered whether or not to trust me in her kitchen. I didn't blame her. I'm not sure I would trust me any more either.

Eventually she nodded her assent, and headed back out into the cold. I filled the largest kettle I could find and optimistically set out four huge mugs, one for each of the search party and one for the elusive Heidi. But once the kettle had boiled, and the silence had returned, I felt at a loss what to do with myself all over again. I couldn't bear to sit there with the anxiety nagging at me. In a bid to distract myself, I set to work tiding up the lounge, throwing away the paper snowflakes and putting the sheets in the laundry basket ready for the next wash. My movements were clumsy and sluggish, but I managed to get the worst of the debris cleared up. I was the one who was responsible for the mess, so I should sort it out. It would be the last thing the search party felt like doing, and, missing guest or no, the rest of the group would still need feeding in the morning.

And then I sat in reception and waited, peering out into the darkness of the outdoors and wondering what was going on out there.

Chapter Seventeen

Just before midnight, there was a hubbub on the front steps. I rushed to the door, hovering anxiously at the threshold, unsure whether I was brave enough to go out and see whatever sight might confront me. I tried to count the shadows moving around, but it was hard to tell how many people were there and what kind of a state they were in. When the door handle eventually opened, everything went into slow motion, and all I could hear was the sound of my own heart thudding.

Johanna was first inside, closely followed by Rudi and then finally Tommi, who shut the door behind him, a solemn expression on his face. I was convinced my worst fears had been realised. The atmosphere in the room grew as cold as outside. A chilling sense of dread filled my veins as I looked between them, fearing the news that I was about to be told. I forced myself to ask the question, but I didn't know if I was strong enough to hear the answer.

'What happened to Heidi?' It was if someone else had

spoken. I barely recognised the quavering, anxious sound of my own whisper. Heidi's name seemed to echo around the room.

At first, I thought Tommi was going to answer me. But his face grew hard and he turned away and walked off, as if the sight of me was too much to endure.

'Rudi, Johanna, please, tell me what's happened,' I begged. Had Tommi gone to ring the authorities? I could already picture the arrival of the emergency services, lights flashing on the snow, sirens muffled, because why turn the siren on when the person you are seeking to rescue is already beyond help. Did Heidi have family back at home waiting for her to return? What would they think when she didn't come back? I knew from my own experience of tragedy that life would never be the same again for them. I didn't care what the rest of the world would think of me when they learned what I had done. After this, I would deserve whatever cruelty they threw at me.

Johanna could obviously see the distress in my features because she took pity on me. Speaking slowly and deliberately, she led me over to the window-seat, sat me down with a mug of hot sweet tea to try to stop my hands shaking, and told me what had happened.

'Heidi went down to the quinzee with only a sleeping bag and her winter coat. She thought it would be fun to camp out there, an adventure to brag about with her friends. But then she mistakenly thought she saw the Northern Lights, so she left her sleeping bag by the quinzee and wandered out onto the lake to find an area where she could get a better look at this sky.'

I felt the bile rising in my throat again.

'We found her staggering around near the bridge, rambling about shooting stars. She was wet and cold, and a few metres from the area where the ice is thin. Fortunately, we managed to reach her before she went too far. There is no sign of frostbite, but she is very, very lucky to still be alive. We have brought her back and put her to bed with extra blankets and a hot drink. Her cabin mate is keeping an eye on her and I will check on her progress during the night. Hypothermia is always a concern, but I am hopeful that we got to her in time. I believe she will be fine in the morning, apart from maybe a hangover;

a small price to pay.'

The feeling of relief was palpable. My hands shook even more now, causing the tea to slop over the edges of the mug and scald my fingers. I barely noticed the pain.

'Oh thank goodness. I'm so glad she's OK, so so glad. I've been going out of my mind with fear and guilt. When I think what could have happened... And it was all my fault. How could I have been so stupid and thoughtless?'

Rudi squeezed my arm. 'Things got a little out of hand, that is all. You did not set out with bad intentions. We were all involved in the party and I feel responsible too. I should have stopped serving many of the guests a long time before I did. Tommi is not happy with me either. I knew the dangers more than you did.'

Johanna piped up. 'I should have kept a closer eye on the guests rather than going back down to the kitchens and leaving you to deal with them alone. If we had all been watching out for our guests as we should have been, Heidi would not have been able to wander off by herself.'

I looked between the two of them, and saw my guilt mirrored in their expressions.

'No, you are absolutely not to blame,' I said fiercely, feeling very moved that they were wanting to share my burden. 'It was my party, I planned it and I roped you two in against your better judgement. And I won't have Tommi believing anything else. You live here. I am only here temporarily and, after this incident, I'll probably be leaving much sooner than expected. I don't want anything to damage your working relationship with him. He already thought I was a waste of space. I'm happy for him to carry on thinking that.'

Except I really wasn't. But Rudi and Johanna had become my good friends, and so I would do anything I could to protect them.

'We'll see. He's very angry at the moment, but I hope he will have calmed down by the morning. You should have seen the look on his face when we found the sleeping bag abandoned by the quinzee. I think it's the first time I've ever seen him look frightened,' said Johanna.

I didn't think it was possible to feel worse than I already did, but perhaps it was. Tommi had shown nothing but kindness to me. Yes, he could be gruff and blunt to the point of rudeness on occasion, but he had taken me in, a complete stranger, because he felt it was the right thing to do, and he'd extended the arm of friendship, even inviting me to join in the activity programme which I knew others had paid a small fortune to experience. He'd shown me the greatest honour by putting his trust in me, and I had chosen to throw it all back in his face. I was the lowest of the low.

Johanna yawned and looked past me into the lounge. She sighed with relief. 'Thank you for tidying away. It's one less thing to do tomorrow,' she said. I thought guiltily of the large pile of washing in the laundry basket. 'It's been a long night and I am more than ready for my bed.'

I nodded in agreement, but I couldn't imagine sleeping peacefully when there was so much on my mind. I could clear away rubbish and make a room look clean and tidy again, but I knew clearing the air with Tommi was going to be a far harder task. And it wasn't just that. Tonight's terrifying events had forced me to take a long, hard look at myself and I really didn't like what I had seen. How had I got myself to this position, when I didn't know when to stop? And how could I turn things around before it was too late?

Needless to say, I struggled to get a wink of sleep. Every time I felt like drifting off, the suffocating sensation of being buried in snow overtook me and I had to push the covers away and lie shivering in the dark until my heart rate steadied again. There were too many thoughts chasing each other around my head. Eventually, I could stand them no longer. I staggered out of bed and rummaged around in my sponge bag until I found a battered box of sleeping tablets. I traced the faded prescription sticker on the side, the feel of the medication in my hand instantly transporting me back to that time when trauma had first intruded, turning idyllic teenage years upside-down. Was that when I had started to spiral out of control?

Forcing back the memories, I dry-swallowed a couple of pills and felt them gouging a painful path down to my stomach. Then I went back to bed and lay flat on my back, my hands folded neatly on my chest and waited for blissful oblivion to overtake me.

Chapter Eighteen

The sensation of cold water dripping down the side of my face and into my ears dragged me groggily back to the surface. Johanna was leaning over me, her expression full of fear. Somewhere at the foot of my bed, I sensed Tommi's disapproving presence bearing down on me.

'Thank goodness,' she said. 'I was beginning to think we were going to have to call for an ambulance.'

I blinked slowly, and experimentally moved my head from side to side. Every movement felt like there was a time delay between the instructions being given by my brain, and my body being able to process them. I grunted, because that was the only noise I currently seemed capable of making.

Now that he'd satisfied himself that I was conscious, if perhaps not quite yet coherent, Tommi fixed me with a stern look.

'I think you and I need to have a conversation,' he said.

I nodded gingerly, hauling myself up to a seated position with a great effort.

Tommi cleared his throat. 'But now is not the time or place. The guests have left and Rudi is escorting them to the airport. I suggest we talk once you've had a shower and some breakfast. I'll be in my office. Come and find me there.'

'Sure thing, will do,' I croaked through dry mouth and claggy throat.

He turned on his heel and strode out of the room.

'I guess a good night's sleep hasn't put him in a better mood,' I said, trying to lighten the tension in the cabin.

Johanna frowned. 'Try to see things from his point of view. You've given us the most terrible fright, Lucy. When you didn't show up at breakfast, we all assumed you were nursing a hangover. Tommi was all for putting you on the coach and sending you home with the guests. But when we couldn't get an answer at your door, and it was too late to keep the transport waiting, we started to get really worried. We had to use the spare key to get in and we've been standing here a good five minutes trying to wake you up. Can you imagine how we felt walking in and seeing you lying here looking like a corpse, a packet of sleeping pills at your side? I was about to call for help when Tommi managed to revive you with the cold water.'

My old companion guilt arrived back with a vengeance.

'I wasn't trying something stupid,' I hurried to reassure her. 'I promise,' I pushed, when her face told me she didn't believe me. 'I was struggling to sleep and remembered I had some tablets to help me knock myself out. I'm guessing they were a little too effective.'

'They probably shouldn't be taken in combination with alcohol,' said Johanna, practical as always.

Another wave of shame hit me. 'They were the last two I had, so it's not going to happen again. Honestly, I can't remember the last time I resorted to taking sleeping pills.'

Johanna handed me a clean towel and gently pushed me in the direction of the shower. 'You'll feel better once you've washed,' she said, the kindness in her voice making me want to weep. 'I'll whip up some scrambled eggs and toast for you, and then things will look much brighter.' She paused at the doorway. 'You know if you ever want to talk about anything, I'm around. We Finns are good at holding our counsel.'

There was a waft of chilly air, and then she was gone.

I followed my instructions to the letter, although I struggled to manage the whole plate of scrambled eggs, but my situation looked no less bleak. My stomach was still churning, whether from the residual panic from last night, or nerves at what Tommi had to say to me, I wasn't sure. It felt like everything was going to be resting on this meeting. I had a feeling that like Mr Darcy, Tommi's good opinion once lost, was lost for ever. But as I never had it in the first place, maybe things couldn't get any worse. I knew I was clutching at straws.

When I could no longer use the excuse of chasing cooling bits of egg around my plate with my fork, I took a deep breath and presented myself at Tommi's office. The door was ajar, but it felt like this was going to be a formal situation, so I tapped politely on the doorframe and hovered nervously, waiting to be summoned in. There was something about the quality of the silence at Wild Zone. It was different every day, a notion which city girl me would have laughed at a few weeks ago. Today, the silence was oppressive, bearing down on me, crushing me with unspoken words of condemnation and guilt. I knocked again, a bit louder this time, the sound of my knuckles on the wood echoing down the corridor. Still no reply. I gently pushed open the door.

Tommi was sitting in an armchair, his long legs stretching out to cover half the space of the tiny room. He didn't look up from his papers. I nervously fiddled with a loose thread on my sleeve while he carried on reading, and when it was clear that he wasn't going to break off until he'd finished the pages, I perched on the edge of the seat opposite him, and waited. I recognised the familiar layout of the feedback forms and subtly leaned forward to try to read what was written on them. Of course, the word 'subtle' and Lucy never go well together, because I nearly tipped the chair over and only just managed to save myself from taking a tumble to the floor.

'If you wanted to read them, you only had to ask,' said Tommi. His blue eyes looked almost grey in here, like the drama of the last twenty-four hours had diminished their light.

'I don't suppose there's a chance they didn't mention me, is there?' I said.

'There were a few choice comments about "Loose Lucy"

and their support for Serenity. I'm assuming that's the person and not a state of mind?'

I felt the tiniest tinge of hope. If he was making a light-hearted comment, then maybe this wasn't going to be the disaster I'd been anticipating.

'Will I ever shake off that nickname? It seems so old fashioned to refer to a woman as "loose" when she's had the audacity to sleep with someone. Not that I did sleep with Jonno. Or do anything at all, for that matter.' It felt important to emphasise this point.

He placed the pile of papers carefully down at his feet and watched me closely. After what felt like forever, he finally started speaking again.

'I wonder if you can appreciate the position I am in, Lucy. Before me sits a woman who is at the top of her field, a radio professional of some renown, but everything has gone so terribly wrong for her, and I have been wondering why.' He leaned back and I felt his gaze reach into my soul and see all the darkness lurking there.

'Well it's obvious. It's all down to that bloody video, of course,' I said.

Tommi's brow furrowed in thought. 'That would seem to be the obvious solution. That is what appears to be the problem on the surface. But if I have learned one thing from living in a place where everything is covered in snow for half the year, it's that you may be able to see one thing on the surface, but beneath that layer of cold and ice, there is a lot more going on. There are creatures buried down in the ground, sleeping until the warm weather appears. There is water, and grass, and reeds, lots of plants that have paused, waiting for that change in temperature when they can start coming to life again. It got me to wondering, what is going on beneath your surface? What are the other things lurking beneath the superficial exterior which make up the true reality of your landscape?'

I squirmed in my chair. This felt uncomfortably like a therapy session. And how dare he speak about my superficial exterior?

'I'll admit I watched the video before you arrived. I was curious about this exile from public opinion that my brother and sister-in-law were sending to me. First of all, let me say that I believe you when you say the sequence of events has been maliciously edited, and I do not think anyone deserves the stream of hatred which has been directed at you. But it did get me thinking about a pattern of behaviour, maybe a destructive pattern. Do you think you know what I am referring to?'

I folded my arms defensively. This was horribly like being back at home and being lectured by my mum.

'Can we stop with the psychoanalysis?' I said. 'I'm sorry about the party getting out of hand last night. I acted with good intentions, but I didn't think about the wider effects of what I was doing. Is that good enough for you?'

'Lucy, do you think you may have a drink problem?'

The statement was so startling, so out of the blue that it almost took my breath away. Had he had the audacity to accuse me of being an alcoholic? There was Finnish bluntness, and then there was being downright rude. The man was unbelievable. But if he'd made the outrageous comment to get a reaction from me, I was determined not to give him the satisfaction.

'Of course I don't,' I said quietly and calmly, although why I felt the need to defend myself to him I don't know.

He remained silent, a classic tactic, and one which I eventually fell for hook, line and sinker.

'I don't have a problem with drink,' I repeated. 'Yes, I enjoy alcohol, but who doesn't? I certainly don't enjoy it to excess and I'm not dependent on it. I'm like everyone else in my profession. I know how to have good fun, and I know when to stop.'

'Not everyone else has a stash of spirits hidden away in their wardrobe. Rudi tells me he's been helping you get hold of booze since you arrived. And from the looks of you last night, you'd had quite a lot at the party. You could barely stand.'

'It was a party. Of course I was letting my hair down. I think you'll find that's what most normal people do. And I happen to be living in a cabin, so there's not a lot of space for storing beverages. If you want to search my accommodation, which I guess you're entitled to do because you own it, you'll also find some fruit and a couple of bottles of water. Is that a problem?'

'You are perfectly entitled to store what you want in your cabin, as long as it is legal that is. But it comes down to how it fits within the pattern and what it consequently suggests about that person. It suggests to me someone who needs the comforting presence of alcohol within their reach as a safety net.'

This cod psychology was really starting to wind me up

now. What gave him the right to make judgements like this about me, having known me for all of a few days? He was way off mark and I wanted to scream and shout at him until he admitted it was all nonsense. But as he continued to fix me with that icy stare of his, a little voice at the back of my mind started niggling at me. It was barely a whisper but it seemed to grow in strength as it kept on repeating to me, 'What if he's right?' I pressed my nails into my palms and tried to drown out the nagging fear, but as my anger with Tommi grew, the self-doubt continued to berate me.

Tommi tried a different tack. 'Heidi told me you were encouraging them all to drink more than they felt comfortable with.'

'Well Heidi was talking bollocks, because she was the worst of the lot,' I snapped back. 'She was knocking it back like it was going out of fashion. If anything, I was the one trying to make her calm it down.' That was how it had gone down, wasn't it?

Tommi shrugged his shoulders in that annoying way of his. 'I will take your word for it.'

'I promise I don't have a problem,' I repeated. I forced myself to calm down. This was so not how I had seen this conversation going. But although Tommi had slandered me, I was at his mercy. The person who'd posted the threats through my letterbox still hadn't been found, the video was still going strong online, and as the reaction from the group in the feedback forms showed, public opinion was still very much stacked against me. If I struggled to deal with it in this tiny settlement on the edge of the wilderness, it would be completely unbearable out in the real world. Home had never felt so far out of my reach. Being stuck in this place of interminable snow and dark frightened me, but at the same time, the thought of going anywhere else was even more terrifying. It was time to turn the conversation around to discovering my fate.

'Am I out on the streets then?' I asked bluntly, crossing my arms and staring back at him defiantly. Might as well get straight to the point, then I could return to my room, pack my stuff and wonder where else there was left for me to hide.

'What would you like to happen?' asked Tommi. The leather of his chair creaked as he stretched his legs out again.

'I'd like to wake up and discover that this whole thing was a horrible dream.' The words hung in the air. I thought I saw a tinge of disappointment darken Tommi's face for the briefest moment. But the second the words were out of my mouth, I realised they were a lie. I'd do almost anything for the circumstances which brought me to this place not to have happened, but, on the other hand, being here hadn't been all bad. The husky sledding had been full of joy. I hoped I'd made lifelong friends in Johanna and Rudi. And then there was Tommi; infuriating and grumpy and interfering as he was.

'But as this is not a fairy story...' prompted Tommi.

Too right. Sleeping Beauty got to nap for a hundred years and only woke up when all her problems were over. Fat chance of me getting to enjoy the same kind of blissful oblivion. No, as usual, I would have to face the consequences of my actions.

'Then I'd like to stay here and make amends for the mess I caused last night. I promise I wasn't making them drink too much, but I did want them to have fun, and I didn't stop things before they got out of hand. It was dangerous and irresponsible, but I won't let it happen again. If you give me another chance, I'll prove that you can trust me.'

Tommi pursed his lips. 'I am in a difficult situation. My head tells me that it is time we say goodbye. These conditions do not give people multiple chances, so why should I give you yet another one?'

I bowed my head, hoping he couldn't see the tears threatening to spill down my cheeks. What was I going to do now? And what would Skye and Henri think when they heard how I'd let them down?

Tommi sighed. 'Come with me,' he said.

I followed him to the entrance hall like a condemned prisoner. My fingers shook as I did up my boots and zipped on my outer clothing. But even the layers of fleece couldn't thaw the cold loneliness which chilled me from within.

Tommi tramped across the drive, and I struggled in his wake to keep up on the slick snow, but instead of turning towards the garage where he kept his car, he turned left and dived into the forest, picking out a track between the trees. We walked for quarter of an hour in silence. At places the snow was above my knees and I struggled to keep my balance, but I persisted, determined not to show any further sign of weakness in front of him. In horror movies, this was exactly how a girl came to a sticky end, heading out into the wilderness with a man she barely knew. But strangely enough, the further we travelled away from the relative civilisation of Wild Zone, the calmer I became. Maybe it was the soft whispering of the trees as they stirred in the breeze, or the gentle crunch from the snow as we compacted it beneath our boots, but the steady rhythm of the walk settled the churning of my stomach and eased the tension between my shoulder blades.

Eventually the regular pattern of densely packed trees fell away into a clearing in a gentle hollow, at the base of which nestled a small wooden hut. It looked like something out a child's story book, with snow drifting over the carved gables, and a simple wooden table and benches set up on the veranda, ready to welcome guests.

Tommi marched up the steps, gave a perfunctory knock on the door, before striding confidently in, beckoning me to follow. It took my eyes a few moments to adjust to the gloom after the bright glare from the snow outside, but the pine-scented darkness felt comforting and homely.

'This is a wilderness hut,' he said, gesturing around us at the simple surroundings. Along two of the wooden-slatted walls, wide shelf beds were ready to receive weary walkers. A stack of chopped wood lay by the hearth, while a collection of bowls and mugs had been placed neatly near the fireplace, which was laid with a pyramid of twigs, ready to be lit by the box of matches on the mantlepiece.

Tommi smiled to himself as he walked around, clearly finding the surroundings to his satisfaction. 'I wonder if you have heard of the wilderness code?' he said.

I shook my head, wondering where he was going with this. As far as I knew, we had walked into someone's private retreat, and I half expected them to turn up at any moment, angrily asking why we had invaded their woodland home.

'The wilderness code is viewed as sacrosanct, especially in this part of Finland. Throughout the forest there are wooden huts like these. They lie here all year round, with a fire set ready in the hearth and tools for wood-cutting and food preparation in the cupboards. These huts are kept unlocked so that any passer-by can let themselves in and shelter from the elements for as long as they need to. There is nothing to stop the greedy hiker from helping themselves to the equipment and walking away, leaving the place in a mess for someone else to clear up. And yet the tools remain in their position, the axe sharp and clean, the hearth set with wood ready to be lit. That is because we Finns are good at putting ourselves in the shoes of other people. We think of the consequences if we were not to act in this way, and how it could prove fatal for someone in desperate need in these unforgiving conditions. We leave things as they are for the next person because we know that they will do the same for the person after that. It is not written in any rulebook, but it is as sacred a system as if it was laid down by law. And if someone is stuck out in the wilderness with nothing to protect them from the elements, they can trust that these huts will provide them shelter and may even save their lives.'

I nodded solemnly, caught up in the seriousness of what he was saying. On the surface it seemed completely irrelevant to my situation, but I'd come to realise that Tommi never said anything without a specific purpose.

'Your actions at the party suggest that I should not trust you and that I would be taking a big risk by giving you another chance. But I am not the sort of man to leave someone in the wilderness fending for themselves. And I wonder if you are in a kind of wilderness of your own. I respect the code, and I hope by giving you this chance, you will learn to respect it for yourself. Do you think that could be possible?'

I looked around at the neat room and the thoughtful touches left by one stranger for another, and for the first time since that video went viral, I felt a tiny burst of hope that maybe the world wasn't such a universally terrible place after all.

'I promise I'll do my best. I really appreciate you giving me yet another chance. I'll try not to let you down. Or myself,' I added as an afterthought.

Tommi nodded. 'You can stay at Wild Zone. In fact, it would be quite difficult for me to get rid of you now.' A slight grin brightened his features. 'Rudi informs me there is a problem with the refuelling system at the airport. Our guests have managed to get their flight, but there will be no more flights landing or taking off for several days until they can get a part sent from Helsinki. But the thing that I ask of you while you continue to stay here, is that you consider what I have said to you. Ask yourself those difficult questions and truly examine your answers. Being honest with yourself can be the hardest thing, but those who are, become better people because of it.' He paused and cleared his throat. 'I apologise. I have been speaking for longer than

I intended. But I hope you will do me the honour of at least thinking about what I have said?'

I nodded numbly. I felt humbled by the trust he was showing in me and the care he had demonstrated in his words. He was a good man. But was I good enough to live up to the responsibility he had placed on my shoulders? After spending the last decade plus running away from myself, did I dare stop now? I wasn't sure I knew how to.

Chapter Nineteen

If I was a better person, I probably should have spent the rest of the day in the wilderness hut, allowing the simplicity of my surroundings to transform me into a Zen-like state of calm during which I'd see the light and all my problems would come to an end. But I needed the loo, and an al fresco pee by a wooden hut with a temperature of minus fifteen degrees centigrade threatening to freeze my nether regions off didn't really appeal, so I tramped back to Wild Zone with Tommi, the route back seeming a lot more direct than the circuitous path he'd taken me on the way out. I wondered if the long walk to the hut had been a deliberate decision to give me time to think.

Returning to the welcoming lights of the main building felt strangely like coming home, mostly because of the overwhelming sense of relief that I wasn't going to have to pack my stuff up and run away once again. But maybe a small part of me was getting used to this strange environment where the weather was cold, but the people surprisingly warm. Before we went our separate ways, Tommi to his office, I to my cabin, he turned to me.

'If you wish to donate your bottles to the bar, I'm sure Rudi would be happy to take them off your hands and reimburse you.' He fixed me with that steady stare of his. 'Please don't put him in the position of getting more for you. He is a good man, but his instinct for doing a deal is strong. Just as you are trying to resist temptation, don't put him in the path of it.'

I fought the urge to salute. I know he had the best intentions, but I'd got the message quite a while ago, and he really didn't need to hammer it home any further. I'd rather not be reminded that my behaviour had had consequences for others too. Before my resolve weakened, I marched to my hut and poured my remaining boozy stash down the sink. It was an overly dramatic way of demonstrating my commitment to being a good girl from now on, but there was something cathartic about seeing the liquid disappearing down the drain and, with every glug, I vowed to resist temptation. Whatever Tommi thought, I knew I wasn't dependent on the stuff. The fumes did give me a bit of an involuntary high, but this was the last time I would ever so much as sniff a bottle of booze, I promised myself. I didn't even keep an emergency inch or two back. Full of enthusiasm, I tramped across to the bins behind the kitchen and threw my empty bottles into the recycling with a satisfying clink. And then I took them out and threw them back in more loudly in the hope that someone, OK I admit it, in the hope that Tommi, would see me doing it and be pleased that I had listened to his words of counsel. But the rest of the Wild Zone crew seemed to have disappeared off the face of the planet and I was left feeling like my big gesture had been a massive anticlimax. I told myself it didn't matter what other people thought of me, that I was doing this for my own sake, but the sentiment didn't ring true.

And then I retreated to my cabin and sat on my bed twiddling my thumbs. Once again, that overbearing silence was closing in on me and I had no idea how to fill it. Naturally, it was already pitch dark outside and, with no guests around, there were no activities I could go and gate-crash in the guise of helping. I needed distraction, something to occupy my mind before it disappeared off to places I'd rather it didn't. I wasn't asking for much. I just wanted a slice of normality, to be able to text Skye about something funny I'd read, and exchange silly gifs with her without fearing what I'd come across online. I wanted to be busy preparing shows, thinking up ways to entertain people and wondering what the big discussion topic of the day was going to be. Heck, I'd even settle for some argy-bargy with Mike over the direction of the programme and which songs we should add to the playlist, anything was preferable to sitting here alone with nothing but self-pitying thoughts to distract me from the darkness.

Eventually, I caved and turned on the radio to fill my surroundings with something other than the noise of my own breathing. I worked my way through the frequencies, but the only station that wasn't filled with static was the same one I'd tried before, with my friend the dullest DJ on the planet once again in the host's chair. This time, however, instead of feeling irritated by his efforts, I started to feel sorry for him. Perhaps the delay in cueing the tracks could be explained by a lack of confidence in the system. And perhaps it was my lack of understanding of the language which was making his intonation seem monotonous. Maybe he was a one-man band who was having to drive the desk, press all the buttons and get all the timings right, at the same time as attempting to be a charismatic presenter. I checked the frequency of the station again. It was a shortwave frequency, one which can only have been broadcasting from somewhere fairly close by. Commercial stations normally occupied a much more powerful place on the airwaves, so maybe this was a smaller, local operation. Perhaps I had been unfairly critiquing someone who did the job on a voluntary basis. I resolved to find out more from one of the Wild Zone staff.

There was a distinctive clink of a glass over the airwaves. I didn't have to speak Finnish to understand the angry, guttural swearing in the background. The radio station abruptly went off the air. I chuckled to myself. It sounded like the DJ had committed the cardinal sin of bringing liquid into the studio and then spilling it on the equipment. I hoped it didn't keep them off the air too long.

Speaking of liquid, I was feeling rather thirsty. I checked my watch. The sun was definitely over the yardarm somewhere in the world. But that was irrelevant to the newly improved, toxin-free Lucy, I told myself fiercely. I padded into the bathroom to fill my glass with fresh water, but I'd forgotten my earlier silliness and the tempting smell of alcohol hit me like a thump to the chest. And that was when the craving for one last drink started. One little glass of something sparkling wouldn't do any harm, I knew that. It wasn't because I *needed* the booze, I just fancied a small tipple to celebrate the fact that I still had a bolthole. Tommi wouldn't begrudge that, and surely having one drink and then stopping would be a better way of proving that the alcohol didn't have any power over me than steering clear of the stuff altogether?

I got as far as stepping onto the porch outside and marching a dozen yards towards the main building when good sense and the cold hit me with a combined frightening sense of clarity. I'd been so focused on the idea of getting a drink, that I'd not even stopped to pull on my coat and boots. I was standing outside in dangerously low temperatures dressed in nothing more substantial than a tracksuit and teddy bear slippers which were already soaked by the snow. Was I going mad? As the wet cold seeped into my toes, I felt the tears pricking behind my eyes once again. Maybe this was what Tommi had been getting at when he asked if I had a problem? I'd always thought alcoholics were those people you felt sorry for when you walked past them in the park, huddled up over a plastic bottle of cider, clothes smelling and skin grimy. I used to pity them for their lack of control. And wasn't there a small part of me who had always felt that I was a better person because I held down a good job, I was clean and had nice clothes? But maybe we weren't so very different after all. Maybe alcohol did have a greater hold over me than I'd realised. When had the scales tipped from drinking for fun, to drinking as a necessity to get by? I wanted to cry with the shame of my realisation, but adding tears to my already-frozen state was not going to help the situation.

I turned and fled to my cabin, desperately hoping that there hadn't been anyone watching me from the warm, welcoming embrace of the main building. It would be too hard to explain what I had been doing wandering around in this silly state.

As soon as I got back indoors, I stripped off my cold, wet clothing and pulled on my thickest, fluffiest pair of pyjamas. And then I huddled under my blankets. But the shivering continued a long time after my limbs thawed out.

The next morning, I woke up in a foul mood and with a raging headache. Apparently my punishment for my improved lifestyle choices was going to be waking with the effects of a hangover without having experienced the fun beforehand. Every time I thought back to the conversation with Tommi yesterday and my own revelation in the snow, I felt embarrassed and exposed. He had seen through me and identified the flaws I worked so hard to keep hidden from the rest of the world. I didn't know if I dared face him again. I pulled the blankets further over my head as if sheltering beneath their comforting thickness would protect me from all the threats of the outside world.

But the outside world apparently wasn't going to let me hide away for ever, because there was a loud knocking on the door of my cabin, and experience told me that whoever it was, wasn't going away.

'Jusaminute,' I called out, my voice muffled and distorted by the comforter I was still sheltering under.

With seemingly no regard for personal space, or etiquette, Tommi strolled into the room, casually whistling.

I sat up abruptly, wrapping my covers around my shoulders like a protective cape.

'Did I say come in?' I snapped.

Tommi shrugged. 'Sorry about that. My English comprehension struggles when words are muffled by blankets and the door. I need some help today, and I thought you might be the one to assist me.'

Checking up on me, of course. I wanted nothing more than to stay in bed and sleep for another few hours until my bad temper and non-hangover hangover went away, but I had a feeling he'd stick around until he got his own way, so I gave in and hauled myself out of bed.

'A coffee might be nice,' I said pointedly, still cocooned by my bedcovers, waiting for him to go before I changed out of my pyjamas.

'Coming right up. And layers would be good today. We're going back into the forest, but it's a strenuous task, so you're bound to warm up quickly.'

I dreaded to think what awaited me.

Although the headache remained, I felt slightly more human once I'd mainlined a black coffee and gulped down a couple of slices of toast which Johanna had thoughtfully thrust into my hands as we passed the main building. The quick-march pace which Tommi set soon had me sweating gently under my layers of fleece, and when we came to a clearing on the other side of the lake, I was glad to pause and take a breather whilst pretending to be looking at the view.

'Enlighten me, what's the task for today? Wood-chopping? Ice-fishing? Going on a bear hunt? I'm beginning to feel like quite the outdoor adventurer.'

'Did I ever tell you what to do if you come across a bear?' said Tommi, matter of factly.

'Bears? I was joking. You're not seriously telling me there are bears in this place, are you?' I looked around, half expecting one to appear at any moment. I love a cute teddy bear as much as the next person, but I'd heard stories that their counterparts in the wild were not necessarily the friendliest of beasts.

'There are a few here and there. The important thing is to make sure you're with someone who can run more slowly than you can. Give them a shove towards the bear, and then start sprinting.' He looked at me for a beat, and then his face crinkled with laughter. 'Nearly got you.'

'Hilarious,' I said, 'especially as I'm guessing in these circumstances, I'm the one getting shoved towards the bear.'

'Why else do you think I brought you along today?' he said. 'No, seriously, in the highly unlikely event you were to encounter a bear in these parts, back away very slowly, don't make any sudden movements, and don't take your eyes off it. It'll probably be more scared of you, than you are of it.' He grinned.

'My mum says that about spiders and I don't believe her either,' I said. 'If a bear comes along, I'm shoving you in its path first. I'm afraid there are some circumstances where it's sensible to be selfish.' I winked at him.

'Well, if that is the case, perhaps you should build up some good karma before you sacrifice me to my fate. I was hoping you would help me with clearing the neighbours' roofs. We've had a few heavy snowfalls of late, and if too much snow collects up on a roof, it can cause it to collapse. I've brought some rope along so we can clear the worst of it away and ease the pressure on the eaves. A lot of the houses around the lake are summer homes belonging to people who live in Helsinki, and they can't always visit as often as they would like during the winter.'

'This place must be very different in the summer,' I said, struggling to imagine what the landscape must look like beneath its concealing layer of snow and ice.

'While darkness dominates our winters, our closeness to the Arctic Circle means that during the summer we get to enjoy nearly endless days of light. Families swim off the jetties and people explore the lake by kayak, while the braver ones try out white water rafting on the river. The only downside is that there are a lot of insects in the marshy areas edging the water. Now, do you want to be the first one up on the roof? It is probably better that you do it as you are the lighter of us.'

I wanted to admit that I wasn't great with heights and that standing on a slippery roof with a long way down to the ground was up there on my list of nightmare scenarios, but I'd already shown enough weakness in front of Tommi and I really wanted to do something which gave him a more positive view of me for a change.

I nodded reluctantly. 'You'll have to tell me what I'm doing though. Funnily enough, there isn't much call for clearing snow from roofs in England. Not even up north, where I'm from.'

'It is very simple,' he said. 'You see that ladder there, climb it, and then walk to the apex of the roof. It's not far up and the snow is quite thick, so you should get a decent grip. Place this rope along the ridgeline, then head back down and I'll show you what happens next.'

He uncoiled a long piece of rope with a hammer tied at one end. He kept that end on the ground and passed me the rest of the coil once I'd gingerly clambered up the ladder. I told myself not to look down and kept on climbing until I was at the top.

'What's the view like up there?' said Tommi cheerily.

I made the mistake of looking in his direction and gulped. Tommi may have said this wasn't high, but I felt as vulnerable as if I was cleaning windows at the Shard without a safety harness. Not caring how silly I looked, I went down onto my hands and knees and crawled nervously along the ridge, thanking my lucky stars that my trousers were better at being waterproof than they were at being flattering. I positioned the rope as instructed, then inelegantly slithered down the ladder at the other end of the roof and launched myself into a thankfully soft pile of snow.

Tommi looped the two ends of rope together and started pulling, a bit like he was moving a cheese wire through a great big block of cheddar.

'Stay back behind me,' he warned. 'Sometimes the snow can slide off without much warning.'

He heaved on the rope, the snow creaking beneath it. I could see very little sign of progress. I started to wonder if this was another of his elaborate mickey-takes or a test to see how far I was prepared to go to stay at Wild Zone. Nevertheless, when the sweat started beading on his forehead, I volunteered to take over for a bit so he could have a breather.

He reluctantly agreed, but only after he'd made me promise to run backwards the second he told me to. Considering that Tommi had made out this was a regular housekeeping duty, it seemed pretty hazardous.

Suddenly there was a change in the rope, a feeling that the resistance had been overcome. I instinctively stepped back as a neat avalanche of snow slipped off the roof and landed at our feet. I whooped with glee. It felt pretty satisfying to have made such an impact. Tommi laughed. 'One roof down, only half a dozen more to go. The neighbours will be very grateful for your community service.'

'We could do with some music to entertain us while we work,' I said. 'Do you have your phone on you? I'm happy to put a playlist together.'

'Still not carrying your own phone?' he asked, a bit too casually.

'You should try it some time,' I said. 'It's amazing how liberating the experience is.' And lonely. 'Besides, when there are such gems on your local radio station, then why would I need to listen to my own music?' I laughed. 'Do you know if it's back on air yet? I think I detected an unfortunate incident involving a spill in the studio last night.'

Tommi pulled a face. 'You can only be speaking about ACFM. That stands for Arctic Circle FM by the way. It's the community radio station. In fact, it's the only local station in these parts. It's run entirely by volunteers, and, funnily enough, it's based in that building over there.'

He gestured in the direction of a group of around five or six houses, the closest thing to a village centre that I'd seen since arriving at Wild Zone. The top of a transmitter poked out of a pile of snow by one of the buildings.

'Right at the heart of everything that's going on then,' I said. 'I wondered if it was a one-man band when I was listening. The presenter seemed, dare I say, a bit hesitant and unsure of what he was doing.'

'You should go and offer your services,' said Tommi. 'They're always on the lookout for new volunteers, and, as you can imagine, they aren't exactly inundated around here.'

I felt a strange mix of excitement and dread. 'Don't be silly. For a start, I can't speak a word of Finnish. And before you say everyone around here speaks English, I don't fancy doing a show full stop. I think it would be against the terms of my contract.' If I even had a job contract still. And I couldn't bear the idea of someone coming across my voice on the airwaves and realising I'd fallen from the heights of hosting my own multi-award-winning breakfast show to DJing at a community radio station in the Arctic Circle for free.

Tommi threw the rope to me, and we started work at clearing the next roof. 'I wasn't thinking of you being a presenter,' he said. 'How about helping behind the scenes? You're good at putting playlists together, and with all your experience, you'd soon find your way around their set-up. I'm sure Aukusti and his gang would be delighted to have your help and the benefit of your knowledge.'

There was another warning creak, and we leaped back as our next roof dramatically cleared. We shovelled a path to the front door through the new pile of snow and carried on around the lake. I realised we were gradually working our way round to the settlement and the radio transmitter.

'As we're in the area, you might as well pop in and introduce yourself,' said Tommi in such a nonchalant manner it convinced me that he'd plotted this ever since I'd mentioned the radio station.

And so I found myself being marched towards the anonymous home of ACFM.

Chapter Twenty

Tommi claimed he could finish the remaining roofs without me, but I noticed he lingered in the vicinity of the radio building long enough to make sure I actually knocked on the door. I tried protesting, saying it was pointless turning up without an appointment, and without an interpreter, but he happily abandoned me hovering on the threshold, as nervous as I had been as a shy fifteen year old when I'd accidentally discovered the studio of the hospital radio station and found there could be some light at the very darkest point of my life after all.

I knocked softly on the heavy wooden door, telling myself my hesitancy was because I didn't want to interrupt the broadcast. After a few minutes, and sensing Tommi's gaze between my shoulder blades, I knocked again, a bit louder this time.

The door swung open and I did a double-take. Had I inadvertently stumbled across Father Christmas? The man in the hallway could certainly give Santa a run for his money with his rotund figure and luscious silvery beard. He leaned against the door frame and addressed me in Finnish.

I felt ashamed all over again that I was yet to pick up more than a couple of words of the language of my host country.

'Hello. Sorry, I don't speak much Finnish. Any Finnish, actually. My name is Lucy Fairweather. I'm staying over at Wild Zone, but back in England I work in radio and I was wondering if I could do some volunteering.'

He slapped his palm against his chest. 'I'm Aku. Follow me.' He accepted my presence as if it was perfectly normal for English DJs to turn up at his front door out of the blue. He waddled back into the studio, humming cheerily. The red transmission light was shining brightly, and I realised with horror that he'd left the microphone transmitting dead air while he answered the door. In fact, the listeners had probably been treated to our exchange at the doorstep. I instantly regretted introducing myself with my full name. Aku muttered to himself as he peered at the desk, fiddling around with faders and dials until finally he alighted on the correct button and set some music playing for his listeners, who must have been wondering by now if the station had been knocked off the air again.

He clicked his fingers at me and gestured towards the messy pile of CDs in the corner. 'That could do with sorting,' he said, before returning to his slow contemplation of the mixing desk.

Grateful as I was for his lack of questions and quiet acceptance of my presence, I was surprised he didn't want to know more about my skills and experience before putting me to work. I guess this was one of those scenarios where I would have to show rather than tell. I unzipped my outer layers and settled myself down on the floor. The set-up in here was so much simpler than the elaborate studio I was used to back at home, but there was something satisfying about the simplicity. The microphone was dominant, a clear reminder that communicating with listeners was at the heart of radio's mission. It felt good to be in a familiar setting, where I could forget about the snow and gloom outside, and enjoy the buzz which I always got from being in a broadcast environment.

I picked my way through the dusty piles of CDs, some of which had clearly been in place since the invention of the medium. I decided to classify them by genre rather than artist, figuring that grouping different styles of music together would be an easy way of helping to guide an inexperienced DJ when they were compiling their show. I worked my way through, checking the CDs inside the boxes corresponded with the packaging on the outside, then I moved onto a pile of discs which were clearly copies. But whoever had taken the time to rip the albums, hadn't bothered to label them with a track list. Aku was in the middle of a very-solemn sounding speech, so I tiptoed my way around the studio, opening cupboards until I found a spare CD player and set of headphones, then I started listening to the music. Without the benefit of my phone, I couldn't use an app to identify the tracks, so I had to dig deep in my music knowledge to try to do the job myself. Every time I listened to a tune, I was transported to the place where I'd first heard the track. It was an exercise in nostalgia, igniting good memories as well as some sad ones. I kept on coming across tracks which my dad loved, but instead of casting them to one side as I would normally have done, I piled them up on their own shelf, creating a playlist which I knew he would have enjoyed. Dad had never got to hear me on the airwaves, but he'd been instrumental in my career. After all, if I hadn't been rushed to his bedside to say goodbye to him on that final day, I might never have stumbled across the hospital radio station where I'd had my first experience of broadcasting. In all my years on air, I'd never played any of these tracks. I hadn't dared. But maybe it was time for that to change.

I put the rest of the unlabelled CDs to one side, vowing to continue the job back at Wild Zone if I had to, then moved onto the final, and biggest collection, which belonged to local Finnish musicians. I didn't have a clue where to start when it came to classifying these ones, but Aku seemed happy enough to indicate with a grunt which genre pile they should be added to. Every so often he swivelled the chair around to check on my progress, and nodded, I hoped in satisfaction, at the work I was doing. Time flew by as I relaxed into my task, feeling productive, useful, and in a familiar space for the first time in ages.

Aku was an undemanding companion, content to get on with his work while I got on with mine. His show was several hours long, but he seemed very relaxed about the process, wandering off to make cups of tea whenever the mood took him, and not worrying about whether there was enough time left on the track to allow him to do this. The first time he did this, I let the dead air play out, but it felt really weird and wrong, so when he disappeared off once again with only fifteen seconds of music left to play, without really thinking about it, I found myself walking over to the desk, loading up a new series of tracks and setting them going in a pleasingly seamless way. It was reassuring to know I hadn't lost the skill.

Aku arrived back after quarter of an hour and nodded approvingly when he saw that I had everything in hand.

'Do you want to come back tomorrow?' he said. 'I could do with the help and the radio station needs fresh blood.'

'I can't present,' I said quickly.

'I wasn't asking you to present. I need a producer,' he said.

I'm not going to lie and say it didn't feel like taking a massive step backwards, going from professional presenter to producer at an amateur station. But on the other hand, doing something, anything in the radio world was better than sitting alone in my cabin twiddling my thumbs. And amateur or professional, what really mattered was being back in that radio environment, and feeling I still had something to offer. Ultimately it wouldn't change my situation, but maybe it would let me feel like I was claiming something back for myself, so that I hadn't allowed the person behind the viral video to take everything from me. I found myself nodding in agreement, while my mind raced ahead with plans for special programmes for the station to feature.

'I will see you tomorrow,' said Aku. 'You might as well stay to help the next person.'

I didn't have anywhere else to rush to. The longer I stayed away from Wild Zone and the siren call of the bar, the better.

To my surprise, it was Johanna who took over from Aku to do the evening show.

'I didn't realise you were a radio star. You should have said something. I'd have listened out for you.'

'It's my night off from Wild Zone,' she explained. 'I only do the occasional show. Obviously, I can't present when I'm busy at the lodge, but it's good to do something for the local community. We're so spread out here, it's nice to be able to bring everyone together across the airwaves.'

'Do you want me to stick around? I mean, I'm sure you're more than capable of driving the show by yourself, but I'm happy to help.'

She smiled. 'That would be lovely. It would be good to have some company. It can be a bit lonely here at the station in the evenings, and it's very easy to fall into the habit of playing long tracks so I can put my feet up and read my book. Perhaps you could help me liven things up a bit? Though maybe not too much,' she added, as we both thought of the disastrous party.

'Let me pull out some tracks for you to play. Do you have a plan for tonight's show? If not, we could play a series of tunes and get listeners to call in and guess what the theme is. Maybe, as you're a chef, we could do a cooking theme? There are loads of tracks with words like "hot" in the title.'

Johanna looked uncertain. 'I'm not sure my knowledge of music is up to that challenge. And I wouldn't know where to start with connecting the calls and putting them on air. To be honest, I like to pretend to myself that no one is actually listening, that way it makes it easier to chat.'

'You don't have to worry about a thing,' I said. 'I can do the technical side, and pick out the tunes so all you have to do is talk. That's the producer's job after all, to make the presenter look great, although I wish someone would tell my producer back at home that. Mike loves trying to make me mess up on air. But never mind that. I promise not to stoop to his level. Given that there aren't many houses occupied around here, it's more than likely that your guests will be people you already know, so it will just be like having a conversation with a friend. You'll be great, I know it.'

Johanna was hesitant at first, but, with my help, she started to relax into it. To be honest, when she'd said she pretended no one was listening, she wasn't far from the actual truth as we only took three phone calls in the whole show, one of which was from Aku and the other Tommi, but with each conversation I could see her confidence growing. When she spoke to the third, unknown caller, she was happy and chatty. With a bit more coaching and some confidence-boosting exercises, she would be as good as some of the professionals at Star FM.

As the music played, I started sketching out more ideas for Aku's show as well. ACFM had the potential to be a great station. As volunteers, the presenters were by their very nature passionate about what they did. It was a matter of channelling that enthusiasm in the right way. The people in this isolated part of the world had given me so much by welcoming me to their home. Perhaps helping their community radio to thrive would be a way in which I could give something back.

Once Johanna's show was over, we put the station into automatic play mode and headed out into the snow. It was a while since I'd felt a sense of satisfaction at a job well done. If I was being truly honest with myself, even before things went so horribly wrong, I'd been getting into a bit of a rut with my show; taking my position for granted and being less diligent than I should have been in my approach to preparing for work. I vowed that if I ever got the chance to return, I would remember this feeling of simple pleasure in getting back to basics, and never allow myself to coast again.

Thinking about work made me come to a decision.

'Johanna, could you do me a favour? Could I borrow your phone?' I said the words quickly, before I had the time to change my mind. It was one thing living in an isolated location, but it was quite another cutting yourself off from the world altogether and increasing that isolation. It was time for me to reach out to my friends back home, and remind myself that there were still people who cared for me. I wasn't brave enough to have my own phone on all the time yet, but maybe making contact on my own terms was a step in the right direction.

When she wasn't working at Wild Zone, Johanna lived in a picture-perfect wooden house in the settlement on the shores of the lake. The downstairs consisted of an open space containing the kitchen and living room combined. It was dominated by a wood-burning stove which filled every corner with a comforting warmth.

'I need to do some chores upstairs, so please make yourself comfortable down here,' Johanna said tactfully.

'Thanks. I'll reimburse you for the phone bill, of course,' I said.

'It's not a problem. Take as long as you need. Help yourself to a drink.'

I fixed myself a hot toddy, leaving out the alcoholic elements. It was the kind of drink I'd normally have when I wasn't feeling well, and the zing of lemon combined with the sweetness of the honey helped settle my nerves before I picked up the phone. It was silly to be anxious about calling Skye, she was my best friend after all, but I was nervous about what she might have to say. After being cut off from the outside world, it felt like a big step to be reaching out from my safe bubble of ignorance.

She answered in Finnish, recognising the international number.

'Skye, is there anything you aren't good at? I didn't realise you spoke Finnish too,' I said, and then had to hold the phone away from my ear while she squealed in delight at hearing my voice.

'Lucy, lovely one, it has been too long. I've missed you. How are you? Tell me all about what you've been getting up to. What do you think of Finland? Isn't it amazing? Such a special country.'

I thought back through my days of husky sledding and cross-country skiing and found myself agreeing with her. It was unlike any place I'd ever visited, and so far out of my comfort zone, but there was something magical about it, plus the effect it was having on me was quite extraordinary. It was making me look at myself in a whole new light, forcing me to question things I had always taken for granted.

'It's definitely growing on me,' I admitted. 'I'm starting to become accustomed to the snow, but the darkness is taking a little longer. I keep on thinking it's the middle of the night and it'll be three in the afternoon or something ridiculous. But, more importantly, how are you? Feeling OK? Is Henri taking good care of you?'

I heard Skye settling herself on the sofa, ready for a long catch up.

'Henri is taking excellent care of me. In fact, I keep telling him he's being almost irritatingly solicitous, running around fetching me stuff and telling me to put my feet up.'

'He should be careful. You'll get used to that kind of treatment.'

Skye laughed. 'I will indeed. Anyway, I've been learning Finnish because we want the baby to be bilingual. Henri's going to speak to him in Finnish and I'll speak in English, but I don't want to feel left out and not know what they're chatting about, so I'm finally knuckling down to language lessons.'

'Wait a minute. Did you just refer to the baby as a him?'

She squealed again. 'We weren't going to find out, but then we changed our minds at the last minute. I've already bought him a "This is what a feminist looks like" babygro. I'm so excited. People keep on texting in during my show to suggest names for him.' Her voice changed suddenly.

'Oh, sorry, I'm such a tactless idiot. Forget I mentioned work.'

'Don't worry,' I tried to reassure her, even though I'd felt my stomach contract at her casual reference to 'my show'. 'But as you brought it up, how is everything at Star FM?'

'Fine, absolutely fine. But tell me about your Finnish exploits. That's way more interesting.'

I had the distinct impression she was trying to change the subject.

'Has HR said anything more about the investigation? Please tell me they're trying to find out who created the video.'

Skye paused for so long that I thought the snow had damaged the connection. When she did speak, her voice was quiet and subdued, most unlike her normal manner.

'Luce, I'm really sorry, but as far as I can tell, they're not doing any investigating at all. The video is still doing the rounds, but they're going on a "no comment" policy and trying to pretend it's not happening.'

'It's like I never existed,' I said glumly. 'Clearly it's a case of out of sight, out of mind.'

'But I'm still speaking up for you,' she said. 'I miss you and your wonderful gift for making people smile. It's not the same without you around. And I feel so bad that my career is being boosted at the expense of yours.'

'I don't begrudge you that for a second. You deserved a promotion, and I'm glad you're getting the opportunity to show what you're made of. I've made a lot of mistakes, and I was getting complacent on the show, but whatever I did, I didn't deserve that video and the hate campaign it generated. But if HR aren't going to bother, I'll have to find some way of clearing my name and making them care. Easier said than done, unfortunately.'

'Things will work out. I know they will,' said Skye. There was something in her voice which made me wonder for a moment whether there was more to her words than just her usual blind faith in fate, but she carried on speaking normally, and I concluded I had imagined it.

It was only after we'd said our goodbyes, and I'd promised to keep in touch more regularly, that I realised that we hadn't discussed one very important issue; how much longer I'd be staying in Finland. But then again, I didn't know the answer to that question myself.

Chapter Twenty-One

Johanna offered to walk with me back across the lake to Wild Zone, but I refused to allow her to spend her night off babysitting me. After promising to tell her when I'd got back safely, she finally let me head off. But despite having reassured her that I was completely fine finding my way around in the dark, it felt strange stepping out on the ice by myself. I told myself that this time would be different to when I got lost in the snow and had to be rescued by Tommi. The landscape was much more familiar to me now, and my experiences following the same wilderness training programme as the guests had made me feel more accustomed to these surroundings.

However, I did feel a pang of fear when my torch died when I was halfway across the lake. Without that warm beam of light chasing away the night, the darkness enveloped me, disorientating my senses and leaving me paralysed in position, too scared to take another step. Logically, I knew the ice was at least thirty centimetres deep throughout the lake, and a lot thicker in some places. I was also certain I was nowhere near the river outlet, the only place where I was at any risk of dropping through into water, but those facts didn't stop me imagining I could hear the sinister creaking of the ice breaking beneath me.

I stopped and took a few deep breaths to try to get my thoughts back together. Closing my eyes, I concentrated on the gentle swish of the breeze through the trees, and allowed the calm to wash over me. The thick snow tended to absorb sound, softening any other noise into a quiet lull, a dense nothingness that was so present in the atmosphere it was like I could reach out and touch it. Maybe I was finally getting used to being in the peace. It was so much easier to do Skye's mindfulness trick here in the serene, pure surroundings of a Finnish national park, than on the polluted road by Star FM. And if someone had asked me at that moment which place I'd prefer to be, I couldn't swear to the answer being back at work.

When I opened my eyes again, I realised that the night wasn't as pitch black as I had initially feared. The light from the quarter moon was reflected in a delicate sheen on the snow, while the rest of the sky glimmered with more stars than I had ever seen in my life. There was such a clarity in the sky, no city diluting the darkness with a distant orange glow, no fug of smog creating a haze on the horizon. I turned slowly on the spot, absorbing the beauty of the moment, surprised at the emotion it stirred in me. And then I started to recognise the inky silhouettes of the summer houses whose roofs Tommi and I had cleared earlier. I traced the direction around, and there, twinkling golden against the monochrome of the forest, were the welcoming lights of Wild Zone and home.

Keeping my gaze fixed on that beacon of light, I made my way across the smooth snowy surface of the lake, enjoying the quiet crunch of my boots on the ice. There was something liberating about being out here alone, trusting my instincts and successfully navigating my way through a landscape which a month ago I would have described as my worst nightmare. I slowed my pace, absorbing every moment of timeless peace.

Finally I drew nearer the shore and recognised the uneven bumps made by the tufts of reeds growing in the marshy border. It was harder going here in the uncompacted snow and I found myself staggering around and falling forward every so often, but each time I picked myself up, dusted the snow from my waterproofs and carried on with a smile. It was only when I stumbled right into the centre of the quinzee encampment that I realised I should stop dawdling and return to the safety of indoors. The quinzees looked no more inviting at night than they had during the day, and I quickened my pace to get away from the reminder of Heidi's near-death experience and my own role in her misadventures. I told myself that that was a different Lucy. The Lucy of now was starting to see her way through the darkness.

Finding the path up through the trees to Wild Zone was a challenge, but I ploughed my own way despite my lack of snowshoes to help me grip onto the untrodden banks of snow. But although it took a while, I felt proud of myself when I eventually emerged into the clearing where the buildings stood. It was the longest time I'd spent outdoors alone in this country without mishap, and I felt I'd proved something important to myself by making it back on my own two feet.

But no sooner had I arrived, then Wild Zone plunged into darkness. Having lost my night vision thanks to the lanterns and fairy lights around the building, it took me a few minutes to readjust to the shadows once again, and I walked slap bang into something solid. Or rather someone.

'Oof,' grunted Tommi as I inadvertently headbutted his chest.

I staggered back, and rubbed my forehead. 'Sorry about that. I promise I'm not making a habit of colliding with you. I lost my bearings when the lights went out. Is there a power cut?'

Tommi shook his head. 'I put them out deliberately. Follow me, I want to show you something,' he said mysteriously. He was dressed in his thickest outdoor gear, the stuff he'd worn for husky sledding. He checked my garb and handed me some handwarmers. 'You've been out for a while. Keep hold of these.'

I sensed my plans of retreating to my hut for a hot shower and early night were going to have to be put to one side. I wasn't that disappointed.

'I've got to tell Johanna I'm back,' I said. 'Where are we going? My mum warned me about the dangers of following strange men on dark nights.'

Tommi chuckled. 'Johanna phoned to say you were on your way. I was looking out for you and I've already sent her a message to say you made it back in one piece. You are welcome to follow your mother's advice and leave me to it, but, when I was looking for you, I thought I spotted the Northern Lights starting to form, and I figured you might like to see them.'

He didn't need to ask me twice. I followed Tommi round to the wide wooden veranda at the back of the main building, all the while leaning my head back, desperate not to miss a moment.

'You'll hurt your neck standing like that,' said Tommi. 'Here, I've got a better idea.' He hurried into the storeroom and emerged carrying some blankets and a couple of the extra-thick camping mats which I knew were reserved for people who were planning to sleep out in a quinzee. He placed them on top of the snow-covered loungers and we laid back, each in a cosy cocoon, and stared up at the sky in companionable silence, watching the countless constellations. And then something changed in the air.

'Look over there, to the right of the moon. I think they're starting to form.' His voice was softer than a whisper, as if he didn't want to frighten the aurora and make it disappear.

At first I thought the grey smudges tracing their way through the sky were clouds, but then I detected the faintest tinge of colour in them as they started to swirl delicately above our heads. Before long, the whole sky had erupted in an enchanted display of muted light and shadows. The colours weren't as vivid as the pictures I'd seen, but the subtle shades were far more beautiful in real life than they were on the screen. In a past existence, I'd have run off to collect my phone so I could record the display and post about it to all my followers. After all, had it really happened if it hadn't been recorded for posterity on Instagram? But I realised now that this was the better experience; enjoying them in the moment without the barrier of a phone screen between me and the mysterious lights. I reached out and traced the path of the aurora with my palm, as if I was conducting the show. The apparitions danced and twirled before us. And then, all at once, they disappeared as if they'd never been there. I let out a breath I didn't even realise I'd been holding.

'Did that really just happen?' I reached across and grabbed Tommi's hand, wanting to feel the warmth of another human to ground me in reality after such a transcendental experience.

He squeezed my hand back. 'I knew you'd feel it too. The Northern Lights are a mystical experience. Every time I am lucky enough to witness the phenomenon, it's like I am seeing it for the first time. I can understand why my ancestors spun such interesting tales around their origins.'

'Tell me,' I asked quietly. It felt sacrilegious to speak at anything louder than a whisper. The whole atmosphere was charged as if electric sparks had been dancing through the air.

'You've been out in the cold for a long time now. You will have been warm from your walk, but it is risky to stay out too long once you've cooled down. Perhaps we should go back inside where it's warmer,' said Tommi. I could hear the reluctance in his voice, and knew that he too wanted to stay out here and savour the magic for as long as possible.

'Another five minutes won't harm,' I said. 'We're dressed in Wild Zone's finest winter weather gear after all.'

I wiggled my thickly gloved hands. 'See, all fingers present and correct, as are my toes.'

'Very well, but promise you'll tell me if you're starting to feel cold or sleepy.' He settled himself back onto the lounger and stared up at the sky. 'Throughout time, the Northern Lights have been seen as having magical powers which we mere humans cannot understand.' He paused and I knew we were both visualising the display which we had just witnessed. 'In Finland, they are also known as *revontulet* or "fox fires". There is an old folk tale that the aurora was caused by a fox running through the tundra. As it ran through the snow, its bushy tail sent sparks of fire spinning up into the sky. The ancient Finns also called magic spells *revontulet*, so another version of the story is that the Northern Lights are spell fires. Whichever interpretation, people always seem to agree that they appear as a mystical omen of things to come.'

I turned on my side and sought out his face in the darkness. 'What kind of things?' I said.

His lips started to form into a smile.

'It depends on which version you want.' His eyes shone with amusement and I smiled back, raising an eyebrow in question.

'Some say it means there is a frost coming, or perhaps even a blizzard. But there is another version of the story, though this may be propaganda put about by the Finnish tourist board to get more visitors to the place.'

'Go on,' I encouraged.

'Well, there is also the school of thought that the Northern Lights are a bringer of fertility, a blessing on developing relationships, and therefore one of the most romantic signs there can be.'

It was hard to tell in the dark, but I thought I detected a slight sparkle in his gaze as he told me this. I realised my hand was still in his. Even through the thickness of our respective gloves, I could feel the warmth and strength of it. I found myself wishing there weren't quite so many layers separating us. The loungers creaked beneath us as first I, and then Tommi leaned in towards each other.

And then a bleep from Tommi's mobile interrupted our moment of quiet togetherness. I willed him to ignore it and to carry on sharing this moment together without the outside world intruding, but the phone beeped insistently again and Tommi stood up. He checked the screen and smiled.

'Sorry, just a message about Gurta. She's doing really well,' he said.

Suddenly the magic of the evening vanished and some instinct told me the Northern Lights wouldn't be returning tonight. If they were a portent of developing relationships, the prophecy wasn't aimed in my direction. I must be mad to be harbouring tender thoughts towards Tommi when he already had a girlfriend.

'It's time for us both to get out of the cold,' said Tommi in a business-like tone. 'It can take you unawares out here, and neither of us have moved in a while. That can be dangerous.'

I wanted to tell him that I felt far from cold.

'I think I'll grab a drink to warm up,' I said casually, wanting to act normally now it was clear that the heightened moment I thought we'd both been experiencing had been more of a one-way thing.

He shot me a concerned look, which immediately irritated me. I stood up and stretched.

'Non-alcoholic, I promise. You can trust me, you know.' I folded my arms defensively.

He didn't say anything, which made me feel even worse.

'You can trust me,' I repeated. 'Oh, what's the point?' I stomped off towards my cabin. The beauty of the last half hour had turned sour and I didn't want him to see how riled I was.

'Perhaps the question isn't whether I trust you, but whether you trust yourself,' he called softly after me. The man was too infuriating for words.

Chapter Twenty-Two

In a defiant mood, I changed direction and decided to visit Rudi in the bar. I had no intention of breaking my vow of temperance, but I didn't see why I should have to avoid the place altogether and stay closeted up in my bedroom while the rest of the world carried on living. Rudi was in an ebullient mood. He made a great show of throwing a cover over the bottles of alcohol and shaking his finger at me in mock disapproval. I knew he was only teasing, but I was feeling fragile and didn't find it very funny. Clearly Tommi had had words with the rest of the staff. I didn't like the idea of him talking about me behind my back.

'Sorry, Lucy, is it too soon?' Rudi asked, slapping his wrist and flinching as he did it a bit too vigorously. 'Rudi by name, rude by nature. Maybe I should let that be my radio catchphrase. I'm trying to persuade Aku to give me my own show, but for some reason he doesn't trust me not to say something inappropriate on air.' He pushed a bowl of nuts across the bar to me. 'Help yourself. On the house, naturally. Maybe Aku would change his mind if I could find a sensible producer who would keep me in line. What do you think? Do you know of anyone who could fulfil that criteria?'

I pretended to think about it. Rudi threw a bag of crisps in my direction.

'Salt and vinegar, my favourite. Well, if this is the standard of producer payment, maybe I could consider helping you out. I'm not sure if I quite come under the banner of "sensible", but I could probably give you the benefit of my vast experience of messing up during live broadcasts so you don't fall into the same traps.'

Rudi punched the air. 'It's a deal. Help yourself to salt and vinegar crisps whenever you like. But maybe don't do it when Tommi's around. Now, let me fix you a *glögi*. It'll warm you through and there isn't a touch of the wicked stuff in it. Just hot berry juice and some raisins in the bottom to liven things up.'

'Sounds exactly what I need.'

I heard the outer door opening, and Tommi arrived in a cloud of cold air. I turned away from him, still angry at the complicated way I felt towards him.

Rudi got up abruptly. 'I remembered I'm out of raisins. Excuse me, boss, I need to go and fetch them.'

He scurried out of the room, leaving Tommi and I alone. I started stacking up the beer mats, not sure what to do with myself. How could I go from feeling so comfortable with him, to feeling so irritated and upset?

'I feel like I should apologise.' He broke the silence first.

'Maybe I have pushed too hard with the whole alcohol thing. I'm not trying to be your nursemaid or tell you what to do. If you say you don't have a problem, then I believe you.' He paused, and when he started speaking again, it was slowly, as if he was carefully searching for each word and weighing it up before he committed to saying it. 'Ever since you arrived here, I detected this sadness in you, something deeper than the drama from which you were fleeing. I founded Wild Zone because I want to give something back to the area which has given me so much. When I first drew up the plans, it wasn't the design of the buildings and the facilities which were most important to me. At the heart of it, I wanted Wild Zone to feel like a place of sanctuary and happiness. A place to be at one with nature and where people can come to an understanding about their place in the world. I guess, in my clumsy way, I was trying to help you find that, but I fear I have been overbearing and bossy, projecting my thoughts onto you, when I should be allowing you and everyone else to find their own path. What I am trying to say is, it is your choice how you find your happiness.'

I nodded, moved by his honesty and perception. There was a quality in his openness, a feeling that the person standing before me was a thoroughly decent and trustworthy man. It inspired me to do something I'd never dared before; open up in return. I turned to face him, determined to stop hiding myself away, even though the thought of laying myself bare in this way utterly terrified me.

'You're right. I don't think I realised it myself at first, but that is one thing which this part of the world gives you; plenty of time to think without distractions. And I've certainly been doing a lot of that since I arrived. I feel a bit like I've been on a treadmill ever since I was a teenager. I think I needed to always be busy, always have a distraction, because if I dared stop and think, I was terrified of being overwhelmed.'

I took a deep breath, knowing that this was the point of no return.

'The thing is, when I was fifteen, my dad was killed by a drink-driver. Dad was driving home from work at lunchtime. He was on a half day so he could come and see me perform in the school show. Someone else had been having a boozy lunchbreak; they missed the stop sign at the junction and that was that. The paramedics rushed Dad to hospital, but all the doctors could do was reduce his pain and call us there in time to say goodbye to him. There are no words to describe what it was like to see him lying in that bed, wires coming out of him, surrounded by machinery which ultimately couldn't make any difference.'

All these years later, I could still picture that exact scene, like it was burned on the back of my eyes. I always tried to avoid talking about that period of my life, even to Mum. Yet here I was, voluntarily pouring my heart out to a man I'd known only a few weeks. But despite our relatively brief acquaintance, I instinctively knew that I could trust him with this raw side of me. He didn't judge, just tried to understand and accept; things that I needed to learn how to do myself. His quiet solidarity inspired me to be honest in a way I had never allowed myself to be before.

'All the time I was standing there at the hospital bedside, I was burning with anger, raging that it was my dad lying there while the other driver had walked away from the crash. It was so unfair, so horribly unfair. But instead of focusing on my dad and saying all the things I wanted to say to him, I could only think about my hatred of that other driver. And so I let that driver steal my goodbye to Dad as well. And I've never forgiven myself for it.' I swallowed a sob. 'How is anyone ever meant to get over something like that?'

Tommi placed his hand next to mine, our little fingers joined by the faintest touch. The gentle gesture of compassion gave me the strength to carry on.

'There is not a day that goes by when I don't wish things could have been different. Whatever success, whatever pleasure I have in life, there is always regret that Dad isn't here to enjoy it. Bereavement like that is an indelible mark, an extra weight I carry with me all the time. You probably think I'm a hypocrite, guzzling booze when my dad was killed by someone who'd been doing just that.'

I searched Tommi's gaze for confirmation that that was exactly what he thought of me, but despite my best efforts to read revulsion in his eyes, I could only see empathy, empathy which I still wasn't sure I deserved.

'I've never drunk and driven; that is a line I have never, would never cross,' I said fiercely. It felt important that Tommi knew that. And then the strength went out of my voice as I tentatively articulated the fear which I had been doing my best to ignore for so long. 'But I will admit that there have been times when I have allowed my consumption to get out of hand. I have acted in a risky way because of alcohol. I've always excused it as the lifestyle I had to lead if I wanted to be a success in my profession, you know, being loud and fun, the party girl everyone loves to listen to. Who was I kidding? Trying to drown the pain is pointless. The scar will always be there. It may fade, but it will always be there. But I am tired of it dictating how I live my life. I want to emerge from the shadows, for me. Not for anyone else. I'm not quite sure what's left behind of the real me, but I guess this is my opportunity to find out. And you're right. The next thing I need to do is to learn how to trust myself again.'

It felt strange to say out loud the thoughts that had been burning away at me since I can't quite remember. I'd always thought confessing to all the fear and crappiness which swirled around in my head would leave me feeling vulnerable and exposed. But in Tommi's quiet, solid presence, it felt safe to pour my heart out and lay bare my fears. He didn't try to interrupt or offer the traditional words of comfort which always felt so hollow to me. Instead he respected my emotions by listening to them, really listening. I could feel the warmth emanating from his hand. I placed my palm on top of his, a quiet gesture of thanks. A heartbeat later, he placed his other hand on top of mine, enclosing it in a gentle hold, sharing his strength with me.

Chapter Twenty-Three

I'm not going to lie and say the next few days passed easily now that I'd got things off my chest and admitted to myself why I'd got into such a destructive pattern. It felt like there was a great lack of purpose in my life, and I had to work hard to remind myself how I used to have fun before I had got side-tracked by the party lifestyle.

As the airport was still closed due to technical problems which prevented new guests from flying in, the pace of life at Wild Zone slowed down even more. Occasionally some hardy souls out hiking would stop by for lunch, but mostly we were left to our own devices to fill our time as we wished. Tommi wasn't around much, to my disappointment. I figured he was probably making the most of his opportunity to spend time with Gurta. I felt a pang of jealousy whenever I thought of her. I hoped she knew how lucky she was to have a man like him in her life.

ACFM meanwhile got the benefit of my unexpected free time and desire to keep myself busy. Every morning I'd hike across the lake to the radio station to open it up, then I'd set up the playlist for Aku's show. I'd even been brave enough to check a couple of news websites; the really serious, strait-laced ones which I didn't think would still be gossiping about Loose Lucy and Team Serenity, so that I could prepare a list of conversation topics Aku could include in his programme. Google Translate had become my best friend as I used it to try to translate my suggestions into Finnish. Occasionally Aku would raise his eyebrows at some of the weirder mistranslations the search engine had come up with, but mostly I felt like I was doing a good job. I had never thought of myself as a behind-the-scenes kind of person before, but I was finding a new satisfaction in performing that role.

Rudi got his wish and did his first-ever live radio show under my close supervision. I was surprised at how nervous he was beforehand, but, just as I had suspected, he was a natural; full of enthusiasm and prepared to have fun with the listeners, all half a dozen of them. I was sure the audience would increase as word spread about the new, improved line-up on ACFM. It felt good to be achieving something in the broadcast sphere again.

As I grew in confidence, I started to wean myself back into communicating with the outside world. This involved me turning my phone on for half an hour each day and forcing myself to go through my emails and messages. Unfortunately, the hate mail was still coming in. Despite my best intentions, it still had the power to reduce me to a quivering wreck of a human, but then I defy anyone to read twenty back-to-back messages describing in graphic detail various terrible fates which I apparently deserved without feeling some kind of fear. I tried to laugh them off by reading bits out in funny voices and rating their inventiveness on a scale of one-to-ten, but they still left me feeling the kind of cold terror that even Wild Zone's roaring fires couldn't chase away.

One morning, Tommi walked in as I was partway through reading one particularly sweary missive out loud.

'Are you still getting that awful stuff?' he said, a look of disgust on his face.

'I'd like to say they're tailing off slightly, but maybe that's wishful thinking. Skye messaged me saying Serenity – that's Jonno's girlfriend – seems to have had a second wind in her career because of videogate, so I wouldn't be surprised if her people are fanning the flames behind the scenes in order to keep her in the public eye. I guess my loss is her gain.'

He slumped onto the sofa next to me and kicked his shoes off. I suppressed a smile when I caught sight of his huskies-in-sunglasses patterned socks.

'I cannot understand that world of so-called celebrity,' he said. 'I hear kids saying they want to be famous, yet they have no idea what they want to be famous for. They seem to have lost sight of the idea of working hard to achieve something. They want instant fame and glory wrapped up in a big bow and handed to them. It's completely bizarre to me that anyone would be so manipulative and condone that kind of abuse of another person in order to get ahead.'

'Sadly, people seem to think that because they write it online, it somehow doesn't count as much. Hopefully they wouldn't dream of saying this kind of stuff to people's faces. I think they forget a real person is on the receiving end of it. And before you say I should ignore it and delete the lot, I did think about that. But a stupidly optimistic part of me hopes that among all the dross will be a clue which might give away who was behind the video in the first place.'

Tommi leaned over to look at the phone screen.

'English is not my first language, but without wishing to appear boastful, I think I've got a better grasp of it than some of these people.'

I laughed. 'Yes, their use of spelling and grammar can sometimes be incredibly bizarre. Actually, it's the ones who can use apostrophes correctly that are the most frightening. I think they're more likely to have the ability to actually follow through on their threats. Though whether some of them are physically possible is another thing altogether.'

I turned my phone off decisively and put it to one side.

'There we go. The torture is over for one day. I've narrowed down a couple of YouTube accounts which seem to have been early broadcasters of the video, so maybe that's a step closer to tracking down my original tormenter. Got to look on the bright side.'

'I'm afraid you might not have so much time for detective work after tomorrow,' said Tommi. 'I've had word from the airport that the runway is open again so our next group of guests will be arriving in the afternoon.'

'That's great news.' I smiled and nudged his shoulder affectionately. We shared a much closer bond after our heart-to-heart, but I was trying my best to keep things on a brother-and-sister level, not wanting to be responsible for coming between him and Gurta. I may have acquired the reputation of being 'Loose Lucy', but it was far from my reality. Although I was starting to wish for more than friendship with Tommi, if that was all he had to offer, then I would settle for it.

'It may also mean you might not be able to do quite so much over at ACFM. I think it really worked having you assist with the demonstrations for some of the wilderness skills, and it would be good if you could help out again, especially as I've got some other tasks in mind for Rudi.'

I glowed inwardly at the praise. I'd happily sacrifice my leisure time to help Tommi out. He looked much brighter now that he knew the guests could fly in again. I knew how worried he'd been for the future of his business. Even though the situation at the airport had been out of his control, it would still have damaged the reputation of Wild Zone as a holiday destination.

Tommi cleared his throat. 'Before the guests arrive and disturb our peace, I was hoping to ask you something.' He shifted awkwardly on the sofa, suddenly looking rather apprehensive. He cleared his throat again.

'Are you coming down with something? I think I've got some cough sweets in my room if you need them,' I offered.

He smiled. 'Sorry, my throat is fine. I was simply remembering what it felt like to be a gawky teenager about to ask out the prettiest girl in school.'

I blinked. Had I heard him correctly?

'I was wondering if you would like to have dinner with me tonight?'

'What, you mean a date?' I asked.

'Yes, a date,' he said, as if it was the most obvious thing in the world. 'I enjoy your company. I hope you enjoy mine. I'd like to spend some more time with you. If that's OK with you.'

'But what about Gurta?' I said.

He looked confused. 'What about Gurta?'

'Won't she be upset about you going on a date with me?'

He laughed. 'I'm sure she'll be fine with it.'

I pulled a face. 'Really? Are you honestly telling me that your girlfriend would be fine with you taking out another woman on a date? Do you not think that would be a little wrong?' I was starting to reassess my opinion of Tommi.

A strange expression crossed his face. Was that a twitch of a grin I saw there? He leaned forward and pulled his shoes back on.

'Perhaps we should go and ask her,' he said, standing up and walking out of the room, seemingly confident I would follow him.

I stayed stubbornly put. I know there are all kinds of relationships nowadays, but being the other woman was definitely not for me.

Tommi poked his head back round the door. 'She's only downstairs. I brought her and the family across just this morning. She's doing really well. It was touch and go at the birth, but she and the little ones are thriving now.'

Something didn't add up. Either Tommi was a massively heartless brute who was asking another woman out on a date shortly after his partner had given birth, or Gurta wasn't quite who I thought she was.

Curiosity got the better of me, and I followed him downstairs. But instead of turning right into the storeroom, he turned left, past the sauna and changing room, and through a doorway I'd not noticed before.

'This leads to my work apartment,' he explained. 'I have a home off base, but when the guests are here, I prefer to be able to stay close at hand in case I am needed.'

I hung back as he turned the door handle, still not quite sure what I was going to encounter.

'Gurta, are you decent?' he called through the open door.

I'd had enough. I knew he was teasing me, but I still hadn't worked out how. The bark gave the game away. I pushed past Tommi and followed the sound of whimpering until I found the famous Gurta. She was stretched out on a sofa, a cloud of wriggling and yelping bundles of fur rolling around on the floor at her paws. She regarded me with interest as I entered the room, but didn't stir from her safe haven out of reach of the puppies. They meanwhile fell on me with glee, pouncing on my feet and taking it in turns to pull at my shoelaces.

'She's a husky. Of course she is,' I said. 'And a very gorgeous one she is too.'

Gurta wagged her tail. I wasn't sure if she was a bilingual pooch, but the language of appreciation is pretty universally understood by dogs.

Tommi arrived at my side, and the puppies swarmed around his ankles. Gurta seemed to grin as soon as she saw her master.

'Gurta, meet Lucy. Lucy wanted me to ask your

permission before I take her out on a date. Do we get your blessing?'

I swear Gurta looked carefully between us, as if pondering her answer, before she finally thumped her tail in agreement.

Tommi grinned. 'If Gurta approves of you, then you must be alright. She's never been wrong in her judgement.'

I waded through the sea of puppies until I reached her. I held my hand out and she sniffed it carefully, then pushed her head towards my palm. I obeyed my instructions and stroked her. Her smooth coat was glossy and I could feel the power of her muscles beneath her skin.

'I'm guessing you like to go sledding, Gurta?' I said. She sat up abruptly and looked hopefully in Tommi's direction. 'Sorry, maybe I shouldn't have said the "s" word.'

Tommi gave up trying to stop the puppies nibbling his shoes, and sat down on the floor, allowing them to use him as a human climbing frame. The puppies looked tiny in comparison to him, each dog scarcely bigger than his hands. His every movement was slow and careful, and even when they nipped him a bit too hard with their razor-sharp teeth, he was kind and gentle when he removed them. The sight of such an attractive man surrounded by a bunch of adorable puppies was enough to set my heart beating faster.

'Yes, the "s" word gets a certain someone very excited,' he said. For a few seconds in my hot-man-with-cute-puppies-induced daze, I wasn't sure what he was referring to. 'Gurta's on maternity leave at the moment, though I'm pretty sure she'd be out like a shot pulling the sleds if I gave her the chance. These little ones are six weeks old now, so it won't be long before she's back to her normal routine. The guys who run the husky trips for Wild Zone have been helping me out by looking after her while she was whelping. It wasn't the best timing to be having puppies and starting a new business, but these things can't be helped.'

'Are you going to keep any of the puppies?' I said. 'How many are there of them? They never seem to stay still long enough for me to count them.'

'There are five, but sometimes it feels like twenty-five. I always said I wouldn't keep one, but I have a feeling I may be changing my mind. Rudi and Johanna have both expressed an interest in taking one, so at least two of them will be regular visitors to Wild Zone. And the guys at the kennels have their eyes on two.'

'Which leaves one left over for you,' I said.

He smiled. 'Maybe. We'll see. Now I know I asked you out for dinner, but actually do you mind if we eat here? I've got Rudi down on puppy-sitting duty tomorrow, but there's no one around to watch them tonight.'

I joined Tommi sitting on the floor and laughed as the puppies pounced at a loose thread on my fleecy trousers. 'I can think of no better place to enjoy an evening. And for future reference, when you're asking a girl out, I'd drop in the fact you've got gorgeous dogs in the first breath. It'll definitely give you a better hit rate.'

'As long as it works on you, that's all that matters to me,' he said. 'Let me go and get you some *glögi*. And if you're really looking to win Gurta's endless devotion, you could help me fix her dinner.' Gurta jumped up from her position on the sofa and let out a single bark. 'Look, there you go, that's another English word she apparently knows. She's far more intelligent than I give her credit for. She gets fed before the puppies. They have a tendency to fall asleep in their food. They're full of energy one minute and then spark out the next.'

Tommi's apartment within Wild Zone was barely bigger than my cabin in the grounds. Add into the mix five puppies and their mum, plus two adults, and there was a lot of bumping into each other and stumbling over small creatures. But there was also a lot of laughter and it felt so natural sitting down to dinner together. Back at home, I wouldn't have been seen dead in the shapeless fleecy top and trouser combo I was rocking today, and I wouldn't have dreamed of going on a first date without an armour of several carefully applied layers of makeup and a decent haircut. After constant exposure to the cold, my hair was currently giving a good demonstration of the frizz-inducing effects of static, and I dreaded to think how my skin looked without my usual confidence-boosting bronzer. But the way Tommi looked at me made me feel beautiful anyway. He was looking pretty fine himself. For the first time, I found myself sending a little vote of thanks to the viral video-maker. Maybe the effects hadn't been entirely bad after all.

'Here we go,' said Tommi, putting the plates down on the table. 'A variation on reindeer stew; I thought tonight we'd go for fish for a change. Freshly caught and local, of course.'

'Lovely. It smells absolutely delicious. But how on earth

do you catch fish at this time of year? Surely the ice makes it pretty difficult.'

Tommi gestured for me to help myself to vegetables. 'It's not the easiest of tasks, and I'm afraid I don't have the patience for it. Aku sent these over. When he's not entertaining us on the airwaves, he enjoys ice fishing. It generally involves cutting through the ice with a chainsaw and then sitting for a long time in the cold until a fish bites on the bait.'

'Were these caught on our lake? And should I be looking out for fishing holes when I walk over to the radio station?' I asked, thinking with horror how many times I'd tramped across there in the dark.

'He prefers the next lake over. He says there are more fish there. And he always cordons off wherever he's been fishing, although it doesn't take long for the ice to form back over the hole as thick as ever.'

The fish practically melted in my mouth. I don't know if it was all the fresh air I was getting nowadays, but I had a huge appetite and everything tasted incredible. The company wasn't bad either. We talked and talked, the conversation wide-ranging and interesting. This was a man who stimulated my brain as well as my senses.

For dessert we had my favourite cloudberry crumble.

'You certainly know the way to a girl's heart,' I said, tucking in eagerly.

'Perhaps you could have another go at making your cloudberry smoothie for the guests. If you want to, that is,' said Tommi, with a smile.

I grimaced as I remembered how my well-intentioned smoothie making had gone so wrong soon after my arrival.

'If I'm feeling brave,' I said with a wink. 'It didn't go down well with the boss last time. Don't want to get on the wrong side of him again. Speaking of cloudberries, you've got a bit of crumble on your face.'

'Help me get rid of it?' he invited. I leaned across the table and brushed it off with my finger. He caught my hand and stood up, pulling me gently towards him.

The stubble on his chin delicately tickled my face as his lips met mine. I ran my hands through his hair and pressed myself closer towards him, relishing the sensation of his body against mine. We backed up towards the sofa and fell onto it, somehow avoiding treading on puppies along the way. I reached up and ran my hands under his top. His firm stomach contracted as my fingers ran over it.

'Sorry, are my hands cold?' I apologised.

'Quite the opposite,' he murmured into my ear, mirroring my movements. This time it was my turn to gasp as his fingers traced their way up my ribs. I stretched my arms over my head and helped him to pull the fleecy layers over my head. We both laughed as the static crackled in my hair. We kissed again with growing intent. My fingers fumbled as I undid Tommi's belt, my body zinging with anticipation. I couldn't get close enough to him.

And then a cold wet nose was pushing us apart and Gurta clambered onto the sofa with a groan, stretching out across our discarded clothes until we were forced to stand up and cede the space to her. She pointedly yawned, closed her eyes and started snoring.

Tommi and I looked at each other and burst out laughing at the ridiculousness of the situation.

'Maybe she isn't quite so approving as we thought,' I suggested.

'I think we're being encouraged to go somewhere more private away from sleepy pups,' said Tommi. 'Shall we?'

He took my hand and led me through to his bedroom where we picked up where we'd left off.

Chapter Twenty-Four

The next morning, I woke to find myself sandwiched between Tommi and a snoring Gurta who had obviously decided to retreat further away from her noisy puppies at some point during the night. It was impossible to move without disturbing either of them, so, with a feeling of great contentment, I smiled, closed my eyes and went back to sleep again.

The second time I woke up, my sleeping companions had left me. There was a note on the pillow from Tommi letting me know he'd taken Gurta out for a walk. I took a leisurely shower, and pulled on yesterday's clothes. At least the advantage of wearing shapeless fleecy stuff every day was that it was much harder to tell when you hadn't put on a fresh outfit. I helped myself to a bowl of cereal and then settled down to play with the puppies, who seemed happily oblivious to the fact that their mum had gone out for a bit.

'Fancy finding you here,' said Rudi, marching in

through the front door without knocking. I thanked my lucky stars I'd got dressed when I had.

'I popped over to play with Gurta's gorgeous offspring,' I said. It wasn't that I was ashamed of spending the night with Tommi, but in such a small place as Wild Zone, I had no desire for our fledgling relationship to be the main topic of conversation.

'Sure you did,' said Rudi, looking pointedly at my breakfast things.

'Which of the gang are you keeping?' I asked, trying to change the subject.

Rudi dived down and picked up one squirming bundle, the biggest boy of the litter.

'This brute. I think he fits my macho image. Actually, I'm sure he'll be a massive softie, but he's a cheeky one, always leading the others into mischief, and I couldn't resist. I still haven't decided on a name, so any suggestions welcome.'

'Maybe you should have a radio phone-in about it,' I suggested.

Rudi gave me a high-five, causing his pet to yelp with excitement.

'Amazing idea! Thanks, Lucy. I'll definitely do that.'

'You might want to put some rules in place though, or he'll end up getting called something like Husky McHuskington. Unless it's just us Brits who love coming up with silly names for things. Every year some council or other launches a competition to name a new gritter and, without fail, someone suggests Spready Mercury or Usain Salt.'

Rudi looked confused.

'I'll explain later,' I said. 'But first I'm going to subject myself to my daily dose of abuse so I can spend the rest of the morning getting ready for the guests.'

'Good luck!' Rudi called after me. 'And I quite like McHuskington for a name. Maybe you could phone in and suggest that.'

What had I started?

I wandered upstairs and removed my phone from the locker behind reception where I'd been storing it for safe-keeping. Taking a deep breath, I turned it on and pushed it away from me as if it was a device that was about to explode. I cringed as I heard the notifications beep go crazy once again. Today, the tone for a text chimed in with the rest.

Praying that the trolls hadn't started texting me as well, I dared myself to look. I relaxed when I saw the message was from Skye, but I didn't say calm for long.

'EMERGENCY. CALL ME ASAP' filled the screen.

My mind instantly went to worst-case scenarios. I hit speed-dial and sat with my heart in my mouth as I waited for her to answer.

'Lucy, love, the important thing is to stay calm,' was Skye's opening gambit, which had the unsurprising effect of making me react in exactly the opposite way. I jumped up and started nervously pacing, unable to sit still while I waited for Skye to drop her bombshell.

'Are you OK? The baby? Henri? My mum?'

'Yes, yes, yes, and I haven't heard anything to the contrary. Your mum has been calling round with lots of knitwear for the little one and she was absolutely on form the last time she visited.'

I heaved a sigh of relief. 'Phew. So what's the big emergency?'

'Before I say anything, I want to apologise. It's entirely my fault and I feel really, really bad. I'm a terrible friend.'

There was genuine distress in her voice. I hurried to reassure her.

'Skye, hon, nothing you could do would make me think you're a terrible friend. But you're really starting to worry me. Could you give me the headline? I'm sure whatever it is can't be that bad.'

'Mike's on his way to Wild Zone because he wants to scout it out as a venue for a winter special show.' She rushed the answer out so quickly it sounded like she was pronouncing one long word rather than a sentence.

My breath caught in my throat as I picked apart what she'd said. The revelation was like being punched in the stomach. The idea of Mike descending on my sanctuary made me feel violated all over again. I forced myself to count slowly to ten before I blurted out something I later regretted.

'Mike. As in *Mike* Mike? Producer Mike? Mike the guy who exulted in my shame and was instrumental in getting me kicked off my show?' Asking for clarification was really only another way of torturing myself, but part of me was still clinging onto the faint hope that I'd misunderstood Skye.

'The very same,' she confirmed. 'And yes, he probably is going to be producer Mike once again. I've heard rumblings that the management are considering taking him off the presenting side of things. I think he's trying to pitch the winter special programme as a last-ditch attempt to impress and get a permanent presenting gig.'

My mind was racing. I'd long been pushing the station to let me go on the road and present the show from interesting locations. Cynics would say there wasn't any point in presenting radio on location as the audience can't see anything that you do, but even if they can't see it, they can still experience a different atmosphere out of the studio, and, guided by a decent presenter, they should be able to visualise a place almost as if they were there themselves. Putting personal animosity aside, I knew Mike would never manage to achieve such a feat. Skye would, but she wasn't the one on a plane heading over here.

'But Wild Zone? What are the odds of him coming to the one place in the world where I am? It's not exactly top of the Google search for winter holiday destinations, is it? Not yet at least,' I added loyally. If Tommi had his way, I suspected it soon would be.

There was a long pause at the other end of the line. 'Ah, I might have something to do with that,' mumbled Skye at last, sounding shamefaced.

'Go on,' I said.

'He knows my husband's from Finland, and when he was talking about Father Christmas living in Sweden, I had to put him right and point out that Lapland is Santa's domain. And I'm super proud of what my brother-in-law has achieved with Wild Zone, so I may have name-dropped the place to one or two people at work. But I swear I never mentioned it to Mike and I never told anyone that's where you are. He must have heard talk of Wild Zone from one of the others.'

My thoughts raced to another very important question.

'But why didn't Tommi warn me he'd be coming?'

Even Mike with his slapdash approach to organisation must have thought ahead to get permission to broadcast from here. There's no way the bosses would have paid for the trip otherwise.

'As far as I can tell, Mike made all the arrangements with Rudi when Tommi was busy off site. It's been sorted out so quickly, I suspect it's going to be as much a surprise to Tommi as it is to you.'

Of course that's how it had happened. I could just imagine Rudi enthusiastically getting swept up in Mike's plans and accepting the booking as if it was any other, without even considering the practicalities or the need to run it past the boss first. I couldn't be too angry with him. He had no way of knowing about Mike's connection to me as I'd avoided getting into specifics about work with him as much as possible. I was certain that Rudi would never have agreed to the trip if he'd had any idea how Mike's arrival at my sanctuary would make me feel, but it was too late now to regret not having confided in him properly before.

'I'm so sorry,' said Skye again, clearly worried by how quiet I'd gone. 'If it's any comfort, I'm pretty sure he has no idea that you're there, and there's still time for you to get away before he lands. Do you want me to book you a flight home?'

I was seriously tempted. It wasn't Mike's presence alone that was making me lean towards fleeing once again, but everything he represented. While I'd been here, I'd worried and stressed about the situation I'd escaped from, but the snowy surroundings of my wilderness hideaway had also created a barrier from the worst of it, wrapping me up in a cocoon of safety, even in spite of the occasional barbed comment from guests. Mike would break straight through that safety barrier, bringing the harsh reality of the outside world in to taint my haven. I knew he'd delight in bringing up the viral video at any opportunity, and he'd probably spend his time crowing over the fact that I was still suspended.

But would running away again really change anything? I wouldn't be returning to the job I loved, and the social media witch hunt was still well underway, never mind the anonymous stalker who'd targeted me at my own house. Who knew what additional threats had been posted through my letterbox by my haters since I'd been away? If I was being completely honest with myself, I'm not sure I'd ever feel safe there again.

And then there was everything I'd be leaving behind in Finland; my new friends, my burgeoning snow skills, ACFM, and, of course, Tommi. No, I couldn't and wouldn't run away from all these good things just because of Mike's unwelcome presence.

I took a deep breath.

'Don't worry about getting me a ticket, Skye. I'm going to stay. If Mike wants to come here, then he's welcome to. I'm not about to let him drive me away. And maybe once he's a captive audience, I can see if he knows more about the viral video than he's letting on.'

I was channelling my radio Lucy persona, hoping I sounded more confident than I felt as I put on enough cheeriness to convince Skye that it was OK for her to hang up and continue going about her day. The joy of last night had vanished, replaced with churning anxiety. I wanted to hide in my room, preferably with a drink powerful enough to numb my fear and give me the confidence to deal with Mike's presence. Shame filled me all over again at the direction my thoughts were going in. I should be strong enough to get through this without having to turn to the booze. But my feeling of vulnerability was fuelling my weakness. I didn't trust myself to stay in the main building, with the temptation of the bar stocked with its colourful bottles of confidence and comfort right to hand. Still, I hovered in place, frozen by my fear-induced dilemma. And then I heard Gurta barking downstairs and the noise jolted me back to my senses. I needed to take action. I hurried to the front door, strapped on my snow shoes and marched myself to the wilderness hut to put some distance between myself and my demons.

Chapter Twenty-Five

The hut felt a lot colder and emptier without Tommi's reassuring presence at my side. In the distance the frosty river was rushing past, the central channel a raging torrent of white foam, while along the bank, ice extended its grip over the slower, deeper waters. The wood stack had grown since our visit, and the chairs had moved position, but the rest of the building was otherwise unchanged; the fire still ready to be lit, the plates set for a friendly gathering of four.

In my haste to leave the main building at Wild Zone, I'd left my gloves behind. I'd realised almost the instant I stepped into the woods, but it seemed more important that I keep moving forward rather than turning back to get them. Despite keeping my hands in my pockets during my walk through the trees, my fingers were still painfully cold and clumsy in their movements and I dropped the match on the floor twice before I was finally able to strike a light and hold it out towards the kindling.

I must have learned *something* from Tommi's wilderness survival lessons, because before long, I'd got a cheery blaze going in the hearth. The brightness of the flames drew the darkness in so the features of the hut disappeared into shadow, but it was a price I was happy to pay for warmth. I held out my palms, the pain of the cold being chased out of my veins almost making me gasp out loud.

Gradually I managed to turn my thoughts away from the panicked craving for something which I knew would do me no good, and I was able to focus on my predicament in a more rational manner. There was nothing I could do to stop Mike arriving here, and there was nothing I could control about his behaviour once he arrived. But I could control my own behaviour and how I reacted to the situation. Whatever muck Mike tried to spread when he realised I was at his mercy, I would have to rise above it all. My Wild Zone family knew the nature of the abuse I'd been fleeing from, and I hoped that we'd built enough of a bond that they would trust in me over him. It was funny that I'd started to think of them as family, but that's the way it felt. Cut off from the rest of the world it was inevitable that bonds would form quickly and tightly. But I liked to think there was more to it than mere geography, that we'd recognised kindred spirits in each other, despite the superficial differences of our backgrounds. At least, that's how it felt with Tommi. Despite my party-girl reputation and former fast-living lifestyle, I normally moved much more slowly in relationships, nervous of showing too much of myself too quickly, wary of trusting and being hurt. But I didn't think that Tommi would hurt me, not intentionally at any rate. He was kind, steady and utterly dependable; characteristics which are all too often dismissed out of hand. I had a feeling that were I to ask it of him, he would refuse to allow Mike to broadcast from Wild Zone, choosing to protect my sensibilities over the benefits which exposure on a popular radio show would bring. The idea was extremely tempting.

I sat and imagined the scene, and I could almost picture the flash of disappointment which would appear on Tommi's face before he would carefully mask it. He would say he wouldn't hold it against me, but what if he did? His fledgling business was fragile. You only had to look at the amount of kit waiting in the storage room for guests to use to know that he must have invested serious amounts of money getting everything ready. The fact that this place was a labour of love was obvious from every inch of beautifully carved wood and carefully selected furnishings. No, I couldn't do it to him. However unsettling the prospect of my former producer's arrival, I would find the strength somewhere to get through it.

I wondered whether I should reveal my connection with Mike to the rest of the Wild Zone staff before his arrival. They would soon work it out for themselves, but it would be good to tell them my side of the story before he muddied the waters. I bet Rudi would fix up Mike with leaky waterproofs if I asked him to. I caught myself. Tommi needed Mike's visit to be a complete success. And I needed to stop gearing myself up for a battle which might never happen. I would keep quiet and attempt to make out it wasn't a big deal. I would endeavour to treat Mike as I would any other guest, proving to myself that I could be the bigger person. Positive thinking was the way ahead. Maybe he would be too focused on the job in hand to waste time tormenting me. Producing a live broadcast outside the comforts of the studio was a big challenge after all.

I shook my head. I knew I was deluding myself. If what Skye had heard was true, Mike's position in front of the microphone was growing increasingly precarious, and he was the type of person who would choose to try to improve his prospects by doing someone else down, rather than looking to himself for the answer. And didn't I know how hard it is to look at yourself rather than blame things that go wrong on external factors? Mike's arrival would test me like nothing else had so far in Finland, but I needed to hold onto this moment of clarity and determination. When things got tough, I would remind myself that I had been through much worse. I gazed at the glowing embers of the fire until they died down into ashy blackness and promised myself that things would be OK. And then I set the hearth again, gathered some extra branches to add to the wood stack and shut the door carefully so the hideaway was ready for the next person.

I took the journey back to Wild Zone at the quickest pace I could muster so my fingers didn't freeze all over again. The fact that I could manage something approximating a run in my snow shoes proved how far I had come since my arrival in the wilderness. I hung onto the knowledge, needing every bit of positivity I could muster.

When I emerged from the treeline I fought the urge to go back to my room and have a quiet lunch of whatever was lurking in my cupboards. Standing in the clearing in front of the main building, I knew I had to face my fear now or it would grow exponentially. I tramped up the steps, kicked off the icy clods from the spikes of my snow shoes, unclipped them and then quietly stepped into the building. My slippers were waiting by the heater inside the door where someone had thoughtfully placed them so they were warm for my return. That small act of kindness gave me more of a glow than the central heating ever could. It also gave me the strength to march straight over to the bar and stare down the bottles like they were personal enemies.

'You are not going to win,' I addressed them, no doubt sounding like a complete idiot. But somehow saying the words out loud imbued me with more confidence in myself. Naturally, they gave no response. They looked so innocuous, and yet they could cause so much trouble. No, I corrected myself. It was the choices of people which caused the trouble; the driver who'd chosen to get behind the wheel of a car even though he knew he was over the limit and then encountered my dad; me choosing to have 'just one more' at too many nights out to the point where alcohol became a crutch. Well, things were different now. I turned my back on the bottles and marched to the kitchen.

'Pleasant walk?' asked Johanna.

I quickly glanced at her face to see if there was more to her question, fearing that she might have heard my little exchange in the bar, but her expression was open and friendly as always.

'It was good to be in the fresh air and get some exercise.'

'I heard you got quite a bit last night,' she replied with a wink.

I grinned and allowed myself to be gently teased. I was beginning to accept there was no point trying to keep my sleepover with Tommi a secret around here.

'I don't kiss and tell,' was as far as I would go.

'That's exactly what Tommi said when Rudi was teasing him.'

Fortunately Johanna was a true Finn in that she had respect for other people's privacy, and that was the extent of the questioning I received.

'Could you help me get ready for the next lot of guests? Perhaps you could make a welcome smoothie for them?'

It was on the tip of my tongue to tell her all about one particular guest, but then I recalled my earlier promise to myself.

'Sure, will do.' I agreed, although I really didn't want to. I put a lot of love into making my smoothies, and frankly Mike didn't deserve the effort. But I reminded myself that if it helped Tommi, that would be all that mattered. But Johanna obviously heard the reluctance in my voice, because she suggested something else.

'Or perhaps you could help me make *Rönttönen* instead?'

For the millionth time, I promised myself I would sit down with a Finnish language book and learn more than just the words for hello, please and thank you.

'Sounds...yummy?' I said hesitantly, not quite sure what I was agreeing to.

Johanna laughed. 'It is, I promise. It is deliciously sweet and filling. You cannot come to Finland without trying one of our traditional pastries. Skye is a particular fan as it is vegan.'

'Then I really had better learn how to make it.'

Johanna poured a pile of potatoes onto the worksurface and indicated that I should start peeling them.

'It's a sweet treat, you say?' I asked, wondering how on earth the potatoes would fit in.

Johanna started sorting through a pile of bright red lingonberries, checking their surfaces for blemishes before she put them in a sieve and rinsed them under the sink.

'Absolutely. The story goes that a woman was storing potatoes in her cellar, and they froze and went all sweet and seemingly unusable. Instead of throwing them away, she mashed them up with wild berries, filled a rye dough crust and created a delicious treat.'

'So I guess the moral of the story is that even when something appears to be ruined, something can still be salvaged from it?'

Her eyes twinkled. 'You are absolutely right, Lucy. Would you like the potato masher?'

I spent the next few hours pondering that idea while I calmed my nerves by pummelling potatoes and kneading dough into submission.

Chapter Twenty-Six

Despite being convinced that I'd spend the whole night awake and worrying about Mike's arrival, I slept surprisingly well. As Tommi had an early start to collect the new guests, he'd suggested I sleep in my own room, so he didn't disturb me when he left, although that hadn't stopped us staying up rather late snuggling on the sofa and continuing our mission to get to know each other better. I missed the comforting warmth of his embrace, but I welcomed the solitude of my own bed as it meant I could concentrate on psyching myself up for the challenges ahead of me. It also meant it was easier for me to keep my promise to myself not to ask Tommi to intervene over Mike's visit.

I scrolled through my phone in bed, trying to see if there had been any developments in my situation since I last checked. With the imminent arrival of my colleague, I'd abandoned my policy of only checking my phone once a day. I figured it was better to be forewarned and forearmed. There did seem to be slightly less vitriol being sent in my direction, although I could have been deluding myself. Maybe I was finally growing immune to the insults and threats of violence. I wished for the thousandth time that internet trolls would remember that there were real living, breathing individuals who were hurting because of their nasty hobby.

I cast it to one side, stretched out my feet and savoured the comforting warmth of my covers. I didn't need to open the shutters to know that it would still be dark outside. I wondered what the snow would look like today. I would never have thought it possible for the white stuff to assume so many different forms, but I was beginning to understand why Scandinavians have so many names for it. I hoped it was a glittering day. I could do with some sparkle in the background to give me a boost.

I knew I should get up, but instead I burrowed down even further, pulling the covers over my head and hiding away. As long as I stayed in bed, I could kid myself that the day hadn't begun, thereby delaying the dreaded moment when I'd have to be in the same room as Mike. I'd about decided that my best course of action was to hibernate for the rest of my stay when my phone buzzed again. Reluctantly, I reached a hand out and scrabbled around until I found it. Like ripping off a plaster, it was probably better to get it over and done with quickly. Thankfully, it was a nice message, this time in the form of a good luck text from Skye urging me to look on the bright side, peppered with her usual liberal use of emojis. In amongst the crossed fingers and the power pose arms, she'd used the sad face multiple times and reinforced her emotions with a gif of a puppy looking very ashamed. I pinged back a text assuring her that I didn't blame her in the slightest bit for Mike's imminent arrival, although the pessimistic part of me wished she hadn't been quite so enthusiastic talking up her brother-in-law's venture to anyone around the radio station who'd listen. But then again, Skye's enthusiasm was one of her most endearing qualities, and I wouldn't really want her to change that.

Vowing for the millionth time to be more like Skye and try to look on the bright side, I finally hauled myself out of bed, and set about getting ready for the day. As was my usual habit, I'd had a shower last night so my skin wasn't doused shortly before it was due to brave the elements. And as I was also following Johanna's advice against washing my face or using any kind of moisturiser, my morning preparations didn't take very long at all. Once I'd brushed my teeth, I stared into the mirror and found myself comparing my appearance to the person who had arrived at Wild Zone all those weeks ago. Gone was the thick layer of makeup and the smattering of stress acne along my jaw. My skin was clear now and brightened by regular exposure to the unpolluted fresh air. My eyes had lost the dull sheen of exhaustion and over-consumption, and were instead sparkling and hopeful, despite the ordeal I was anticipating. My body felt powerful and stronger, rather than bloated and worn-out, thanks to a combination of regular, healthy meals and the physical challenges of living in a snowbound hideaway. Skye was right. Out of every bad situation, there was always something positive to be found. I smiled encouragingly at my reflection, giving myself a private pep talk. You've got this.

Putting on my fleeces to go outside and meet the minibus felt like strapping on armour, every layer providing extra protection against the malevolent forces about to invade my safe space. I reminded myself that the first step of getting through this was to try not to think of Mike as the enemy. He was just another guest. I promised myself I would be the better person in this and not let him get to me. I zipped up my Wild Zone staff jacket decisively and then went to join Johanna and Rudi on the steps of the main building.

I gazed around Wild Zone and tried to distract myself from my nerves by imagining how the place would appear to Mike. When I'd first arrived, I'd been so overwhelmed by sensation akin to the shock of capture that I'd been oblivious to the beauty of the location. Now full of affection for my refuge and especially its owner, everything seemed touched by magic, a picture-perfect scene which wouldn't look out of place on a Christmas card. Even the climbing wall which normally utterly terrified me with its lethal surface of sheer ice looked enticing and special. How could Mike not fall for the place? I bristled at the idea of him criticising anything about it, while simultaneously hoping he'd not like it too much so he'd stay for the minimum duration possible.

Bang on time, the minibus hove into view on the top of the hill with Tommi behind the wheel, and my promise to have a positive mindset took a nosedive. Although I attempted to wave cheerily with my Wild Zone colleagues, every movement of my arm felt like an effort and my grin was forced; more like I was baring my teeth at the orthodontist than genuinely welcoming anyone. I caught Johanna throwing a concerned look in my direction, but I couldn't even summon enough strength to try to explain why I was so jumpy.

Tommi pulled up smartly alongside the main building, the brakes squeaking only slightly as the sturdy winter tyres of the vehicle gripped the ice firmly. I hurried to the back of the bus to start offloading everyone's luggage, keeping well out of the way, and still hoping against hope that there had been some big misunderstanding and that Mike wasn't really here after all.

Unfortunately, there was no mistaking the harsh tones of his voice over the babble of the other guests as he jumped off the bus and swore at the cold. What did he expect, visiting Finland in winter? I ignored the voice at the back of my head which tried to remind me that I had been similarly blindsided by the conditions on my arrival. I peeked around the corner of the minibus, making sure most of me was concealed by the raised lid of the boot. Mike looked like he'd stepped straight out of the radio station and onto the plane. He'd obviously tried to smarten up his act a bit since my departure, replacing his usual faded sweatshirt and tatty trousers with a flowery shirt and jacket, styled with stonewashed jeans. He looked like a cross between an *Antiques Roadshow* presenter and an estate agent. The Star FM baseball cap added to the slightly bizarre look. I reminded myself I was in no position to pass judgement from a fashion perspective, dressed head to toe in my baggy fleeces, but at least I was warm and protected from the elements.

Mike stepped to one side, and then another surprise awaited me. Following him off the bus was Jonno, my unwitting co-star in the viral video which had destroyed my reputation while at the same time bolstering his. What on earth was he doing here? Skye hadn't mentioned that he would be on the trip too. Come to think of it, why *was* he here, and Skye wasn't? She wasn't far enough along in her pregnancy to be banned from flying, and if this was a breakfast show recce, then she really ought to be included, given that she'd been filling in for me. I hoped it wasn't an indication that she was about to be side-lined in favour of Jonno.

I watched Jonno carefully, trying to read the reason behind his presence in the smallest of movements. What was going on here? I pulled my head back and took a few deep breaths trying to calm my racing heart. Every instinct told me to flee while I still could. I could see trouble ahead, and I'd had enough of being caught up in drama. I certainly didn't want Tommi and the others to get swept up in it too. Perhaps I could rough it at the wilderness hut for the duration of their stay? Mike on his own would have been bad enough, but Jonno's presence added a whole extra layer of potential embarrassment and awkwardness. How could I face him after that video? I cringed as the image of me apparently lunging towards him loomed in front of my mind. Did he blame me for causing difficulties between himself and Serenity? They'd appeared to put on a united front in the tabloids, but who knew what had been going on behind the scenes. But I wasn't going to feel too sorry for him. After all, he'd endorsed her statements about forgiveness when he knew full well that nothing we'd done was worthy of apology in the first place.

And then there was the effect Jonno could have on my growing closeness to Tommi. Tommi was bound to have recognised him from the video. What if Tommi believed the line the viral video sold and thought I'd invited Jonno to Wild Zone for round two? I told myself I was being ridiculously paranoid, and that Tommi was far too sensible to think that kind of nonsense. But insecurity is hard to ignore, and part of me feared Tommi was so far out of my league that the slightest thing could cause problems. Our relationship, such as it was, was too new to be adding this kind of complication into the mix.

'My luggage will have frozen if that's how long it's going to take to bring it inside.' Mike's braying tones gave me a vital second to try to pull myself together before he marched around the corner and appeared beside me, his unsuitable shoes making him slither in the snow.

'Do you even speak English?' He was speaking loudly and slowly, like he was addressing someone who was very hard of hearing.

I tried to hide my face in the boot of the minibus, but it was too late.

'Shit. Lucy. What the hell are you doing here?' He sounded genuinely surprised, but I couldn't decide whether that was because he didn't know I was here in Finland full stop, or whether it was because he hadn't expected to encounter me practically hiding in the boot of the minibus.

His face flushed, and, for a brief couple of seconds, it felt like I had the upper hand. I could practically see his brain working at a million miles an hour as he tried to process the shock of my presence. He cleared his throat awkwardly, then reached out to grab his bag from me, as if he didn't want it to be tainted by my touch. I twitched it out of his reach, for some desperate reason thinking that if I carried it into the building, I would demonstrate how strong and capable I was and maybe make him think twice before starting to bully me. Mike lunged forward and tried to grab it again. His feet went from under him and he landed with an audible thump on the frost-covered snow.

I tried to apologise, although I knew I had nothing to apologise for, but he brushed it away, like it was the buzz of an annoying fly.

'That's a nice welcome,' he snarled, also refusing my offer of help to get back up, and instead turning onto all fours and scrabbling around until his leather-soled shoes finally got a purchase. If I hadn't been so horrified by the situation, it would have been funny to see him sliding around doing his best Bambi impression. When he finally hauled himself back up, the knees of his jeans were soaked through.

'Are you OK?' I asked nervously, already knowing the effect the loss of dignity would have had on his mood.

'No thanks to you.' He sent a hatred-filled look in my direction and then shuffled gingerly towards the main entrance, his arms waving around like windmills as he tried to avoid a repeat of his fall.

I sank down to perch on the edge of the boot, holding

my head in my hands as I replayed what had happened. The only way it could have gone any worse would have been if Jonno had also fallen over. Thank goodness he'd chosen to march straight towards reception, not bothering to check whether his luggage would be following him or not.

Common sense made me realise it was too cold to sit around wallowing, so before I spiralled any further, I forced myself to get back up and carry on with the task in hand.

Tommi walked around the side of the minibus, his face lighting up when he saw me standing there. I felt an answering surge of joy looking at his lovely presence, but when he leaned forward to kiss me, I stepped away. Busying myself with the suitcases, I tried to make it look like I wasn't deliberately swerving from this sign of affection. I was torn because I really wanted to kiss him back, but every instinct warned me that I shouldn't be showing any weakness in front of Mike, and my burgeoning feelings for Tommi were exactly the kind of thing he would leap upon and try to exploit.

'Are you OK?' Tommi asked, looking hurt that I'd dodged his greeting. Tommi wasn't a hugely demonstrative man in public, well, as public as it ever got at Wild Zone, and I knew that for him to have made such a move was a big deal, which made me feel even worse.

'Where's my room so I can change into some dry clothes?' Mike's loud demand from the front step stopped me before I could explain. I saw Tommi glance across at Jonno and then back at me. His face grew shuttered, and he turned to pick up the luggage, swinging three large suitcases over his shoulder as if they weighed less than a bag of flour.

'Tommi,' I started, filled with dread at the thoughts I feared were running through his head.

'We'll talk later. Perhaps you could show Mike where his quarters are?' was his only reply.

I flinched. If he wanted to punish me for some perceived wrong, then he had just found a very effective way of doing it.

'Tommi,' I tried again, but he was already marching up the steps of the main building, luggage and supplies in tow.

I sighed and wondered if it was too late to throw myself into one of Aku's fishing holes in the lake. Then I painted on my biggest smile and tried to pretend that everything was tippity-top as I marched over to play the role of happy, welcoming host.

'Mike, so exciting to have you here. Would you like to follow me? I'll show you to your room.'

I knew I'd got my radio voice again and that my speech must have sounded very forced and unnatural to my Wild Zone friends, but if I had to channel my Lucy Fairweather, Wacky Radio Presenter guise to get through this, then that's what I would do.

Mike's only response was to send a look of pure disgust in my direction. I felt pretty disgusted with myself too.

Chapter Twenty-Seven

I tried to ignore Mike's jibes as I showed him around his cabin. I also tried to ignore them as he insisted I accompany him to the kit room to collect his cold weather gear, and when I ended up having to give him the guided tour of Wild Zone because Tommi had mysteriously disappeared. However, when he settled down for a production meeting with Jonno in the main reception and tried to make me stay to act as a waitress/runner/general dogsbody, I put my foot down and said I had business to attend to. I pulled on my cross-country skis and set off across the lake, not aiming at anywhere in particular, just wanting to get out of the way. At least in the centre of the lake I could look up to the wide, open sky and feel like I wasn't being crowded by my former colleagues.

Even though I was surrounded by what I'd come to realise was one of the most beautiful panoramas in the world, I still found myself unable to appreciate it today as I instead replayed every interaction with Mike. He was very sneaky, I'll give him that. He hadn't said anything which would have been deemed unacceptable if I relayed the conversation back to other people, but it was the manner in which he addressed me and the undercurrents in every sentence which stung me so much. He left me questioning everything, doubting my abilities, and blaming myself for my predicament. The fact that I couldn't quite put a finger on what exactly it was within the conversation that had made me feel so uncomfortable added to my sense of unease.

But now I thought about it more carefully, hadn't every conversation with Mike been like that before, even in the days when I was succeeding in my job and wasn't a social pariah? What he did probably counted as a form of gaslighting, but putting a name to it didn't make me feel any more confident in dealing with it all. How are you meant to tackle something so intangible and slippery? But I knew I would have to deal with it. Being a victim did not sit comfortably with me. Wild Zone was my home, for the time being at least, and I wasn't prepared to put up with this sanctuary being destroyed by Mike and his snarkiness.

I used my ski pole to trace out a skull and crossbones design in the snow as I pondered the situation, imagining Mike as the gap-toothed skeleton. Then I drew two big lines through the picture, scraping the icy surface until every trace of it had disappeared as if it had never been there. If only it was so easy to destroy my demons and start fresh in the rest of my life.

My toes were starting to get cold from standing around doing nothing, so I pushed myself back into motion and started skiing another loop of the frozen lake. Everyone who lived on its shores was so independent and capable, forced to become that way because of the harsh environment in which they lived. But although they prided themselves on standing on their own two feet, they knew when it was important to ask for help, when doing so would avert a much bigger catastrophe. I'd never been good at doing that. Even Skye and Henri's intervention had only happened because they had been proactive in looking out for me. Perhaps the time had come for me to be brave and ask for help? But who could I trust? The answer came to me immediately. Tommi.

I set off skiing towards the shore as I rehearsed in my head what I would say to him. I imagined the feeling of relief I would get after discussing it all with him. I pictured him listening in that quiet, dependable way of his, nodding sympathetically and supportively offering his take on the situation, but only after I'd invited him to do so.

And then another fear intruded, and, once I'd thought of it, I couldn't dismiss it, even as I tried to tell myself I was being ridiculous. What if he didn't see things the way I did? What if my explanation of Mike's behaviour made me look like the unreasonable individual rather than him? When I'd voiced my suspicions before that Mike could have something to do with the viral video, Tommi had asked me what proof I could offer and I'd been unable to demonstrate any. Once again, there was nothing really tangible I could offer now to prove Mike was in the wrong. Tommi had been kind and supportive of me so far, but what if showing too many of my anxieties frightened him off? I couldn't and wouldn't allow Mike to destroy something so new and precious.

Maybe I should leave Tommi out of it and see what Jonno thought of Mike's behaviour. If I spoke to him, he might be able to offer some insight into whether I was overreacting. After all, he'd been present throughout the guided tour, and he knew Mike of old. In fact, I had a vague memory that they'd been at another radio station together before they joined Star FM at a similar time, although that was hardly unusual. The commercial radio world was shrinking rapidly as technology took over and costs were cut, and it had always been fairly incestuous to start with. Jonno's long-standing knowledge of Mike and his behaviour might prove to be advantageous.

Jonno was always so laidback, he was practically horizontal, but he'd never been anything but decent with me, even when I inadvertently insulted his listeners by accidentally referring to them as 'Wednesday whiners.' And OK, I was still really hurt that he hadn't exactly gone out of his way to reach out to me following videogate, or stand up and speak the truth, but then again, it had been an impossibly difficult situation. Once the trolls started tormenting me, I'd gone to ground, making it hard for even my closest friends to help me. Of course Jonno had put his girlfriend first. Besides, any communication between us could have been misinterpreted.

I took a deep breath, and relished the sensation of the crisp coldness seeping into my lungs and clearing my mind. Perhaps I was overthinking things. Dwelling on negativity wasn't going to help me feel any better, nor was getting myself wound up about what Mike had or hadn't said when he arrived. Maybe his nastiness had been his shocked reaction to my presence at Wild Zone. It was time to move on. We were both adults, and we could, and should, put this behind us. Fired up by my new-found clarity of thought, I picked up the pace and skimmed my way back to base.

———————

It's one thing promising yourself to look on the bright side of a situation when you're in the middle of nowhere, surrounded by nothing but sparkling snow. It's quite another to put it into practice when you're stuck in a room and once again being the butt of another person's cruel 'banter'. The few hours we had spent apart seemed to have replenished Mike's stock of nastiness and he continued his subtle taunting throughout dinner, although it grew increasingly less subtle as the evening wore on and he indulged in Wild Zone's well-stocked bar. He noticed, in a most uncharacteristically perceptive way, that I was not partaking in the wine that everyone else was sharing. Rather than accepting it and moving on, he kept on bringing the conversation back around to the topic of booze, regaling his audience with tale after tale of occasions from industry parties where I'd ended up doing something stupid and making a spectacle of myself. He did it in the guise of being entertaining, but I knew it was really because he got a kick out of seeing me squirm.

'And then she ended up ripping her dress and she nearly flashed the entire audience.'

Mike roared while I prayed for the ground to swallow me up, just as I had done when that particular mishap had occurred. For once, my clumsiness hadn't been as a result of me making the most of the open bar which is normally on offer at awards ceremonies, but was instead caused by the demanding dress code for us ladies who were expected to dazzle in skyscraper heels and cinched-in gowns while the male guests got to prance about in comfy flats and simple black tie. I'd like to see Mike try to negotiate a steep flight of steps while wearing a dress that's about two feet too long for him. Besides, that particular awards ceremony had been on the anniversary of my dad's death. The unspeakable pain of that date and the added poignancy of wondering what Dad would have made of his little girl winning a national broadcast prize had touched everything that night with the physical ache of grief. It was hardly surprising I hadn't been paying attention to where I put my feet.

My knife and fork landed on my plate with a clatter. For the first time since I'd landed in Finland, I'd left most of my food untouched. I was so tense I could barely chew, and nothing tasted right tonight. Mike sat up straighter, seeming to grow in strength as he sapped the energy from me with his bullying.

'Oh and do you remember when she got locked out of her house wearing nothing but a towel, and had to wait on the doorstep for two hours until a locksmith could let her back in?'

He howled with laughter. Yes, nearly getting hypothermia and being half embarrassed to death at the same time was hilarious. I was not going to carry on rolling over and letting Mike trample on me like this.

'It was mostly an act,' I insisted, determined to try to reclaim my reputation before it became too tarnished. 'Listeners liked hearing about Loopy Lucy's exploits. It gave them a laugh in the morning. They knew those incidents were mostly tall tales, given a bit of an extra spin for added amusement.'

Mike's eyes gleamed triumphantly and my heart sank as I realised I'd fallen straight into the trap he'd set for me.

'Ah, Loopy Lucy. That takes me back. Loose Lucy is more your style nowadays, eh, Luce?'

I glared at Mike as he shot a smug glance in Tommi's direction, taking great delight in showing me up in front of him. He'd cottoned on to another of my weak points far too quickly for my liking. I tried to tell myself that Tommi wouldn't care, but just because he was aware of the video and my horrid nickname from the trolls, didn't mean I wanted his face rubbed in it by my former producer with such glee.

Tommi, bless him, tried to change the topic of conversation away from my misdemeanours, but I quickly wished he hadn't bothered.

'Did you know that we have our own community radio station here?' he said, the pride evident in his voice. 'It's called Arctic Circle FM.' My bad feeling started to get a whole lot worse and I willed him to stop before he said anything more. Sadly, my telepathy skills were clearly not up to scratch because he ploughed on regardless. 'In fact, ever since Lucy came to join us here, she has been helping out, training the volunteers at the radio station and acting as a producer for them. Haven't you, Lucy?'

His face was full of pleasure and affection, but I barely noticed because all I could see was Mike's smirk.

'Wow, well done you,' he said, in the most patronising tone imaginable. 'Community radio. And in the Arctic Circle of all places. What a gig. Although you might want to have a word with Charlie to check that it's permissible for you to work at another station when you're still on leave from Star FM. But of course, that might not be the case for very much longer.'

Stupid hope welled in my chest that this might mean my exile would soon be over, and then it was almost immediately crushed by Mike's next statement.

'Oh, sorry, Lucy, don't want you to get the wrong idea. I believe they've nearly finished their investigation, and I think there might be some shuffling at HQ. I've been saying all along that the easiest thing for them to do would be to quietly let you go, and I'm sure Charlie agrees. And then Arctic Circle FM could have you all to itself. Lucky community radio. I bet both the listeners would be delighted. Don't you agree, Jonno?'

'Don't bring me into this.' Jonno at least had the good grace to look embarrassed by Mike's now-overt malice. 'You know I keep my head well out of politics and I haven't got a clue about HR's investigation, apart from them checking in with me to make sure I was OK after the video went viral, of course.'

I found myself nodding, although I was livid to discover that HR had been demonstrating a much greater commitment to their duty of care towards him than they had towards me.

'The breakfast show is the flagship show, and it should be presented by the best person for the job, pure and simple. I'm not sure an appearance in a viral video is either here or there,' concluded Jonno, instantly making me forgive him for coming out of this situation as the blue-eyed boy, cosseted by HR and protected from all the trauma that I'd been through. I sent a warm smile in his direction as I hugged to myself the implication that he thought I was still the best presenter for the show.

'Does anyone want any dessert?' said Tommi, scraping his chair back and standing up abruptly.

'No, thank you,' said Mike. 'Got to watch the old figure in this business.'

'It's radio, Mike. No one gives a damn what anyone looks like,' I couldn't resist answering him back. If anyone had a face for radio, it was old Mikey.

'Ah, but since we arrived and saw the many interesting attractions there are in this place, I thought it would be a good idea to stream our broadcast live on a webcam,' he replied smugly, knowing exactly how the revelation would make me feel. 'Just so the listeners can get the full effect of the location. We want to show them everything we see here. Everything and everyone.'

The threat was obvious. My mood took a further nosedive. That was all I needed, Mike and Jonno turning this trip into an all-singing, all-dancing spectacle live-streamed to the world for anyone to watch. And from the sounds of it, Mike would take great pleasure in making sure the camera caught me, even though he must know that it would set the trolls going all over again. Once again I wondered whether he might be the person behind the original video. Well, if that was the case, I wasn't going to let him win this time. I would keep well out of the way so nobody would catch even the briefest glimpse of me at Wild Zone. I couldn't bear it if the poison pen letters caught up with me here and tainted this place too.

'Lucy, could you help me with the plates?' asked Tommi, interrupting my racing thoughts with a perfectly reasonable request.

'If I have to,' I said shortly, my irritation and upset at Mike leaking out in the form of biting Tommi's head off, which I immediately felt bad about.

Mike looked between the pair of us and chuckled, which didn't make me feel any better.

My hands were shaking with frustration and anger as I collected up the plates, only just resisting the urge to tip the remainder of my dinner over his head. I was in such a state by the time I got to the kitchen that I tripped over my own feet in the doorway and only Tommi's quick-thinking stopped me dropping all the plates on the floor.

'Hey, this is Finland, not Greece.' He caught my arms and gently took the plates from my grasp.

But I was in no mood for being teased.

'Don't I know it,' I retorted, then instantly regretted snapping. 'I'm sorry. Ignore me being horrid. I obviously got out of bed the wrong side this morning.'

Tommi squeezed my shoulder gently as he walked past

me to start stacking the plates in the dishwasher, like nothing bad had happened.

'You certainly did. I missed waking up next to you.' He sighed, and leaned against the worksurface, folding his arms and watching my expression closely. 'Look, I realise that Mike and Jonno are probably the last people you would like to see here. I am very sorry that Rudi didn't consult me about the booking, as I wouldn't have accepted it. Mike is clearly not a pleasant man. He obviously gets a kick out of making you the butt of his jokes and worse. But don't let them dictate your life and spoil what we have. They're here now, and we might as well make the most of the exposure they will give to Wild Zone. They will be busy doing their thing during their stay, and you will be busy doing yours. There is no need for you to be upset by their presence.'

'But what is my thing?' I burst out. 'Up until a couple of months ago, I was a respected radio presenter, with my own show, and bosses who respected me and my talent. I'd even won awards. But now what am I? A chalet maid in the middle of nowhere, cleaning up after my former colleagues and being told to be grateful for it while the rest of the world carries on hating me for fun. What if I'm tired of being targeted, tired of being glad of the opportunity to hide away for the rest of my life? What if I'm sick of being at the mercy of other people's kindness?'

Angry tears were welling in my eyes, and I brushed them away with the back of my hand, frustrated at myself for being so weak.

Tommi let me rant on. 'I am sorry you feel that way.'

His quiet acceptance of my rage made me feel even

303

worse, especially as I knew that I must be hurting him with my unkind comments. But in my own pain, I couldn't seem to help lashing out and wounding others.

'You are not a burden,' he added quietly. 'I thought you might perhaps get in the way when you first arrived, especially when you did not even have a coat with a functioning zip.' Tommi's eyes sparkled, although I couldn't even summon the strength to smile at the memory. 'But you have settled in and you are part of the team now.' He studied my face, as if he was trying to see into my brain and understand all the hurt and anger which was whizzing around there. 'I know it was never your dream to live and work in the wilderness. But it is mine, and I am grateful that you have been so supportive of what I am trying to do here.' He paused, and when he carried on speaking there was a gravelly tone to his voice which hadn't been there before. 'I shall miss you when the time comes for you to return to England.'

Despite my rant, the idea of going back to England and leaving all of this behind hurt me almost as much as Mike's behaviour had done. And I was in such a state that I wilfully misunderstood Tommi's point and interpreted it as a sign that he was keen to get rid of me.

The tears spilled over in earnest now, and I shook my hair forward hurriedly, trying to shield my expression, not wanting Tommi to see my moment of weakness. If he could talk so calmly about the idea of me leaving, then I would pretend that I could be blasé about it too.

'Bring it on,' I said. 'The sooner things return to normal and I get my life back, the better.'

I saw the disappointment and hurt in Tommi's face before he quickly masked his expression.

'Please don't allow me to hold you back. I would never wish to do that.' And then he turned away and carried on stacking the dishwasher as if there was nothing else he would rather be doing.

Chapter Twenty-Eight

Not for the first time, I wished someone would invent a time machine so I could return to the evening before last and relive the joyous time I spent with Tommi, laughing together over the antics of Gurta and her puppies, and then loving together. Everything had been much less complicated then, and even the troubles which had driven me to this country in the first place had seemed a long way away. Of course, if time machines really existed, I guess I would have been able to go even further back and change the pattern of events to make it so that I never appeared in the viral video in the first place. But although that idea was appealing on a superficial level, I wasn't sure I would be prepared to pay the price for it. Skye says that there's always something good that comes out of something bad. For a long time I was dismissive of what I viewed as her naive, silver lining attitude. But there have been a few things which have made me rethink and wonder if she has a point. I'm not sure I would have discovered radio, the place that makes my soul sing, if it hadn't been for stumbling across that hospital radio studio on my darkest of days. And if I hadn't been hounded out of the UK by the evil trolls, I wouldn't have met Tommi and spent all this magical time with him in a country I was also falling in love with.

I reminded myself of that when Rudi arrived on the steps of my cabin the next morning and roped me into helping him with a 'very important task'.

'Are you sure I'm the only person who can assist? I was planning to work in the kitchen with Johanna today.' I hopped around on one foot as I tried to pull on my heavy boots without undoing the laces which I'd lazily left tied up last night, too tired and too defeated to find the energy to ease out the knots.

Rudi rolled his eyes. 'I know exactly what you're doing, and you're not going to distract me by pretending you can't even do your boots up.'

'I don't know what you're talking about.'

'None of us are stupid. We all know how difficult it is having your old boss turn up here. I'm really sorry that I didn't realise who he was when I took his call.'

'He was *not* my boss.' The boot fell out of my hands with a clatter, and I gave up the fight and started working away at the laces.

'Whatever. Boss, colleague, he's still an arse and we understand how him being here must make you feel. But that is not a good enough reason to hide away in the kitchen like you are Cinderella.' He trilled the name like he was auditioning for a musical.

I couldn't help but laugh at that. 'You constantly

surprise me, Rudi. I would never have put you down as a Disney fan. And so what if I want to hide in the kitchen? Maybe I feel safer there.'

'You are safe everywhere. Tommi won't let them do anything to you while they are here.'

'Hmm. I have a feeling Tommi would think life was a whole lot easier if I was just out of the way.' I pretended to be completely absorbed in fastening my laces. 'Besides, I don't need Tommi to protect me,' I added as an afterthought, the feminist in me torn equally between lust and disgust at the image which had sprung into my head of Tommi in Viking warrior guise, fighting off barbarians with his bare hands while I swooned gracefully.

'He knows that and I know that. But there is nothing wrong with having someone look out for you.' The spider tattoo did its usual dance as Rudi raised his eyebrows and fixed me with an expression which warned he refused to be argued with.

'Thanks, oh wise Rudi. Perhaps you could look out for me by letting me hide myself in the safety of the Mike-free kitchen which, yes, is what I would be doing.'

Rudi handed me my coat and hat and hustled me out into the cold.

'I think not. This way is better.'

When I realised that Rudi's way involved me spending the morning with my ex-colleagues, presumably as some kind of immunisation by exposure experiment, I was tempted to shove a handful of snow down the back of his neck.

'Good morning, Mike, Jonno. I hope you slept well.

Lucy has kindly offered to come with us today when you check out the ACFM studio. There's no one who knows the set-up better than she does.'

Rudi gestured proudly at me, looking relaxed and happy. I guess he thought he was making me look good to the others. Mike barely deigned to glance in my direction, while Jonno sent a brief apologetic glance at me before he returned to tapping away on his phone with his touchscreen sensitive gloves.

I forced a smile which I'm pretty sure looked more like a grimace. Not only had Rudi tricked me into coming face to face with my nemesis once again, he was also making me take him to my particular sanctuary, my cosy piece of radio heaven in the snowy wilderness. The last thing I wanted was for my beloved studio to be tainted with images of Mike.

'Ready to go?' said the man himself, clapping me vigorously between the shoulder blades.

'Nurgh,' was the only noise I found myself capable of making as I rubbed my back and prayed Rudi stopped interfering with my life and returned to his usual occupation of doing slightly shady deals.

'Lead on, Lucy,' said Jonno, finally putting his phone away and starting to show a bit of interest in proceedings. For a guy who was planning to do a live outside broadcast for a massive audience in just a few days' time, he seemed pretty unbothered about the logistics, but then Jonno's always been happy to leave the details to others.

I took a deep breath and told myself I could act like a grown up and be the better person.

'What's the plan for ACFM, then, guys?' I possibly went overboard in my attempt to sound casual and relaxed.

'We want to check it out for use as our location for the big special. It's great that there's a ready-made studio in the area which we can have access to for the live show; everything set up and easy to use,' said Mike, apparently missing the entire purpose of an outside broadcast. If they were going to do it from the cosy confines of a studio with its complete lack of background atmosphere thanks to its soundproofing, soundproofing which I had been working to improve can I point out, then they might as well have just done it from home.

Although Mike was the last person I wanted to do a favour for, my broadcaster instincts meant I couldn't help speaking up.

'I thought the whole purpose of the trip was to scout out a good location which would give the listeners a real sense of where you are doing the shows from? Sure, ACFM is in Finland, but one studio is pretty much the same as another. You'll sound exactly like you would do back at home in Sheffield.'

Mike put his ear muffs on and pretended to ignore me, while muttering under his breath something about not needing to take broadcasting advice from a cleaner.

I turned so hot with embarrassment I thought the snow might melt under my feet. The Lucy of old would have come right back at him with a smart retort, but I was so taken by surprise by his downright cruel comment that I couldn't find the words.

Jonno at least had the good grace to look embarrassed at

Mike's dismissive behaviour. 'Mate, give her a rest. Whatever menial stuff she's doing now, she still has a good idea what she's talking about from a radio point of view.'

I couldn't decide whether I should be feeling supported or patronised by him. But his comments gave me enough of a boot up the backside to snap myself out of my shame trance. I firmly told myself that I was the better person in this situation. Let these guys think whatever they liked about me; I knew the reality, and I knew they'd be better off taking my advice. Besides, this was about much more than me. After last night's near squabble with Tommi, I felt I had a lot of ground to make up. I wanted Star FM's Finnish broadcast to work well for his sake and, for his sake, I would swallow my pride, put up with the jibes, and push for what I knew would make for a good radio programme.

I forced myself to remain calm, and carried on speaking as if nothing had happened. 'You'll be looking for a location with plenty of atmosphere, but also with easy access to amenities, especially if you're planning presenter-led discussion segments between the music. You'll also want things to see and talk about, and the potential for good background noise, without it being too much so that it would dominate the conversation.'

Mike started nodding vigorously as he recognised the sense of what I was saying. Then he realised what he was doing and froze, trying to look uninterested. I could tell he was itching to get out his phone and make a note of my suggestions so he could reel them off to the bosses at home and make them all sound like his ideas.

'I wonder if the veranda around the side of the main

building would work?' I continued, my instinct to show Wild Zone at its best still winning out, despite great provocation. 'It would be easy to run the cables from there to a power source, so you're not reliant on battery power, especially as batteries tend not to last as long as you want them to in these cold conditions. We can set up chairs and a table so it's like a studio. Plus, you have a beautiful panoramic view from there which would work well on the live web stream, and you're only a few steps from the climbing wall and the sledge run, should you wish to try some winter activities to provide more of a spectacle for the listeners. If you're going to be here, you might as well tell them all about the amazing things to do. And you can nip inside to warm up and use the facilities while the songs are on. Doesn't it sound perfect?'

Jonno shrugged his shoulders, happy to go with whatever offered him the easiest life. Mike was clearly torn between his desire to reject my suggestion, and his recognition that everything I had said made sense. I watched his features twitching as he fought an internal battle about what to do.

Rudi decided enough was enough. 'Good plan,' he said, intervening at last. 'Follow me, gents.' He glanced across at me, the apology obvious in his face. He had underestimated Mike's levels of pettiness and I knew he felt bad for putting me in this position. He herded them around the side of the building and out of my way, in the manner of a sheepdog chasing the flock to exactly where he wants it to go.

It would have been so much easier to slink away to hide in the kitchen with Johanna, but I wasn't going to let Mike get away with treating me like a minion. Besides, I felt invested in the outside broadcast now, and I wanted to see if they would take up my suggestions.

I rushed after them before I lost courage. While Rudi pointed out various sites of interest to Mike and Jonno, I moved the loungers out of their way, trying to ignore the flashbacks to the night Tommi and I had reclined here as the Northern Lights danced above our heads. Would we be able to enjoy another evening like that, or had I ruined everything with my hurtful comments and thoughtlessness?

'Do you agree?'

Rudi's question brought me back to my current reality.

'I'm sorry, I was miles away. Can you say that again?'

I heard Mike mutter something insulting about me living on a different planet and heavily implying there was a chemical reason for that.

Rudi's vengeance was unsubtle and immediate. He picked up one of the snow shovels and set to work, ostensibly clearing a wider space for us to stand in, but in reality making sure that the excess snow headed in Mike's direction.

'That's better,' Rudi said, as Mike scurried behind Jonno and started brushing the ice off his clothes. I saw him open his mouth, and then shut it hurriedly as Rudi looked at him with a bland expression. My former producer was apparently too much of a coward to pick on someone his own size.

Rudi grinned, and turned back to me. 'I was suggesting that we could set up the table here and run some extra cables out, perhaps even power a small heater so the team could spend longer doing their live links. I know I'm only an amateur, but that's the way I would do it for ACFM. Perhaps we should try it ourselves one day.'

'Excellent plan. It would be great to do an ACFM special broadcast.' My mind was already buzzing with ideas. 'And there's no such thing as "only an amateur". Amateurs are people who are so passionate about what they do, they do it for free.'

The pep talk had started out as encouragement for Rudi, but the words resonated with me too, and I felt much better for saying out loud what I had started to think. Whether I was paid to do radio or not, I still loved it and I was grateful that my current fluid employment status hadn't prevented me from continuing my passion.

Mike snorted, but I refused to be bowed by him any longer. If Mike wanted to continue playing games, then that was his prerogative. But it was time I did something about it. He was on my territory now, and I was determined not to let him get the better of me.

Chapter Twenty-Nine

Showing Mike and Jonno the veranda had at least distracted them from visiting the Arctic Circle FM studio today, but I knew I'd have to face that challenge sooner or later. Mike liked his comforts, and I suspected he'd want to do at least half the show in the familiar surroundings of a proper studio, whatever I said about the benefits of location sound.

Jonno headed back to his room, muttering something about calling Serenity, while Rudi took Mike off, ostensibly to scout out another broadcasting position, although I had a feeling he was hoping to get some business by showing him his stash of 'extras'.

I retreated to the main building, glad to be free of them all for a bit. I wanted to track Tommi down and speak to him properly about what had happened last night. I was still hurt by his apparently casual attitude towards the idea of me leaving Wild Zone. However, I was self-aware enough to know that I'd been in the kind of mood where I was over-sensitive to everything, perhaps creating something out of nothing, seeing problems where maybe there weren't any. I wanted to talk to him and be open about where my head was at. I was done with keeping secrets and bottling things up inside. I had ruined relationships in the past by keeping a barrier up in a misguided attempt to protect myself, and Tommi mattered too much to me to allow history to repeat itself. Tommi was honest to the point of bluntness. If he wasn't interested in me any longer, he would be open about it. But I hoped that wasn't the case.

I knocked on the door of his flat, and waited, half hoping and half dreading his appearance. But there was no answering scuffle from Gurta and the puppies, and I could sense the emptiness within. I went upstairs and tried his office instead, but yet again there was silence from inside. I tried the handle, in case he hadn't heard me knock. The door creaked open, but no smiling Tommi looked up from the leather armchair. There was no need for me to cross the threshold and go in, but somehow that's exactly what I found myself doing. I knew it was an invasion of his privacy to go into his space like this without his permission, but after locking horns with Mike this morning, I wanted the reassurance which only speaking to Tommi could offer me. He wasn't here, but I could feel his presence in the office, and even that was in some way calming.

I wandered over to his desk and idly lifted up a picture of Tommi posing happily with Henri and Skye at a family gathering. As I did so, my hand brushed against the mouse and the computer sprang to life with a loud beep. I stepped back, knowing how it would look if anyone walked in and found me apparently prying through Tommi's things. I was about to hurry out of the room, when the video on the screen started automatically playing. The tinny music sent chills down my spine as I recognised the tune.

Like a rubbernecker on the motorway, I couldn't help turning back to have a look. It was the video, the one which went viral, the one which made me feel physically sick whenever I thought about it. I'd seen it a thousand times, and I didn't need to see it again, but something drew me closer to the screen. The shots were horribly familiar, and yet there was something different about it, something I couldn't quite put my finger on. I pulled Tommi's chair up to the desk and scrolled through the video, examining each shot frame by frame, trying to ignore the nauseous churning of my stomach.

It happened so quickly I almost didn't spot it. But my brain was so attuned to what it was expecting to see, that when it didn't happen, alarm bells rang in my subconscious. There was definitely something off. While this had the familiar sequence of the boomerang effect drinking and the lunge towards Jonno, at the point where the original video faded to suggestive nothingness, this one continued playing for a couple of seconds longer. There was no fade to black but instead the camera fell down as if whoever was wielding it had dropped it to the ground.

I hit pause and leaned forward to examine the image on the screen. Yes, there was definitely a flash moment when you could see Jonno and I move apart from each other, several inches of glorious space between our faces as he looked off camera into the distance and I turned away. Then, of even greater interest, just as the camera fell to the ground, there was a fleeting glimpse of something else. My heart leaped with optimism. Had the mysterious Peeping Tom accidentally caught themselves on film? I tried increasing the magnification on the screen to try and see more, but unfortunately it just made the image even more pixelated and hard to make out.

Nevertheless, the knowledge that this video even existed made me feel a surge of hope. At last, there was something concrete which could take me a step closer to my goal of proving that I'd been set up and clearing my name. I wondered where Tommi had found it and how he had managed to track it down. Perhaps it was thanks to the friend of Rudi he'd mentioned as having good computer skills. I didn't realise he'd actually followed through on his offer of help, and the knowledge that he'd been working behind the scenes to assist me made me feel all warm and fuzzy inside.

I examined the image frozen on the screen again. The shot was so dark and blurry, it was hard to be a hundred percent sure exactly what it was, but the more I looked at it, the more I was convinced it was a trouser leg, and a rather grimy, dishevelled-looking one at that. Without anything to get a sense of scale, it was hard to work out the size of said leg, how tall the person might be or what their build was. But the longer I stared at it, the more I convinced myself that the leg belonged to Mike. He was notorious for wearing tatty clothes during his producer shifts at the station, even if he seemed to have gone slightly more upmarket for his trip to Finland. Dropping the camera on the ground was exactly the kind of clumsy thing he would do, plus wasn't he the person I'd suspected all along as he had the most to gain from ousting me from my breakfast show? My evidence was flimsy, in fact, calling it evidence in the first place was massively overstating it, but my gut feeling was that I was right.

In the past, I would have rung Skye to get her take on things, but I didn't want to put her in a difficult position. She still had to work with Mike, after all. But I needed to speak to someone, to say what I was thinking out loud.

I wondered what Tommi would make of my suspicions. He'd obviously been looking at the video himself, so he must have drawn his own conclusions about it. And perhaps there was more he could tell me about how he'd found the video and where it might have come from in the first place. I quickly emailed myself a copy of the link to the footage, and prayed it didn't disappear from the internet as mysteriously as it had appeared in the first place. Then I hurried out of the office and did a quick sweep of the main building. But there was no sign of Tommi anywhere, and, when I popped my head around the kitchen door, Johanna informed me he'd taken Gurta and the puppies to the vet for a check-up.

'Give him a ring on his mobile, I'm sure he won't mind,' she said, as she busily peeled and chopped vegetables for the evening meal.

I knew I should stay to help her with the food preparation, but my selfish need to address the video situation was giving me tunnel vision, so I waved my thanks and hurried off to use the phone in the visitors' lounge. It seemed to take ages to connect, and then the phone rang endlessly, but Tommi didn't pick up. I took a deep breath and told myself to calm down. The video had been around for weeks. Tommi would be back at Wild Zone in time for the evening meal and I could discuss things with him then. Another few hours weren't going to make any difference to the situation long term.

But there was someone else who had been affected by appearing in the video, albeit in a much more positive way than me. Jonno hadn't exactly gone out of his way to talk to me about how we'd gone viral, but surely he'd be up for the conversation now there was another video which could make people look at the situation in a different way? And didn't he have just as much of a right as me to know of this video's existence? Admittedly, I didn't really have any more concrete facts to present him with, but it would be interesting to see what he thought, and whether he'd had any similar suspicions about Mike.

I swung by reception to pick up my mobile phone, and checked that the email had landed with the link to the new video, doing my best to ignore all the other messages in my inbox. A girl could only take so much stress and drama in one day. And then I pulled on my outdoor layers and hurried across the darkening grounds to Jonno's cabin, the nerves rising as I rehearsed in my head what I wanted to say to him.

The light from his hut was spilling out through the curtains and onto the snow, the warm glow making everything around it seem that much more gloomy. I experienced a moment of misgiving, but I took a deep breath and knocked on the door before I lost courage altogether. There was a shuffling from within, and the curtain twitched slightly as if the occupant was checking who the guest was before they decided to open the door and welcome me in. He'd probably had enough of hanging out with work colleagues and wanted to spend a bit of time to himself. I couldn't really blame him.

'Jonno, it's me, Lucy. Do you have a moment?' I called through the wooden door, trying to keep my voice low in case the snow with its weird acoustic powers echoed my words in places I'd rather they weren't heard. If Mike came over to see what I was up to, I'm not sure what excuse I'd be able to come up with, and I didn't trust myself not to jump right in and accuse him straight off, which probably would not be the brightest of ideas.

I rattled the door again. I didn't want to appear desperate, but the cold was starting to seep through, despite my many outdoor layers. Or maybe it was the nerves that were chilling me to the bone. There was still a voice niggling at the back of my mind that maybe I shouldn't dive straight in and have this conversation until I'd thought about the situation properly.

There was another long pause and then, eventually, Jonno stuck his head out of the cabin. He didn't look particularly pleased to see me, although the pained expression on his face could equally have been reluctance at having to let cold air into his cosy room.

'Can I have a quick word?' I repeated, stepping forward

across the threshold and kicking my boots off before either of us changed our minds.

'Sure, why not.' He stood back to let me pass, and then checked outside carefully before he shut the door behind me. I wondered why he was so jumpy.

He opened his wardrobe, pulled out a bottle of gin, and poured himself a generous measure before proffering the bottle towards me.

'Join me for a pre-dinner snifter?'

I shook my head and tried not to imagine the sweet, refreshing taste of the clear liquid trickling down my throat and warming me from within.

'Sorry, tactless of me,' he said. 'You're doing a great thing, giving up the sauce.'

'New location, new me. I thought it best to make a fresh start.' I tried not to think about the terrifying incident with Heidi which had made me reassess my life and decide to make better choices for myself.

'I should probably do the same. I'm not sure I can afford to keep on the booze for the rest of the trip. That Rudi charges a fortune for his secret stash, and the Wild Zone bar isn't much better.'

'That's Finland for you.' I smiled as I remembered how outraged I'd felt when I arrived and realised quite how pricey alcohol was in this country.

'Hmm, another reason why I can't wait to go home. I only agreed to come on the trip because I thought it would help my demo tape for the job...anyway, ignore me, how can I help you?'

He waved the gin bottle in my direction again, as if he

hoped to use it to distract me from what he'd just said. His avoidance made me all the more interested. I wondered what job Jonno had in mind. Had he decided it was time to move on from Star FM? I'd have to ask Skye if she had any insider gossip. And then I firmly told myself to stop being so nosy. The internal politics and job moves of Star FM were really none of my business any more, and I'd only be torturing myself by trying to find out.

I once again gestured for him to put the bottle out of reach.

'Can I speak honestly with you, Jonno? I'm going to tell you something and it might be completely mad, but, then again, it might not. But, either way, I'd really appreciate it if it didn't go any further and stayed between the two of us.' This wasn't the clear, well-thought out speech I'd planned, but he'd thrown me off-balance first with the booze, then with the hint at the job move, and now I sounded like a complete numpty with my garbled speech.

'That sounds complicated.' He took another deep gulp of gin. 'But I guess I haven't got anything else to do on a cold night in the Antarctic, so shoot.'

I resisted the urge to correct his geography, disappointed in his apparent reluctance to be a confidant. Was I being foolish to even consider talking to him about this? But he'd been in the video too. Surely he would want to know about this development, even though the video hadn't had such a devastating effect on his life as it had on mine?

'It's about Mike,' I said, speaking quickly before I changed my mind. 'Do you think that he's the one behind the video? I've been thinking carefully about it. He was at

Bazzer's leaving do, and he wasn't at the radio station when the bit in the pub car park was filmed, I checked with Skye. Out of everyone involved, he's gained the most. After all, it's thanks to the video that he got to start presenting.'

'Him and Skye,' corrected Jonno.

'Yes, but there's no way on earth that Skye is behind the video. She doesn't have it in her. It wouldn't even cross her mind.' I was angry at Jonno for suggesting such a preposterous idea.

He pulled a face as if he took what I was saying with a pinch of salt, but when my expression remained stony, he held his hands up as if in surrender.

'Fine, if that's what you want to believe.' His voice still hinted at incredulity. 'But why do you think Mike would do something like that? I mean, he's not exactly the cheeriest guy on the block, but that doesn't mean anything. And do you think he'd really have the brainpower to come up with such a devious scheme?'

'I wouldn't underestimate him. He's got hidden depths, and not in a good way. He's always had a problem with me. At first I thought it was just women in authority he disliked in general, but I soon realised I was singled out for special consideration in his gallery of hatred. He actively pushed for HR to be involved when I was late for work, and he's shown no consideration nor care since the moment I left the station, despite it being patently obvious how distressed I was about the video.'

Now I was actually speaking to Jonno about it, I realised how flimsy my reasoning was.

'But that's Mike for you. Sure, he can be a bit of a sexist

bastard at times, but that's just his way. Doing the whole touchy-feely caring thing isn't his style. It doesn't mean he's not bothered because he's not checked in with you.'

I shook my head, amazed at how dismissive Jonno was being.

'And why do you think it's someone at the radio station who's behind this in the first place?' he continued. 'Wouldn't it make more sense that it's a random punter who put the thing together for a laugh, and it got out of hand? Everyone's wanting to go viral nowadays and get their chance at a shot of fame.'

'But who wants fame at this price? And would a random punter have been at Bazzer's leaving do, and then have been lurking around in the pub car park the next day? It seems pretty unlikely, doesn't it?' I knew I was clutching at straws, but without my Mike theory I was back at square one, and that felt like I was being tormented all over again.

'It could have been Chris.'

How could Jonno be so casual about this? He sounded like he really couldn't care less whether the perpetrator was caught.

I nearly laughed at how ridiculous his suggestion was. 'Sure, because the landlord of The Crown is going to film footage of one of his best customers and make it look like she's getting herself into trouble. And yes, I'm saying it as it is. I was one of the most frequent customers at The Crown, but I never did anything which would have offended Chris to the point where he'd put out a malicious video.'

'Then I'm all out of ideas,' said Jonno with a shrug. 'But I wouldn't go around accusing Mike. I think you're overthinking all this, Luce. Let bygones be bygones. You seem to have got yourself fairly sorted here. Why worry about something which happened in the past? Move on.'

And with that, he hustled me out of the cabin so quickly I didn't even have time to tie up my boot laces, let alone zip up my coat. I stood outside in the cold and replayed the conversation in my head as I tried to sort out my outer layers. How come speaking to Jonno had made me feel so much worse?

Chapter Thirty

I hovered on the porch, trying to get myself sorted before I caught frostbite. Far from putting my mind at ease, the conversation with Jonno had set my thoughts racing off in a very interesting direction. He'd been evasive, shifty, avoided my gaze and done everything he could to get rid of me as quickly as possible. Maybe he was still feeling uncomfortable about being in the same room as me because of the video, but maybe there was something more to it. Had he been in a hurry for me to leave because he felt guilty? Did he know more about the video than he was letting on? I'd always thought it strange that he'd come out of it so well, especially as he was the one who appeared to be playing away from home, while I'd been the single one, free to do what I wanted with who I wanted. I'd been so shocked by the video's appearance and taken so utterly by surprise at the rate everything had spiralled, that by the time I'd got my head around it, the story had been set and it was too late for me to speak out and defend myself.

But Jonno, on the other hand, had emerged as the blue-eyed boy, the innocent victim taken advantage of by a predatory female, the loving boyfriend determined to make amends with his glamorous reality star girlfriend. The narrative had been so shaped in his favour, it was almost like he'd known what was coming before it had even happened, and had prepared for it so he came out on top, with a higher public profile to boot. Perhaps that had been his intention all along.

I shook my head. This was ridiculous. I was letting my imagination run away with me, seeing conspiracy theories wherever I looked. Getting all paranoid wasn't going to change my situation.

'Move on, Lucy,' I told myself.

'Are you alright?' Tommi emerged from the shadows. He had his thickest coat on, the ice crystals in its creases suggesting he'd been out in the forest for quite some time.

I finished zipping up my coat and hurried down the steps from Jonno's cabin, feeling doubly stupid for the direction my thoughts had been going in, and for being caught by Tommi talking to myself.

'All good,' I said in an overly cheery voice, trying to compensate.

'How is Jonno?' asked Tommi.

'What do you mean? Why would I know?' I said, like a first-class idiot. I evaded the question because I was sick of thinking about the man and didn't want to spend precious time with Tommi talking about my ridiculous theories. It was only later that I realised quite how suspicious I made myself look, standing there on Jonno's front steps straightening my clothing and avoiding answering a simple question when I'd so obviously just been in to visit him.

Tommi, to give him credit, didn't pursue the issue, but he was perhaps more quiet than usual as we walked back across the main building together. Instead of taking the opportunity to ask him about where he'd found the new video, and to be honest with him about what was going through my mind, I fell back into radio presenter mode and tried to fill the silence with a steady stream of inane chatter which probably made my behaviour appear even more shifty. The conversation with Jonno had increased my feeling of vulnerability and, for now, it felt safer to keep the barriers up and protect myself.

Dinner that evening was an uncomfortable affair. Jonno was clearly keeping away from me in case I repeated my madcap theories, and I was attempting to avoid him for a similar reason. Mike was being his usual self, veering between being patronising and downright rude, while Tommi's mind appeared to be somewhere else, and he kept on having to ask people to repeat what they'd said. Only Rudi and Johanna seemed to be enjoying themselves as they served the meal to the rest of the guests, but by the time we'd moved onto dessert, the tense atmosphere had got to them too, and they quickly made their excuses after finishing dinner service and retreated to their own homes rather than staying to be sociable as they would normally have done.

Thankfully, most of the guests didn't stick around too late either, and then it was just Tommi and I together in the kitchen, stacking the dishwasher and making sure everything was prepared for breakfast in the morning.

'Could you finish up in here? I have something I need to see to,' said Tommi.

'No problem,' I said, trying to sound like I didn't mind. I'd half been hoping that we'd finish the chores together and then maybe retreat to his rooms downstairs for an encore of the other night. I wanted the simple reassurance of being close with him again, because being with Tommi made me happy, and helped me escape from the dark places my mind kept going to. I couldn't help feeling hurt that he didn't seem to need me as much as I needed him. Later, when I was lying alone in my cabin, sleep dodging my grasp, I started wondering if my evasive behaviour earlier had had something to do with Tommi avoiding my company. Had it made him wrongly suspect that there was something going on between me and Jonno? I turned over in bed and tried to push the thought from my head. Tommi wasn't that kind of person. If he had suspicions, he wouldn't keep them to himself, and he would ask me outright. Once again, I promised myself to have an honest, straightforward conversation with him and get everything out in the open. But although I told myself that everything would be OK once we'd talked and that things would look better in the morning, it didn't stop me tossing and turning for half the night.

Chapter Thirty-One

Things did not look better in the morning. As I pulled on my fleecy layers, I practised out loud what I intended to say to Tommi, but I was struggling to find the right words. I was scared that I would only make things worse, either by planting an idea in his head that wasn't already there, or by not explaining things properly and making myself appear even more suspicious in the process. My head was aching from lack of sleep and it felt like anxiety-induced gremlins were doing high kicks in my stomach. I knew I was being ridiculous, getting myself in such a state about potentially nothing, but my mind seemed to be feeding on the negativity spiral. It was time to act before I really freaked myself out.

I took myself off for a vigorous walk around the perimeter of Wild Zone, letting the shimmering snow and calming fractals of the trees work their magic on me. By the time I was on my third lap, my cheeks were stinging with cold, but my head felt clearer, and the endorphins from the exercise had boosted my spirits sufficiently to make me feel able to face Tommi and the challenges of the day with confidence. When I spotted Mike and Jonno walking off together in the direction of the Arctic Circle FM studio, I felt relieved more than anything. It had been inevitable that they would visit at some point, but at least I wouldn't have to be there to witness it.

And even better, they wouldn't be around to spoil my breakfast. I hurried over to the main building, the exercise having replaced the anxiety gremlins with hunger pangs. As I opened the door to reception, I could smell the delicious scent of bacon cooking and my stomach grumbled in response.

'Sorry, I'm absolutely ravenous,' I explained to a startled-looking Rudi as I hopped on one foot, trying to pull my boots off and get my slippers on.

'Lucy, thank goodness, I need to speak to you,' he said. But at the same moment, Tommi walked into the room from his office. My insides flip-flopped as nerves and affection and desire zinged around my body simultaneously. I caught his gaze and felt myself sinking into the gorgeous pool of his eyes.

'Sure, Rudi, but do you mind if we chat later?' I said, still looking at Tommi, trying to read what was going through his mind. 'I want to speak to Tommi first.'

'It's important,' Rudi started to say, but the phone rang, and he zipped across to answer it.

His friendly Finnish greeting soon switched to cutting English.

'I told you before, she has no comment to make. Do not

call this number again.' Then he slammed the phone down and stood in front of it, as if trying to block it from my sight.

And in an instant, the anxiety gremlins reappeared with a vengeance.

'What was all that about?' I asked, trying to keep my voice light, as if I wasn't dreading the answer.

'Nothing,' said Rudi in a very unconvincing way. His eyes darted nervously between me and Tommi, and my feeling of impending doom increased.

'Who was it?' asked Tommi.

'Nobody.' Rudi sounded even more unsure of himself now. It was one thing being evasive with me, but quite another when you were avoiding answering your boss.

'Strange way to respond if nobody was there,' said Tommi.

Rudi started staring at his feet as if they were the most fascinating things in the world. Tommi was about to try another tack, when the phone rang again. Rudi dived for the receiver, but Tommi got there first. He picked it up and didn't say anything beyond 'Hello' in Finnish. Whoever it was at the other end obviously had a lot to say for themselves. He turned his back on us so we couldn't see his expression, but I could sense the tension in his broad shoulders.

'I see,' he said in English. 'As my colleague told you, there will be no comment. Kindly stop calling.'

He put the receiver down quietly, leaned across the counter to unplug the phone, then turned tail and walked out of the building without stopping to speak to either of us.

'Rudi, please, tell me what's going on,' I begged. My bad feeling had developed into something much worse. I had a horrible idea about the nature of the phone call, and until Rudi confirmed or averted my suspicions, my tendency to jump to the worst-case scenario was ruling my emotions. I wanted to run after Tommi and ask the same questions of him, but knew I would be in a better position if Rudi filled me in first rather than me blundering in headlong and potentially making a bad situation worse.

Rudi was pale-faced with concern, clearly torn as to what to do.

'I don't want to upset you,' he said, with a slight stammer in his speech. His voice was also more accented than usual, another sign that he was feeling under pressure.

'If it helps, not knowing is making me feel upset already. I'd rather be armed with the facts so at least I know what I'm facing. I assume I am the "she" you said had no comment to make.'

He nodded sadly but still remained frustratingly silent. I led him into the lounge, hoping that getting him away from the sight of the unplugged phone might help him to start speaking. Inside I was screaming at him to talk, but I knew that wouldn't help the situation.

'Let me take a wild guess and suggest that it was someone from the English tabloids at the other end of the line. They've worked out where I'm hiding, and they've got some follow-up muck they'd like to publish, but they're doing their due diligence of trying to get a response from me before they do so.' I kept my voice slow and calm, as if I was trying to reassure a small child caught eating sweets before dinner that they weren't in trouble.

Rudi sighed and muttered, 'Yes,' under his breath as if he barely dared to utter the word out loud.

'And what is the story they're wanting a response to now?' I asked, dreading the answer.

This time, Rudi seemed fascinated by his fingernails. Then he took a deep breath and turned towards me, although he couldn't quite bring himself to look directly at me and instead stared at a point on the wall beyond my left shoulder. He spoke quickly, as if talking fast would help this difficult situation disappear speedily too.

'Someone sent them a picture of you walking out of Jonno's cabin.'

I actually laughed out loud. Better than crying with disappointment that my hideaway had been rumbled.

'Shock horror, woman visits man in his cabin. Last time I checked, it wasn't the eighteenth century and it's perfectly acceptable for a woman to talk to a man unchaperoned. Besides, I'm working here. Of course I go into guests' cabins. I mean it's really not ideal that they know where I am, but surely even the grubbiest of gossipmongers couldn't spin something suggestive out of that.'

'I don't think they need to. Jonno told them that you tried to come onto him again.'

The revelation literally took my breath away as if I'd been punched in the stomach. The slimy, sneaking, two-faced bastard. How dare he lie about me like that? I jumped up from the sofa and started pacing about the room, my rage sending so much adrenalin surging around my body that I couldn't sit still. I cursed Jonno with all kinds of unrepeatable names, and then added Mike into the mix, because who else but him could have taken the picture and sent it into the hands of a hack in the first place? What were they playing at? If they'd done this, then surely I must be right in thinking they'd also been behind the viral video, just as I'd suspected? But why? What had I ever done to them to warrant such cruel behaviour? And what did they hope to achieve by it?

And then I had another horrifying realisation.

'Oh my goodness, Tommi.'

Tommi had answered the second call, and he'd given a no comment on my behalf, just as Rudi had. But he'd stayed on the line long enough for the hack to spin their sordid tale. My whole body went cold with horror.

'Tommi wouldn't have believed it, any more than I did,' said Rudi. This time he did meet my gaze, striding across the room and holding my shoulders so he could address me face to face.

I swallowed. 'You're right. Tommi wouldn't believe that.' The words rang hollow to my ears. What if I was wrong? What if he had taken the hack at his or her word? After all, as soon as he'd put the phone down, he'd walked straight out of the building. He'd not stopped to speak to me, he hadn't even looked me in the eye.

No, he was too sensible to be taken in by gossip, to trust the word of a stranger over mine. He knew that I would never betray him like that. But then I thought about how he himself had seen me standing on Jonno's front porch, and how I had been stupidly evasive when he had asked me a simple question. I'd acted like I had something to hide and, yes, I had been concealing stuff from him because I was scared to open up. But I hadn't been shifty because of this, never this. I felt physically sick. Why hadn't I been honest with him when I'd had the opportunity? If I explained it to him now, would he even believe me?

The sadness and hurt of having my hideaway revealed and once more being thrust into the limelight for a fabricated situation paled into insignificance next to the pain of wounding someone I had come to care dearly for. My career was clearly down the pan, my name was mud, but I knew I would find a way to overcome those hurdles eventually. But if Tommi became collateral damage in the disaster that was my life, then I would never forgive myself.

I needed to find him and explain the situation.

Chapter Thirty-Two

I hauled my outdoor clothing back on as quickly as possible. I had to track down Tommi, but getting frostbite in the process would not help my situation. Rudi flung an extra scarf and pair of gloves in my direction, recognising that I wouldn't pay attention even if he tried to stop me, and then I burst out into the fresh air, welcoming the pain of the biting cold, glad to have an excuse for the tears stinging in my eyes.

Think, Lucy, think, where would he have gone? He'd headed straight out of the main door, so he wasn't hiding in his office or his rooms downstairs. I replayed the scene in my mind, torturing myself with it frame by frame as I tried to interpret what had been going through his head as he'd walked out. And then I firmly told myself to stop. I needed to concentrate on finding him. Once I was with him, I would find the right words, somehow.

You'd have thought it would be easy to track someone down in such an isolated place, especially as footprints in the snow were a dead giveaway about which direction people had been walking in. Unfortunately, as the main building was the hub of Wild Zone, there were far too many sets of footprints for me to work out which ones belonged to Tommi. I would have to rely on my instinct. At first, I wondered if he'd gone off to the wilderness hut in the forest. As I knew myself, its peaceful isolation was a perfect haven for gathering one's thoughts.

I set off at a run, regretting the fact that I wasn't wearing snow shoes, but not wanting to waste any more time by turning back to fetch them. The path into the forest was compacted hard, with a lethal layer of ice on top of it. My boots didn't leave a trace on the surface, so I knew that if Tommi had headed this way, there would be no sign of it. But as I got further into the trees, my pace slowed. It sounds silly, but the woods felt empty. I'm not saying I'd developed a weird sixth sense for the presence of other people, but maybe over the weeks I'd been here I'd become attuned enough with my surroundings to detect the small changes which occur when there are other humans around, even if they were so minute that they didn't properly register in my consciousness. Somehow I knew that Tommi wasn't ahead of me. I swerved off to the left, slipping and sliding down the steep slope until I found myself standing on the shore of the frozen lake. The snowy mounds of the quinzees made by the last guests had nearly merged back into the landscape thanks to the regular snowfall of the last few days. I remembered how I had mixed the tunes as they dug the snow, Tommi and I working together as a team to make sure the visitors enjoyed every moment of their holiday.

Would he ever look at me again with such laughter in his eyes?

Once again I fiercely told myself to get it together, and then I set out across the lake. I don't know why I chose to head towards ACFM, but I felt drawn towards it, like there was a homing beacon on top of the building. I guess I was thinking that if I couldn't find Tommi, at least I could confront Mike and Jonno and tell them I knew what they'd been up to, even if I still couldn't understand what had motivated them to such behaviour in the first place. They must have known I'd work it out eventually, especially after they'd been so brazen as to leak a picture of me in Finland. The video back home could have been shot by anyone, but the pool of suspects at Wild Zone was ridiculously small. They weren't as clever as they thought they were.

It was hard work walking across the lake, ploughing my way through the thick snow without the assistance of skis or snow shoes. I would even have been grateful for a pair of gaiters, anything to stop the snow sneaking into the gap between my boot and my leg, and then melting down into my socks. I wriggled my toes. I could still feel them, but it wasn't ideal that they were getting so wet. I tried to increase my pace, knowing I was walking a fine line between frostbite and falling headfirst into the snow.

By the time I staggered up the steps and into the ACFM studio, my heart was pounding and I was gently perspiring with the effort of my trek, whilst simultaneously shaking from the cold. I pulled off my damp outer layers and soaking boots, and stood shivering in my base layers. It was not exactly the calm, collected demeanour I'd been planning to display when I challenged Jonno and Mike.

But there was another person in the studio, someone whose presence put all thought of everyone else out of my head.

'Tommi, I...' I rushed towards him, then stopped in my tracks, suddenly fearful in case I saw rejection and disgust in his features. 'I didn't realise you had an interest in the radio,' I said, cautiously.

Tommi waved at the mixing desk. 'I may have asked Aku to show me a few things. It's important to you, so it's important to me.'

I forgot that I was cold, I forgot that my feet were wet and that I was standing there in the arctic equivalent of underwear. I looked at Tommi, really looked at him, and without anything more being said, somehow I knew that everything would be alright between us.

'I would take Aku's guidance any day over those two,' I replied, nodding my head towards Jonno and Mike. 'You can't trust a word they say.'

'Oh I know,' he agreed. 'I was about to say as much to them. I guess you came here for the same reason I did. I'm sorry I didn't stay with you in reception after that phone call. I know I should have been with you, but I was hoping to make things right for you first.'

He closed the distance between us and I reached out to take his hand.

'That's very lovely of you, Tommi. But you know you don't have to save me, right?'

He chuckled; a wonderful sound which wrapped its way around my heart.

'I know that very well. You are more than capable of doing whatever you put your mind to. But I am here to help, should you wish me to. You only have to ask.'

He squeezed my palm, and I felt his strength alongside mine. Provided this kind, generous man believed in me, it didn't matter so much what the rest of the world thought.

Mike cleared his throat. 'Can we stop with the touching reunion? Only some of us have work to do.'

OK, so the opinion of the rest of the world wasn't my top priority, but I still cared that those two jokers had tried to make me a victim for their own reasons.

I turned around and fixed Jonno and Mike with the steeliest of stares. And then I confronted them with exactly what I'd worked out. Tommi stood back, a silent source of solidarity in the background, as I laid out my evidence.

I'm a radio presenter. I know how to relate a story in the clearest, most effective way possible. By the time I'd finished, Mike and Jonno were left in no doubt that they were rumbled. There was only one part of my accusation I wasn't so sure about, and that was the reason behind it. But I knew they would never tell me unless provoked, so I took a stab in the dark.

'I can't believe you did all of this over some poxy job. Mike, you had your eyes on my role from the start and, Jonno, well, you've got your heart set on something much bigger. The next rung on the ladder. A TV job, perhaps? Only you knew you weren't high profile enough to get your name into the mix despite your famous girlfriend, so you conspired with Mike here to generate some extra publicity for yourself. That way both of you could get what you wanted, and who cares about the price that I've had to pay? Did you even go so far as to post the threats through my letterbox? How low can you go? And when it looked like it still wouldn't work – yes, I've heard the rumours about the reshuffle at Star FM – you thought you'd try round two with a pathetic photo of me innocently standing on Jonno's porch and a silly story about me throwing myself at him all over again. You know what, I feel sorry for you both. I feel sorry that you didn't believe in your own abilities enough to trust that you'd be able to get the jobs on your own merit.'

I think it was my expression of pity that finally made Mike blow up. Whilst Jonno had shrunk further and further into the corner of the room to the point where I thought he might actually climb out of the window to escape the shame, Mike had been pacing and posturing, muttering, 'The woman's deluded' and other such choice phrases. But when I said I felt sorry for him, he turned and actually snarled at me.

'How dare you, you stupid woman. Yeah, so we set you up, big deal. But if you can't handle playing with the big boys, then get out of the playground.'

I burst out laughing at that, which infuriated him even more.

He actually stamped his foot on the ground. 'Laugh all you like, but do you really think anyone's going to believe you? There is not a shred of physical proof that we did it, not even on those silly newspaper clippings. You try peddling that line around, and you're going to get a reputation as a nutter as well as a desperate slut.'

Tommi cleared his throat. I followed the direction of his gaze to the open fader, then across to the faces of my colleagues, distorted and ugly in their deception, and then back again to that open fader. And I knew exactly what he had done.

There is one very important thing that you are always told on your first day working at a radio station; if you are in a studio, always assume that the microphones are live and that whatever you say can be heard by the listening public or, at the very least, your nosy colleagues listening in the control room. But when you spend all day surrounded by microphones it is easy to forget that important piece of advice, and even to stop registering the fact that you are in a live broadcast environment. Combine that with the media world's propensity for gossip, and it's easy to understand why there is very rarely such a thing as a proper secret in a radio station. In fact, it was pretty surprising that the pair of them had managed to keep this particular secret so long.

They still hadn't realised what I had. Tommi leaned back in his creaky chair and put his arms behind his head, looking completely unperturbed by the scene happening in front of him. I tried to follow suit, perching as casually as I could on the edge of the mixing desk, trying to maintain a calm exterior while my insides were a seething mass of nerves and anticipation. A tiny bud of hope was unfurling within while my heart thudded against my ribs. My senses were hyper alert, adrenalin running through my veins in expectation and fear of what was to come next.

'I don't know why you're looking so pleased with yourself,' said Mike, catching the slight twitch of a grin which had escaped from my lips involuntarily. 'But just because you know who was behind it all, it doesn't mean that you'll ever be able to prove it. Jonno is the golden boy of the airwaves, and I'm your precious Skye's right-hand man. Do you think she'd be half so successful on the breakfast show if she didn't have me holding her hand? And do you really think anyone is going to believe you if you go around shooting your mouth off and trying to blame everything on us? You'll end up looking like a bitter, twisted, has-been, trying to get fame at any cost.'

'Goodness, Mike, it really sounds like you're describing yourself there.' His jibe about Skye had been the final straw. I was done with taking his abuse. I'd always known he'd had a problem with women, but I hadn't realised how deeply entrenched the misogyny was. It was about time he realised it was the twenty-first century, and got used to the idea that we're not some kind of inferior sub species.

'For a start, it's obvious to anyone who has a pair of ears that Skye has been keeping you afloat on the airwaves, and that you'd be a wallowing mess without her. And if you think Jonno is the golden boy, then you are very much mistaken. What kind of golden boy needs to resort to dirty tricks and intimidation in order to get his big break? I suppose I should be flattered that the two of you felt so threatened by me that you needed to come up with such a ridiculous scheme. No, I'm not going to call it ridiculous, because that really underestimates the true cost it has had on me. It was a nasty, malicious, cruel scheme which it's no exaggeration to say left me fearing for my life and sent me to a very dark place. But I am a stronger, better person than either of you, and I will not let this be the end of me and what I want to achieve in my career. However, it may well spell the end of your ambitions. While you saw that happen to me, and crowed over me, I am not going to lower myself to that kind of behaviour. In fact, I will pity you, because I know what you will be going through.'

Mike continued with his blustering and chuntering, but Jonno followed my gaze and finally cottoned on to what Tommi had done.

He lunged towards the desk and tried to switch off the fader of the open microphone. But before he could reach it, Tommi casually stood up to block him, and folded his arms. He said a very guttural, stern-sounding 'Ei', and then repeated 'No' in English, in case Jonno hadn't got the point.

Jonno hovered on the spot, torn between his need to stop the microphone broadcasting everything to the world, and his desire not to get squashed by such a quietly strong man. His indecision made him look like a toddler who was desperate to go to the loo.

Mike, meanwhile, still hadn't realised that his ranting was being broadcasted live on Arctic Circle FM. Admittedly, the listenership wasn't the biggest in the world, but I more than anybody had a good idea of how quickly this kind of content would spread far beyond its original audience.

I gestured to Tommi to follow me when he was ready, then I turned my back on the scene and started pulling on my outdoor clothing. I had seen enough.

When I had first arrived, the bulky fleece jumpers and

jackets felt constricting and at times too heavy for me to endure. But now, every extra layer I added, I felt a corresponding lightening of my soul. I had been vindicated. The truth was out there. And although I suspected the viral video would always be somewhere in the background, wherever I went and whatever I did, the recording which revealed what had really happened would also be alongside it. I could reclaim my name and my position. The future was mine to choose.

Chapter Thirty-Three

Once again my phone was buzzing, the screen flaring with a constant stream of notifications and messages. I pushed it away from me, not daring to look.

'Do you want me to check?' asked Tommi quietly, reading my mind with that uncanny ability of his.

We were snuggled up together in front of the fire in his living room, Gurta and the puppies curled at our feet. Rudi had taken Mike and Jonno to the airport. They'd returned from the ACFM studio to find their bags already packed and loaded into the minibus. Johanna told me Rudi had been all for dumping their stuff in one of Aku's fishing holes in the lake, but she'd managed to persuade him that it was better to take the moral high ground in this kind of situation. I didn't know what they'd be returning to, although judging by the stony expression on their faces as they'd driven away, I think they'd got a fair idea that they were in for a stormy time. Now that everything was out in the open and the horrible duo had left, my soul felt lighter, but a nagging fear was still lurking deep down. It felt too good to be true for everything to come right so suddenly.

I tore my gaze from the phone and tried to smile at Tommi.

'I know it shouldn't matter to me one bit what a load of anonymous strangers think of me. All that matters is the opinion of the people I care about, who care about me. And yet, not knowing is almost worse. My imagination is running wild and you know me…'

'You've jumped immediately to the worst-case scenario.' Tommi finished my sentence.

I spread my palms. 'I can't help it. Perhaps it's a self-protection thing; thinking the worst so I'm not so surprised and shocked when it comes to fruition.'

'But what is the worst-case scenario?'

'The notoriety continues despite the truth being out there. People still hate me. My reputation is tainted for ever so I can't get another job. Basically what happened to me when the video first appeared.'

Tommi nodded. 'That would be upsetting.'

'I can hear a "but" in there.' I said.

Tommi shrugged and remained silent. He reached across and interlaced his fingers with mine, squeezing them comfortingly.

'…but it would not be the end of the world,' I said what I knew he was thinking. 'My life would carry on. People would forget eventually, and those who care for me will know the truth. And ACFM is always going to need a producer to keep you all in line. I am better than this.'

As I said the words out loud, I realised they were true.

Yes, a part of me would be horribly upset and hurt if the trolls still had me in their sights, but it would not be a fatal blow. I was a stronger person than the one who had slunk to Finland terrified of her own shadow and desperate to hide away from the world. I had learned so much about myself since I had been here. My self-respect had returned and, just as importantly, my self-belief. I knew I was strong enough to face whatever was thrown at me.

'Yes. We who love you know who you really are and we don't care about a silly video and the uninformed opinions of people on social media.'

For a moment I didn't register the full meaning of what he had just said. And then, when the words did sink in, my worries vanished into the background as I instead concentrated on demonstrating to Tommi that I felt the same way about him.

A while later, Gurta finally managed to divert us from our embrace by picking up my phone and dropping it back on Tommi's lap.

'I think she's hinting that we should stop being distracted and concentrate on putting your mind at rest.'

'Trust me, my mind is definitely elsewhere right now,' I mumbled, tracing the delicious curve of Tommi's collarbone.

I felt the vibration of his warm chuckle against my fingers.

'I'm afraid Gurta thinks it's best we find out now, rather than putting off the moment.'

There was a pause as he started scrolling.

'Well don't keep me in suspense,' I said, making a not-very-concerted effort to take the phone from his hands. He answered by tickling me until I retreated.

Then he sat up and looked serious.

'You appear to be trending once again on social media,' he said. 'But as the hero of the hour. Someone has already put the confrontation to music, and the hashtag "Listen to Lucy" has got tens of thousands of retweets.'

Before I could respond, the phone started ringing.

'It's Skye,' said Tommi, offering to pass it across.

'Put her on speakerphone.'

We both recoiled at the volume of the excited squealing that came out of the phone. She started talking so fast that neither of us could understand a word she was saying.

'Skye, lovely, slow down a minute,' I pleaded, as Tommi simultaneously said something along the same lines.

'Ooh, you guys sound like you're getting on well. I knew you'd love each other. I said as much to Henri, but he said I shouldn't interfere and to let you find out in your own time.'

Tommi winked at me as I rolled my eyes in mock annoyance at Skye's matchmaking aspirations.

'What do you want, Skye? Apart from to claim you've been playing cupid all along?' I said. 'Without being rude, we were quite busy when you rang.'

She giggled. 'I bet you were. The reason I rang was to let you know that the MD and Charlie are trying to get hold of you. They'd like to offer you your old show back. How amazing is that?'

I'd longed for this moment so much that it had even

invaded my dreams, but now it was actually happening, it felt hollow.

'But what about you, Skye? You're doing so well on the breakfast show. I don't want to steal it away from you.'

'Silly me, I didn't make myself clear. They want us to double head it. You and me; besties together on the airwaves.' She whooped again, and this time I joined in.

'When do they want us to start?'

'As soon as possible, although if I were you, I'd make the most of being the woman of the hour and say you're going to take some more time enjoying Finnish hospitality. You might as well make them sweat after the way they treated you.'

When we finally hung up the call, my mind was buzzing with ideas for the new show. Tommi wrapped me up in a big bear hug.

'I am so pleased for you,' he said sincerely.

'We'll make it work,' I replied, addressing the concern I knew he'd have, but was too decent to say. 'The start of my new radio chapter does not mean an end for us, I promise.'

'I am glad,' he said simply. Then Gurta started nudging our knees with her nose. 'I think somebody wants her dinner. Fancy helping?'

As we clattered around the kitchen pouring dog food in bowls, I thought how much I would miss this comfortable companionship when I returned to my normal life in Sheffield. But then an idea struck me. It would take a bit of arranging, but I thought it would be possible. And, as Skye said, the bosses did owe me after everything I'd been through. I looked across at Tommi, marvelling at how someone dressed in such unflattering base layers could nevertheless look so sexy as he dished out the food to the hungry puppies and their mum. I hoped he'd be as delighted with my plan as I was. And then I put all plotting to one side as Tommi led me back to the sofa and we picked up where we'd left off.

Chapter Thirty-Four

Tommi handed me a flaming torch and beckoned for me to follow. The path which had been ploughed through the waist-deep snow was only wide enough for us to walk in single file. Although there were at least a dozen of us in the group, we were silent, almost reverential, as we followed our guide. It was early afternoon, but thick darkness surrounded us, only disrupted by the flickering flames from our torches. The mist from our breath hung in the air, adding to the mysterious atmosphere. It felt like we'd stepped back several centuries. And then the path suddenly widened until we were able to fan out and stand in a huddle. Our guide gestured around him and explained something to the group in Finnish. Tommi leaned towards me and quietly translated, but I'd already gleaned some meaning from the reactions of those who surrounded me. We were standing on the Arctic Circle, the geographical point marking the crossover into an even colder and wilder land. Some people started jumping back and forth, grinning as they posed for selfies. Others looked around in wonderment at the quiet glory of the wild landscape.

I stood on the invisible boundary and thought about how much I'd changed since arriving in this captivating country. I'd realised I was capable of more than I'd ever imagined. I'd seen the darker side of my party-loving ways and found a different approach to living my life. And I'd finally found the courage to open up about my dad's death, first by telling Tommi what had happened, and then, last night, by talking to Mum about it properly. It was the first time we'd really been honest with each other about our terrible loss and how it made us feel. I knew we had a long way to go in our grieving process and in our relationship, but it felt like we were moving closing together in our understanding of each other. Mum had ended the call by saying that Dad would have been proud of me.

As I remembered those precious words, Tommi reached down and took my hand. Our gloves were so thick it was like holding hands with a bundle of fabric, but then he squeezed my palm and I felt that glorious connection with him all over again.

'What do you think?' he asked.

I gazed around me. Don't get me wrong, if the Lucy who had first come to Finland had arrived here, I think she would have been seriously unimpressed by the lack of a fuss. But now I appreciated the quiet understatement of the place. It would have been wrong for there to be a big tourist spectacle here. The lack of a fanfare allowed everyone to appreciate their surroundings in their own way.

'There's something magical about it,' I found myself

confessing. 'I can't really explain it. It's not like the landscape looks very different from the environment at Wild Zone, but I feel like I'm reacting to it in here.' I thumped a gloved hand against my chest.

Tommi nodded. I couldn't see his face properly beneath his balaclava and thick hat, but I knew he was grinning.

'I knew you'd feel it too.'

He pulled me closer, wrapping me in his arms as if he was scared to let me go. Then he started talking quietly. 'I wanted you to see this place before you return home. It is special to me. I hope you will remember our walk together here when you are hurrying into work after those early morning alarm calls.' He took a deep breath. 'I have debated whether to say this to you, but I will. Please don't take this as me trying to hold you back, because I want nothing more than for you to be happy and to succeed in what you want to do, but I'm going to miss you when you're gone. I know we will make long-distance work, but I shall be sad not to experience the ordinariness of daily life by each other's side.'

I hastily blinked back the moisture which came to my eyes at the beauty of his speech. I couldn't risk frozen tears right now when I had something very important to say.

'We don't have to be long-distance, if you don't want to,' I said, carefully. 'I've spoken to the management at Star FM and said I would return if they met two conditions.'

'Oh yes?'

'Number one, that Skye and I do the drivetime show, rather than breakfast. That would be better with the time difference here. And number two, that I do the drivetime show remotely, using the studio facilities of ACFM. They can put in a special line to the back room, so I can use that as my studio and won't disrupt ACFM's programming. Aku and the others put it to the vote. They're more than happy for me to use the place, as long as I help out with some volunteer producing on the side. What do you think?'

Tommi remained silent for so long that I thought I'd made a mistake.

'Of course, I could still go back to Sheffield and broadcast from there and we can be long-distance, if that's what you'd prefer,' I added hurriedly.

'No, I would love for you to stay here. It was destroying me, the thought of you going, but I didn't want to stand in your way.' He reached out and gently brushed the ice from the loose tendrils of hair which were sticking out from under my hat. 'I am sorry I didn't reply straight away. I was so overwhelmed, the English words went right out of my mind.'

I was so happy, I half expected to see the snow melting away underneath me from the warm joy which was filling my body.

'Ah, that's another condition of me staying here. You'll have to teach me Finnish. Even Gurta is bilingual. I refuse to be put to shame by a dog.'

Tommi laughed. 'I would be delighted to.'

And then he took my hand, and we walked back across the magical line of the Arctic Circle and onwards through the snow together.

Acknowledgments

It's been such a joy writing *Meet Me Under the Northern Lights* and being able to make the journey to Finland in my imagination while travel has been so restricted because of the pandemic. Finland is a beautiful country, so thanks have to go to Fran and Liz for suggesting our winter holiday there a few years ago... and for not laughing too hard when I fell off the husky sled, just like Lucy ended up doing!

A huge thank you to Jennie, Charlotte, Sara, and all the lovely team at One More Chapter for your support, encouragement, and general marvellousness. It's a pleasure to work with you. And thank you also to my wonderful agent, Amanda, who is a cheerleader, sounding board, and source of wisdom, all rolled up into one!

To the Book Campers, thank you for all your friendship and support. I'm so lucky to know such a talented and inspirational group of women.

A special shout out to the team at Tempo FM who prove

the value of community radio and are a valuable friend to many over the airwaves.

As always, thank you to my beloved family for being there for me, and also for gifting me with a love of reading and writing.

And finally, thank you to you, the readers, for picking up this book. I hope you've enjoyed reading it as much as I've enjoyed writing it.

Read on for a preview of *Duvet Day*, another uplifting and funny romcom from Emily Kerr…

Young lawyer Alexa Humphries's one true love is her precious duvet, yet she is torn from its comforting embrace every morning while the foxes are still scavenging the bins outside and doesn't get back until long after most normal people are already asleep.

Worn down by the endless demands of her suspicious boss and her competitive, high-flying housemate and fellow lawyer, Zara, Alexa barely recognises herself anymore.

This wasn't how life was supposed to be.

But today is different. Today, Alexa just cannot get out of bed to face the world.

Everyone deserves a duvet day, don't they?

Duvet Day: Chapter One

Tuesday 23rd April

4.57 a.m.

There's nothing quite like snuggling in the warm embrace of my one true love. It's where I feel utterly content. Here I am safe, happy, and briefly able to remove the mask of sensible, Grown-Up Lawyer that I have to show to the rest of the world. Here, for a few blissful moments, I can finally feel like Alexa Humphries, actual human being, rather than Alexa Humphries, corporate drone. But the trouble is, that's all it ever is. A few blissful moments. For my darling, king-size, 13.5 tog duvet and I spend most of our time apart, cruelly separated by the ever-growing demands of my job, which has become more of a lifestyle choice than just a career. This is so not how I imagined my dream life in London would turn out.

Take today, for example. It's still dark outside. The foxes are scavenging by the bins on the street corner, and the noise of traffic has quietened to an occasional grumble from its usual constant roar. Anyone with any sense is deep in the land of nod, and according to my employment contract, I'm not expected at work for at least another four hours. But whereas lawyers are steely-eyed and detail-oriented in pretty much every other aspect of our business, when it comes to following the letter of our own working hours, we're expected to become forgetful and instead do what is necessary. And it turns out that my employers consider it necessary for me to be on call. Permanently. Which is why I didn't get to my beloved bed until nearly 1.30 a.m. and why I've been awake for the last half hour stressing about the day ahead and panic-reading obscure bits of contract law for a particularly complicated merger that's looming on the horizon.

It's not like I'm extremely senior and important either. When it comes to the food chain of office politics, I know I'm the pond life. But if I want to make it from plant to herbivore and beyond, I need to play the game. I'm just not sure I like this particular game that much any more.

Despite that old cliché of lawyers being bloodsuckers out to make as much money as possible, whatever the cost to others, I've always had a rosy-eyed view of the profession. It started when I was six and the local solicitor helped my grandma prevent developers from forcibly buying the family farm, and then was solidified by my addiction to the movie *Legally Blonde* during my formative years. Sure, the main character, Elle, went through tough times, being patronised by a pervy professor and being constantly underestimated because of her hair colour. But she triumphed as the underdog and rose to great heights, all while wearing killer heels and carrying her faithful pooch in her designer handbag. I would sit in my teenage bedroom, teeth aching from my latest trip to the orthodontist, face covered in bits of toothpaste in a vain attempt to dry out my spots, and promise myself that, one day, I would be like Elle: a confident, successful woman full of integrity, standing up for justice, and fighting for those without the power to fight for themselves.

The spots vanished (mostly), and the teeth were straightened, but somewhere between law school and venturing into the big, wide world, I got lost. It's been two years since I became the envy of my university buddies by joining Richmond Woods. But I didn't realise when I signed on the dotted line that I might as well have signed in blood. It's one of London's leading law firms, notable for having one of the biggest budgets for pro bono work in the city, which is why I was so desperate to get the job in the first place. Alas, while the people on the fifth floor get to make use of that philanthropic power and do some good in the world, I'm trapped on a treadmill on the second floor, charged with applying my skills to help a lot of rich, bossy men become even richer and bossier. The richer bit is from using my legal know-how to help them negotiate company mergers and takeovers, the bossier bit is from being a real-life Alexa who they can enjoy ordering around with the same lack of respect they use to operate their voice-activated devices. The only way it could be worse was if I was called Siri instead.

I stretch out my toes to take full advantage of the still-toasty hot-water bottle at my feet. My room in the house-share has beautiful big windows, making it a light and airy space, or so the girl moving out promised me when she showed me round. I unfortunately failed to consider the fact that the stately Victorian sash windows with their glorious view of the squat opposite were single-glazed. Add into the mix ill-fitting wooden frames which are suspiciously squishy, and it's a recipe for a permanent draught akin to a gale. Even during last summer's heatwave, there was only about one week where I didn't need some extra form of warmth to get me through the night. I suppose what I could really do with is a hot bedmate – in both senses of the word – but as I appear to have formed an unhealthy, all-encompassing relationship with my job, I can't see that happening any time soon.

Instead, I'm trying to keep warm with my current bed attire, an anything-but-sexy unicorn onesie. It's all the colours of the rainbow, fleece-lined, with a furry exterior, complete with tail and silver horn. Don't get me wrong, I love a cosy pair of PJs as much as the next girl, but a unicorn onesie is definitely at the extreme end of things, and when my twin brother Charlie handed it over to me for Christmas with a wicked grin on his face, I swore I'd never lower myself to actually wearing it. But what can I say? Needs must. My laundry pile has been growing its own ecosystem because I've been getting back from work late, and I'm too scared of incurring the wrath of my Queen Bee housemate Zara to turn on the washing machine after dark. In desperation last night, I'd dug out this little number from the back of my wardrobe, where it had been languishing in a cocoon of torn wrapping paper. I'm trying not to imagine the look of triumph on Charlie's face if he knew I was wearing it. He's always on at me to "Chill out and go with the flow", which is all well and good if you're content coasting your way through life by occasionally busking in the local market town back home, like he does, but it doesn't really cut it in the corporate world I've ended up stuck in.

The windows rattle as a lorry rumbles down the road, sending another chilly blast of morning air over my face, and making the curtains flutter. Shards of orange light from the streetlamps dance their way around the walls, sharpening the fuzzy details of my room. I gaze around, nostalgic thoughts of my childhood home making me see my current surroundings as if for the first time. I'm barely ever in here when I'm not sleeping, and I can't remember when I last actually paused and considered my surroundings. It's a depressing sight; wardrobe doors hanging open to reveal a row of identikit suits, the pile of dirty washing overflowing out of a bag in the corner, and stacks of musty legal tomes leaning precariously by the bed. It's more of a habitat than a bedroom, certainly not what someone would associate with a so-called professional woman in her mid-twenties. The only uplifting feature is the collection of pictures on my walls. They're bright abstract prints of some of the most famous London landmarks, images which adorned my student bedroom to inspire me during the long days of learning case law and wading through incomprehensible legal jargon.

When I first moved here, I had visions of changing the world during the week, and then ticking off each famous landmark during the weekends, but I'm always too knackered to be bothered. Most of my weekends are spent comatose, wrapped up in my duvet and trying to catch up on all the sleep I've missed out on during the weekdays of corporate kowtowing. The realisation saddens me. It's like I've blinked and suddenly two years have passed without me getting any closer to the dreams of making a difference that I'd once held so dear. How have I let things get to this position?

I turn onto my side, blocking out the too-cheery images, and try to ignore the crushing sense of failure which threatens to overwhelm me. I need to get a grip. Nobody likes a misery-guts and this one-person pity party needs to stop. Time to focus on the day ahead. Right on cue, my phone buzzes, warning me that yet another email has landed in my inbox. When I first started at Richmond Woods, being gifted a work phone and being told that I could also use it for my personal calls felt like a demonstration of trust and respect. However, after the thrill of being able to ring utility companies' premium-rate phone lines without having to worry about the cost had worn off, I realised the hard reality of the apparently generous gesture. I started to resent the fact that I was expected to carry a device akin to my own personal slave master in my pocket all the time. Even in my supposed downtime I find myself obsessively checking messages and feeling stressed if I don't reply to my seniors within half an hour. Sometimes it feels like my head might explode with the pressure of keeping on top of everything.

Despite my best efforts last night, my inbox is still at the higher end of double figures, and suddenly it seems impossible that I'll ever get through it all. Several of the emails have been sent with bright red exclamation marks in the subject line to denote them as extremely urgent, and just in case I haven't got the message, "SORT THIS NOW" has been added in shouty capital letters. I cringe as if I was actually being yelled at. Of course, no one at Richmond Woods would be so coarse as to raise their voice in person, but they've developed all kinds of passive-aggressive methods of creating the same horrible effect on us lowly minions.

I know I should start chipping away at my replies, but I'm desperate for just a few more minutes of peace. I find myself grabbing my own battered mobile and falling into my usual procrastination habit of scrolling through Instagram, trying to escape reality into a world of hashtags promising glossy positivity.

Pictures of cute animals and gorgeous holiday destinations normally do the trick in cheering me up, but today all I can notice are my friends' posts about their perfect lives. Instead of putting a smile on my face, they increase my sense of melancholy. I gaze at the shiny picture of my best friend from school, carefree and laughing with her fiancé on Sydney Harbour Bridge, and try to remember the last time I saw any of these people in real life.

When I make my weekly call to my parents, they always

ask after my old school and uni mates, and the answers trip off my tongue. Laura's engaged, Michael's got another promotion and oh, did I tell you that Sara thought she bumped into Prince William at Waitrose the other day? But now I'm stopping and actually thinking about it, I realise my friends haven't told me these charming anecdotes personally. They've made general announcements to me and several hundred others of their closest online followers. I've double-tapped my appreciation and sometimes there's even been the briefest exchange in the comments along the lines of, "Congratulations lovely, we must meet for a proper catch up soon", but I can't remember the last time it actually translated into a real-life interaction. Have I allowed social media to paper over the cracks of where an actual social life should be? I always assumed everyone was too busy, but a growing fear is telling me that maybe I'm the only one struggling, while everyone else really has got it sorted so that they're #livingthedream.

Suddenly my body jerks and the sick sensation of being about to fall off a cliff jolts me back to full consciousness. That was close. Much as I need the sleep, I can't afford to drift off again. Regretfully, I push the hot-water bottle out of reach so I don't get too comfortable. I know I should be getting on with work. The senior partner I report to has flown out to Japan to help a client finalise a deal, and her flight is due to land in Tokyo at any moment. I'd be prepared to bet next month's rent money that she'll ping a dozen missives my way as soon as she does. Genevieve's notorious for expecting an instant acknowledgement and I daren't let her down. Besides, she's on the appointments board for the pro bono department and maybe, just maybe, one day she'll recognise my hard work and reward me for it with a position there, and then all this will have been worth it. Or that's what I keep telling myself, anyway.

My work phone buzzes once again as the expected emails arrive. My fingers hover over the screen, but just the thought of sending even one more reply makes me feel like a steel band is tightening around my head, and I find myself pushing the phone away. Despite my good intentions, I shuffle back down my mattress, burrowing myself into my duvet like a hibernating animal. If I can't see the emails, maybe I can pretend they don't exist, I tell myself, much like a small child playing hide and seek by merely covering their eyes.

The phone's buzzing continues, and through the thin party wall, I hear the distinctive thumps of Zara jumping out of bed and switching her light on. It's a badge of pride among us junior lawyers if we can count the number of hours of sleep we've had on one hand. Zara claims to thrive on this, but anything less than six hours and I find my brain becoming sluggish and my reactions slowing until I feel like I have jet lag. Sometimes, I'll have a whole conversation with someone and feel like they're talking to me on a time delay, so it takes me several seconds to be able to process what they're saying and be able to respond appropriately.

Now she's in circulation, I know I should look at my emails. Zara and I work for the same firm and in the same department – another reason why I feel I can't even switch off when I get home. When I first moved to London, it seemed like the easiest solution to share a house with a colleague. Yes, I know, what was I thinking? But by the time I'd realised quite how ruthlessly competitive Zara is, I'd already signed a six-month lease. Somehow, it's gone on a lot longer than that initial agreement, but I'll just add that to my long list of things that I've let slip. I barely have time to buy a pint of milk, let alone look into moving house. And on the plus side, our other housemate Sam is no bother. In fact, she's no bother to the point that we've only ever communicated through the house WhatsApp group. She moved in at Christmas when I was home visiting my family for a brief forty-eight hours, and she appears to work weird shifts too. Or maybe the reason we've never met is that she's got a much better social life than me. Most people have, after all.

Now the clattering sound of Zara typing on her laptop punches its way into my room. She's attacking the keys as if they are promotion rivals. Even when I pull a pillow over my head, I can still hear her tapping away, each jab nagging at my growing sense of anxiety. It's like she's doing it deliberately, making sure I know she's already hard at work while I'm being a lazy layabout. I know I should pick up the work phone again, send out my own replies and signal that my working day has begun. But somehow today it seems impossible. The very thought of rolling out of bed, getting dressed and dragging myself into the office for yet another day of thrashing myself to the limit is enough to make me groan out loud. I wish I could carry on pretending to myself that everything is OK, but this morning, I just don't have the energy to even try.

I poke my nose out of my duvet and stare wistfully at

the family picture teetering precariously on what was meant to be my dressing table, but which I use instead as a makeshift desk. It's a classic Humphries image, illustrating the family pecking order perfectly, with me the default target for teasing. My older brothers are cracking up, my mum and dad are hiding their amusement with mock outrage, while I'm rolling my eyes at Charlie who was taking the picture. I can remember the suggestion he made to elicit such a response. I'd been in a hurry to make my train back to London, and being delayed for a family snap was not helping my stress levels. After dragging me back to the doorstep and plonking me in position, Charlie had peeked above the lens of the ancient camera and fixed me with a stern stare as I protested my urgent need to get going, right now.

"Lighten up, sis. Just throw a sickie. What's the worst that can happen?"

His words echo around my mind.

Throw a sickie…

I can't.

Charlie wouldn't think twice about it. But I'm the sensible twin. It would be completely out of character for me to do something so spontaneous and rebellious. I'm expected at work. I've got deadlines to meet, clients to appease, bosses to impress. I can't let my colleagues down. But Charlie's voice in my head is insistent.

What's the worst that can happen?

I know the answer to this. A day out of the loop could leave me on the back foot for weeks. I could lose the respect and trust of my colleagues, my job even, were I to get found out. I can't do it. It would be foolhardy.

But even as I try to bully myself into getting up and getting on with what needs to be done, my gaze travels back to those pictures of London, images which used to stand for hope and now represent nothing but personal failure. How long can I keep lying to myself that things are going to get better? I realise I've had enough. I am done with feeling like this. I need to do something about it.

Before I lose courage, I reach out, pick up my phone and find myself typing an email I never imagined I would dare to write. It's time I took my destiny into my own hands.

Don't forget to order your copy of *Duvet Day* to find out what happens next...